ACCLAIM FOR MELISSA TAGG

NOW AND THEN AND ALWAYS

"Powerful. I've always loved Melissa Tagg's stories, but this one is something special. Lyrical, yes. Enchanting, of course. But her story about a broken man meeting an equally broken woman and their journey to healing touched unexpected places in my heart. An absolutely beautiful, compelling read."

-**Susan May Warren**, *USA Today* bestselling, RITA Award-winning author of the Montana Marshalls series

"Charming! Set in an old bed and breakfast in need of love, *Now and Then and Always* delights the reader with mystery and romance. Tagg continues to set herself apart as a classic romance storyteller."

-**Rachel Hauck**, *New York Times* bestselling author

"Melissa Tagg is the kind of writer who makes me fall in love with story every single time I read one of her novels. In *Now and Then and Always* she does it again. Tagg's writing draws you into the pages—into the Storyworld she creates in such a powerful way, threaded through with humor, romance and, yes, mystery. I closed the book happy and satisfied—except that I wished the story hadn't ended."

-**Beth K. Vogt**, Christy Award-winning author

"With her trademark wit and stunning word pictures, Melissa Tagg has penned a romance that drew me in from the very first sentence. *Now and Then and Always* is a heartbreakingly beautiful romance sprinkled with characters who felt more like friends. Truly, a story that will capture your heart."

-**Courtney Walsh**, *New York Times* and *USA Today* bestselling author

"*Now and Then and Always* is a beautiful story of an old house that brings people together to find healing and wholeness in their brokenness and the family they never expected. Tagg's well-written novel is the perfect blend of smiles, tears, and happily-ever-after with a touch of intrigue. The characters linger long after the pages have been turned and The Everwood makes me wish it was real so I could have my own life-changing experience."

-**Lisa Jordan**, Carol Award-winning author for Love Inspired

WALKER FAMILY SERIES

"Tagg crafts a beautiful romance filled with humor, mystery, and heartfelt emotion . . . Tagg's moving story beautifully explores themes of redemption and the nature of home."

-**Publisher's Weekly**, for *All This Time*

"Bear and Raegan are endearing and intriguing characters, and readers can't help but fall in love with them. Tagg excels at fleshing out the hints we've been given throughout the series and developing them into layered, authentic backstories...A doozy of a first kiss is completely worth the wait, and even a little suspense is skillfully worked into the plot—in case pulses weren't already racing. (They were.)"

-**RT Book Reviews**, 4½ Stars TOP PICK! for *All This Time*

"With her inimitable style, Melissa Tagg has penned a gem of a story, one that will delight longtime fans and entrance new ones. Replete with swoon-worthy moments, unwrapping Bear's complicated history and discovering Raegan's hidden struggles make this a love story that resonates on a deeper level."

-**RelzReviewz.com**, for *From the Start*

"With profound truths on one page and laugh-out-loud hilarity on the next, *Like Never Before* quickly becomes one of those novels I didn't want to end. Melissa Tagg has penned a delightful story that took hold of my heart and didn't let go. Superbly well done!"

-**Katie Ganshert**, bestselling, award-winning author

"In *Like Never Before,* readers are invited to revisit the much-loved Walker clan that delivers on the promise that even if lost once, love can be found again. In true Melissa Tagg style, the dialogue is smart and the romance is real and raw in all the right places. This series is witty story-telling at its best."

-**Kristy Cambron**, bestselling, award-winning author

"Tagg (*Made To Last; Here To Stay*) writes heartfelt and humorous gentle romances with a wisp of faith woven throughout. Fans of her previous two books will want this one. And devotees of Rachel Hauck and Robin Lee Hatcher will embrace a promising new author."

-**Library Journal**, for *From the Start*

"Tagg excels at creating wholesome romances featuring strong young career women, gentle humor, and an unobtrusive but heartfelt infusion of faith."

-**Booklist**, for *From the Start*

BOOKS BY MELISSA TAGG

MAPLE VALLEY SERIES

Now and Then and Always

Some Bright Someday

WALKER FAMILY SERIES

Three Little Words (prequel e-novella)

From the Start

Like Never Before

Keep Holding On

All This Time

ENCHANTED CHRISTMAS COLLECTION

One Enchanted Christmas

One Enchanted Eve

One Enchanted Noël

WHERE LOVE BEGINS SERIES

Made to Last

Here to Stay

NOVELLAS

A Place to Belong

One Royal Christmas

SOME
Bright
SOMEDAY

MELISSA TAGG

To the One who holds all my todays and all my somedays in His hands and keeps whispering, "Trust Me."

$\mathcal{T}$his high up, where the first faint breaths of autumn filled his ready lungs and a glowing, harvest sun leaned into the west, Lucas could almost remember what it felt like to be whole.

What it felt like *before.*

Before the scars—not only the ones hidden under his long sleeves that still itched even all these years later, but also those etched in deeper, hollow places. Before the shame and before the secrets.

Up here, at least for these few fleeting moments, he could be a hero.

He adjusted his grip on the outdoor climbing wall's nearest handhold, his harness jangling as he hefted himself another foot closer to the spindly, trembling body plastered to the wall above him. Third kid today to make the climb then freeze at the top. The last one he'd fetched had about broken his eardrums with her screams.

This girl, however, was as silent and still as a barren Afghan desert.

He lifted his shoe, found his footing. Almost there.

A breeze tinged with cinnamon and cider tugged strands of his overly long hair free from his haphazard ponytail. Probably should've gotten a proper haircut for this weekend's event—Apple Fest at the Valley Orchard. He might as well have shaved, too, and buttoned up the flannel shirt currently whipping in the wind over his plain tee.

But then, why did it matter how he looked? This was his sister's big day, not his. Between the hayrides and the petting zoo and this new climbing wall, Kit had taken the old family orchard and turned it into a true tourist attraction. Though they'd technically been open to visitors since August, Apple Fest on the last weekend in September always ushered in the beginning of their busy season. Their Friday crowd was helped along by the fact that there wasn't school in Maple Valley today. So the place had been packed since ten this morning.

Which meant Kit had been beaming since this morning.

Which meant he definitely couldn't tell her he was leaving again. Not today.

It was bad enough he planned to duck out early tonight. He was due in town for his friends' surprise engagement party in an hour.

He closed the last inches between him and the girl. "Hey, your name's Haddie, right? I'm Lucas Danby. I'm here to help you down."

Her blond curls fluttered around her face, her white-knuckled grip on the wall tightening. "I-I wasn't scared u-until I looked down."

He nodded as he fished around in his pocket for the spare carabiner. "That's usually how it goes. Took my first chopper ride when I was nineteen. Didn't think I'd be scared at all. But then when we were somewhere over the Wakhan Corridor—that's in the Middle East, by the way—I happened to look down, and well, let's just say I wished I'd skipped the mess tent earlier." He used the metal clip to hook Haddie's harness to his own then detached her belay cable, chatting just to keep her distracted.

She slid him a cautious glance. "You talk a lot, Mr. Lucas."

His cable jostled with his low rumble of laughter. "You should tell that to my sister. Always says I'm too quiet." As did the friends who'd become like family in these past months. Mara and Marshall, engaged as of last week. Sam, who'd been here earlier with his daughter. And Jen . . .

Jenessa Belville.

The heart of the group and probably the only person in the world who could successfully charm him into helping plan tonight's little party for Mara and Marsh.

Pathetic, maybe, but he wished Jen were here now, watching down on the ground with the circle of onlookers. Maybe if she witnessed him scaling a wall and rappelling his way down, a kid tucked under one arm, she'd get a glimpse of the man he might've been. If not for Afghanistan. The court-martial. Prison.

If not for the label time refused to erase. *Dishonorable.*

Didn't matter what he'd done since—the shadowed heroics not even his sister knew about—he was still the Lucas Danby who'd gone off to war fifteen years ago, fresh out of high school, only to desert his post and disappear.

"Mr. Lucas?"

He blinked, released a taut breath. "Sorry, kid. Mind wandered for a sec." To a place he shouldn't let it linger. He needed to think about his future, not his past.

And his future was in D.C. with Bridgewell, the paramilitary company that'd given his life meaning again, even if it did draw him away from Maple Valley for the better part of each year.

He just wished he could figure out why Flagg hadn't

called him in yet. Usually by now he was back in D.C., readying for his next assignment with the team of elite citizen specialists he served alongside. But then, the last mission—a raid on a drug cartel down in South America—hadn't gone according to plan. There'd been that incident with his teammate Courtney, and right before that, he'd taken a pesky bullet to the thigh. Barely more than a scratch but it'd been enough for Flagg to send him home earlier than usual for his annual leave. Four months had stretched into six, and he'd begun to feel like he was in timeout.

On the other hand, there were days when he caught himself imagining what it might be like to stay here in Maple Valley, to have some kind of normal life. Sometimes it almost felt like the past couldn't touch him here, like he might have a future as wide open and golden as the rolling hills beyond the groves of sun-glazed apple trees that once belonged to his grandparents.

If he did stay, if he actually settled down, maybe he could muster up the nerve to have *that* conversation with *that* girl. The one with the dark hair and midnight blue eyes and—

"Why are you smiling like that, Mr. Lucas?"

"Because sometimes long shots are worth smiling about." He couldn't help reaching out to ruffle Haddie's hair. "You can call me Luke, by the way. Now, what do you say you let go of the wall and hang on to me instead?"

She shook her head. "I don't think so."

"Hmm, what's the problem? Do I smell?"

Her giggle drifted on the breeze. "No."

"It's my hair, isn't it? You don't like long hair on dudes, huh?"

"I like your hair."

"You do? Then let's stop stalling." He shifted, his harness digging into his thighs. He almost felt silly wearing the

4

thing. This was an amateur climbing wall, after all. Nothing compared to the grueling, muddied courses he'd barreled through in boot camp.

"I can't. I'm too scared."

"Oh, I think you can. I have a theory that all of us are a little braver than we think. Sometimes we just need another person to notice it." He waited until Haddie looked up to go on. "So let me be the one to point out that you are a very brave girl. Lots of other kids have come by the wall, taken one look at it, and scurried off to the hay-bale maze instead."

"Really?"

"Really. All you have to do is let go and hang on to me." A better option than forcibly prying her loose. "You're already hooked to me, so you won't fall. Promise."

She took a ragged breath, her shoulders lifting, and . . .

Two skinny arms flung toward him, wrapping around his neck as he got a mouthful of hair. "Easy, kid, don't strangle me. Can't rappel us down if I can't breathe."

She only tightened her hold, and he found himself laughing, strangely exhilarated. He gave a quick glance over his shoulder to Beckett, his brother-in-law, down on the ground, holding the line. "All right, Beck. We're—"

A whoosh of shock stole his next words as a figure winding through the orchard grounds seized his attention. Lucas twisted his body sideways, pulling Haddie along with him, gaze straining. He couldn't see the man's face, but that imposing, rigid stature—ever a soldier's gait—and that sharp profile . . .

No. Flagg wouldn't come here. Not when he knew how carefully Lucas separated his two worlds. If Kit knew where Lucas really was all the months when she thought he was down in Mexico working on a fruit farm, nursing his wounds—

"Luke?" Beckett's voice rose from below. "You ready?"

He took a breath and tore his focus away from the man who *wasn't* Flagg. He patted Haddie's back with one hand and, with his other, released his hold on the wall to cling to the cable. "Here we go."

With a huff, he pushed away, his palm scraping against the line as his weight sent him gliding until his feet hit the wood planks once more. Beckett slackened the rope and Lucas pushed off again.

Moments later, he landed in the grass. He unclipped the carabiner from Haddie's harness then crouched to let her slide free. But she lunged for him all over again, kissing his cheek and squeezing his neck.

"Someone has a fan club."

He glanced up to meet his sister's smirk. "Well, I did rescue her."

"Didn't mean her." Kit folded her arms as Lucas rose and Haddie skipped away to her mother. "I meant them." She nodded her head toward a group of teen girls gathered near the parking lot.

Beckett stepped forward to take Lucas's harness. "I give it two minutes before one of them comes over, makes the climb, then pretends to get scared at the top—just so Superman here can race to the rescue." He slipped his arm around Kit and kissed the top of her head. "Installing the climbing wall was genius, Mrs. Walker. Good for business and for your brother's image."

Lucas pasted on his best scowl. "You guys are ridiculous, you know that?" Not to mention they acted as much like newlyweds as ever, never mind they'd been married almost two years.

Which was exactly why he'd been staying at the Everwood B&B all spring and summer instead of the orchard farmhouse he'd grown up in. 'Course, it helped that all his friends lived there at the moment, too—Mara in the owner's private living quarters on the first floor, and Sam, Marshall, and Lucas in a row of rooms upstairs.

Even Jen had taken to staying at the B&B in recent weeks. She said it was to avoid the overbearing mess of the house she'd inherited from her parents, but he had a feeling she just didn't want to be left out of their little group. After all, she was the reason they were all so connected in the first place. She'd befriended each of them separately, eventually stitching individual threads of friendship into something sturdy and complete.

Speaking of, he had somewhere to be soon. "Beck, you okay to man the wall on your own now? I've got that engagement party tonight, but I want to check the hitch on the tractor before I head out."

"It'll disappoint your fan club to see you go, but yeah, I can handle it from here. Kit can help if any more rescues are required. Or my dad—he's around here somewhere."

Lucas turned to his sister. "Kit, today was perfect. You've built this place into something incredible. Grandma and Grandpa would be proud."

"Lucas, I . . ." She paused. "I can't decide whether to tear up because of how sweet it is of you to say something like that or go into shock over you going to any kind of party at all."

"I'm not a total hermit."

"Says the man who routinely disappears for more than half a year at a time. And when he is home, chooses to live in a B&B instead of with family. And treats extended silences like first-rate entertainment."

Was it just him or was there an underlying hint of . . . something he couldn't decipher in his sister's tone? But as quickly as he detected it, she shook it off. "Go on. I'll help Beck at the wall. He's *my* first-rate entertainment."

7

Lucas played up his scowl. "Gross. And you wonder why I don't live with you guys." At Kit's laugh, he turned, still smiling . . . but froze before taking a single step.

Arthur G. Flagg stood not ten feet away, thick eyebrows raised. "Danby."

Lucas thrust a glance over his shoulder to Kit. For once, he was grateful for her constant adoration of her husband. Meant she was too busy flirting with Beckett to notice Flagg, entirely out of place in his starched slacks and crisp shirt and tie.

He marched forward and motioned for Flagg to follow. More strands of hair escaped his ponytail and the wind whipped the ends of his shirt. He scratched at the scars underneath his sleeves as he walked. "What are you doing here?"

"You called me three times this week. Would've thought I might get a warmer welcome."

Yes, and if Flagg had actually come all this way instead of simply returning his calls, he must have bad news to deliver. Was he cutting Lucas from the elite team? Moving him back to basic contractor status? "My family doesn't know—"

"Lucas."

Every muscle in his body clenched at Flagg's granite tone and the steel in his eyes and what it must mean. At the realization that whatever it was he'd begun to feel here in Maple Valley, it was only wishful thinking. A false hope.

No match for the truth that his past could always, *always* find him. If not in his nightmares, then right here where he stood.

---

2

*I*t was the letter that finally made her do it.

Crinkled yet unopened. Scribbled words faded, blue ink smeared. *Return to Sender.*

Jenessa's final attempt, as fruitless as all the others.

When she'd spotted the envelope peeking out from the pile of mail on her newsroom desk, something inside of her —the last of a decades-old brittle hope—had snapped.

So here she stood, swallowed up in the long, late-afternoon shadow of Belville Park, feet rooted to the sidewalk just outside the wrought-iron gate. Her childhood home peered back at her from yawning windows evenly spaced between slabs of white-gray stone, braided ivy climbing the west wall.

It waited, stately and still, as if sensing the coming goodbye—this house that had never been the same after Aunt Lauren disappeared.

"So, are we going in?" Paige Parker's thick Southern drawl did little to veil her curiosity, anticipation swimming in the younger woman's eyes.

Probably a normal reaction for anyone taking in Belville

Park for the first time. After all, the massive house and surrounding grounds looked like the kind of estate that belonged on the outskirts of a wealthy New England neighborhood or, better, the English countryside . . . not in the middle of small-town Iowa.

"I should warn you it's not as impressive inside. I mean, yeah, there's twenty-four rooms, including a master suite that's bigger than the whole *Maple Valley News* office, but my parents weren't exactly up to Marie Kondo standards by the end."

A hoarder's paradise—that's what Lucas had called the house once.

He wasn't wrong.

Although, it wasn't fair to entirely blame Mom and Dad for the state of the house. While it was their shared four decades' worth of possessions cluttering the mansion, Jenessa was the one who'd left half-packed boxes and bags strewn about the place before giving up on the overwhelming task of sorting through their things.

The interior might be a neglected mess, but she had every intention of whipping the patio out back into shape for tonight's gathering with her best friends—a little celebration of Mara and Marshall's engagement. She'd have rather hosted the small party at the Everwood where they all lived at the moment, but considering Mara owned the place, keeping it a surprise would've been impossible.

Paige shifted the boxes in her hands, her short brown braids peeking out underneath her ball cap, tangled twinkle lights spilling out of the top box. "Well, I still want a tour, no matter what it looks like inside. Why do you think I offered to help you lug all these decorations here?"

Jenessa grinned. "I thought maybe you were still brown-nosing, trying to impress the ol' boss by going above and beyond the call of duty." And it wouldn't be the first time.

Honestly, hiring Paige at the newspaper this summer might've been the smartest business move Jenessa had ever made.

Sure, buying the *News* three years ago and bringing it back from the brink of financial ruin had been a fun challenge at the time, a nice distraction from the difficulties of caring for both Mom and Dad in their final years. But the thrill of running it singlehandedly had lost some of its luster lately.

Or maybe it was just the weight of this house and all it represented dragging down her spirits in recent weeks—months, really. Maybe once she let go, decluttered her life a little, she'd feel a glimmer of the old Jenessa. The one who didn't have to force her buoyant disposition or stay busy to convince herself the life she'd chosen was actually the life she wanted.

"Let me get this sign in the ground and then we'll go in."

A light nudge was all it took for the gate to swing wide, creaking into the pull of the wind. Curled leaves tumbled over the sprawling lawn, the branches of the towering walnut tree in the front yard rustling against the usual quiet of the neighborhood.

Jenessa tucked her chin into the collar of her denim coat and stepped onto the brick path that led to the massive front door. The entrance was flanked on both sides by empty bronze urns and topped by a half-circle window of swirled glass. Prickly, untrimmed hedges lined the walkway and fanned out in front of the house.

Not exactly the homiest of pictures—no cozy porch or swaying wooden swing—but then, Belville Park hadn't felt like home in years.

Which was exactly why she'd decided it was finally time. Mom had been gone a year; Dad, nearly two. And this place was far too big and, worse, far too crowded with memories, old sights and sounds she'd never be able to shake.

Dad's yells and Mom's tears and Aunt Lauren running from the house . . .

Closure, that's what she needed. No more stalling, hoping if she waited long enough all her old questions might somehow find new answers. Wasn't going to happen. The returned letter Aunt Lauren, Mom's sister, hadn't even bothered to open made that much clear.

She halted halfway up the brick path and pulled the *For Sale by Owner* sign from underneath her arm. Grass and dirt gave way easily when she pressed the metal stakes down, using the wedged heel of her ankle boot to push the sign into place.

She took a step back, resolve or maybe relief filling her sigh. And then, a smile. Because she was being dramatic. Sam would make fun of her if he were here. Mara and Marshall would laugh. Lucas would stand by, quiet as ever at first, but then he'd most likely be the first to ask if she was sure she wanted to do this.

"Yes, I'm sure." The wind hushed her whisper.

But Paige must've heard it anyway. "Um, if you're, like, having a moment or something, I can wait back at the car."

A laugh pushed free. "I can't help being theatrical. It's in my blood. My mom was an actress back in the day." Before she'd married Dad and settled into her role as a senator's wife.

Jenessa hurried to the entrance, balancing her box in one hand and with her other, plucking a key from the pocket of her maroon skirt—a perfect match for the scarf taming her near-black waves. The moment she opened the door, the familiar scent of Mom's old lavender perfume wafted over her. Stupefying, how it managed to linger even after all these months.

Paige's gasp accompanied the sound of her steps as she followed Jenessa.

"I'm telling you, Parker, don't let the foyer fool you. It goes downhill from here."

"The floor is marble." Paige set her box on the antique accent table near the bottom of the open, winding staircase.

"And ridiculously cold in the winter." Jenessa draped her jacket over the stairway banister, then moved into the sitting room. With its pale blue walls and gaping windows bordered by paisley-print curtains, it was the most formal of all twenty-four rooms.

The most cluttered, too. Mom and Dad had loved their things—figurines, books, travel souvenirs. A mess of carelessly packed boxes edged up to one wall.

"Jen, this place is . . . it's . . ."

"Prim and overly decorous?"

"Elegant and incredible." Paige was already moving through the room, skirting around the pearl-hued, tufted chaise lounge and craning her neck to take in the tray ceiling. She crossed into the music room, where the only thing more impressive than the floor-to-ceiling white bookshelves on the far wall was the grand piano in the corner.

Paige's gasps trailed from room to room—Dad's mahogany wood-paneled study, the adjoining library, the dining room with its waist-high wainscoting and crystal chandelier, family living room, spacious kitchen.

She could understand Paige's awe, she supposed. The house itself was in good shape—modern enough for daily living, yet awash with the kind of character that came only from age and craftmanship. It just needed a thorough purging and some homier touches.

Finally, they passed through the French doors that led into the sunroom at the back of the house. Orange sunlight poured through generous windows, skimming over the surfaces of the wicker loveseat and glass table.

For the first time since they'd stepped into the house, Jenessa grinned. "Did you finally run out of gasps?"

"Maybe words, too." Paige's gaze was fixed on the expansive yard—two acres of land including Mom's once-glorious flower gardens, a riot of color in years past, complete with a quaint stone path and a fountain, currently nonfunctional, in the center. A thicket of ancient, craggy trees bordered the property.

And there at the back, nestled in the brush—the little caretaker's cottage with the pretty blue shutters and matching flowerboxes Aunt Lauren used to fill like clock-work each spring.

Paige turned to her. "I can't believe you're really going to sell this. It might be a little messy but—"

"A little messy? Paige, this house is like a massive garage sale gone wrong." Maybe she could hire someone to sort through everything or organize an auction or estate sale. She'd need to do something about the overgrown gardens, too. The broken fountain. That tree that had fallen down during the tornado of 2014 and crushed the shed.

Huh, perhaps sticking that *For Sale* sign in the ground had been a little hasty. Still, it was the symbolism of it all. She might feel differently about the whole thing if the family legacy hadn't crumbled years ago. If she wasn't the last Belville left.

But it had and she was and she just couldn't see what good it would do anymore to pretend there was anything left for her here.

"Think of what you could do with it, though. You could turn it into an inn."

"And compete with the Everwood? Which happens to be run by one of my best friends?" A friend who would be here

14

soon. Jenessa opened the patio door and stepped outside. Yes, a few twinkle lights, some candles, the cupcakes she'd picked up at the Sugar Lane Bakery, and a couple of pizzas from Petey's and they'd have a perfect little celebration.

"Fine, it could be a bookstore," Paige said, following her outside. "Or a fancy restaurant—like a London tearoom where ladies wear posh hats and eat tiny sandwiches with their pinkies in the air."

Jenessa chuckled as she righted a weathered cushion on a rattan chair. "Sometimes I forget how new you are around here. This is small-town Iowa. We don't do posh." Then again, Mom had thrown any number of glittering, lavish galas out in the backyard once upon a time. They'd been pretty amazing, actually—lights and music and the gorgeous splendor of Mom's gardens. Her parents had been in their element then. They'd been . . . happy.

But that had been before Dad's fall from grace. Before Mom's drinking grew worse. Before . . . everything.

See, this is why you're selling. The memories—

She halted, gaze snagging on the cottage for a moment. On one of its windows and . . . had she just seen light, a movement?

"What is it?" Paige came up beside her.

Jenessa peered across the lawn, eyes narrowing as she took in the cottage's little wooden door, the sloping roof, the windows, each line and arch so familiar and beckoning she could almost hear Aunt Lauren's voice.

"This can be your safe haven, too, Jen. Yours and mine. We'll dream about a future that's brighter than either one of us can even imagine."

That had been Aunt Lauren—whimsical and imaginative and artsy. She'd taught Jenessa to dream in vivid color, to picture life as the beautiful adventure it could be.

If only she'd given her some warning about what

happened when the dream faded. When life at thirty-five—
however it might appear—just felt a little too . . . meander-
ing. Less an adventure and more a wandering. And sometimes, a lonely one. Even with the best of friends filling her
days.

"Jen?"

Paige's voice snapped her back to the present. "Sorry,
thought I saw something for a sec, but I was wrong." Just
like she'd been wrong when she'd hoped her aunt might
answer her latest letter.

But no. Not once had her aunt responded to a letter, an
email, a phone call. Twenty-three years of silence. *No more
waiting.*

Jenessa exhaled and turned to Paige. "Come on, I've got
a party to get ready for." A gathering that might as well
serve two purposes. A celebration for Mara and Marshall's
engagement . . . and her own little personal goodbye party.

To this house and that cottage and everything else best
laid to rest.

3

"*S*ir, if you're going to cut me from the team, I wish you'd just say so."

Lights beamed from the windows of the Everwood Bed & Breakfast just down the lane. Blue-black shadows brushed rolling fields in the distance. Was rain on the way? The rumbling engine of Arthur Flagg's rental sedan rose over the crunching of gravel.

Lucas was pretty sure he'd seen Kit spot the pair of them leaving the orchard. Which on its own was reason for concern, but then to find out Flagg had checked in at the Everwood? Asked Mara where to find Lucas?

Lucas might as well just give it up, spill his secrets to his family, his friends.

I haven't been spending winters working on a fruit farm in Mexico. I'm part of Bridgewell Elite, a civilian black-ops team. I was recruited ten years ago. I started out as a regular private military contractor but now . . .

How many times had he mentally rehearsed the explanation? And how could the thought of saying the words out loud feel so tempting and so terrible all at the same time?

And why . . . why was Flagg here? Why hadn't he said more than a few words on the ten-minute drive from the orchard to the Everwood?

"Lucas." Flagg cut the engine with a flick of his wrist. "I'm not here to let you go."

"Then why—"

"But I'm not here to call you back either."

Lucas could only stare at the older man. Flagg's hair was grayer than when he'd last seen him and new creases had joined the web of wrinkles in his face. His was a weathered sturdiness, and the glint in his pale blue eyes was as compassionate as it was firm.

Compassion—that was always the thing that undid Lucas. Because he didn't deserve it. Just like he didn't deserve any of Flagg's kindness. Not after all he'd done. Not with those two words marring his record—*dishonorable discharge.*

But Flagg had a soft spot for ex-soldiers, convicts, scarred men with blemished pasts—all of which described Lucas.

"I'm supposed to be at a friend's house now. I need to change." He was already late. He pushed his door open and slid from the vehicle. The lofty, three-story Victorian house tucked away on a small homestead, encircled by a grove of dogwood and shagbark trees, had become as familiar to him as his childhood home.

Flagg's steps sounded in the grass behind him. "I know it's probably been killing you—not hearing from me. I'll admit, Danby, I've been struggling to know what the right course is when it comes to you."

Lucas climbed the porch stairs, no longer as rickety as they'd been when he first moved in. "If this is about Courtney, sir, I swear I didn't realize . . . I didn't know . . ." Hadn't a clue his teammate had developed . . . *feelings* for him.

It'd all been so ridiculous. He'd been in the hospital after getting shot and she'd come to visit. Had kissed him and he'd overreacted, practically pushing her into the nurse who'd come into the room and—well, everything had gotten awkward from there. Frankly, he'd been more than a little relieved when Flagg had suggested a longer hiatus post-mission this time.

But to let something like that break up the team indefinitely? When they had so many years of successful missions under their belts?

Lucas stepped over the Everwood's threshold and moved to the open staircase.

Flagg followed—relentless. "Why would it be about Courtney? Please don't tell me—"

"Nothing happened." Save a working relationship turned uncomfortable. But Court would've gotten over it by now, right? She was a professional. "And if it's not that—"

"You didn't have to take that bullet in Venezuela, son."

Lucas paused halfway up the stairs.

"You broke protocol. You took a risk no one asked you to take. You could've blown the operation."

"But I didn't." The raid had been successful and they'd managed to bust up the entire cartel without any hint of the U.S. government's involvement—the whole point of their team.

He finished climbing the stairs and reached his room in seconds, Flagg just behind him. The familiar scents of cedar and clean linens tugged him forward. It was a simply arranged room—queen bed, chest of drawers, closet in the corner. But there was something satisfying about the space. Maybe it was the fact that he'd painted it himself during the months Mara and Marshall had worked to renovate the bed and breakfast.

In fact, he'd helped all around the place in between shifts at the orchard. He'd peeled off old wallpaper, hauled out broken furniture, carried in replacement mattresses.

And all the while, his ties had deepened—to this house and this town and the four friends who'd somehow burrowed past his reserve. His team back in D.C. operated on camaraderie and trust in each other's skills. But these friendships back home? They went deeper.

So why was he so set on returning to D.C.? So needled at the thought that Flagg might not want him back?

Because after having been so sure at one time that he'd squandered and spoiled any opportunity to serve his country, his work with Bridgewell, high-risk and secretive as it was, had given him an undeserved second chance. He owed all his loyalty and dedication to the company, to Flagg.

He opened a dresser drawer, pausing as his gaze lifted to the mirror above. The B&B wasn't the only thing that had transformed during his six months here. Weeks of work outside had bronzed his skin and his dusty brown hair was longer and wavier than ever. Just because he could, he always went two or three days without shaving when he was off the company clock. But more significantly, gone were the shadows under his eyes, the gauntness in his cheeks he always brought home from missions.

Flagg came up beside him. "You haven't been to see Clayborne in some time."

His therapist. The one Flagg had insisted he begin meeting with after he'd first recruited him. He met Flagg's eyes in the mirror. "If you're worried my actions in Venezuela were some kind of PTSD-induced brain malfunction, don't. That's been under control for a long time. I simply saw an opening and made a split-second decision. I'm sorry if it was the wrong one, but we completed the assignment."

He reached behind his head to free his hair from its limp ponytail before pulling a clean shirt from his dresser drawer. Jenessa would lecture him for being late, and he would take it like he always did—with quiet amusement and no small degree of gratitude.

Because in a town filled with people who still only saw him as the hometown kid who couldn't make good, who'd shamed his family and his country, Jen and the others were his saving grace.

"Art?" His voice went low as he dropped the shirt, turned. Flagg had perched on the edge of his bed. "Why haven't you ever asked me why I deserted?"

Everyone else had. The MPs who'd finally hauled him back to the States for his court-martial in 2008. The JAG who'd been assigned to his case. The reporters who'd dragged his name through the headlines after the military tribunal had sentenced him to three years in prison, longer than any American deserter since Vietnam.

And Dad. Career Army man himself, he'd done more prodding than anyone. Had demanded an explanation the moment Lucas stepped onto the tarmac upon his return. No hug. No handshake.

But he shouldn't have been surprised. Lucas's mother had died when he was only a toddler. It would've been nice if his remaining parent had at least tried to fill in the gaps. But instead Dad had let other relatives care for Lucas and Kit for several years before bringing them to their grandparents in Iowa and returning to his base. They saw less and less of him throughout their teenage years.

"I did ask," Flagg countered. "That first day I came to see you in prison."

"No, you asked me if I had a good reason. You never asked what the reason was."

"Well, you said you did. That was enough for me.

Besides, I knew you were only two years out of high school when you went AWOL. I knew about the IED. I knew . . . about the boy."

Tashfeen.

Just the name hovering at the edges of his mind was enough to make him twist away.

Don't think about Dad. Don't think about Tashfeen. He slipped one hand under the sleeve of the opposite arm, scraped his fingers over the mottled skin.

"They still bother you?"

Lucas closed his eyes, scratched the other arm.

"How about the nightmares?"

Lucas shrugged, forced his eyes open. He crossed the room to the window and opened it, wished the fresh air and the rural landscape and this place he'd come to love could work some kind of magic. Make him forget. Just for a while. The wind rustled, bending the limber branches of a row of young, scrawny trees below.

Years ago, when the nightmares had first begun, he'd tried praying them away. But his faith had proven as fragile as his honor.

Flagg rose and came to stand beside him once more. He placed his palm on Lucas's shoulder. "I do have an assignment for you, son. I'll tell you right off the bat, you're probably not going to like it. But I want you to take it on and take it seriously."

Son. It was the second time Flagg had called him that. Lucas would do just about anything for Flagg. The man had to know that.

"Someone else is on his way to Iowa. Name's Noah Johannson. Twenty-seven. Medically discharged last fall and he's not happy about it. Got in some legal trouble over the winter."

Lucas turned away from the window. "Another one of

your not-so-lost causes?" It was the phrase he'd used on Lucas when he'd come to the prison to see him. Back when Lucas had been wasting away in his shame, so painfully sure the only thing waiting for him on the horizon was a future of disgrace.

"He needs a change of scenery. Some time to consider his options." Flagg held his focus captive. "Needs a mentor."

Wait . . . no. "Sir, I'm the last person—"

"I want you to spend the next four or five weeks with him. Already reserved him a room across the hall. He'll be here tomorrow."

"What? What am I supposed to—"

"Take him under your wing. Swap Army stories. Give him a realistic view of what signing on with Bridgewell means." Flagg leaned against the dresser behind him. "Maybe test his mettle a little. I'll check in with you periodically, see how it's going."

"But, sir—"

"This is the assignment, Lucas. Complete it with the same focus you've completed every other mission and come November, we'll talk about your return to D.C."

In other words, his future with Bridgewell Elite depended on this. On playing big brother to a stranger.

"Now," Flagg said, clapping his palms together and crossing the room, "where's a man get something to eat in a town like this?"

"I vote if Lucas doesn't show up in the next ten minutes, one of us drives over to the orchard and drags him here."

Jenessa flopped onto the lawn chair closest to the stone fireplace at the edge of the patio. With the lights and candles and *Congratulations* banner, she'd pulled off a nice little celebration if she did say so herself. Even the weather was cooperating, dusk just beginning to paint the sky in autumn colors—streaks of red and amber and yellow. As long as those pillowy gray clouds in the distance managed to stay away.

Mara and Marshall had arrived half an hour ago, expecting to pick up Jenessa and head downtown for dinner out. Instead, she'd coaxed them through the house and out to the patio, where the surprise engagement party awaited—only their small friend group since Lucas had talked her out of her original plan of a larger, grander shindig in the town square. Paige hadn't even stuck around, so it was just the four of them so far.

Sam, thankfully, had come bearing firewood. He crouched near the fireplace now, arranging logs, concentration etched into his wrinkled brow. "Lucas will get here when he gets here."

"Yeah, but the pizza's going to be delivered any minute. That boy is always late to everything." And speaking of missing people, shouldn't Mara and Marsh be back out here by now? They'd gone inside to fetch cans of pop from the fridge.

Sam straightened a log, gave a satisfied nod, then stood. He crossed his arms—his usual police chief stance—and cocked one dark eyebrow. "*That boy* is only two years younger than you and he'd cringe if he heard you call him that."

"No, he'll cringe when he hears my lecture if he doesn't get here soon. He's terrified of my lectures. It's why he finally agreed to drive the *News*'s float in the Fourth of July parade. And came to the Labor Day picnic. And shows up to church now and then."

Sam pressed his lips together, his standard scowl and

the hint of premature gray at his temples always making him look so much older than mid-thirties. "Yeah, Jen. He's scared of you. Sure."

A chilly draft swept over the patio and she pulled her legs onto the cushion, having traded her ankle boots for simple canvas flats earlier. Leggings and a skirt might not have been the best option for a cool near-fall night, but soon enough the fire would warm her up.

As would the presence of these friends she loved so. Sam, who'd she'd known longer than the others. Mara and Marshall, who'd only come into her life this past spring. Lucas, if he ever got here.

A makeshift family, that's what they'd become, somehow all ending up at the Everwood right when they'd needed each other most.

"You could've told me, you know."

She glanced up in time to see a flicker of concern—or maybe something more like frustration—flash in Sam's brown eyes. But he suppressed it in a blink, only the slight tic in his jaw giving away any hint of emotion. "Told you what?"

"The house. You're finally selling."

"You saw the sign out front—"

"I'm not blind. Of course I did." He dropped his arms and plopped onto the chair beside her. "And even if I hadn't, I heard about it before I got here. This is Maple Valley. Gossip spreads faster than the flu. You know that."

"So that's why you're extra grumpy tonight? Because I didn't tell you before the local rumor mill?"

"I'm not extra grumpy."

"You're glowering."

"And you're—" He clipped his words but gave his glare a few more seconds to fade before softening his tone. "It's just . . . I know how much history there is in this place."

Personal history, he meant, though considering her ancestors had practically built Maple Valley, there was plenty of actual history, too. And truthfully, Sam didn't know the half of it. Sure, he knew how hard it'd been for her those few years of caring for her ailing parents before they'd passed. He knew about the breakup she'd gone through back then, too—an old relationship that had gone on far too long.

But he didn't know about the early years. About the cottage and Aunt Lauren and the cold, unrelenting silence after she disappeared. About the toll of Dad's campaigns and the harsh realities of Mom's up-and-down battle with alcoholism.

About the part Jenessa had played in it all.

"She's a liability, Granger. Surely that's clear to you by now." The voice of Dad's old campaign advisor murmured through her mind. As clear now as it'd been when she was only twelve years old and unequipped to handle the grief of Aunt Lauren's leaving.

That was when she'd first learned the importance of controlling her emotions.

Hiding them, more like.

"Jen."

She met Sam's eyes. He wore that look that was as much scrutinizing cop as it was observant friend—keen and probing. "I know it must be hard. You've been putting it off for a long time. We're all here for you."

"It's okay, Sam. You don't have to make a speech."

"I wasn't making a speech." His eyes narrowed. "I suppose you think I was going to offer you a hug or something, too."

Another gust of wind whooshed through the trees, shaking the twinkle lights and blowing out one of the candles. She laughed. "Come on, let's go figure out what happened to M&M. And maybe one of us should text Lucas while we're at it." At this rate, those clouds in the distance would roll in before he did.

Sam's steps lumbered behind her. "By the way, what are you going to do with all the money?"

"Money?" She slid open the patio door.

"When you sell the house. Didn't your parents already leave you an inheritance? You're going to be loaded once you find someone to buy this place. Don't tell me you don't have plans for what you're going to do with it."

"Actually, I don't."

"I don't believe it. You're Jen Belville. You always have a plan. And you're obviously bored at the newspaper so—"

"You can tell?"

He grunted as he trailed her through the sunroom. "Everyone can tell."

"Paige said instead of selling the house I should turn it into a bookstore or something. Maybe she has a point. I mean, I have been a little . . ." She paused with her palm on the knob of the French doors.

"A little what?" Sam prodded.

Restless. Discontent.

Unhappy. That was the nonsensical gist of it. Nonsensical because she couldn't explain it. Knew that if she tried, Sam would probably look at her the same way her parents had too many times.

Better to smile and laugh and be the breezy Jenessa Belville everyone knew. "Oh, nothing, Sam."

He followed her to the kitchen where they found Marshall leaning against a counter and Mara perched on the island , her feet dangling over the edge. Marshall flashed an easy grin. "Hey, guys, what's up?"

Sam folded his arms. "Guess you forgot you were supposed to be grabbing drinks, huh?"

Mara's pink cheeks and burst of laughter, the constant joy she wore these days, made it almost impossible to believe this was the same wary, wounded woman Jenessa had first met six months ago.

Marshall radiated the same contentedness as his fiancée. He'd come to Maple Valley last spring a broken man, but a person would never know it by looking at him tonight. In Mara, he'd found unexpected healing and happiness, and in the Everwood, a home.

And so had Jenessa. More and more, the Everwood had become her happy place, a needed distraction from the dissatisfaction she'd begun to feel with her life. She'd gotten used to sharing a morning coffee with Mara before heading into the newspaper office. To Saturday evening movies in the B&B den and the sound of Sam's snores echoing down the hallway most nights.

Or the floorboards creaking as Lucas paced after one of the nightmares he probably thought none of them knew about.

"All right, who wants to be the one to call Lucas and interrogate him about his whereabouts? I've already texted him twice so—" She broke off at the unwelcome sound pattering from outside. "Please tell me that's not rain." She twisted to look over her shoulder, out the window above the kitchen sink.

Sam gave her an apologetic look. "It appears we might have to move the party inside."

"The cupcakes!" She'd left them sitting out on the patio table, the box open, along with paper plates and plastic silverware and—Jenessa froze, her gaze locked on the view out the window. On Aunt Lauren's cottage. A gushing wind grappled with the branches of the trees around the little stone house and a thin sheet of rain blurred her view.

But she could see enough. Movement. A glint of light.

She whirled.

"What is it?" Mara's voice called after her.

"I'll grab the cupcakes." Sam hurried beside her. "You get the plates and napkins."

"No, it's not that." She burst outside, a new chill sweeping in with the clouds overhead. She pointed past the unkept gardens, raindrops tapping on her shoulders. "Do you see that? Someone's in the cottage." She stepped off the patio, but Sam's hand on her arm stopped her.

"Yeah, I see it. You stay. Save the cupcakes. I'll check it out."

She pulled away and pitched forward, grass already growing damp and slick underneath her shoes as she headed toward the trees. "I'm sure it's just a couple of bored teens looking for cheap entertainment, Sam. The last thing we need is the chief of police scaring them half to death."

Even as the words left her mouth, she could feel a foolish, irrational hope bubbling up inside of her. She swiped at the rivulets running down her cheeks and picked up her pace.

Don't let your thoughts go there. It's not her.

"If it's teens trespassing, isn't a cop exactly what you need?" Sam's voice rose over the increasing wind. She could hear Mara and Marshall following as well, and the huff of her own breath as her steps turned into a run.

Stop it. It's not her. She didn't even open the letter. She didn't respond to a single email. Twenty-three years and not one word. She didn't even say goodbye.

She nearly tripped over a sprawling, leafy vine at the edge of Mom's garden, and as the rain thickened, it matted her hair to her face, caught in her eyelashes, and forced her to slow.

Until finally, she reached the arched wooden door, and

despite the nagging voice of her logic, breathless words released in a gasp as she pushed inside. "Aunt Lauren?"

But it wasn't her aunt who gaped at her from the center of the little room. Two small faces with wide, scared eyes—no, three, the third bundled in a blanket, encased in the arms of a girl who couldn't be older than ten or eleven.

Sam came up beside her, breath heavy. "What in the—"

The baby's wail cut him off.

Convincing the kids she'd found in Aunt Lauren's cottage to come to the house had been hard enough. But getting them to talk? Nearly impossible.

Jenessa stood at the island counter in her parents' kitchen, eyes glued to the two girls huddled together at the breakfast nook in the corner. She'd been wrong about the one who'd held the baby earlier—Colie. She'd thought the girl must be around ten years old, but in the few sparse sentences she'd offered, she'd discovered Colie was twelve.

Violet, who'd already tucked away two pieces of pepperoni pizza, was six. The baby, Cade, was nine months old. Mara held him now, perched on the bench across the girls with Marshall at her side, Cade's small body scrunched against her chest and his head nestled against her shoulder, the both of them looking perfectly content.

Colie glanced to her younger brother in between every bite of pizza, as suspicious and protective as she'd been since the moment Jenessa had burst into the cottage.

Thunder rumbled outside the kitchen window, what had started as a light rain now a full-on storm. Wind hurled itself against the house.

"You should go change, Jen." Sam's voice was low beside her. "Put on some dry clothes."

They'd managed to keep the kids from getting too wet on the hurried trek to the house, but Jenessa's sweater still clung to her skin and moisture had seeped through her canvas shoes. "What do I do with them?" she whispered.

"Well, I think feeding them was a good start. Petey's delivery had good timing, at least."

Yes, it hadn't taken more than a few minutes to figure out the kids hadn't eaten since morning. Cade, at least, had apparently had a full bottle recently, but the girls . . .

Her gaze swept over them again—Colie's stick-straight dark hair the opposite of Violet's blond spirals, both girls thin and their clothing worn and faded. Violet happened to look up just then, her cheeks bulging. She swallowed then lifted one corner of her mouth in a shy half-smile.

Something warm and welcome spread through Jenessa, momentarily crowding out the chill of her wet clothing and her complete cluelessness as to what to do next. She couldn't stop from smiling in return, a quiet chuckle pushing out when Violet took another enormous bite.

"I think normally if someone found three abandoned children squatting on their property, they'd call the police," Sam said quietly. Lightning flashed at the window behind him. "But considering I am the police, well . . ." He reached for the pizza box on the counter and lifted a slice. "We probably need to call DHS."

The Department of Human Services. "But it's the weekend."

"I'm sure there's an emergency number. I'll look into it."

Jenessa pushed away from the counter. "At least let me try to get a little more information first." Although they'd all seen how well that had gone so far. She didn't even know the kids' last name—or names. She'd assumed they were siblings. Colie's protectiveness surely seemed like that of an older sister. But all Colie had been willing to say to this point was to confirm that they were alone. That they'd only stayed in the cottage one night. That they hadn't run away from home because they didn't have a home *to* run away from.

But what exactly that meant, Jenessa wasn't sure. She ambled to the table now, careful to keep her smile in place and the closest thing to ease she could manage in her movements. "Can we get either of you more pizza?"

Colie shook her head, but Violet nodded, her curls bouncing around her heart-shaped face. Sam carried over the pizza box and set a piece on Violet's plate.

Jenessa glanced at Mara before speaking. Cade was sound asleep now.

"So girls, um, I was wondering . . . well, is there anyone who might need to know where you are right now? Parents or grandparents?"

"It's just us," Colie said quickly.

"But you can't be entirely on your own. How'd you even get here? Did someone drive you or—"

"They took Momma's car," Violet cut in.

"Vi," the older girl hissed.

"What? They did." She set down her half-eaten slice of pizza. "First they took Momma. Then they took the car. And Colie says they're gonna take the house, too, so we might as well leave. We walked and walked and pretended to be exp'orers and then we found the little house."

Colie's green eyes flashed with censure as she glared at her sister.

So they'd just stumbled upon the cottage? "What do you mean someone took your mom?"

"Not like that." Colie's tone was flat. "She died. The ambulance took her."

At Jenessa's side, Mara's quick inhale matched her own shock, tinged with a well of pity for these children. "And . . . and your father?"

Silence.

"Could you at least tell me your last name?"

Violet brightened. "It's Hollis! I'm Violet Jeamine Hollis."

Colie rolled her eyes. "Jeanine."

"And what was your mom's name?" She nearly tripped over that word in the middle—*was*. What the reality of it meant for these kids. How long ago had she died? Was there no father in the picture? Had they somehow slipped through the cracks, been left to fend for themselves? Maybe they were in foster care.

Everything in her wanted to fire more questions at them and push for answers. But there were already shadows under Colie's eyes and Violet's chewing had paused, her slow blink attesting to the possibility that she might fall asleep at any moment, mouth still full.

"Tessa," Colie finally answered.

Tessa Hollis.

Jenessa looked over her shoulder at Sam. He nodded. He'd do his cop thing—look up the name, confirm what little they knew of the kids' story. But for now . . .

"Colie, I don't want to bombard you with questions. But I really do need to know if you're sure there's no one worried about where you are right now."

Quiet seconds ticked by until, finally, for the first time since she'd discovered Colie, Violet, and Cade Hollis in the cottage, the oldest girl met her eyes. "I'm sure."

Well, at least she knew one thing, then. She wouldn't be returning to the Everwood tonight.

4

*H*e heard the explosion before he saw it. Its heart-stopping boom shook the earth—rattling the ground underneath his Army-issued boots until his knees hit the grass.

The smoke came next—acrid and black—tumbling over him in a cloud.

Then, when his eyes dared to squint and open, the sight of the flames, grappling toward the sky even as they fanned in every direction.

And finally, the realization. *The village boys.*

The ones who came out to watch every day as Lucas's unit worked on the fence around freshly plowed fields. The ones who spoke in broken English while laughing at his attempts to master Dari.

The ones who'd been kicking around a ball in the same place where a scorching blaze devoured the terrain.

He was on his feet and running, yelling—at the boys, at his walkie-talkie, at his closest buddy working a mile away. And no one could hear him—no one—he knew it.

And then he saw the bodies.

He saw Tashfeen.

He . . .

Lucas sat up with a jolt, heart thrashing against his chest and the searing pain he knew too well racing up his arms. Great, he'd been scratching at them in his sleep again. His bed sheet was twisted around his legs, and he must've thrown off his comforter at some point.

He glanced at the clock on his nightstand. Only 11:15?

He fell back against his pillows, willing his panting breaths to slow. Same old nightmare but at least he'd woken earlier than usual. And come to think of it, he'd gone a good three and a half weeks without the dream.

Regardless, he'd need to get up, walk it off, if he had any hope of sleeping the rest of the night. He forced himself to sit up again, swing his legs over the edge of the bed. He stood and padded, barefoot, across the room and back again.

After half a year living in this room, he'd probably tread a pattern into the tasseled area rug by now. Jen had joked once that even from across and down the hall she could hear the creaking of old floorboards at night when he paced. He'd mumbled something about being a fussy sleeper.

But she wasn't dumb. Kit had picked up on the nightmares in recent summers when he'd stayed at the farmhouse. Jen and the others likely had, too.

He paused halfway across the room. *Wait . . . Jen.*

Had she ever come back to the Everwood tonight? He'd heard Mara and Marshall return nearly two hours ago, their voices carrying upstairs. He'd seen Sam's vehicle pull into the lot soon after and had considered going downstairs to check in. But then of course they'd ask why he'd never shown up at Jen's house for the party and he'd be caught between giving a vague explanation about Flagg's presence, which would only invite more questions, or flat-out lying, which would only leave him feeling guilty.

So he'd holed up in his room instead. And apparently the rest of them had taken his lack of response to any of their earlier texts and calls as a signal that he didn't want to be bothered. He should've been relieved.

But later when he'd heard footsteps on the stairs, in the hallway, there'd been a pair missing. He'd recognized Sam's heavy steps and Marshall's usual gait. Where was Jen?

Lucas moved to his guestroom door. Wouldn't hurt to check on her real quick. But he stopped himself before leaving his room, realizing he only wore his gym shorts. He backtracked, grabbed a t-shirt, and pulled it over his head. Paused again.

It's not like Jen had never seen his scars.

Still.

He reached for a hoodie and tugged it on as he edged into the hallway. Keeping his steps light, he covered the distance to Jen's room and stopped outside her closed door. Should he knock? What if she was asleep? But how else would he know . . . ?

Her car.

Obviously.

He moved to the open staircase and made his way down. Cold night air enfolded him as he stepped onto the Everwood's porch, its boards chilled under his feet. He walked to the far edge and peered into the dark, looking for Jen's car. There were only a few guests this weekend, so it wouldn't be hard to pick out.

If it were here. Which it clearly wasn't.

Where are you, Jen?

Jenessa crouched behind the old, ripped chair in her parents' attic—*her* attic—squinting into the dark, looking for the moving shape that had chased her here. She'd come up here on a whim, hoping to find a crib for Cade among the mess of abandoned furniture and boxes and bags filled with who knew what.

Instead, she'd found a bat. Or rather, it'd found her. Which was when instinct had taken over and she'd gone into hiding.

But she couldn't stay up here forever. She had three sleeping kids downstairs, all huddled into one guest bedroom on the second floor—Colie and Violet sharing the bed and Cade in an emptied-out dresser drawer she'd fashioned into a temporary cradle.

Either kill the bat or make a run for the door. Fight or flight, fight or flight . . .

Musty, chilled air wrapped around her and she blinked against the dark as a flutter of wings sounded overhead. The bat's blurry outline whooshed and dove toward the opposite wall, then perched in front of the circle window where moonlight slanted in. *Now's your chance.*

Jenessa crept forward, the tap of her slippers hopefully soft enough not to alert the creature, her fingers clenched around the handle of an old badminton racquet. She could do this—just whack the bat and pray the racquet did its job.

But if she did manage to kill it, what then? What did a person do with a dead bat?

At least she was dressed for the battle—sweatpants and a tee, hair piled into a messy knot underneath an old football helmet she'd found after first encountering the bat. She neared the window, the helmet heavy on her head. She held her breath, lifted the racquet—

A knock bellowed through the house, echoing upward and quaking the bat into flight once more. It plunged past

Jenessa's head and she couldn't help the shriek that escaped. Who would be at the door this late? Maybe it was about the kids. Maybe Colie had lied and someone really was looking for them.

Another knock rattled from below and the bat lunged again, wings flapping. This time she let out a full-fledged scream, her racquet clattering to the wood planks underfoot.

Any and all bravado fled in an instant. She tripped over a plastic tub, lost a slipper, and didn't bother reaching for it. Instead, she righted herself and wound through the maze of forgotten belongings, one hand holding her helmet in place. She needed to get out of here, needed to see who was at the door, check on the kids, and—

A crash of shattering glass sounded from below. *What was happening? Was someone breaking in?*

She darted to the stairs, her heart pounding almost as loudly as her footsteps.

Except those weren't her footsteps. She slowed, telltale thumps sounding from down below. Yes, someone was in the house and making his or her way up to the second floor. *The kids.*

Cold, clammy air stilled around her as grim resolve cemented in her stomach. Her muscles stiffened as she whirled around, ignored a hiss of air and flutter of wings. She found her racquet and barreled down the attic stairs. If she could get to her phone before whoever was down there got to her—

A flood of light gushed into the stairway and before she could slow her steps, she rammed into something solid and warm. And apparently off-balance. Because suddenly she was tumbling, squealing, crashing into the walls around the staircase, tangling with a mess of arms and legs . . .

And then landing with a thud on top of a man, her

helmet smacking into his chest. One of her arms was jammed under his shoulder, but even if she'd been able to move, shock froze her in place.

Until a groan rumbled underneath her.

Her trapped breath released in a yelp and she rolled off him, attempted to yank her arm free.

"Nice helmet."

Wait, she knew that voice. "Lucas?" She moved just enough to free her arm and scrambled to her knees. The amber light of the sconces lining the second-floor hallway was dim but it was enough to confirm it was definitely Lucas she'd just landed on. "What are you doing here? Are you okay? Can you move?" She bent over his prostrate form. "Should I call 9-1-1?"

"Easy, Belville. Need a sec before I'm up to a game of twenty questions." He peered up at her through eyes the color of sandstone—hazel with streaks of brown and gray.

She pulled off her helmet, her hair spilling free from its unruly bun, and bent closer to Lucas's face. "I'm trying to remember the signs of a concussion. Your pupils don't look dilated. You know what day it is, right? You know your name? And my name?"

She sank back on her knees as he sat up, revealing the badminton racquet he must've landed on. He winced, stretching his neck from side to side. "I just said your name, didn't I?" He glanced over his shoulder. "Was the racquet for me?"

Remembrance rushed in and she bolted to her feet, slammed the attic door to stop any attempted escape by the bat, and leaned with her back against it. "The racquet was for a bat originally. 'Til I heard someone breaking in."

He was propped with both hands on the floor behind him. "I knocked. You didn't answer. And then I heard you screaming." He lifted one corner of his mouth in a sheepish half-grin. "I busted a window to get in."

"Oh. Okay. That's . . . that's fine." Now she just had a broken window to take care of and probably glass to clean up. Add that to the list of all she needed to do to get this house ready to sell. Although why she was thinking about the house when she had three children currently sleeping just down the hall, she didn't know. At least, she hoped they were still sleeping, considering all the noise they'd just made.

And to think, just this afternoon she'd been pondering decluttering her life.

"Hey, you okay, Jen?" Lucas's upward gaze was fastened on her face from his spot on the floor, and apparently her nod wasn't good enough for him. Not according to the concern narrowing his eyes. "I'm sorry about the window. I was just worried."

"It's fine. I'll call somebody. S-someone who fixes windows. A window-fixer. Except it's late so I can't do that until tomorrow. And tomorrow's Saturday, so I guess I'll need to wait until Monday. Which is fine, because I've definitely got more immediate things to take care of in the meantime. Like finding some tarp or something to cover the window and—"

"I think maybe what you should do right now is sit down."

She squeezed her eyes closed as she slid her back along the attic door until she was on the floor again. Knees bent, head tipped.

A warm hand settled over her forehead.

She opened her eyes to see Lucas crouched in front of her. "What are you doing?"

He shrugged. "Making sure you don't have a fever. You're pale. You're suddenly quiet." His focus traveled from her face to her bare feet—where had her other slipper gone?—and back again. "You're wearing sweatpants. Never in the three years since you walked up to me that day in Coffee Coffee and demanded we be friends have I seen you in sweatpants."

Her stomach growled. Why hadn't she downed a piece of pizza earlier? "I wasn't expecting company, thank you very much."

"I'm just not used to seeing Casual Jen." He grinned and stood.

"What are you doing here anyway?"

"You never came home. Someone had to check on you."

Home. Strange how perfectly the word fit her little room at the B&B and not this house she'd spent most of her life in. She glanced up at Lucas, took in his mussed hair—long, and damp at the tips. He always showered at night, which might be a weird thing to know about a man she wasn't related to. But then, they lived in the same house. His rhythm was as familiar to her as his hawk-like features—straight nose, high cheekbones.

But there were times she wondered if she truly knew *him.* She had a feeling Lucas Danby held more secrets behind those hazel eyes of his than even this house.

"Where were you earlier tonight, Luke? You never showed up for the engagement party." Not that they'd had much of a party after finding the kids. No bonfire. No cupcakes.

No Lucas.

"I . . ." He closed his mouth. Opened it again. "Something came up."

"You could've at least called."

"I'm sorry." He held out his hand and she placed her palm in his, let him tow her to her feet. She came up mere inches from him, though a head shorter, and huh, maybe she didn't know all his patterns. Because whatever soap or shampoo he'd used tonight, she didn't recognize it. Made her think of the trees out back, of a glistening first frost on a late-autumn morning.

Lucas looked back at her, a hint of a grin forming above his shadowed jawline.

"What?"

"Just thinking about you trying to kill a bat with a badminton racquet."

"Luke, if you tell Sam and the others about this—"

"And the way you looked running down the attic steps wearing that helmet—best thing I've seen in a long time, Belville." He barked a laugh.

"Not so loud."

"And then when you knocked me down the stairs. If I had been a home intruder, you would've scared me straight." His laughter filled the hallway. "I'm going to wake up sorer tomorrow than when I was in boot—"

She slapped her palm over his mouth. "Pipe down."

He still shook with laughter, grabbing hold of her wrist and moving it away. But just as quickly, she whipped her other hand into place.

"Lucas, you'll wake them up."

"Wake who up?" Her hand muffled his question.

She glanced behind her, at the door down the hall she'd left a few inches open at Violet's insistence. "The kids. Cade already woke up crying once. And I don't blame him considering he's sleeping in a dresser drawer. That's why I was in the attic. I was trying to find a crib."

She looked back to Lucas just in time to see his amusement from seconds ago give way to complete confusion. "What kids?"

She opened her mouth to answer, but a squeaking voice spoke first. "Jessa?"

She turned to find Violet hovering in the bedroom doorway, a stained rag doll dangling limp in her hand and tears streaking down her face.

Lucas couldn't get it out of his head—the picture of Jen kneeling in front of that little girl, whoever she was, and whispering gentle words. Eventually Jenessa had pulled her into a hug and then lifted her into her arms, carrying her into the bedroom.

He'd followed, pausing at the doorway, taking stock of another kid already in the bed, the baby in a dresser drawer just like Jen had said.

He stood in her kitchen now, pouring pancake batter onto a hot griddle. What was Jenessa Belville doing with a trio of kids? Did she have nieces and a nephew she'd never mentioned? No, she didn't have any siblings. A friend's kids, perhaps? But they shared most of the same friends.

What were the children doing here and when had they arrived and—

And how was it possible that a woman who was usually dressed with clothing and jewelry and shoes effortlessly coordinated could look even more beautiful in sweatpants and a floppy t-shirt? And when she'd lifted that little girl into her arms as if it were the most natural thing in the world . . .

She'd looked downright maternal. Not a word he'd ever thought in association with Jenessa Belville.

Bubbly and gorgeous and bold, yes.

But maternal? Not so much. The only kid he'd ever even seen her with was Sam's daughter, and Jen had always seemed to hang back a little when Sam brought Mackenzie around. But then, they all did. Sam never had nearly as much time with his daughter as he wanted and the situation with Mackenzie's mother was complicated and, well, some things were off-limits . . . even between friends.

Sometimes especially between friends.

Like the thoughts Lucas shouldn't have let himself entertain as he'd watched Jen with that girl. Like what a perfect picture she made. How he'd used to imagine that exact picture for himself. A family, kids to tuck in at night . . . . a wife.

But his future was with Bridgewell. Assuming he didn't make a mess of this mentoring thing with a guy, Noah, whose last name he'd already forgotten. But how in the world did Flagg expect him to make some kind of positive difference in someone else's life when he'd spent so many years making a mess of his own?

Maybe in the morning he should try arguing with Flagg once more. Convince him to find someone else to buddy up to Noah and let Lucas go back to doing what he was good at—overseas missions with a strategic protocol and clear end game. Flagg was the wise, counseling type. Not him.

"You're making pancakes?"

He spun around. Jenessa stood in the doorway between the kitchen and dining room. She'd thrown an oversized sweatshirt over her tee and tidied her hair into a ponytail, but a few loose strands still straggled around her face.

"Your stomach was growling."

"But you don't have to feed me, Lucas."

"Maybe not, but I wasn't about to leave without finding out why you've got three kids camped out upstairs. Who are they? What are they doing here? How long are they staying?"

"I don't know, I don't know, and I don't know." She sat on a stool at the island. "Actually, that's not quite true. I know their names—Colie, Violet, and Cade Hollis. We found them out in the caretaker's cottage earlier. We weren't able to get much info out of them, but from what we did get, Sam was able to confirm that they're from Maple Valley. They lived with their mom and grandmother over on Ashton Circle."

Hmm, not the nicest part of town. "Lived?"

"She died almost three months ago—cancer. Their grandmother took care of them after that, but apparently she died a few days ago—long-time health problems. Sam put those pieces together after stopping at their house. He called the hospital. Seems they'd been trying to get ahold of a next-of-kin, but no one had gotten as far as realizing there were three kids in the picture. Oh, and Sam said there's an eviction notice on the front door of their rental house. We think that's why they left home."

And apparently ended up in the cottage behind Jen's house. "Their father?" Lucas asked.

"They clammed up when we asked."

"And how long have they been in the cottage?"

"A night and a day."

Three kids—alone in an empty cottage. No electricity. No adults. Dealing with the recent loss of their mother and now their grandmother's death on top of it.

"Sam says I need to call DHS in the morning, and I know he's right, but what's going to happen to them? I can't bear the thought of what they've been going through. Colie —she's only twelve but she's been taking care of her siblings alone for days."

Jenessa lifted her eyes—a deep, dark blue, they penetrated with so many emotions just now he couldn't make out one from another. Until they brightened under the tawny light of the fixture overhead and she grinned. "That frilly apron is a good look on you, Luke."

He glanced down. He'd forgotten he'd even put on the silly thing. Only had because he'd figured it'd make Jen laugh.

"Do you smell burning?"

Shoot. He whipped around, slid the spatula under the pancake, and freed it from the heat. Not burnt, just a smidge overly brown. He dropped it on a plate, half-covering another, and turned back to Jen, setting the plate in front of her. "You can start eating these now, but how about scrambled eggs, too?"

"Sure, thanks. Although if you're being so good to me because you're hoping to avoid a lecture for missing the party tonight . . ." She shrugged. "Well, then you've completely succeeded."

He'd been in Jenessa's kitchen often enough to know where to find her silverware. He pulled open a drawer and nabbed a fork, plunked it and a bottle of syrup in front of Jen. "I saw the *For Sale* sign, by the way. You're finally going to sell this place?"

She nodded as she cut into a pancake. "I think so. I have a feeling I was premature in putting up the sign, though. I'm not sure I'll get any takers with the property in its current condition—especially out back."

She was probably right. Although, personally, if he had a house this nice, even cluttered as it was, he'd think twice about selling. The kitchen alone was impressive. A person didn't have to be a gourmet chef to appreciate the gray marble countertops and cupboards painted a stylish navy blue filling the spacious kitchen. He especially liked the exposed wooden beam overhead.

He still remembered the first time he'd seen the inside of Belville Park—after Jen's dad had passed but before her mom had followed. It'd been all he could do to hide his shock at the size of the place. Sure, it was crowded—boxes, bric-a-brac, books—as if someone, probably Jenessa, had begun the job of organizing the overabundance of possessions but quit mid-mission.

Yet the hardwood floors and ornate woodworking, the walls painted in an array of neutrals and pastels were all in good condition. Swap out some of the overly fancy furniture for comfortable couches and chairs, move all the boxes and clutter out of sight, and this place could make an amazing home for a family.

Jenessa, though, had seemed embarrassed about the messiness the first time she'd given Sam and Lucas a tour. She'd also been exhausted, grieving her father, worried over her mother, buried in work at the newspaper. It'd been one of his first hints that all wasn't as idyllic in the Belville family home as he'd once thought.

He grabbed a carton of milk from the fridge. Expired a week ago, but they could risk it. The fact that he'd found any groceries at all in the pantry was a surprise given that Jen had all but moved in at the Everwood.

"Hey, Luke?" Jen had paused with her fork in midair. "I didn't really demand we be friends, did I?"

He grinned at her echo of his earlier words. "That's exactly what you did." He cracked two eggs into a bowl. "You waltzed into the coffee shop one day, practically dragging Sam along with you, and came right up to me as I was stirring creamer into my coffee. You said, 'I'm Jenessa Belville and this is my friend Sam Ross and we're in the market for another member of our inner circle. Which makes us sound cult-ish, but I promise we're not.'"

"I sound like a nutcase."

"Well, I joined your little inner circle, so what does that make me?" He poured milk into the bowl and whisked. He remembered vaguely recognizing her when she'd approached him that day. They'd both grown up in

Maple Valley, after all, she a couple years ahead of him in school.

She smiled around a bite. "A friend. That's what it makes you."

It took every ounce of self-control in him not to wince. To keep whisking the globby mix of eggs and milk and pretend that one little word—*friend*—didn't feel so ill-fitting.

"A mysterious friend, but a friend all the same."

"I'm not mysterious, Jen."

"You are. You never talk about yourself. But I don't mind. I'm good at cracking mysteries. One day I will discover all your secrets."

Well, that was the most disconcerting thing anyone had ever said to him. He pointed his whisk at her. "Just eat, Belville."

Although if ever there was a person he might wish to let in, it was Jen. Something told him that if he someday spilled everything to her—told her about the explosion and Tashfeen and the decisions he'd made after—she'd understand.

But then he'd have to tell her the rest. About Tashfeen's mother. About Flagg and Bridgewell. About how long he'd been lying to them all. And that might be enough to ruin his chances—

He cut the thought off before it could go any further. What *chances*? Anything more than friendship with Jen had always been out of the question. Because of his secrets. Because he spent half the year or more overseas doing things he'd never be able to talk about.

Because Jenessa Belville deserved someone more whole than he could ever hope to be.

He rubbed a palm over his arm, felt the ridges of his scars through the cotton. Then, realizing what he was doing, he stopped, picked up the bowl of eggs, and carried it to the griddle. "Why don't you take your plate into the sunroom? It'll be more comfortable there. I'll bring the eggs in when they're done."

Jen nodded and stood, lifting her plate. But she paused halfway across the kitchen. "You know what the odd thing is?" She glanced around the room. "Ever since I put that sign in the ground, I've had this strange feeling that as much as I might want to be done with this house, maybe it's not done with me. And then . . . those kids. What if there's a reason they're here?" She shrugged, a chunk of dark hair falling free from her ponytail. "I sound silly. I must be overly tired."

No, she sounded like the Jenessa Belville he knew. She always saw the potential in things. Like the way she'd seen something in him, later Mara and Marshall—sensed the possibility of deep friendship when they'd been little more than strangers.

It inspired him. Made him think of Noah, of the mission Flagg had assigned him. He should take a cue from Jen. Look for the potential and possibility in this assignment. Cling to the promise of securing his future with Bridgewell.

If only that future didn't mean once again saying goodbye to the woman currently disappearing into the sunroom. He dragged a fork through sizzling eggs. At least he still had another month in Maple Valley.

He'd make it count. Spend as much time as possible with his friends, with Kit and Beckett. He'd mentor Noah as best he could. He'd enjoy each and every encounter with Jen even though he knew they didn't belong together.

And maybe somehow, he'd convince his stubborn heart to let go.

5

*J*enessa woke up to the warmth of the sun on her face and the welcome weight of her quilt tucked up to her chin, the lull of a fan or some other whirring sound gently coaxing her to consciousness. And something else . . .

A sense of calm and comfort. As if she wasn't alone in her bedroom.

She opened her eyes and sat up slowly, bleary gaze coming into focus, and she felt her forehead wrinkle in confusion. She'd slept in the sunroom?

She flopped back against a nest of throw pillows, trying to make her morning brain function. There was a plate on the end table and—*oh!* Lucas had been here last night. Had made her pancakes—and eggs, too, although she didn't remember eating them. She must've fallen asleep . . .

A flurry of whispered voices passed the room.

The kids!

How could she have forgotten? She jumped from the loveseat, gaze zooming to the small antique clock on a wall shelf. 8:02. For all she knew, the children had been up for hours while she slept.

She moved quickly, tripping over the quilt at her feet, catching herself on the back of the rocking chair. The kids were probably hungry. Maybe she could take a cue from Lucas—make some pancakes and eggs.

She emerged into the kitchen. Wait, who'd started a pot of coffee? Its tantalizing scent wrapped around her as the sound of shuffling from the dining room snagged her attention. What were those kids up to?

"Come on, Vi." Colie's hissed words carried as Jenessa hurried to reach them, finally catching up just as they moved into the entryway.

"I don't want to leave." Violet dragged a bag behind her. No, not a bag. A pillowcase? Filled with what? It clanked over the mudroom floor.

"We have to." Colie shifted her own armful—Cade—and pulled open the front door. "Hurry up. She'll wake up any minute."

"She's already awake."

At the sound of Jenessa's voice, both girls whirled and Cade let out a squeal at the quick movement, dimples she hadn't noticed last night peeking from both cheeks. Oh, he was adorable. And a spitting image of Violet, whose sleep-tousled blond hair, large green eyes, and full cheeks made for an even cuter picture in the light of day than they had last night.

Only Colie glared at Jenessa, long lashes rimming her narrowed gaze and her hold on her brother tightening. She didn't say a word.

"You don't have to leave. Especially without breakfast."

"Colie says we'll eat breakfast later. But I don't think it's going to be good." Violet wrinkled her nose as she plopped the pillowcase on the floor. A metal can rolled out.

"Green beans, huh? Not my preferred breakfast either."

"Colie says we weren't stealing. Just borrowing."

Jenessa took a few steps closer. "Did Colie also happen to mention where you're going?"

"It's not really any of your business."

Oh, so Colie had decided to speak, had she? "Hate to argue with you, but considering it's my cottage you trespassed in, my guest bedroom you slept in last night, and"—she glanced at the bulging pillowcase—"my pantry you apparently raided, I think it might be my business, after all." It was all she could do to keep from smiling. Something told her Colie would not appreciate her amusement at their attempted getaway.

The older girl bent to let Cade slide free. "We'll pay you back when we can."

"I've got a better idea. Stick around for a little bit. Have some breakfast. I'm no Betty Crocker, but I can whip up something a little more appetizing than canned green beans."

Cade had begun crawling across the entryway and he reached Jenessa just as Colie opened her mouth, an argument clearly at the ready. But she paused as Jenessa knelt in front of Cade. Because she'd realized cold vegetables wouldn't work for her baby brother's morning meal?

Or perhaps she was smart enough to know Jenessa might be pretending to give her a choice, but there wasn't a chance she was about to let three kids simply wander off.

"I want to stay, Colie." Violet looked up at her sister, a pleading in her emerald eyes. "I like Jessa." ·

Jessa. Same shortened version of her name the little girl had used last night when she'd wandered into the hallway, heavy-lidded and half asleep. It'd been enough to capture Jenessa's heart in the moment—and it seemed it was enough now to soften Colie at least somewhat. Because after another moment of hesitation, she finally nodded.

Then marched forward and scooped up Cade. "But don't get attached. We're not staying long." With that, she disappeared into the sitting room.

Jenessa couldn't help it then—she let out a grin. "Not sure if she was talking to you or me, Violet."

Violet's dimples were a perfect match for Cade's. "You can call me Vi if you want."

"All right, Vi." She stretched over the little girl to close the front door, a blast of cold air catching her before it latched. She reached for whatever jacket or sweatshirt she'd left on the staircase railing last time she came in the house and slid it on, then picked up the pillowcase. "Shall we go see what we can find for breakfast?"

Violet grinned up at her and took hold of her free hand. "I really like Pop-Tarts. And cereal. Cheerios are okay but my favorite is the kind with the colored circles."

"Froot Loops?"

Violet nodded as they entered the sitting room. "But the best breakfast is donuts with sprinkles."

Hmm, maybe Jenessa could run up to the bakery to grab a box of donuts. But no, she could hardly leave the kids here alone, not with the possibility of them running off again. She couldn't pile them into her car either. Cade would need a car seat and probably Vi too and—

She stopped in the middle of the room, a sudden realization trekking through her. Something was off about the room. It was different. It was . . . clean. Not clean as in dusted and vacuumed, but clean as in no boxes. Not a single one. No displaced knickknacks either. No pile of newspapers on the chaise lounge.

She started moving again, fingers still closed around Vi's

hand. She gasped as they stepped into the music room. Same thing—no boxes or bags or stacks. None of the untidy chaos she was used to.

What . . . who . . . how?

And why did this jacket smell like something spiced and woodsy? She glanced down. Oh, it wasn't her jacket at all. It was a hooded sweatshirt. Lucas's probably.

The slam of a screen door echoed through the house. She darted toward the kitchen once more, pacing her steps solely for the sake of little Vi at her side.

She halted in the doorway at the sight of Mara and Marshall together in the center of the kitchen, plopping a heap of overflowing grocery sacks on the island counter. Mara broke into a grin and unzipped her fleece coat. "Hey, you're awake. And the kids are too, I see."

"And you're . . . here." The overly long sleeves of Lucas's hoodie dangled at her sides. Colie had already settled into the breakfast nook, Cade on her lap and a look of impatience etched into her face. Violet ran over to them. Jenessa looked back to Mara.

Marshall gave a small wave. "Morning, Jen." He came around the counter to squeeze his fiancée's shoulder. "I'll get the rest of the bags." He left through the kitchen's side door.

"I don't understand. What are you doing here?"

Mara opened a sack and started pulling out items. "Well, you've got company. And according to Lucas, there wasn't much in your fridge, so we thought we'd get you stocked up. Don't even try to protest or insist on paying me back." Her grin widened. "Besides, Marshall paid."

Jen plodded to the counter as Violet joined Colie. "But . . . why? Did you make the coffee, too?"

Mara shook her head. "I think Lucas got it ready and used the delay-brew setting."

The coffeepot had a delay-brew setting? And wait . . . *Lucas*. The cleaned-up rooms. That was his doing, wasn't it? Goodness, he had to have spent half the night here. Maybe the whole night.

She dropped onto a stool, thoroughly flummoxed, tangled hair flopping about her shoulders.

Mara pulled a bag of apples from a sack. "We just got a few staples. It was Lucas's suggestion. I only saw him for a minute this morning before he left to take someone to the airport. Some guy from out East who checked in yesterday. He knows him, apparently."

Lucas had someone in town visiting him? He hadn't mentioned that last night. Must be the reason he hadn't shown up for the engagement party. "It's weird to think of Lucas having friends other than us. And talk about a fast visit. The guy just checked in yesterday and he's already leaving?"

Mara shrugged and carried an armful of produce to the fridge. "I think Lucas left a note for you." She nudged her head toward the refrigerator door, where a magnet held a scribbled message in place.

Jen slid off her stool and retrieved it, before opening the door for Mara.

Took care of the broken window. And the bat. But now I owe you a badminton racquet. It didn't survive the fight. —L

All the puzzlement of this morning dissipated in the wake of her laughter now. And her gratitude. "I'll never be able to thank him for all of this."

Mara peeked around the refrigerator door. "Veggies in the bottom drawer?"

Jenessa nodded. Mara rose and closed the fridge. She

marched to the coffeepot, pulled a cup from the mug tree nearby, filled it up, and handed it to Jenessa.

"I don't know how I ended up with friends like you guys."

Mara went back to unpacking groceries. "I do. You came waltzing into my world when I didn't even know how much I needed you. Marsh would say the same."

"Waltzing, huh? According to Lucas, I barreled into his life and demanded he become my friend."

Mara grinned. "And my guess is he, in particular, thanks his lucky stars for that every day."

"Why him in particular?"

Marshall came in before Mara could answer, Sam on his heels. He was here, too? He pushed his sunglasses up to the top of his head, glanced at the kids and then at Jenessa. "Nice hoodie."

"Lucas left it here." Why that fact would make Sam's forehead crease, she didn't know. But she had three hungry kids waiting on breakfast and no clue what to make them, so—

"Froot Loops!" Violet's squeal broke in and Jenessa followed the direction of her gaze to where Mara was pulling a box of cereal from a grocery bag.

All right, cereal it is. Not exactly the hot breakfast she'd envisioned, but it'd make at least one kid happy.

"Can I talk to you for a sec, Jen?" Sam took off his sunglasses and dropped them in his front pocket.

"But the kids . . ."

"I can get them situated," Mara offered. "I got milk to replace your expired gallon, by the way. Another instruction from Luke. Oh, and he mentioned a baby, so just in case, I grabbed formula."

She thanked Mara, then followed Sam into the dining

room. "Let me guess. Luke told you about the helmet and the badminton racquet and the bat."

His forehead creased all over again. "What?"

"He didn't tell you about falling down the attic steps?"

"I didn't even know he was here last night. I came to check on the kids. And to give you this." He handed her a scrap of paper with a scribbled telephone number on it. "An emergency number for a DHS contact."

Oh. Right. Making that call should take precedence over anything else this morning. And yet . . .

She could see into the kitchen over Sam's shoulder, to where Violet was bouncing up and down in her seat as Mara poured her a bowl of cereal. Cade had already grabbed a fistful of Froot Loops and was shoving them in his mouth.

And Colie . . . she stared back at Jenessa. Even from here she could read the knowing in the girl's eyes. The dread.

"Sam—"

"You have to make the call, Jen."

She met Sam's firm gaze, kept her voice low. "What if they can't find their father? What if they do and he's awful? Or what if the kids have to go into foster care? They could get split up."

"Jen—"

"I know I have to make the call, I do." It's not like she could keep the kids here indefinitely. But Vi looked so happy and Cade seemed so content and Colie . . . a full night of sleep hadn't erased the shadows under her eyes. She might need a respite more than any of them. "What's the harm in waiting a bit?"

"The harm is that despite what Colie says, there could be some frantic person—a guardian of some sort—worried to death right now."

"They're from right here in Maple Valley. If they had a

guardian worrying over them, that person would've gone to the police. Which happens to be you. We'd know if there was someone looking for them."

"Even so." Sam sighed. "Please, Jen. Make the call. Or I will."

The headache Lucas had woken up with after only three scant hours of sleep still hadn't faded.

The only upside was that it'd given him a legitimate excuse when he'd called Kit to tell her he'd be a little late to Apple Fest this morning. He felt guilty about it, though. With today being Saturday, the orchard would be even busier than yesterday.

Flagg hadn't necessarily needed a ride to the airport, what with the rental car and all, but Noah's flight was scheduled to arrive around the same time Flagg's departed. Lucas preferred the idea of meeting the younger man there, away from Maple Valley. It'd give him time to assess Noah.

And decide what to tell everyone about the situation. Perhaps he could just keep it vague. Call Noah a fellow former soldier in need of a getaway. Say a mutual friend had connected them.

Flagg pulled his small carry-on bag from the cab of Lucas's truck. They'd dropped the rental off in Ames and driven the rest of the way together. "Have to say, I love an airport so small you don't have to arrive more than forty minutes before your flight."

"I'm with you there." And for an international airport, the Des Moines airfield was about as small as they came. They crossed the road that separated the parking ramp from the main building, and Lucas followed Flagg into the revolving door that led into the ticketing area. "My sister's not as big of a fan of this airport, though. She lived in London for six or seven years after college. I didn't see her a ton in those years, but the few times I did, she never failed to complain about all the stops she had to make between here and there."

"For what it's worth, I would've enjoyed meeting your sister." Flagg slowed as they neared the escalator. He'd already checked in to his flight online.

Lucas stretched one arm and then the other, squelching a yawn in the process. He wasn't sure whether the sore muscles in his arms and back came from that climbing wall yesterday or the fall down Jen's attic stairs last night—or all the trips he'd made up them later, carrying one armload of boxes after another.

Nor was he sure what exactly had prompted him to take charge of the task. She'd still have to sort through all her parents' belongings at some point, after all. But he'd figured if it were him, it'd be easier to do so in small doses. Seeing it all scattered about the house surely made it feel more overwhelming.

And anyway, after finding her sound asleep in the sunroom, he simply hadn't been in a hurry to leave her house. Even though every speck of common sense told him the best thing he could do for himself was to put some space between them. Get used to the idea of not seeing her every day anymore.

"Did you hear me, Lucas? I said I would've liked to meet your family."

"But, sir, you understand why that's impossible, right? You know Kit doesn't know . . ." *Anything.*

And tired as he was of the secrets and half-truths, the thought of revealing everything to his sister only made him feel worse. She'd be angry that he'd kept it from her this long. Confused as to why.

Sometimes *he* was even confused. He'd told himself for so long that he didn't want Kit worrying every time he left on a mission. That so much of it was classified, it wasn't as if he'd be able to tell her much, anyway.

But maybe, truthfully, there was more to it. Maybe, down deep where the shadows of his past lurked, there was still a piece of him that was scared of another mistake. Scared something with Bridgewell might go wrong and he'd fail again and she and anyone else he told would *know.*

Maybe that's why he'd called Flagg so many times last week. Why, even now, he knew he had to make this thing with Noah Johansson work. Because he had to return to Bridgewell.

His life in Maple Valley gave him a sense of peace. But Bridgewell gave him purpose—and probably the closest thing he'd ever get to redemption.

"I better get to the security line." Flagg clasped his palm in a handshake.

"I'm sorry I was rude when you first got here yesterday."

Flagg grinned. "I'd hold a grudge except, honestly, it was highly amusing seeing you so upended and frantic."

"I don't think you're capable of holding a grudge." No, underneath his soldierly exterior, Flagg was far too compassionate for that. He was a man of quiet, but strong, faith—in God, in forgiveness, in the power of prayer and the possibility of redemption.

There'd been a time when Lucas had that sort of belief, too. Might even still be there inside somewhere, but it was worn and eroded now. His prayers were few and far between.

"Well, I'll tell you what, son, I know a thing or two about what *you're* capable of. I know you don't see the sense in this assignment. But give it some time. Get to know Noah and let him get to know you. You have more to offer than you realize."

"Thank you, sir."

"Don't think I don't know how badly you want to argue with me right now." Flagg chuckled and slung his bag over his shoulder. "Now, I've got a plane to catch. And Noah's should be landing any minute."

Already had according to the flight schedule behind Flagg. Another handshake and the older man was off. Lucas crossed from the escalators to the baggage claim and found a seat.

"You have more to offer than you realize."

Flagg was right—not about that, but about how much he'd wanted to argue. To say he didn't have a thing to offer Noah. That there had to be someone better.

But this was the assignment. Somehow he had to figure out how to treat it the way he did all his other assignments. *Accept the mission. Identify the strategy. Complete the mission.*

From his pocket, his phone pinged. Kit checking on his whereabouts? Or Beckett nagging him for leaving him alone at the climbing wall today. Or perhaps Flagg had given Noah his number.

Better than all three—Jen.

Thank you, thank you, THANK YOU. I would've said it sooner but I temporarily lost my phone.

Despite the fatigue clinging to every bone in his body, he grinned and replied to her text.

Everything going ok? With the kids and stuff?

His phone dinged again.

Acknowledge my gratitude, Lucas!! (And yes. Everyone's still alive, anyway.)

Gratitude acknowledged. You're welcome, obviously.

"Are you Lucas?"

He looked up from his phone. "Noah?"

A younger man stood in front of him, his clean-shaven cheeks and a light blue button-down a contrast to the tattoos marking both arms, the leather jacket tied around his duffel.

Lucas stood. "Nice to meet you." He held out his palm, but Noah didn't move to take it. He dropped his hand. "I know this is a little awkward. Don't know about you, but Flagg didn't give me much lead time here. But I'm hopeful—"

"You can keep your hope. I don't need it."

"Okay. Uh, listen—"

Noah's pale eyes glinted with stubbornness. "What I need is to make the Bridgewell Elite team. I doubt you want me here any more than I want to be here. But if it's what I have to do to make the team, I'll do it. Just don't expect me to be happy about it. I'm not looking for a new best friend."

Lucas adopted Sam's usual look—folded his arms, lifted an eyebrow. "You finished?"

"Yeah."

"Good. You got a suitcase or anything?"

Noah nodded.

"I'll wait."

The younger man turned toward the baggage claim but Lucas called after him. "Not for nothing, but I've already got plenty of friends. And you might want to consider that the guy you just brushed off holds the key to your future with that team you want to join."

Noah's back stiffened.

Same way his own sore muscles tightened at the thought that the reverse was equally true. His own future with Bridgewell rested with the sullen man currently walking away from him.

Peachy. Just . . . peachy.

Colie wouldn't get out of the borrowed minivan.

Jenessa shifted Cade on her hip, a cool breeze sending sand from the orchard's gravel parking lot dusting over her black-and-white-striped canvas shoes. She kept hold of Violet's hand to keep her from excitedly running toward the goats she'd already spotted in the petting zoo.

"Please come with us, Colie. It's a really cool orchard."

Coming to the orchard late in the afternoon had been a whim, sparked by a desire to distract the children from all the turmoil they'd experienced since their grandmother's passing. Maybe distract herself too. Violet had asked her at least twenty times if they'd be staying at the house again tonight. Colie had cast her countless skeptical scowls all day long. After calling that emergency DHS number three times without an answer, she'd been helpless to know what else to do other than tell Violet that, yes, they probably would be staying another night and come up with some sort of activity—anything—to fill the rest of their Saturday.

And if Lucas was here, she could take the opportunity to thank him again for all he'd done last night.

Transportation had been her only obstacle, but Sam had come through. One of his deputies had a minivan he didn't need for the day.

"I want to see the goats, Jessa." Violet tugged on her hand.

"Please, Colie?" She tried again.

"I don't feel like it."

How many times had she heard that exact phrase today? Colie hadn't felt like eating peanut butter and jelly sandwiches at lunch. She hadn't felt like explaining Cade's napping routine. She certainly hadn't felt like talking at all about what had happened with her grandmother a few days ago.

But Jenessa had pieced together enough from Violet. Their grandmother—who Violet had repeatedly referred to as mean—hadn't come out of her bedroom by lunchtime on Wednesday. Colie had found her unresponsive in her bed and had called 9-1-1.

But so much didn't make sense. Were there truly no other adults in the kids' lives? And why weren't they in school? Had Colie had a plan when they'd left their house?

According to Sam, the eviction notice on their front door was a week old. Which meant the grandmother had known about it. Had *she* had a plan?

For all she didn't understand about the Hollis family's situation, subtle questions to Violet here and there had filled in a few gaps. They hadn't had a happy home life even before Tessa Hollis's death, it seemed. Tessa and the grandmother hadn't gotten along. Sometimes her mom had a job and sometimes she didn't, Violet said. And their father rarely made an appearance.

Colie was slouched in her seat in the minivan now, her arms crossed. Jenessa couldn't just leave her here. Or could she? If she took Violet and Cade over to the petting zoo, the van would still be within her eyesight. Maybe she just needed to give the girl a few minutes alone.

"All right. We'll go see the goats. If you want to join us,

we'll be right over there." Colie didn't look to see where she pointed. For the love, the girl could be exasperating.

And yet, Jenessa didn't doubt for a moment Colie's stubborn, hard shell was just that—a shell covering a tender hurt she likely didn't know what to do with. For what had to be the hundredth time today, her heart ached for these children and longed to do something more than give them a bed to sleep in again tonight.

But what? *I'm at a loss here, God.*

The thought was part prayer, part complaint. It'd been a long time since she'd felt any sort of divine direction in her life. Her own fault, probably. But she just got tired sometimes—of trying to say and do all the right things. Why was it her faith at times felt more like a performance than something real?

"Jessa!" Violet's voice had gone from impatient to downright vexation.

Jenessa shook off her thoughts and couldn't help a laugh, even as she gave Colie one more assessing glance. Ten minutes and then she'd come back to check on her.

But they only made it halfway to the petting zoo when a voice calling her name slowed her steps. Mayor Milt?

"Ms. Belville, the very woman I need to speak with." Maple Valley's longtime town leader shuffled toward her from the direction of the old barn Lucas's sister had turned into a community center. "A moment, if you please."

Cade was growing heavy and poor Violet wasn't going to last much longer if she didn't get to see her goats soon. "It's nice to see you, Mayor, but as you can see, I've kind of got my hands full and—"

"It's about the house, Ms. Belville. About Belville Park." His snow-white mustache twitched with each word, his usual sweater vest a fitting pattern of fall colors today.

"You've known me my whole life. I think you can call

me Jen." She smiled despite Violet's fingernails scraping her palm as she attempted to pull Jenessa toward the goats. "Could we walk while we talk?"

She had a strong feeling she knew what was coming. In a town like Maple Valley, personal business tended to be everyone's business. But now wasn't the time for discussing whatever gossip might be flying about her plans to sell the house.

Mayor Milt fell in step beside her. "No, I think I'll keep calling you Ms. Belville because I'm not talking to you as a friend or even the mayor right now. I'm talking to you as a concerned citizen *and* president of the local historical society. Belville Park is a historic landmark in Maple Valley. Your ancestors founded this town. How can you even consider selling it?"

"I'm not considering selling it. I *am* selling it. It's too much house for one person and—"

Violet's squeal cut her off as a goat came trotting over the grass, heading straight for the little girl. Why wasn't this one behind a fence with the others? Had it escaped?

"Ms. Belville—"

"This really isn't the best time." Violet's grin took over her whole face as she petted the friendly goat, Cade's giggles joining in as the goat nipped at his feet. "I guess one of the little critters got free."

"Flynnie's not part of the petting zoo." A new voice swept in.

"Lucas, I was hoping you'd be here." She angled to see him nearing, his jeans faded at the knees and his plaid shirt untucked. He certainly appeared to fit in better at the orchard than she did—her bright yellow, knee-length cardigan, striped shirt, and black leggings not exactly farm wear. But she'd needed just one thing to feel normal today. "Who's Flynnie?"

He reached her side, giving the mayor a nod of greeting. "Kit's pet. A gift from Beckett."

Violet had moved to the nearby fence, her hand outstretched through the wood planks that penned off the other goats—the ones who *weren't* pets and therefore not as privileged as Flynnie, who apparently enjoyed free rein of the orchard grounds.

"Mr. Danby, good afternoon—well, almost evening." If Mayor Milt was annoyed at being interrupted, he didn't show it as he returned his attention to Jenessa. "Perhaps we can continue this discussion another time, Ms. Belville? It's not only the house we need to talk about. Surely you remember that Founder's Day is on the horizon."

Founder's Day? But why would he want to talk . . . *oh.* Good grief, he didn't have some notion of resurrecting the old Founder's Day Gala Mom used to throw, did he? Mom had spent months planning those things.

"Mayor Milt, I hope you're not thinking—"

He gave her a jolly shake of his head. "Another time."

She'd argue but knew Mayor Milt well enough to know he'd track her down regardless. She glanced at Lucas as the mayor strolled away, moving a squirming Cade to her other hip. "You should really have a white horse when you do stuff like that."

"I wasn't riding to your rescue, *Ms. Belville.*" He copied the mayor's address, only the faintest circles under his eyes giving away what must've been an incredibly short night of sleep last night. "Just providing a timely interruption."

Violet was back to petting Flynnie. "So this is a pet? Interesting. Most guys opt for flowers or chocolate." She bent to let Cade get a closer look at the animal.

"Beckett's not most guys. Where's the oldest girl?"

"Colie Hollis is not exactly my greatest fan." She let out a long, dramatic sigh. "Refused to budge from the car."

"So I guess you never got ahold of DHS?"

She nodded. "Sam's not happy. But I don't know what else he wants me to do at this point. Other than take care of them until I can call the office number on Monday. And maybe give them some fun weekend memories in the meantime. What's so wrong with that?" She straightened, lifting Cade with her.

"Not a thing."

There was something reassuring about Lucas's presence. Always had been. Did he realize that? "That's why I borrowed a minivan and brought them here. Well and because, I know I said thank you in a text, but—"

He held up one hand. "Jen, you don't have to."

"You fixed the window. You killed the bat. You carried a thousand boxes to the attic and the garage and wherever else they all ended up."

"There's a few in the basement." He seemed almost embarrassed as he rubbed his chin and looked away. "All I did was clear out some space. And I was just doing what anyone would—"

"No, not anyone would do it, and you need to stop interrupting me. Just stand there and let me thank you and take it like a man."

He laughed. "Fine, then. You're welcome. Again."

Violet's squeal cut in. "He nicked me. He nicked me."

Jenessa jostled Cade. "Do you think she means nipped or licked?"

"Maybe both. Hey, want to feed the goats, Violet?"

Violet looked to Lucas, her expression turning shy. Did she recognize him from the hallway last night or had she been too drowsy to take much notice of him then? He pulled a quarter from his pocket and moved to a glass case packed with dried corn, slipped the coin in, and turned the crank.

Jenessa watched as he knelt next to Violet and opened his palm. She cast him another shy smile before plucking a handful of corn from his fingers. He stayed beside her for another minute or two, pointing out his favorite of the goats—a black and white kid less than a month old—and showing her how to scratch between its ears.

When he stood again, he must've caught her stare. "What?"

"You're good with her." And how had she never noticed before the way the corners of his eyes crinkled when he smiled? Were his smiles really that rare?

They shouldn't be. The one he wore now lit up his sandstone irises.

"Any chance you'd be willing to watch both of them for a minute while I check on Colie?"

"Of course." He held out his hands and she handed Cade over.

And for a moment both delightful and somehow poignant, she observed their first interaction—Lucas figuring out how to fit the nine-month-old against him, Cade lifting one pudgy hand to touch Lucas's cheek. "I think something's happening to me, Lucas."

"What's that?"

"These kids, I just . . . I don't know. Once at lunch today, I looked over at Vi and she was chewing with her mouth open, and for some reason I thought it was the most adorable thing ever. When I laid Cade down for his nap, it took me twenty whole minutes to make myself leave the room. Even Colie—it's like I can feel the hurt radiating from her and every little thing inside of me longs to wrap her in my arms and promise her I'll make it better, even though I know I can't."

She looked over her shoulder, straining for sight of Colie's form in the minivan.

"Here the mayor was going on about the house, but all I could think about was this trio that landed in my world for this tiny slice of time. And I wish it would stretch out." She shrugged. "I know it's crazy. I have all those boxes to sort. A house to get ready to sell. And the backyard is a whole project on its own. Between the gardens and the destroyed shed and everything, I probably need to hire someone—a handyman? A landscaper?" She met Lucas's eyes. "But I'm struggling to remember why any of that's important."

She wasn't sure why she was telling him any of this. Nor why his simple, silent response—a dip of his head, a golden glimmer of understanding in his eyes—affected her so. How could he be so comforting without saying a word?

"I'll be back in a minute." Hopefully with Colie in tow. She turned.

"Jen, wait."

His expression had shifted again. He was mulling something now—she could see it. "What?"

"I might've just come up with a genius idea."

Maybe it wasn't so much genius as an idea born of desperation.

But as Lucas stood outside Noah's door in the Everwood hallway now, he couldn't bring himself to regret the impulsive offer he'd made Jenessa an hour ago.

Because even more than he needed to figure out what to do with the guy he'd picked up at the airport earlier today, Lucas craved what his spontaneous idea offered: the chance to be Jenessa Belville's hero. No matter how small the opportunity.

"You mentioned your yard. The gardens. I've actually got

landscaping experience—I worked for MV Garden & Turf in high school. And I could have a new shed up for you in no time. I don't know much about flowers per se, but—"

"No, Luke," Jenessa had argued. "You've already done enough for me."

"But you'd be doing something for me. There's this kid I'm supposed to mentor." Not a kid, really. At twenty-seven, Noah was only five years his junior. But he'd acted like a child when they'd arrived at the Everwood hours ago, escaping to his room and practically slamming the door in Lucas's face.

But Kit had needed him at Apple Fest, and he'd figured maybe the guy could use some time to adjust to his current circumstances, anyway.

He'd explained his own current circumstances to Jenessa in vague terms. Any other time and she probably would've drilled him for more information on Noah. But she'd had her eyes on Violet and likely her mind on Colie.

The more he'd talked, the more he'd realized this might be the perfect solution. Flagg had said to come up with a project, after all. "You'd be doing me a favor if you'd let me take on the yard, with Noah's help. I'll probably still help Kit at the orchard on weekends, but she doesn't really need me on weekdays."

"I'll think about it." But he'd seen the way she'd perked up at the idea. She'd accept, he didn't doubt it.

So he lifted his fist to knock on Noah's door now. No response. He knocked again, shrugged, and opened the door.

"Hey, a little privacy might be nice." Rancor filled Noah's voice from his slouched spot on his bed.

None of this was going to be easy, that was clear as anything. But at least he had a path forward now. "You get one day, Johansson."

The younger man's forehead wrinkled, though his glare was unwavering.

"Do whatever you want tomorrow. Sleep in. Go to church. Take a self-guided tour around town. Whatever. But I want to see you downstairs ready to go Monday morning. That's when the work starts."

"What work?"

He ignored the question. "Seven a.m. Don't be late."

6

*J*enessa didn't know what she'd expected the social worker from the Department of Human Services to look like, but it wasn't this: baggy jeans, close-fitting striped top, hoop earrings almost as large as the bangles on both wrists.

Carmen Rodriguez had maybe a couple years on Jenessa, tops.

A sticky, cloying reluctance had clung to her as she'd called the DHS office in Ames at 8:00 a.m. on the dot this morning. Especially after yesterday. She might've been in a daze for most of Saturday, but Sunday had been near-perfection. She'd opted to skip church, figuring it might be too much for the kids . . . and for her.

Instead, she'd spent the day channeling Aunt Lauren. Coaxing giggles, indulging whims. Spoiling the kids.

She'd picked up donuts from the bakery the evening before—with sprinkles for Violet. She'd played hide and seek with Vi, taught Cade how to give a high-five, built a fort from blankets and old bed sheets she'd found in the hallway closet upstairs. And in the evening, as they chomped on homemade popcorn and watched *Toy Story*, she might've even caught Colie smiling once or twice.

But any ground she'd gained with the older girl had dissipated when Jenessa had discovered her listening in on this morning's phone call. Even now, two and a half hours later, Colie's look of complete betrayal was enough to set her stomach churning all over again.

I had to make the call. It was the right thing to do.

She poured Carmen a second cup of coffee, eyes glued to the scene in the dining room—Carmen with patience etched into every inch of her expression, seated across from Colie. Quiet as ever.

Surly, more like. Her one-word answers to the social worker were as monosyllabic as all Jenessa's interactions with her had been in the past two days. She'd bet her entire inheritance on the fact that the only reason the girl hadn't tried sneaking away again was how content her younger siblings seemed.

Which attested to the fact that somewhere underneath Colie's leaden gaze and sullen silence was a big sister's caring heart.

"And the last time you remember seeing your father was . . . when?" Carmen's slight accent added an extra softness to her voice.

But so far, her gentleness had done nothing to ease Colie. "I already said it was a long time ago." She huffed, and apparently decided to throw Carmen a bone. "It was last Thanksgiving."

Jenessa replaced the carafe and picked up Carmen's mug. She'd tried not to intrude too often as Carmen spoke first with Violet and then Colie. But she hadn't liked the idea of leaving the girls alone with a stranger either.

Carmen had let Violet off the hook only a few minutes into their conversation. Thankfully, the younger girl seemed completely oblivious to the import and implication of Carmen's presence. She was happily occupied by *Toy Story 2* in the living room now.

Jenessa carried the mug into the dining room and set it in front of Carmen. She darted a glance at Colie, but the girl refused to meet her eyes.

Carmen gave Jenessa a thankful nod. If she was bothered by Jenessa's loitering in the past thirty minutes, she hadn't let on. "Is there anything else you can tell me about your dad, Colie? Something that might help us locate him? I know you said he drives semis. When he came home in the past, how long did he stay?"

"A few days." Colie slouched in her chair. "Sometimes a week."

"And were he and your mother . . . friendly to one another? Was he nice to you and your sister?"

A shrug.

"He never met Cade?"

A shake of Colie's head.

"Was there ever a time—maybe a long time ago—when he wasn't traveling all the time? Did he ever live with your family?"

Colie's hooded gaze was trained on her lap. "When I was little."

"Little like Violet? Or like Cade?"

Jenessa nearly jumped from her perch under the kitchen doorframe when Colie slapped her palms to the tabletop. "I'm not a child. You don't have to treat me like I'm dumb or something. I was seven, okay? That's when he left the first time, and I didn't see him again until I was nine. And I don't know where he is now and he probably doesn't even know Mom's dead. Or Grandma."

A deafening silence filled the room. And if Jenessa had felt a pull at her heartstrings when she'd first laid eyes on the kids in her cottage Friday night, if her heart had twisted and melted with each hour spent with them over the weekend . . . it simply fell apart now. Not at the blunt anger in Colie's voice, but in the haunting pain hovering just behind it.

The urge had become all too familiar—to go to Colie and pull her into a hug whether she liked it or not.

But before she could move, the squeak of Colie's chair lanced into the pulsing quiet. She stood. "Is that all?"

Carmen laid down her pen, wrapped both hands around her mug. She nodded.

Without the barest glance Jenessa's way, Colie stalked from the room.

"It's only been a few months since her mom passed. And with her grandma, I'm sure that accounts for her . . . irritability." Although Colie had confirmed what Violet had implied earlier—that their relationship with the grandmother hadn't been at all affectionate. That theirs hadn't been a happy home. Jenessa dropped into the chair Colie had abandoned.

"She's scared and hurting," Carmen affirmed. "I just wish she'd been able to tell us a little more about"—she glanced down at her notes—"Dustin Hollis. Even so, it shouldn't take too long to locate him. We'll work closely with law enforcement. Until then, there's another staff member at DHS who will be able to help with arrangements for the grandmother."

"And then what? What if the father's not fit to take care of them? You heard Colie. He didn't even come home for the birth of his son."

Carmen sipped her coffee. "Yes, but we don't know the situation. Until we know more, we have to take this one step at a time. Meanwhile, I made some calls on my way here. I've got a respite placement lined up already. If it takes more than a few days to locate Mr. Hollis, we'll look into alternate arrangements. That is, unless we can locate other relatives, although from everything Colie says and my quick initial background work, I'm not thinking that's going to happen. So foster care is probably—"

"Wait. Please. I . . ." Respite placement? Foster care? She'd known that was the likely course of action, but the thought of it had kept her awake half the night. "They've already had to deal with so much change. They had to leave their house, they camped out in my cottage, then settled in here. They've been through so much and . . ."

And the idea that had set her tossing and turning overnight spilled out now. "Why can't they stay here?"

Carmen eyed her over the rim of her coffee mug, her expression impossible to read.

"I've clearly got plenty of space."

"Didn't I see a *For Sale* sign out front?"

"It's going to take me a while to get the place ready to sell." Although, now that Lucas had practically begged to help, it might go faster than she'd anticipated. She still couldn't make sense of his offer. But she'd been so focused on the kids Saturday night, she'd barely given it any thought.

Other than to send a quick and grateful text of acceptance Sunday afternoon. *If you're sure you want the job, it's yours. But I'm going to pay you.*

He'd texted back minutes later. *Better idea: Let Noah and I stay in the cottage rent-free. That's compensation enough.*

That made even less sense than his insistence on helping in the first place. Why would he want to give up a comfortable room at the Everwood to stay in a neglected little four-room house? And where had this Noah come from anyway?

But once again, she'd been too distracted by the kids to

argue. So at some point today, Lucas would be showing up with his mentee and moving in to Aunt Lauren's cottage.

"Miss Belville—" Carmen began.

"Jen."

"Okay, Jen, I can see you have a lot of compassion for the children. And you've obviously taken good care of them in the past couple of days. But you're not a trained foster parent. This could go on indefinitely and I'm not sure you're prepared—"

"Will they be split up if they're placed in foster care?"

"Obviously, we'll do our best to keep them together but—"

"You can't separate them. They need each other."

"Jen—"

"I can childproof all the cabinets. I'll double-check all the smoke detectors, the carbon monoxide detector. If the crib I found in the attic won't work, I can buy a new one. And car seats, too. I can provide food, shelter, and safety."

Carmen pushed her mug away. "What about school? We're already nearly a month into the fall semester. Colie and Violet should be there right now. And I'm assuming you have a job. What are you going to do with Cade while you're working?"

"I'll figure it out. My job's flexible. I own the local news-paper. I'm financially secure." Frankly, thanks to the money her parents had left her, she could shut down the paper today and have plenty of savings to live off of for years to come.

"Jen."

"Do a background check on me. I've literally never even had a speeding ticket."

"Please, slow down."

"No, I'm asking *you* to slow down. Don't force these children away from a place where they're stable and comfortable, maybe for the first time since their mother died." Or maybe even since before she died, if the hints of past unhappiness she'd picked up just in the past couple of days were on the mark. "Come back and check on us as often as you need to, but don't take this away from them."

Don't take them away from me.

The force of her own desire surprised her even as it coursed through her, settling deep into her bones. For the first time since her own mother had died, she felt needed. Purposeful.

Sam had said she was bored at the newspaper. And he was right. She'd been restless for months, using her busyness, maybe even her friendships, as a distraction from her lack of direction. Full days were a cover for the buried emotions she'd been just as reluctant to sort through as all her parents' belongings, for the sense of discontent she didn't know what to do with.

For her . . . loneliness.

I'm not lonely. I have Mara and Marshall and Sam and Lucas. She had Paige at the paper and a town full of people she'd known her whole life.

Yes, but do they know you?

It wasn't the first time she'd entertained the thought that no one knew the real her. Not even the friends she'd wrangled into a family. Truth was, this house she'd avoided for so long had seen more of the real Jenessa Belville than her friends had. It had witnessed the anxiety that had riddled her teenage years, the angst of her guilt over all that had happened with Mom and Dad . . .

The tears she saved for nighttime after Aunt Lauren left.

She looked up, meeting Carmen's brown eyes. "I was only a little younger than Colie when I lost someone very close to me. It's not the same situation, but I think . . . I truly think I have something to offer her, to offer all three of them."

Carmen's studying stare bore into her.

"Please give me a chance."

"Not that the B&B is a five-star hotel or anything, but we're giving up rooms there for this?" Noah dropped his duffel bag to the cottage floor and it sent dust and dirt pluming at their feet.

Okay, so it was dirty.

And dark despite the sunlight flooding the sprawling back lawn of Belville Park. Removing the dingy curtains from the main room's windows would help with that. And the city utilities office had promised to send someone out by the end of the day to turn on the electricity.

"A little cleaning and it'll be plenty livable." Lucas crossed the room, passed the small kitchenette against the back wall, and peeked into one of the two tiny bedrooms. No bed, but he'd slept on hard ground plenty of times through the years. A sleeping bag on the floor would suit him just fine tonight.

And if Noah didn't like that, well, he could take that faded couch in the main room.

Point was, they were Army men, former soldiers. They'd get by. Because whatever else the cottage might lack, it offered two things the Everwood didn't—privacy and space.

He'd realized first thing Sunday morning that he and Noah couldn't stay at the Everwood. Noah had already shot him a strange look when he'd made vague introductions to Mara, Marshall, and Sam. And though none of his friends had necessarily pried for information, they'd asked just enough questions to convince Lucas he'd be better off finding somewhere else to stay.

"Grab the bucket of cleaning supplies from my truck, will you? I'm going to check out all the faucets." Supposedly the water already had been turned on, but whether the sinks and shower and toilet would work after years of disuse, who knew.

But Noah didn't budge from the doorway. "So . . . what? We live in a sardine box and clean up a yard that looks like it was hit by a tornado?"

Lucas twisted the faucet handle over the kitchenette's small sink. After a second or two, a trickle of water dripped into the rusted drain below. "Actually it *was* hit by a tornado. We got a bad one in 2014." And for once, he'd even been around at the time.

After serving out his prison sentence, he'd gone straight to work with Flagg. But three years into his time with Bridgewell, he'd received the call about Grandpa's passing. He'd actually come home for a couple of years then, worked the orchard at Dad's insistence before Kit had moved back from London and taken over.

But he'd known all through those two years that he didn't belong at the orchard. Probably didn't even belong in Maple Valley. He'd itched to get back to Bridgewell. Never had understood why Dad had turned the orchard over to him, especially considering the years of distance between them, his father's refusal to so much as shake his hand when he'd finally come back to the States.

Of course, Dad hadn't known about Bridgewell. Probably thought Lucas needed the work, the discipline. *Probably thought he was doing me a favor.*

Right. As if Dad had ever gone out of his way to actually be a part of his son and daughter's lives.

"And somehow playing gardener is supposed to get me ready to join Bridgewell Elite?"

Oh, they were going to do more than garden. It'd take a full day alone to saw that fallen tree into smaller pieces and haul it away, along with all the debris from the destroyed shed. Then they'd need to rebuild the shed. Between that and the neglected gardens, the broken fountain, the landscaping, they'd have plenty to keep them occupied for the next month, at least.

And frankly, he liked the challenge of it. Of the physical labor, anyway, if not necessarily the company. But he couldn't forget that Noah *was* his work. His mission.

"Noah, Bridgewell Elite is a team. It's a close-knit group of soldiers who haven't just mastered a series of skills and tools. We've perfected the art of working together. It's not the physical training that makes us elite, it's the fact that we can communicate silently, read each other's minds."

Well, almost anyway. He hadn't picked up on Courtney's, uh . . . feelings or anything. Nor had he done a good job—or any job at all—silently communicating his break in protocol when they'd been in Venezuela.

Still. He might've taken a bullet, but he'd completed the mission.

And he'd complete this one. No matter how many scowls Noah sent his way.

"We need to start tackling this place if we want to be able to sleep tonight without inhaling dust. I thought maybe while we work, you could tell me a little about your experience in Iraq."

"Flagg said you're my mentor, not my counselor."

"Yeah, well, he also told me he could see promise and potential in you. Maybe he misled both of us." Probably not the best thing to say to get on the guy's good side, but just how much was he supposed to put up with here? He sure as heck hadn't been this insolent when Flagg had first taken him under his wing.

No, he'd been entirely too desperate to be anything but pliable and grateful.

"Lucas!"

The distant sound of Jen's voice broke in. He crossed the room in three long strides and brushed past Noah. Jenessa was flying across the lawn, the loose maroon dress she wore over a pair of black leggings billowing around her. Why was she barefoot? Today was the first day of October —the ground was cold.

"What's wrong?"

"Nothing," she gasped through panting breaths, covering the last of the grassy space between them. "Nothing at all." She gulped for air. "They're staying. At least for now. I had to practically beg Carmen and apparently she has to get some temporary emergency order or something from a judge somewhere and there's this whole checklist of stuff I'll have to do, foster parent training and . . ." She again attempted to catch her breath. "The point is, I can keep them . . . at least until . . . further notice."

Before he could say a word, she flung her arms around his neck. She released him a second later, stepped back, and glanced over his shoulder.

"Oh, hi. You must be Noah."

He should say something. Congratulate her. Introduce her. But no, one fast-as-lightning hug and he'd gone mute. He barely heard Noah's mumbled "hi" behind him.

"I'm Jenessa. I own this place." She turned her sparkling eyes back on Lucas. "Are you sure you want to stay in the cottage, Luke? It's not exactly modern. Although you should've seen it back when my aunt lived here. It was my favorite place in the world back then and—oh, I can't stay.

Cade's going to wake up from his nap any minute. I just wanted to tell you the good news."

Words. Just cobble a few together. "I'm happy for you."

She beamed. "I'm happy for me, too."

And then she did it a second time. Hugged him all over again and suddenly he was convinced that moving to the cottage was both the best and stupidest thing he'd ever done.

As quickly as she'd appeared, she was gone, racing back to the house, her ponytail swaying behind her.

"I get it now."

He was still absurdly out of breath when he turned. "Get what?"

Noah rose from the chair at the large paint-splattered table in the corner. "Why we ditched the B&B for this place."

"What do you mean?" He stepped into the cottage, irritated as much by the tone in Noah's voice as the knowing look in his eyes. Just what exactly did he think he knew?

"You're sleeping with her, aren't you?"

Lucas went still. "Say something like that again and—"

"And you'll what?" Noah leaned his hip against the kitchenette counter. "Tell Flagg you're giving up on me?"

"Tell him *he* should give up on you. I'm serious. Disrespect Jen one more time in front of me and I'll send you packing so fast you won't know what hit you." He plucked Noah's bag from the floor and tossed it in a bedroom. "Now go get the cleaning supplies and get to work."

She couldn't stop staring at the baby in her arms.

The creak of her rocking chair was a lullaby in the

silence of the room she'd picked out for Cade—breezy yellow walls, tasseled rug with a geometric pattern of blue, white, and gray. Marshall had helped her carry the old crib down from the attic on Saturday, but up until today, it'd been in the room down the hall where Colie and Violet slept.

But now that she knew the kids were staying indefinitely, it made sense to give them their own rooms. Not like she didn't have plenty to spare. She'd rolled the crib in here and had given the girls the pick of the remaining rooms.

Jenessa leaned closer to little Cade, the scent of baby lotion lifting from his soft, pink skin. He'd spent half the day crying. He'd pooped through his diaper. He'd made Violet shriek when he'd grabbed a fistful of her hair at suppertime.

But right now? With his little chest rising with each deep breath and his impossibly long eyelashes resting on his cheeks? It felt like she was holding a piece of heaven in her arms.

"Jessa?"

Her gaze flitted to the bedroom door. The light from the hallway spilled into the room, creating a silhouette around Violet's thin form. "Hey, you."

Violet wore a *Little Mermaid* pajama top with red-and green-striped Christmas bottoms and held a bright pink toothbrush in one hand. Carmen had stopped by Tessa Hollis's house earlier in the day, picked up clothing and other items—Cade's high chair, a plastic grocery sack filled with a few toys, several pairs of shoes, car seats—and dropped them off at Jenessa's. But none of their belongings had excited Violet as much as the new toothbrush Jenessa had produced later.

She had Mara to thank for that. Her friend had swung

by the mini-mart this evening and then dropped off a few things.

And thankfully, Jenessa had found a temporary solution to the vehicle situation, leasing a mid-sized SUV from a local dealership that had delivered it right to her driveway.

"I can't reach the toothpaste, Jessa."

Jenessa blinked and stood. She kissed Cade's cheek once more before crossing the room and laying him in the crib. She turned on the baby monitor, another item Carmen had found in Tessa Hollis's rental house.

What would happen to the rest of the stuff the kids had left behind? To all of Tessa Hollis's belongings? Maybe Jenessa should bring the kids over there at some point. Let Colie and Vi pick through whatever was there and identify anything else they wanted to make sure to keep.

Or maybe that was a job better left to their father. Assuming he could be found before the home's owner took it upon himself to empty out the place.

She reached Violet and took the little girl's hand, leading her across the hall and into the bathroom. Moments later, Jenessa had the pink toothbrush loaded with toothpaste. "Are you old enough to brush your own teeth?" Colie had been in the bathroom with Violet the past two nights.

From her perch on the bathroom footstool, Vi's chiming giggle was almost as cute as her dimpled grin and her mismatched pajamas. "You're silly, Jessa."

Or just tragically inexperienced at taking care of kids. But she'd done okay so far, hadn't she? At least two out of the three liked her.

The other barely tolerated her. But at least Colie hadn't seemed overly upset when Jenessa had told her she'd be staying. Had hardly reacted at all, really.

But there'd been so much to do all day that she hadn't had much of a chance to try to soothe any of Colie's perpetually ruffled feathers. Meals and bath time and what felt like a hundred diaper changes had chipped away at her energy. Cade had seemed fussier today than the past two days, and Violet had bulleted questions nonstop.

"How long do we get to live here? Who was that lady with the bracelets? Why did she ask so many questions? Why do we get our own rooms now? Is Colie mad that we're staying?"

Was Colie ever not mad?

"Are you daydreaming?"

Jenessa's eyes jolted open—when had she closed them? Toothpaste foam rimmed Violet's mouth and her adorable little ears angled out between limp curls. "Does it count as daydreaming if it's nighttime?" Jenessa asked.

Violet put one hand on her waist. "I don't know. I'm only six."

"You know what, Vi? I think we're going to get along really well."

Violet swiped the back of her arm over her mouth and hopped off the footstool. "Now what?"

"Now you go hop into bed while I check on your sister. Then I'll tuck you in."

"Okay." Violet swung her arms as she moved to the bathroom door. But she stopped and turned back to Jenessa. She curled and wriggled her pointer finger and Jenessa obeyed the motion, crouching in front of the girl. The moment she lowered, Violet wrapped her skinny arms around Jenessa's neck. "I really miss my mom, but I like it here, Jessa. I think I'm happy we're staying."

A damp mess of curls ended up in her mouth, tickled her nose, and the apple scent of the tangle-free shampoo Mara had picked up engulfed her.

And it was as if Jenessa's heart stopped, just for a second, a moment of poignant silence and stillness for what this six-year-old had already endured. What anguish surely gripped her older sister. What her younger brother would miss out on.

But even as the heartbreak swirled around her, the same feeling that had held her willingly captive a few minutes ago as she rocked Cade came over her again. A feeling of rightness and belonging. She was so far past falling for these kids—even Colie with her constantly crossed arms and resolute silence.

"I'm happy you're staying too."

Violet kissed Jenessa's cheek and then skipped away.

Leaving her to stand in the fluorescent light of the bathroom, staring at herself in the mirror. Her ponytail hung limp to one side and since when did her dress have a whiteish stain on one sleeve? *Cade's formula.* Right. She needed to invest in some spill-free bottles and sippy cups. And probably ask someone somewhere at what age to switch from formula to milk and . . .

And she needed to get in the habit of reminding herself this was only temporary.

With a sigh, she flicked off the bathroom light and roamed down the hall. She paused outside of Colie's room. "Colie?" She kept her voice low in case the girl had gone to bed already. But a sliver of light under the door told her that wasn't the case. "I just wanted to check on you."

No answer.

She reached for the doorknob, hesitated. *You need to at least make sure she's in there.* She inched the door open and glanced inside.

Standing in the middle of the room, Colie instantly whirled away, turning her back to Jenessa. But she hadn't been fast enough to hide the redness of her eyes and nose. The tracks on her cheeks. "You ever hear of knocking?"

Jenessa lingered in the doorway, uncertain whether to pretend she hadn't noticed Colie's tears and congested voice or try to comfort her. Anytime she'd attempted the latter so far, it hadn't ended well.

"I just wanted to see if you need anything, especially since this is a different room and—"

"I'm fine." Fists clenched at her sides, Colie trudged to her bed.

She took a hesitant step into the room. "Colie, I—"

"I don't really want to talk. I just want to go to bed." She pulled her covers back but didn't make a move to slip under the sheets.

"Okay, well . . . I know these past couple of days have been really weird for you. And staying here might feel odd, too. But I'm going to try my best to make sure you and your siblings are as comfortable as possible, okay?" She paused. "Maybe you can help me with that. You're clearly a great big sister and I think you might know more about what Violet and Cade need than I do. Maybe we can work together?"

The tense, dogged silence that seemed to accompany Colie no matter where she went clogged the space between them now. But finally, she nodded and crawled into bed, face still turned away.

"Well, goodnight, then."

Jenessa stepped into the hallway, gently closed the door. It hadn't necessarily been a success of a conversation. But it was a start.

7

*J*enessa had been convinced that getting all three kids out the door this morning would be the most difficult part of her day.

She hadn't counted on the ambush awaiting her at the *Maple Valley News* office.

Four or five voices all pecked at her at once, filling the pressroom with more noise than it had ever had since she'd made the decision to outsource the printing of each weekly issue and sold off the old, barely functioning press. This room served little purpose now other than to house shelves of oversized bound black books, each one holding a year's worth of old newspapers and decade's worth of dust.

And today, apparently, the space played host to an impromptu gathering with the mayor, half the city council, the president of the Chamber of Commerce, and several others.

"Mayor Milt, everyone, please. It's production day and I've got a paper to finish laying out." And then several rounds of proofing before sending it on to the print vendor.

Not to mention she had three kids currently hunkered

down in her tiny office at the corner of the newsroom, visible through the pressroom window. That cartoon on Netflix might keep them occupied for another half an hour or so, but she couldn't expect poor Paige to play babysitter much longer.

"I know you're all concerned about my plans for my parents' house—"

"Not just your parents' house," the mayor interjected from his perch on a metal stool near an old counter with a backlit tabletop, useful back in the days of literally cutting and pasting the paper together but long since abandoned. How did Mayor Milt manage to look so friendly and stern at the same time? "Belville Park was your grandparents' and your great-grandparents' before them and all the way back to Jessup Belville, who—"

"Founded Maple Valley in the fall of 1869 and was our first mayor and went on to serve in the state senate. I know my family history." She attempted a sip from the travel mug she'd stuffed in the overflowing diaper bag she'd lugged to the office today. But she'd already finished off the coffee.

Would've brought a second mug if she'd known what was in store.

The mayor dipped his head. "Well, you left out the part about how Jessup Belville built Belville Park with his own two hands. How can you think of selling it? What if an outsider comes in and tears the whole place down? Just like that, we lose an historic landmark."

"But—"

Belinda, the president of the Chamber of Commerce, cut in now. "And it's not just the house. It's those gorgeous gardens your mother spent over forty years cultivating."

She hadn't done it alone. Aunt Lauren had helped her nurture the flower beds and pick out new varieties of plants every summer that she'd lived in the cottage out back.

Those were the only times Jenessa remembered Mom and her sister getting along, actually.

Most of the time, Mom was endlessly frustrated with Aunt Lauren. She'd complained about her sister's flightiness, described her as artsy—not a compliment in the tone Mom used—and overly emotional. As a child, Jenessa had often wondered if that was why Aunt Lauren had been relegated to living in the cottage—because Mom simply hadn't the patience to have her any closer.

But oh, how Jenessa had loved spending time at the cottage with Aunt Lauren. That little home with its mismatched furniture and splashes of color, thanks to the very artistic bent Mom didn't appreciate, had held more life and happiness than any one of the twenty-four rooms back at the main house.

And Jenessa—she'd somehow always felt more . . . well, *herself* in Aunt Lauren's cottage.

But Mom and Dad tried. In their own way, they'd loved her, hadn't they?

"Ms. Belville, are you even listening?"

Should she answer that honestly or . . . ?

"Mayor Milt, perhaps we should tell her the real reason we're all here."

It was a new voice that spoke, piping up from the back of the crowd. Leigh Renwycke? *No, Pierce.* Right, the woman around Jenessa's age had gotten married just recently. They'd had one of the cutest wedding photos she'd ever placed on page 4.

Leigh worked for the city these days, didn't she? Part-time event coordinator or something along those lines.

"You're not here about Belville Park?" Jenessa set her empty travel mug aside, casting a quick glance through the horizontal window that peeked into the newsroom. She could just make out the girls in her office, still perched in front of her laptop. Hopefully Cade remained asleep in his port-a-crib.

What she wouldn't give for a nap herself. She'd been exhausted when she'd dropped into bed last night, had expected to drift to sleep in seconds. But Violet had come padding to her door the moment she'd closed her eyes.

"Jessa? I've never slept in my own room. I don't know if I like it."

She'd ended up curling next to Jenessa, spending the whole night there. Jenessa probably hadn't slept more than two hours at a time the rest of the night without waking up to a heel in her shin.

Leigh moved to the front of the group. "They—we—are here about your property. But not just because of town history." Leigh gave the mayor a look of expectation.

His white mustache twitched. "Very well. As you know, Founder's Day is less than a month away—October twenty-seventh. In years past, your family used to host the Founder's Day Gala."

Oh dear. Already she didn't like the direction this was headed.

"Obviously in more recent years, your parents had to step away from the gala due to their health. It's the only annual event that's ever fallen off our calendar under my watch."

He was being generous. Yes, Dad's emphysema had flared up horribly before his death. And Mom's final relapse had led to such severe liver problems there was no undoing the damage.

But that wasn't why the Belvilles had stopped hosting the gala. Their involvement had waned more than a decade ago right after Dad was forced to withdraw from the gubernatorial race he'd spent his career building up to. Word had gotten out about the degenerative disease, how he'd tried to mislead voters, and his campaign had died before it'd even gotten off the ground.

At least that time he hadn't blamed his public disgrace on her.

She laced her fingers together to keep from fidgeting. "Mayor Milt, I hope you're not about to suggest—"

"It's not a suggestion, Jen. It's a heartfelt request. We'd like to revive the gala, and we have a specific reason for asking. We just found out Maple Valley is going to be featured in the November issue of *Iowa History*, so it's the perfect opportunity to talk about Founder's Day and our town history. We could invite the writer of the article to attend, take photos. Just think of it, your childhood home, your mother's gardens—you could make the cover."

"But, Mayor, you don't understand. Those gardens—"

"Don't you have Lucas Danby working on them?"

Wow, leave it to Maple Valley to get that news circulated in speedy fashion.

"I know it's a nervy request," Leigh piped in. "But you wouldn't have to coordinate the actual event. We're just asking to host it in your yard. Our Plan B is the town square, and we'll all completely understand if you'd rather not—"

"Speak for yourself," the mayor grumbled with a good-natured grin.

Leigh gave him an exaggerated look of reproof before turning back to Jen. "I'd be handling all the details. The catering, the decorations, the promotion."

"And you'd be helping us out tremendously." Mayor Milt hopped down from his stool. "Landing the feature story in *Iowa History* is a big deal. You're a journalist, Ms. Belville. You know this. I want to make a splash."

But to do so, she'd have to take down that *For Sale* sign in her yard. At least temporarily. How would it impact

Lucas's timeline? He'd said Noah was in town for four or five weeks. Could they finish their cleanup and landscaping work in a month's time?

"Uh, Jen?" Paige ducked her head through the pressroom door. "You're needed."

Something with the kids? She offered her visitors an apologetic shrug and stepped into the newsroom. She halted. "Oh my word. That smell."

Paige's dramatic nod accompanied her crossed arms. "My brown-nosing efforts only stretch so far, boss. I draw the line at changing dirty diapers."

That pungent smell didn't indicate dirty. It indicated a full-on explosion. Lovely. She crossed to her office in the corner. "Sorry, Paige. You shouldn't have been stuck babysitting in the first place."

Hopefully she wouldn't need to bring all three kids to work many more days. She had a meeting with the junior high principal later today, which meant Colie's school situation would be figured out soon. And she'd set up an appointment with the elementary school principal tomorrow.

As for Cade . . . well, she'd ponder that pickle later. Preferably when it wasn't deadline day. When she didn't have a cluster of townspeople gathered in the pressroom.

And when she wasn't surrounded by a deadly stench. She pulled Cade from the port-a-crib and made quick work of the cleanup. Violet was still perfectly content watching her cartoon, and Colie had a book open.

"All right, buddy," she said as she snapped Cade's cute little corduroys. "Now when I shoo all those people out of the pressroom, hopefully no one will pass out from the smell."

As if he understood her words, he gave her a grin and a giggle. Man, she was a sucker for those two tiny bottom teeth of his. And the way Violet was leaned over Jen's desk, her chin propped in her fist—just adorable. And Colie with her book . . .

Jenessa's first official day as the temporary guardian of the Hollis children might've gotten off to a hectic start. She might not have any idea what to expect for the rest of the week. When she was going to find time to shop for school supplies. What she'd fix for supper tonight.

But she knew—she *knew*—this was right.

"Why are you staring at me?" Colie's sarcastic voice cut in.

Jenessa felt the width and warmth of her own smile. "Because you guys make me happy, Colie. That's why."

For once, the girl didn't scowl. Rolled her eyes, yes, but the lack of glower felt like progress.

Jenessa propped Cade on her hip and prepared to face the mayor and his gathered crowd once more. But she stopped in her office door, catching sight of the framed photo atop a filing cabinet—Mom and Dad and herself. Taken almost twenty-five years ago, it showed Dad still hale and hearty and Mom wearing one of her glitzier dresses. Some campaign occasion, surely, back when Jenessa had still been allowed to attend.

Before she'd embarrassed Dad at his first event after Aunt Lauren's disappearance. Broken down in front of his guests. Been whisked away by Mom and called a liability by Dad's advisor.

They'd still been a happy family back then.

"Jen?" Mayor Milt stood in the pressroom doorway. "Are you coming back?"

She tightened her hold on Cade and nodded.

Lucas should've expected this. Two and a half hours—almost three—since he'd sent Noah to the hardware store for new chainsaw blades and he still hadn't returned, leaving Lucas without his assistant and without his truck.

Nor had Noah picked up when Lucas called or deigned to respond to a text.

Maybe this was what Jen and the rest of his friends had felt like last Friday night when he'd failed to show up for that little engagement party. Taste of his own non-communicative medicine, as it were.

He tipped his sunglasses over his eyes as he strode down Main Avenue. He'd already been by Klassen's Hardware, only to find out Noah had been in and out two hours ago.

Noah wanted to play hide and seek? Fine. He'd track the guy down easily enough. Because he knew something Noah didn't—new faces stuck out in Maple Valley like sore thumbs. All he had to do was stop in at whichever local hub he pleased and someone was sure to have seen the guy.

When he spotted Sam's squad car parked along the riverfront, it made his decision for him. *Coffee Coffee, it is.* Even if Sam hadn't seen Noah, surely someone in the place had.

Bells jangled overhead as he entered the shop, crowded even this close to noon. It was an eclectic little place with black-and-white-checkered flooring and brightly colored leather furniture. He gave a nod toward the barista up front —owner, actually—with the jet-black hair. He liked Megan Hampton. She was probably the youngest business owner in town and she had a sarcastic sense of humor he could appreciate.

"Luke?"

Good, Sam *was* here. He turned at the sound of his friend's voice, spotted him at a table in the corner with four other men, two he recognized and two he didn't. He wound his way through a congested maze of customers. "Hey, man. Thought I saw your car."

Sam rose, glancing at the other men at his table. Were those Bibles open in front of them? Shoot, what had he just interrupted?

Sam caught the question in his eyes. "Uh, men's Bible study. What are you doing here? Thought you'd be working at Jen's."

"I should be. But I lost my coworker."

He'd introduced Noah to Sam Sunday morning. The conversation had lasted all of five minutes—partially because of Noah's hostile silence, mostly because Sam had been out the door on his way to church. Huh, he'd known Sam was a more dedicated churchgoer than himself, but Bible study, too?

And why was the fellow with the gray hair at the end of the table giving off a less-than-friendly vibe as he watched Lucas? Maybe they'd been mid-prayer or something.

Or maybe it was his appearance. He could still feel his arms vibrating from hours of chainsaw use this morning as he'd worked on that fallen tree. He looked down at his dirt-and grass-stained white t-shirt and flannel shirt. His faded jeans fared little better, and he couldn't remember when he'd last shaved.

He returned his focus to Sam. "Any chance you've seen Noah?"

Sam shook his head. "No, but ask around and you'll find him easily enough."

"That's what I figured. I'll let you get back to what you were doing."

He was halfway across the coffee shop, debating whether it was worth waiting in line so he could ask Megan if Noah had been by, when he heard Sam call after him.

"Wait up, Luke."

He paused, felt the warmth of streaming sunlight pouring through the coffee shop's front windows. Perfect day to be working outside. He shouldn't be wasting it chasing down someone who couldn't appreciate the value of a good day's work.

"You didn't need to leave your study, Sam. Sorry I interrupted."

Sam waved off the apology and motioned toward the exit. "We were almost done. Besides, been meaning to talk to you. But considering you apparently don't live at the Everwood anymore, it's not as easy to catch you these days."

Was there an undercurrent of tension in Sam's tone? He stepped into the sunlight, a crisp, autumn cool washing over him. The trees across the road dotting the grassy knoll that curved toward the riverbank were just beginning to speckle with color.

"It makes sense to stay at Jen's cottage. I'm kind of working for her now."

Sam didn't reply right away, and for a strange moment, Lucas almost wished he hadn't honed his skills of observation quite so keenly in his years with Bridgewell. Then maybe he wouldn't have noticed the way Sam's grip on his Bible tightened. Or that one vein in his neck that protruded just so whenever he was on the brink of getting upset.

But why the heck should he care that Lucas had offered to help Jen? Or was it the living-in-the-cottage part that bothered him?

"About that Bible study group, by the way," Sam said. "I've thought about inviting you a few times but—"

"It's okay, Sam. I'm not pouting at being left out. And I've got a missing guy to find so I should be on my way." He moved toward the crosswalk. The next most crowded place in town would likely be the bakery. He'd try there next.

But Sam's voice from behind slowed his steps. "When are you leaving?"

He felt the breath in his lungs go cold, a rigid and strained silence stretching in the air between them as he turned. He squinted against the bright rays of the sun. "What?"

"I know you, Luke. You've been antsy for weeks. You might've stayed in Maple Valley longer this stint, but I can't shake the feeling it's only a matter of time."

"You have a feeling." His own voice came out murky and hoarse. Antsy? Is that what Sam thought? That he was driven by restlessness?

"I'm a cop. I get feelings. And they're usually on the mark."

"Then I don't know why you're asking me anything if you're so sure of your intuition." He crossed the street, moving toward the path that traced the river. This wasn't what he'd come downtown for. He needed to find Noah and get back to work at Jen's and figure out how to get the kid talking.

Sam's long strides matched his own. "I don't know why you're being weird about this. It was a simple question."

Except it had anything but a simple answer. "Sam—"

"You have friends who care about you, Danby. You have a family. If you're planning on skipping town again—"

Frustration crowded out his reticence. "Fine, yes, I'm leaving, okay? Is that what you wanted to hear?" He could feel the force of Sam's hard stare. "I'm not exactly sure when, but I'll probably be gone by Thanksgiving. You wanted to know and now you know."

"Have you told Jen? She hates it when you leave every fall and now you've promised to help her out, all the while knowing you're going to be heading out again."

Was that why Sam had seemed bothered earlier? Not

because he had a hunch Lucas would leave soon, but because he was worried about how Jen would take it? Worried Lucas was going to leave her hanging halfway into that backyard project?

And why wouldn't he think you'd do something like that? You're the guy who ditched your Army unit. You're the guy who leaves everyone behind every single year.

Why wouldn't Sam question his ability to finish what he started?

They walked in silence for a few moments before Sam spoke again. "There's no fruit farm in Mexico, is there?"

Lucas's steps slowed to a complete halt. How could Sam know that? *He's a cop. He gets feelings.* He couldn't make himself meet his friend's eyes.

"Tell me the truth or don't. Whatever." Sam raked his fingers through his hair. "But think about Jen. You're inserting yourself so fully into her life that it's only going to be harder for her when you leave."

"I'm trying to help her." Why couldn't Sam see that?

Sam stared at him for a long moment. "You're going to hurt her, Danby."

It sounded less like an accusation and more like a regret. "Thanks for the vote of confidence." He walked away.

One way or another, Jenessa had to find a way to focus on this meeting. To mentally set aside Mayor Milt and his posse and that irrational promise they'd wrangled out of her long enough to get through this meeting with Principal Willard.

Jeremiah Willard had been a fixture at Maple Valley Junior High since Jenessa's days as a teenager. His once-black hair had grayed entirely in the couple of decades since, but he still wore that ever-patient expression she remembered.

And if ever there was a time he needed it, it was now. Colie couldn't have appeared more bored from her spot in the vinyl chair next to Jen's. And if she popped one more bubble with her gum—

"So remind me, Colie, were you involved in any extra-curriculars last year?" It was the third time Principal Willard had tried to engage her. The poor man was probably regretting asking Jenessa to bring her along.

And she was regretting scheduling this meeting for today. Production day at the paper rarely sapped her energy, but she'd been running on empty from the start. Whatever meager vigor she'd started with had been utterly depleted by Mayor Milt's visit.

If only he hadn't kept bringing up Mom and Dad. The Belville legacy. All the galas of yore. Tugging on her guilt.

If only she hadn't been pricked with some groundless sense of responsibility to her family name. To the memory of her parents, who'd been so unhappy in the end. Mom would've liked the thought of another grand party. Dad would've appreciated a renewed standing in town.

Another pop of Colie's gum pulled her to attention. Had she even answered Principal Willard's question?

". . . sure it's not too late to talk with Coach Bertelli about joining the team again this year," the principal was saying.

Apparently, Colie had answered. She played a sport?

"You probably know the varsity volleyball team took second in our division at State last year and our JV team made a darn good showing as well. Coach Bertelli does a great job getting our younger players ready for the high school teams."

Volleyball? Finally, something she might actually be able to use to connect with Colie. "Hey, I played volleyball, too."

Remembrance lit the principal's eyes as he slipped off his glasses and laid them on his desk. "That's right. You were a star spiker."

Jenessa grinned, tugging a wavy chunk of hair behind her ear. "A good, healthy way to get out my teenage emotion." Which she'd always seemed to have too much of.

"I'm a setter," Colie said now, punctuating the statement with another bubble.

Jen swallowed her sigh, hoping Principal Willard could catch the apology in her eyes. He folded his hands over the manila folder on his desk, the one he'd been studying when they'd first entered his office. Probably Colie's transcript.

"Colie, I wonder if you'd mind if I chat with Miss Belville for a few minutes alone." He pointed out the glass wall that separated his office from the school secretary's domain. "Would you mind taking a seat out there for a bit?"

Colie answered with a shrug and stood, not even looking to Jen.

Jen watched the girl trundle from the room. She wore a too-small denim jacket, its sleeves pulling up at her wrists when she slumped into a chair near the secretary's desk. Discouragement pinched at the edges of her fatigue as she turned back to the principal, her fingers gripping the strap of the purse in her lap.

"I'm sorry she's not a little more . . . friendly."

Understanding hovered in the principal's expression. "You said you found her in a shed behind your house?

"A cottage, actually. I'm acting as a temporary guardian. It's been a whirlwind, to say the least." Thankfully, Mara had offered to watch Violet and Cade during this meeting.

"Wow." He replaced his glasses and opened the manila

folder, spreading out Colie's files in front of him. "We do need to talk about Colie's grade placement."

"What do you mean? She's in seventh grade."

His brow furrowed as he fingered through the papers. "She missed quite a few days last year. And she's already missed several weeks this year."

"I wish I knew why her grandmother didn't get her enrolled. Her health, perhaps."

He tapped the top page. "It's not only her attendance. Her grades are far from exceptional and her Iowa Test of Basic Skills scores were low last year. Plus, at her age, she's one of the youngest in our seventh-grade class."

"What are you saying?"

"Given her past attendance, her standardized test scores, and all the change she's already enduring now, I believe we'd be better off placing her in the sixth grade."

The leather of Jen's purse squeaked against her twisting palms. "You want to hold her back?"

"I really think it'd be the best thing for her."

She fought to keep her voice steady. "Embarrassing her would be the best thing for her?" She moved her purse to the chair Colie had vacated, just to keep herself from fidgeting. "Principal Willard, please. I haven't been able to connect with Colie at all, and now you want me to go out there and tell her she's being sent back a grade?"

"Would you rather wait until she's struggling in her classes? Do you really want to risk starting her off at a level she's not ready for only to have to tell her two or three or four months in that she's going to have to move back?"

"How can you be that sure she's not ready?"

"Because I know kids." He took off his glasses once more, as if willing her to see the truth in his eyes. "We're a small enough school, not to mention a small enough town, that it's relatively easy to spot at-risk children. I believe

Colie took on more responsibility at home for years than a child should have to."

Jenessa had pieced that together as well from comments here and there. Violet had talked about Colie making supper each night, doing laundry and other things. It was good for kids to have chores, of course, but Jenessa got the feeling Colie's responsibilities went beyond that.

Had Tessa Hollis worked evenings? Surely the cancer had made keeping up with things at home a hardship near the end.

"I'm not trying to make Colie's life—or your own, for that matter—any harder," Principal Willard said. "I'm trying to make this transition easier. For both of you."

Resignation settled over her, a heavy shroud she couldn't shake for the rest of the conversation. Within minutes, she was standing and shaking his hand. Reaching for her purse and forcing the closest thing she had to a smile as she left his office and approached Colie.

The halls of the school were silent as they walked, save the muted voices of teachers and students drifting from each classroom door they passed. Somewhere a locker door slammed. Colie didn't say a word as their footsteps echoed on the hard floor, nor as they emerged into the afternoon sunlight.

Jenessa waited until they'd reached the car and Colie was buckled in to face the girl. "Hey."

Colie didn't respond, only leaned her arm on the door, chin in her fist.

"So volleyball, huh?"

Nothing. Maybe it'd be better to get straight to it.

"How do you feel about waiting a couple of days to start school? Maybe Thursday or even Friday? Principal Willard says it's okay, and it'd give you a little time to get settled in at the house."

At least she got a shrug at that.

"There's one thing, though. Principal Willard . . . he, uh, he thinks you'd be happier this year in sixth grade."

Colie dropped her arm. "What?"

"You missed quite a bit of school at the end of the year last spring."

Colie actually looked her straight in the eye. "Yeah, my mom was sick."

It was as if she'd hurled a piercing arrow toward Jen. One that turned around in midair and pointed straight back at the girl. Because, oh, the torment she saw in Colie's eyes. The mix of anger and dismay.

"I'm sorry, Colie. I'm so—"

Colie shoved herself out the passenger door. Jen cut the engine and hurried out after her. "Colie, please—"

The girl whirled around on the sidewalk. "It doesn't matter anyway. I'm not staying here long. We'll leave eventually."

Where exactly did she think they'd go? "I know this is hard. But please . . . let's try to talk this out. In the car. School's going to let out soon and this parking lot will be a zoo."

"Whatever." Colie budged past her, moving once again in the direction of the car.

"Colie—"

"I said, whatever." She slammed the door and sank into her seat.

Leaving Jen to round the car, heart sinking.

8

The beads of hot water soaking his hair and pummeling his skin might slick away the grime of this day, but they couldn't come close to warding off Lucas's exhaustion.

He stood in the shower, eyes closed, forcing himself not to lean against a tiled wall lest he nod off right here and now. It wasn't just the work, the hours spent hacking up that tree and hauling logs and limbs in the wheelbarrow. It was last night's less-than-restful sleep due to the hard floor —he must've gone soft from months on that comfortable mattress at the B&B.

It was concern over the fact that he never had been able to find Noah today, and he was legit beginning to wonder if he'd ever get his truck back.

It was that conversation with Sam. He couldn't decide which rankled him most. Sam having picked up on his plans to leave and his lies about Mexico.

Or his friend's complete lack of faith in him.

He turned off the water and shoved the shower curtain

aside, reaching for a towel. Humidity thickened the air in the cottage's small bathroom and clouded the medicine cabinet mirror. Towel wrapped around his waist, he scrubbed a circle into the mirror and spared himself a brief glance. Should he take the time to shave?

His focus roamed lower—to the pinched skin of his arms. The burn marks started on his wrists and climbed all the way past both elbows, darker and more mottled in some spots than others, but an eyesore all the same.

Wasn't so much the sight of them that bothered him. He wasn't vain, and anyway it was easy enough to cover them.

It was the memories they induced. The sensations they still managed to resurrect even all these years later. The smell of burning flesh—not all his own. The weight of the body he'd carried through the village. The anguished cries of the child's mother . . .

His own yells when he'd awakened from the darkness later. The searing pain.

Stop.

He whirled away from the mirror, bent to swipe his discarded clothing from the floor, then ducked his head out the bathroom door. One of Noah's shirts was slung over the old couch in the middle of the living room and from here he could see the guy's duffel through an open bedroom door.

Noah might not have returned to the cottage, but he hadn't left entirely. That, at least, was something. But just how long was he supposed to hang around waiting for Noah to return? And why—*why?*—had Flagg thought this was a good idea?

On a whim, he snatched his cell phone from the kitchenette counter as he padded to the back bedroom, leaving wet prints on the wood planks underfoot. A voice answered on the second ring.

But not the voice he expected. "Hey, Danby."

"Uh, hey, Court. Why're you answering Doug's phone?"

"Doug's dealing with a burnt pizza situation. We're all at his place. Pizza. Football. You know the drill."

Right, because when the Bridgewell Elite team was stateside, Mondays were training days at the gym. Which meant during the NFL season, no one ever got home in time for whatever game was airing that night. They'd made a habit of gathering on Tuesday evenings and watching a recorded game.

He could picture them now in Doug's apartment—as sparse as the rest of the group's. Courtney with her cropped hair, usually in track pants and a Cowboys tee. She hadn't lived in Texas in almost twenty years, but she remained loyal to her home team. Doug, Jamar, and Kelvin would be there, too. Mariana was the only married member of the elite team, so she didn't always join in the after-hours gatherings.

"Everyone misses you, by the way."

Had she taken extra care to emphasize the *everyone* or was that just wishful thinking on his part? Surely after this many months of distance, the feelings she'd expressed last spring had dissipated some, right?

"Believe me, I thought I'd be back by now. But Flagg has me on an impossible mission at the moment."

"Right. The kid from Boston."

"Wow, you know where he's from? That's more than I've gotten out of him. You meet him or something?"

"No, but Flagg mentioned him."

He grabbed his last pair of clean jeans from his open suitcase. Should he ask Jen about using her washer and dryer at some point? Or maybe he could bring a load over to Kit's—like a college student lugging dirty laundry home.

Just another reminder that his life didn't look anything

like that of other thirty-three-year-olds. The closest thing he had to a landing spot was his own boxy apartment back in D.C. But it'd never felt as homey as his room at the B&B. It never beckoned him back the way Maple Valley did.

He put his phone on speaker and laid it on the sole piece of furniture in the room—a rickety end table with one leg superglued together. "I wish he'd talked to me a little more about him. I can't get a word out of the guy. I thought I had a good idea for working together. Thought it might give us a chance to talk or connect or something, but now he's AWOL." He reached for a clean t-shirt and pulled it over his head.

"I guess you know a little about that, don't you?"

Her harsh words stunned him. No, they flat-out pummeled him. Finding all the bruises that never faded and pressing down. Hard.

No one on the team ever brought up his desertion. They didn't bring up the dishonorable discharge, the prison sentence, any of it.

Was Courtney really still that angry? Had he hurt her that much when he hadn't kissed her back? What about what she'd said just a moment ago about the team missing him? Just forced politeness?

He picked his phone back up. "Court, I . . . I'm—"

"Don't want to talk about it, Luke."

"But don't we have to at some point? I'm still a part of the team and I want to know we can still work together and—"

"Cowboys just got a first down. Now's not the time. Why'd you call?"

"I don't know. Wanted advice, I guess. Wanted to know if anyone else knows something I don't about this Noah guy. Wanted to know why Flagg is doing this to me and—"

His train of thought completely derailed as his gaze

hooked on the sight outside his bedroom window. Was that smoke curling from the back of the main house?

What the—? He squinted, peering through the near-dark of the evening. Definitely smoke.

He scoured the tiny room for his shoes.

"Luke?" Courtney's muffled voice sounded from the phone.

He didn't even bother ending the call, just tossed his phone on the bed, yanked on his shoes. He ran from the room and burst out of the cottage. Black tendrils curled from the kitchen's back window and that distant beeping sound was probably the smoke detector.

He raced across the lawn and pushed his way in through the sunroom doors. "Jen?"

Cade's screams wailed through the house. Lucas surged into the kitchen in mission mode—focus homing in on the scene in front of him. Cade pounding on his high-chair tray, Violet bouncing up and down on the bench at the breakfast nook, Colie unmoving and unhelpful across from her.

And Jenessa over by the oven, waving a hot pad over whatever it was in that glass pan in front of her, burnt to a black crisp. *Not a fire.* But smoke fogged around her and . . . were those tears tracking down her cheeks?

He snapped into action. *Accept the mission. Identify the strategy.* Long, determined strides propelled him to the island counter. He hefted himself up and reached the detector with ease. *Complete the mission.*

The moment the incessant beeping quieted, so did Cade's cries. Lucas hopped down as sudden, blessed silence echoed in the room.

Until Violet's tinny, timid question. "What happened to your arms?"

He looked down so fast his neck cricked. He hadn't

pulled on his usual long sleeves. He opened his mouth, but no words came out.

"Do they hurt?" Violet's eyes were wide.

Jenessa brushed past him. She scooped Cade from his high chair and reached for Violet's hand. "I'm sorry supper's going to be a little while longer. Colie, take your brother. We never did start *Toy Story 3* last night, but the disc is already in the Blu-ray player."

She shooed them from the room and turned to Lucas. "I'm sorry about . . ." She flicked a glance to his arms. "Anyway, I guess now you know my kitchen skills are lacking. Worse, in this short of a time, I've become that caretaker who plops kids in front of a TV when she needs a break."

It took everything in him not to rub his palms over his arms, scratch at the scars, hide them behind his back. *She's seen them before.* But what they represented . . .

He swallowed. "You're not the first person to burn supper. And *Toy Story 3* is the best of the series so—" At the pools in her eyes, he forgot all about his arms. "Hey, what is this? It's just food, Jen. Want me to whip something up?"

She yanked open the silverware drawer. "It's not just dinner, it's this whole day. I'm in completely over my head. I should've known when we could barely make it out the door this morning in one piece."

Why was she choosing now to straighten the silverware? Forks, spoons, knives. The movement of her hands was almost frantic.

"I made a really stupid promise to Mayor Milt. Paige and I almost missed the cutoff for getting the paper to the printer. I have a whole checklist of stuff to do for Carmen. And then there's Colie and school and . . . seriously, what was I thinking, Lucas? What made me think I'm capable of taking care of three kids?"

He moved to her side and reached one hand to cover both of hers. "Did you have time to take a shower this morning, Jen?"

She turned her glistening blue eyes on him. "What? I smell, too?"

He gave her a half-grin. "No. Well, that is, I suppose considering the charred casserole or whatever it is . . . was—"

"Lasagna. Mara dropped it off."

"Right. So there's a bit of a smoky smell to everything right now, including you, but that isn't why I asked. You said something about barely making it out the door this morning and I made an educated guess. And I'm also gonna guess that maybe you could use ten or fifteen minutes alone."

"But the kids—"

"I'll feed them. If you'll remember, I make great pancakes. Maybe I'll even get fancy and do French toast. Go get cleaned up. I can handle this."

He'd blown it with Noah today. With Sam. With Courtney. But at least he could do this—make Jen's night a little easier.

Lucas Danby was a miracle-worker and a godsend in one blessed package. The low rumble of his voice carried from Violet's bedroom, where he'd made himself at home in the chair beside her bed. Jenessa had peeked in a minute ago, just in time to catch Violet giggling over the book he was reading.

And now she hovered outside the door, back against the

hallway wall, arms wrapped around the front of her pink fleece pullover.

He'd made supper. He'd convinced her not to feel guilty for letting the kids eat in front of the TV. Had even pulled Cade's high chair into the den and fed him bite sized pieces of syrup-drenched French toast and cut-up scrambled eggs.

And then, while the kids finished their movie, he'd let Jenessa spill every frustrating minute of her day. From the mayor's ambush, to her worries about how to keep up with the newspaper while caring for the kids, to that meeting with the principal and her disastrous conversation with Colie afterward. He'd even looked at Carmen's list of requirements for the house and helped her come up with a plan.

He really was a remarkable listener. Everyone liked to tease Lucas about his quiet ways, but beyond his reticence to talk about himself was a skill at making space for others to free their burdens. Maybe that's why he was mentoring that younger guy.

"Time to turn the page, Vi." Lucas's low tones reached into the hallway again.

"Mr. Luke?"

She heard the sound of a page's shuffle. Lucas's murmured, "Hmm?"

"Can't you tell me why your arms are like that? Colie said it isn't polite to ask, but I know I won't be able to sleep if I don't."

Jenessa tipped her head to the side. By the time she'd returned to the kitchen after her shower two hours ago, Lucas had apparently found the hoodie he'd left here the other night. He'd been wearing it ever since. How would he answer Vi now?

"Well, I got some burns a long time ago. They were

pretty bad and I never got to a hospital, so they didn't heal as well as they might've otherwise."

It was a vague answer, but apparently it was enough, because Violet let him go on reading. Until a couple pages later. "They don't hurt you?"

"No. They itch sometimes, but that's it."

Yes, she'd seen him rubbing his arms often enough. But he'd never given her any more of his story than he gave Violet.

She allowed her posture to sag against the wall as her gaze wandered to the attic doorway. She really ought to bring a couple of boxes down. If she went through two or three each night, she'd at least make some kind of progress on sorting through everything. But just the thought made her already tired brain flinch.

Somehow she had to get up tomorrow and do all of this over again. What if the meeting with the elementary school principal went as poorly as today's meeting had? Had Colie said even one word to her the rest of the day?

"Jen?"

She jerked away from the wall at the surprise of Lucas's baritone voice. "Finished the book already?"

The dim hallway lighting did funny things to Lucas's eyes, bringing out a tawny, almost amber tint. She'd always sort of wondered why he let his hair grow so long. But now she wondered why she ever wondered that in the first place. It gave him a sort of rugged appeal. Or maybe that was the beard.

Yikes, how long had she just stared at him? She really was tired.

"You keep coming to the rescue, Luke. I keep having more and more reasons to thank you."

He cast a glance down the hallway, to where a sliver of light shone under Colie's door. "She's a quiet one."

"She's an angry one. Doesn't want to be here. Doesn't like me."

"Everyone likes you, Jen. Just give her a little time." He rubbed both palms over his cheeks. "Which is the same advice I'm trying to give myself regarding Noah."

"You know I still don't entirely understand what your deal is with him. Frankly, I don't know how I've let you off the hook for this long. Normally I'd have lured all the details out of you by now—who he is and where he's from and how you know him." She knew enough not to interrogate Lucas about his time in the Army or the hard few years after, but his present-day life wasn't usually off-limits.

The part of it he spent in Maple Valley, anyway. Rarely did he have much to say about the months he spent working down in Mexico. Maybe there simply wasn't that much to say about it.

"I told you. He's an Army acquaintance in need of . . . I don't know. Guidance, I guess."

"And you're the one providing it?"

He lifted one corner of his mouth. "Shocking, I know."

"Actually, it's not."

Now the other corner of his mouth lifted, too. "So what are you up to now? Early bedtime? Clandestine, kid-free viewing of *Toy Story 4*?"

"I was trying to convince myself I had the energy to retrieve a couple of boxes from the attic. I can't sell this house if it's still crammed to the gills with my parents' things."

The color in his eyes shifted again—a light gold brightening his irises. "Well, if you're going up, I'm going too. Because I've got something to show you."

What could he have to show her in her own attic? He was already moving down the hallway and in seconds, they were making their way up the dusty attic steps.

"By the way, that helmet is right at the top of the steps. In case we run into any more bats."

She whacked the back of his leg as she climbed the stairs behind him. "Not funny."

"Just looking out for you, Belville." He reached the top of the steps, then grabbed hold of her hand when she emerged onto the landing. "Come on. Over here." He tugged her through the labyrinth of boxes and furniture.

He let go of her hand as soon as he reached the circle window at the far end of the attic. "I've always wondered why there's a little balcony high up outside your house when there's no door leading to it."

"My aunt used to say the same thing."

"Well, the other night when I was hauling boxes up here, I realized the balcony's just outside this window. Why whoever built this house put a window here instead of a door, who knows. But the point is, the balcony's accessible." He stretched and fiddled with a latch on the window, pushing it open. He gave her a conspiratorial wink. "Let's go."

She eyed the window. "Through that small space? I don't think so."

"I tried it myself Friday night. I'm twice your size. If I can fit, you can too." He pushed a box over and held out his hand. "Stop stalling. Climb on up and shimmy through. The view's worth it."

She might argue again if not for the slant of drowsy moonlight peeking through the glass. Just enough to make out the curve of his grin and the twinkle in his eyes. He'd saved her night from going up in smoke—almost literally. If he wanted her to climb through a tiny window, fine.

His warm fingers closed around hers as she stepped onto the box, then loosened as she peered at the window.

"Legs first," he instructed.

She nodded and lifted one leg over the sill, found her footing on the small balcony landing, then brought the other leg over and slid herself the rest of the way through. Awkward, but doable.

A gust of cold evening air rushed over her, rattling the open window. At a second whoosh, it pushed the window closed altogether. "You better not leave me out here alone, Lucas."

The window muffled his chuckle until he pushed it open again. He climbed through with ease, the landing creaking under their feet. He shot her another smile. "Now we just pray this balcony holds us."

Instinct pushed her closer to his side. "Tell me you're not serious. Tell me this thing is one hundred percent stable."

He jumped then shrugged. "Seems stable to me. And you really should've told me you're scared of heights. I wouldn't have forced you out here."

"I'm not scared of heights."

"You're white as a ghost."

"Well, I haven't had much sunlight lately."

He chuckled, touching the back of her arm to lightly steer her to the balcony railing. "If you're truly not scared, then check out the view. Was I right or was I right?"

She let her gaze travel the nighttime landscape stretching out in front of them. Moonlight polished rooftops and skimmed over the tops of trees. Stars winked from a sky of midnight blue and, in the distance, the river that ran through the middle of Maple Valley glistened. The chilly air smelled of autumn and . . .

Well, the man next to her. How was it she could spend an inordinate amount of time with a friend over the years and only just now realize what good taste he had in cologne or shampoo or aftershave . . .

No, not aftershave. He clearly hadn't shaved anytime in the last couple of days. And this train of thought was making her uncomfortable. She'd certainly never put this much thought into his hygiene habits when they'd both lived at the Everwood.

"Can I ask you something, Jen?"

She swallowed, willing her scrambled thoughts into some kind of order. "Sure."

"You mentioned your aunt a minute ago. You brought her up at the cottage yesterday, too. I don't know if I've ever heard you talk about her before the past few days."

"My Aunt Lauren lived in the cottage when I was a kid. She was kind of like a second mom to me. A best friend, really. I spent a ton of time in that cottage with her." Even after she'd left, Jenessa had found herself escaping to the little house out back.

Until the day Mom had found her out there, messing around with Aunt Lauren's old camera. She'd taken away the camera, made Jen come back to the house. And the next time she'd gone out to the cottage, the lock had been changed.

"She left when I was twelve," she went on. "I never knew why. Or where she went." Only that something had happened. Something that had caused her dad to yell and her mother to sob in a way she'd never heard before.

But in the days that followed, it'd all been swept away. Her parents had refused to talk about whatever had happened. They'd avoided her questions, waved off her emotions. *"Stop overreacting, Jen. Lauren's always been flighty. She's on to her next whim. Enough with the tearful theatrics. Don't be so emotional."*

Mom had done the verbal scolding, but Dad's constant expression of irritation had been just as potent. She'd done her best to save her tears for nighttime. But months later, without so much as a single call from her aunt, she'd broken down during one of Dad's campaign events.

"She's a liability, Granger."

Her fingernails dug into her palms as she willed the memory away. She lowered to the balcony floor, moving to the edge and letting her legs dangle through the openings between railings.

"You haven't seen her since then?" Lucas sat beside her.

She shook her head. "I found her years ago. Wasn't hard. But no matter how many times I've tried reaching out, she apparently doesn't want anything to do with me. Of course, I've never gone so far as to show up on her doorstep or anything, but . . . I just don't get it. We were so close. I really thought . . ."

That she loved me as much as I loved her. Maybe even needed Jenessa. They were the same. They were the family members who didn't quite fit in with their austere surroundings.

"She was really artsy and had like a dozen hobbies. Photography, sculpting, painting, she could do it all."

"Oh, that explains the table at the cottage. It's got dabs of paint all over it."

She remembered that table. Remembered it well. So many days spent sitting beside her aunt—doing crafts together, eating sugary snacks Mom never would've allowed if she'd known.

"Is she the one who painted the shutters that bright blue?"

Jenessa nodded with a wistful grin. "Mom and Dad were not exactly happy about that." But Aunt Lauren had insisted the cottage needed the color. Had even tried talking Mom and Dad into painting the trim of the mansion in the same shade. Her grin faded. "Anyway, I tried one more letter recently. I thought surely she wouldn't be able to ignore a handwritten letter. But it came back. Return to sender. That was Friday."

Understanding brushed over Lucas's expression. "The day you decided to sell the house."

"I guess that's the real reason I put it off for so long. For years I let myself think that she'd return someday. That maybe . . ." But she was done with that particular *someday*, that unlikely *maybe*. Her parents might've been the ones to push Aunt Lauren away, but the fact remained that Jenessa wasn't reason enough for her to stay. Or return. "Anyway, now I've let the mayor talk me into stalling again."

She'd explained the whole situation to Lucas earlier—the promise she'd made to Mayor Milt not to sell the house until after Founder's Day, to let him revive the gala and host it here at the end of October.

"If I know you, Jenessa Belville," he said now, "and I'm pretty sure I do, I think there's probably a piece of you that doesn't entirely hate the thought of having some big party out on the back lawn, complete with lights and a working fountain and fancy little appetizers."

She slid him a glance. "Is that what you think?"

"I think you might even like the idea."

Perhaps there'd been a minute when Mayor Milt was talking this morning that she'd started picturing the gardens as they used to be—lush with autumn flowers and hardy plants, solar lights tracing the walking path, and lanterns hanging from brushed-nickel stands scattered throughout.

"You do realize that by me agreeing to this, I've put your backyard mission on a timeline?"

"Lucky for you I work all the better under pressure."

It *was* lucky for her. Everything about Lucas Danby's presence in her life lately was an unexpected gift.

"I'm really glad you didn't go back to Mexico this fall, Lucas."

He didn't reply. Didn't move his eyes from whatever far-off point in the moonlit landscape they'd latched on to.

Until a pair of headlights cut into the dark, turning into the drive of Belville Park.

"He came back," he murmured, rising, turning to the window.

And Jenessa couldn't help wishing Noah had waited just a little longer.

Lucas trod through the garden, ignoring the pathway, not bothering to sidestep the ropey, limp sunflower vines. He kicked a tipped bush out of the way and marched to the cottage.

He could run away from Jen, but he couldn't escape the impact of her words.

"I'm really glad you didn't go back to Mexico this fall, Lucas."

Sam was right. He was going to hurt her, wasn't he? She assumed because he hadn't left when he usually did, it meant he was staying long-term. But no, he was going to leave and the same pain that she'd felt when her aunt had abandoned her would needle her again.

Except not the same. Whatever his own feelings, he and Jen were friends. *Only* friends.

She and her aunt—they'd had some kind of special bond. He'd heard it in her wavering voice as she'd talked. Now he understood why she didn't bring her up more often.

He passed his truck, parked at a careless angle in front of the cottage, and barged through the front door.

Noah was sprawled on the couch, a McDonald's bag next to him. "Hey."

Lucas stopped a few feet in front of him. "Hey? *Hey?* You disappear for the whole day and that's your greeting now?"

"I got extra fries in case—"

"Did it occur to you that I might need my truck? That I was waiting on those saw blades? That even though I have very little reason to like you at this point, I might've been worried?" He combed his fingers through his long hair as Noah simply stared at him. What could he say to get through to the guy?

Noah stuffed a fry in his mouth.

"I don't know what your deal is, Noah. I don't know what you've been through and I sure as heck don't know what you need." He towed off his sweatshirt and held out his arms. "But if you think you're the only one who's been through something horrific, take a good look at me."

If the younger man felt any shock at the sight of Lucas's mottled arms, he held it in. He spared Lucas's scars only a momentary glance before meeting his gaze head-on.

"Flagg had to have told you about me, didn't he? About the desertion and the dishonorable and the prison sentence." He tossed his sweatshirt onto the kitchenette counter. "Well? Didn't he?"

Noah still watched him, his gaze steady. "He did."

"All of that is because I didn't respond to all of this and what caused it"—he held up his arms again—"with any ounce of dignity or maturity. Take it from me, Noah, it's worth stopping the downward spiral before it picks up speed. That's what Flagg's trying to do for you. That's what I'd really like to do for you if you'd just give me one measly chance."

Tense, soundless seconds passed.

Until, finally, Noah rose. Slowly and with the first hint

at all that there might be some speck of humility in him. "I won't disappear on you again."

Lucas let his glare bore into Noah one moment more. To his credit, the guy didn't flinch.

"All right. Tomorrow we build a new shed."

9

*J*enessa stopped in the middle of the town square, the boisterous noise of the Maple Valley varsity football team drifting from where they gathered in the band shell. How had she managed to remember her camera bag, her notebook, and even a pair of furry cream-colored gloves but not her wallet?

Maybe if she hadn't spent nearly all day distractedly checking her phone, she might not have been so frazzled as she'd left the newspaper office. But today was Colie's first day of school and Jenessa was more nervous about it than the girl herself. Colie had stayed after school for her first volleyball practice.

Sam's tall form leaning against a tree over by the apple cider stand caught her eye. Ah, he could help. She shifted her bag and tossed one end of her knit, mustard yellow scarf over her shoulder. Her fleece-lined, wine-red jacket wrapped her in warmth as she hurried toward Sam.

The auction—one of Maple Valley's zanier events—was already under way. It was the football team's annual fundraiser during which they auctioned off, well, them-selves and a Saturday's worth of work. Always amusing, if nothing else, as the football players showed off for the bidders.

"Sam," she called as she neared her friend. He was out of uniform today. Was he here alone or . . . ? She glanced around the crowded square. No sign of Sam's daughter. No Mara or Marshall.

Lucas, of course, was back at the house. She'd seen him for just a minute this morning. He seemed pleased with the progress he and Noah had made in the past few days out back. When she'd mentioned needing to cover the auction this afternoon, he'd offered to watch Violet and Cade.

Jenessa nabbed a cup of cider as she passed the stand manned by Kit and Beckett Walker, offering the pair a wave before pouncing on Sam. "I need a loan, Sam. I left my wallet at home and—"

He interrupted her with a scoff. "Don't tell me you're actually participating in this nonsense."

"Technically, I'm on the clock. Need to grab a few pics for next week's paper. But yeah, I was totally planning to bid on a few guys 'til I left my wallet behind."

Sam shook his head. "You ever stop to think about how bizarre this town really is? Doesn't this auction break child labor laws?"

She let her camera bag drop to the grass and lifted her cup of steaming apple cider to her lips. "What's got you so moody today?"

"Nothing. Tell me why you're in the market for a foot-ball player."

"Actually, I'm in the market for two or three. Maybe four. I'm going to put them to work in my attic."

The idea had come to her late last night as she'd been thinking ahead to today's schedule. She could bid on a few players and have them sort through boxes, pack up things like clothes and shoes and old home decorations. Maybe they could even haul everything to a thrift store. She'd tell them to set aside anything that looked like it might have sentimental value for her to pick through later.

A brilliant plan, if she did say so herself. But to pull it off she needed cash. "Please tell me you've got some money on you. I'll pay you back ASAP. I've got my eye on the Meyer kid and oh, who's number forty-two? He looks stocky and strong."

Sam pulled out his wallet. "Has it ever occurred to you to just ask your friends to help? I do have days off now and then. And considering how much time you spent helping Mara and Marsh at the Everwood—"

She shook her head. "No way. Mara has already dropped off multiple meals this week. And Lucas practically lives in my backyard now."

His expression turned to a scowl. "Yeah."

Mayor Milt's voice boomed through his megaphone from the band shell, where he was playing auctioneer like always. "What's that look supposed to mean?"

"Nothing. How much do you need, anyway?"

"I don't know. What's a Saturday of work go for these days?"

Before Sam could answer, Leigh Pierce came ambling through the gathered crowd, her gaze set on Jenessa and one hand lifting in a wave. Sam thrust a couple of twenties in her hand, mumbled something about stopping at an ATM for whatever else she needed, and moved off.

She was still watching his retreat when Leigh reached her.

"I was hoping I'd run into you here, Jen. Ever since Tuesday . . ." She paused. "Something wrong?"

Sam disappeared behind the band shell and she shook

her head. "I hope not." But why had Sam seemed so weird today? His grumpiness was nothing unusual, but he'd stiffened at the mention of Lucas. Was something going on between them?

Maybe he was just annoyed that the pair of them had ditched him at the Everwood. But finding three kids in her cottage hadn't exactly been planned. As for Lucas . . . she still didn't know what had prompted him to offer to help with her yard or suggest moving into the cottage, but she was more grateful than ever that he had.

Leigh cupped her fingers around her cider. "I've been meaning to talk to you. Apologize for letting you get roped into the gala. The whole thing's my fault, I'm afraid."

Jenessa ducked her chin into her scarf. In these first days of October, the last warmth of an Indian summer had given way to the brisk chill of autumn. And she loved it. Loved the tinge of color—burgundy and orange and yellow—ornamenting the trees in the square and the seasonal wreaths on so many of the doors of the small-town businesses that wrapped around the square. Baskets filled with fall mums hung from the old-fashioned lampposts that dotted the downtown.

She loved how the feeling in the air hinted at change and a sparkling sort of newness.

Goodness knew her own life looked completely different today than it had just one week ago. But she'd found something of a rhythm in the past few days. She'd worked only a few hours at the office each morning. She had Paige to thank for that, and her little circle of friends for the fact that she hadn't needed to bring the kids with her. Mara and Marshall had hung out at the house on Wednesday morning. Sam had stopped by on Thursday. Lucas had insisted on helping today.

Lucas . . . he was another part of her routine. Joining

them for meals here and there, happily putting up with Violet's constant requests for bedtime stories, even managing to pull Colie into conversation a time or two. Last night Noah had joined them for dinner in the den. He'd seemed friendly enough, if not overly talkative.

And for the first time last night, when Violet had climbed into Jenessa's bed sometime around midnight as she'd done all week—never mind that she'd been tucked into her own hours earlier—Jenessa had barely stirred.

She'd gone from almost ready to give up on Tuesday evening when she'd burned supper to somewhat well-adjusted in just a few days' time. She'd even managed to accomplish most of what Carmen required.

Gratitude—the real thing—coursed through her. Nothing forced about it or the prayer humming under the surface. *Thank you, God.*

Leigh was still talking. "I was having my monthly meeting with the mayor a couple of weeks ago and we were talking about Founder's Day. I'm the one who brought up the old galas your mom used to host and that planted the idea in his head. It's my fault you got guilted into hosting it so last minute."

Leigh wrung her hands together, her wedding band glistening in the sun. She'd just married recently—her groom a cowboy from Texas who'd helped restore the little movie theater downtown.

Jenessa swigged the last of her cider. "It's okay. Really. I've had a few days to acclimate to the whole thing, and I'm not as opposed to the idea as I was at first."

"Well, I promise you won't have to take care of any of the event details. As I said the other day, I'll have everything from the catering to the decorations covered."

"I just hope the weather's okay." And that Lucas would have the time he needed to get the backyard in shape. He hadn't seemed at all bothered by the deadline. The man really was a knight in shining armor.

Up in the band shell, the mayor had just auctioned off the team's star quarterback. She'd probably better start paying attention before she lost her chance to bid.

"I've already looked into renting some outdoor space heaters if we need them," Leigh added. "And get this, I found out Bear McKinley and Logan Walker are going to be back in town that weekend. I'm hoping I can convince them to team up for some live music."

Logan Walker was going to be in town? She pretty much owed the person she was today to that man. He'd sold her the newspaper three years ago when she'd needed a fresh start. Running the paper might not fill her with contentment at the moment, but back then, it'd felt meant-to-be.

She really was so much like Aunt Lauren. Spontaneously pouncing on anything that looked like an exciting opportunity. How many times through the years had she wondered what whim had pulled her aunt away from Belville Park?

I would've understood. If she just would've said goodbye. Kept in touch.

Sam strode back into view, a wad of bills in his hands.

"You're a lifesaver, Chief Ross."

He lifted his eyes to the sky, frown in place. "Avoid Josh Turner. Jonas from the bank hired him to clean out his gutters last year and the kid only got half of them done in six hours."

"Got it. No Josh."

"And I stopped Corbin Delmar for speeding last week. Second time this month. So take him off your list."

She chuckled. "Just because he's got a lead foot doesn't mean he couldn't put in a good day's worth of—" The ring of her phone cut her off. "Sorry, I better answer this." She directed the apology at both Sam and Leigh. Could be

Lucas about the kids or—she glanced at the screen—the school?

She moved a few feet away, concern scraping through her as she lifted the phone.

"Ms. Belville, this is Principal Willard. Can you get down here as soon as possible? There's been a fight."

"All right, one more ride in the wheelbarrow, then Noah and I have to get back to work."

A golden harvest sun combed through the trees around the cottage, stippling the grass, even flecking the air with splotches of color. Violet's giggles rang out over the wind that tangled through her curls.

"Keep your arms around your brother, okay?"

"Yes, Mr. Luuu—" His name was lost to her squeal as he pushed her over the bumpy ground, the muscles in his legs, his arms, his back—all of them sore from day after day of work.

He relished the feeling almost as much as he savored the sounds of Violet and Cade's delight as he gave them what had to be their twentieth ride across the lawn. Up ahead, near the broken fountain, Noah waited with what might actually be a full-fledged smile.

A miracle in and of itself.

Or maybe not, considering the way he'd loosened a little more with every day spent working outside. He seemed to be enjoying the added task of watching the kids nearly as much as Lucas.

He curved around a craggy root protruding from the grass and jostled the wheelbarrow into the stone path that wound through the garden.

"Don't crash into Mr. Noah!" Violet's shriek pulled a laugh from somewhere deep inside him.

Until he hit another bump, felt the wheelbarrow tilt. *Yikes.*

Noah rushed forward to help just as it tipped, grabbing hold of Cade before he could spill out alongside Violet. She rolled into the grass, her giggles a relief even as Lucas's own chuckles joined her. "Thanks, Noah. That could've been bad."

"Ah, you weren't going that fast."

Really? The cramps in his legs said otherwise.

Violet hopped up from the ground. "Again, please?"

"Oh, don't you dare turn those doe-eyes on me, Private Vi. I told you Private Noah and I have work to finish, didn't I?" Work in the form of continuing to dig up old flowers, plants, and hedges in the old gardens to make room for new landscaping. It felt a little more tedious compared to the past two days of labor—clearing up the debris from the old wrecked shed on Wednesday, putting a new one in place yesterday.

They had not actually *built* a new shed. Not after he'd gone down to the hardware store and realized how much easier it'd be to order a pre-fab structure. Still, it'd taken the better part of the day to get to the store, load it onto a trailer, and set it up in place of the old one.

"Don't understand why I'm a private. Made it up to Sergeant E-5 in my time." Noah swiped the back of his hand over his forehead. Didn't matter that the temps had barely reached the high forties today. Both of their shirts were streaked with sweat—not to mention grass and dirt and grime.

Violet barely fared any better, with leaves in her hair and a green stain on her pink coat. Lucas had pulled her hood up and knotted the tie under her chin at least four times this afternoon already, but somehow it always wound up hanging behind her head.

How Cade had managed to keep his own little hat on, he really didn't know. Noah lowered him into the Pack 'n Play Lucas had set up earlier, and Violet had apparently accepted the end to her wheelbarrow rides. She skipped to the blanket near Cade and plucked a doll from the ground.

"Good call on the wheelbarrow rides, Noah. Pretty sure we made both of their days."

He shrugged, grabbing the hoe he'd leaned against a tree. "My dad did the same thing once. He wasn't around a whole lot when I was a kid, but when he was, he was pretty good about, I don't know, having fun, I guess."

"Military guy?" A shot in the dark. There were certainly plenty of other reasons a father might not be around. Dedication to the Army just happened to be the one Lucas had firsthand experience with.

And he was right. Noah nodded.

"Mine too. Except no wheelbarrow rides. I lived with an aunt and uncle for my first ten years. Then Dad brought us to my grandparents here in Maple Valley. Spent the rest of my growing-up years on the orchard."

"The one your sister runs now."

His turn to nod. Wasn't often he had a reason to talk about Dad. Wasn't often he wanted to. But if it was something he had in common with Noah, well, he'd been searching for an in. They'd worked well together since that uncertain truce Tuesday night, but conversation had lingered at the surface.

With another glance at Violet, happily brushing her doll's hair, he reached for the shovel he'd been using earlier to dig up dead roots. "There was this one summer when my dad came home, though. Stayed at the orchard all the way 'til about this time of year. Don't know why but I was convinced he meant to stay that time. Kinda killed me when he left."

It wasn't just the leaving, though. It was the lecture the night before. The instructions. *"You're nearly a man now, Luke."* He'd been thirteen. *"I don't want you crying about this like Katherine. You're old enough to understand the call of duty and responsibility. Set a good example for your sister and be a help to your grandparents."*

And in place of a hug, a handshake.

Looking back, he supposed he should've been grateful for that much. It was more than he'd received in the years since.

He reached down to grasp a root and tossed it to the side, felt the ache in his back at the movement. He straightened, stretched his neck, gaze catching on a dogwood tree nearby, the border of bright red around its leaves.

Lazy, lingering autumns were always his favorite. Too often, a storm or two blew through or the weather turned cold too quickly. And the leaves turned and fell in a matter of meager weeks.

Had Violet ever jumped into piles of crunchy leaves before? She'd love it—Cade, too. Maybe there'd even be a way of coaxing Colie outside. Then again, would the kids even be here by the time the trees were stripped bare?

Would he?

"Is your dad the reason you enlisted?"

He blinked, looked over. Might be the first time Noah had asked him anything close to a personal question. "Not sure, actually." He picked up his shovel once more. "At the time, it was patriotism. It was only a couple years after 9/11. But I guess if I'm being honest . . . yeah, maybe Dad had something to do with it." He couldn't deny he'd thought following in his father's footsteps might earn him a place in his father's attention.

Instead, Lucas had gone and thrown away any last chance at a relationship with the man. When he'd deserted, he'd humiliated his father. He was surprised Dad had even shown up for the court-martial.

"How about you?" He'd tried asking Noah yesterday what had ended his military career. Hadn't gotten far. Maybe he'd have better luck asking what had led to it.

"Because of my dad, too. Not in a good way, though. I got expelled my senior year of high school. Had to finish the year in alternative school. College was out of the picture." He shrugged. "Dad drove me to the recruiter's office himself."

Lucas speared his shovel into the ground, used his work boot to give it an extra shunt. "I really want to ask you how you felt about that, but I'm thinking if I do, you'll call me a shrink. Or accuse me of trying to be your counselor again."

Noah actually grinned at that. Used his hoe to turn over a patch of fresh dirt. "Well, I wasn't excited about it, I can tell you that. Helped a little that my best friend was enlisting, too." His smile faded.

Lucas might have asked about that. Might've risked Noah clamming up altogether and gone ahead and pried.

If not for the scream from the corner of the yard.

She should be lecturing Colie about the fight right now. She should be deluging her with questions—how had the argument started and why and what on God's green earth had made her think pushing the other girl was a good idea?

Instead, she was pacing a waiting room that smelled of disinfectant and stale coffee, on the verge of telling that grumpy-looking receptionist to take a hike. How long was she supposed to wait out here, worrying and wondering and—?

"Jen!"

Oh, thank God.

Lucas was practically sprinting down the hospital corridor, his dirt-stained clothes and rumpled hair barely registering as she felt her pulse rise. "How is she? What happened? Is she okay? You've got to learn to do a better job communicating, Luke. Your short text was offensively unhelpful."

He stopped in front of her, his breath heavy. "She's fine. Broken arm, is all."

"Broken arm, is *all?*" Her voice pitched high at the end.

He clasped her elbow and steered her toward the waiting room, where Colie had jumped up from her chair in the corner.

"What are you doing? I need to go see her."

"She's getting her cast on now. There's paperwork I wasn't able to do—"

"Paperwork? Are you serious right now?"

He moved both hands to her shoulders. "Jen, please, take a seat. You're not going to do her any favors by rushing in there all panicked. Give yourself a second to calm down."

Calm down. Were there any two words she hated more? So many times they'd been flung at her. In Dad's exasperated grumble. In Mom's overly syrupy tone.

Calm down, Jen, you don't need to get so worked up.

Calm down, Jenessa Marie. Why are you so emotional?

Calm down, Jen. Can't you see you're making a scene?

She wrenched away from him. Forced her hands to still but refused to sit. "What happened, Luke?"

"I looked away for a few minutes. Just a few minutes. I'm so sorry. All that wood we'd piled up by the new shed. I guess she tried to climb up it."

Jenessa clamped her lips closed lest she screech at him.

"We heard her scream just as the logs started rolling. But her arm—the doctor says it's not even a full break. Hairline fracture, he said. She'll only be in a cast a few weeks—"

"She broke her arm, Lucas. On your watch."

"Jen—"

"I don't know what I was thinking leaving her with you. I should've brought her to town with me. I should've—" She gasped. "Where's Cade?"

There was an ashen tint to Lucas's face and a storm in his hazel eyes. "He's with Noah at the house." His voice was flat. "He texted a few minutes ago. Everything's going fine. They're inside. They're . . . fine."

She shouldn't have hurled such accusatory words at him. She should apologize. But she couldn't. Not now. Not with worry still throbbing through her.

"Can we please go see her?"

They both turned at the sound of Colie's soft voice.

"Please?"

For the first time, Jenessa noticed the nurse standing off to the side. At her nod, Colie hurried past them. Jenessa glanced back to Lucas.

"Go on."

"Luke—"

"Go."

The nurse was already disappearing around a corner with Colie in tow. She turned to catch up to them. She'd apologize to Lucas later. She'd smooth it over. Somehow.

The nurse opened a door and Colie hovered just outside. "Well, look who's here, little Miss Violet." A doctor's voice rang out from inside. "I do believe you have a visitor."

Jenessa slipped inside, waving for Colie to follow her in.

"Two visitors!" Violet exclaimed. She held a sucker in

137

one hand, her other arm propped on her lap, a neon pink cast already in place. "Look, my first cast."

"Aw, Vi, I'm so sorry this happ—" Jenessa began, but Colie interrupted.

"Violet!" Colie hopped onto the exam table beside her, flung her arms around her sister, and leaned against her. At least she'd picked the side without the cast. Her abrupt show of affection was surprise enough.

But when she burst into tears a moment later, even Violet looked stunned.

The doctor stood. "We'll give you three a moment." The nurse followed him out.

What should Jenessa do? Leave the room, too? Give the sisters time together? But how could she possibly leave with the sound of Colie's cries piercing her heart?

"They said you were in the h-hospital." Colie's voice shook through her sobs. "I-I didn't know what happened. I couldn't stop th-thinking about Mom. I was so scared."

"You're hurting my arm, Colie," Violet whined, sticking her sucker between her teeth.

Jenessa took a tentative step toward the table. "Colie, honey, maybe don't squeeze her quite so much."

"I'm s-staying with you. You and me and Cade. No one's going to make us be apart."

She was sobbing so heavily now, Violet's bottom lip was beginning to quiver. From the pain in her arm or sheer shock at her sister's crying, Jenessa didn't know. But she had to do something.

Ever so carefully, she reached for Violet and eased her from Colie's hold. She helped her down to the floor, then took her place on the table beside Colie, finally letting herself do what she'd longed to for days. She wrapped her arms around the girl, tucked her head against her chest.

And let her cry.

10

*M*aybe she shouldn't leave the kids.

Oh, Mara and Marshall would keep a watchful eye on them. It was only a short hayride around the orchard. Violet was loving the attention her hot pink cast received and Cade was all smiles. Even Colie seemed cautiously content this morning.

It was as if the girl's breakdown in the hospital room last night had begun a slow thaw of the icy divide between them. At some point, Jenessa still needed to talk to her about the fight at the school, but she hadn't wanted to lose the tentative progress they'd gained. So she'd decided it could wait.

What couldn't wait was an apology to Lucas. But when she'd gone looking for him at the cottage this morning, he was already gone. Right, he was still devoting Saturdays to helping Kit at the orchard.

It'd been pure luck, discovering Mara and Marshall in the parking lot when she'd arrived. Since they'd missed out on Apple Fest last weekend, apparently they'd planned a date for today. *So you really shouldn't be saddling them with the kids.*

But that wasn't the real reason she was hesitating. It was the residual fear left over from yesterday. It was needing to know the children were okay in every moment. Was this what parents went through on a daily basis?

"Look, Jen! Mara signed my cast." Violet held up her injured arm from her perch next to Colie. Curls peeked out from the pointy little hood tied under her chin and her cheeks were rosy. Probably more from excitement than the nip in the air.

"Better get Marsh's autograph next," she called back, then looked to Lucas's sister, who stood at the back of the wagon, ushering the last of the riders on board. That pet goat of hers—Lucas had said her name was Flynnie, hadn't he?—was at her side. "It's only a ten- or fifteen-minute ride, right?" Oh, why was she being such a worrywart?

Kit nodded, reaching down to scratch Flynnie between her ears. "And the wagon's sturdy and the hitch connecting it to the tractor is stable and Beckett's a safe driver."

Was her anxiety that obvious?

Mara laughed from the wagon bed. "Jen, you're forgetting I was a nanny for a long time. They'll be fine with us. Go find Luke. And make sure to tell him about dinner at the Everwood tonight."

She turned to Kit. "You said he's in the south field?"

"Far south. Fixing a fence. He was way too moody to be around orchard guests today so I took him off climbing wall duty."

"There's a slight possibility I'm at fault for that." More like a strong likelihood.

And maybe Kit knew it. Maybe Lucas had told her what Jenessa had said last night. Perhaps that's why Kit couldn't quite hide the tint of annoyance behind her eyes as she latched the door of the wagon bed and motioned toward Beckett. The grumbling tractor gave a lurch, and Jenessa lifted her hand to wave at the kids.

Violet and Cade's return waves had her cheeks stretching, but it was Colie's that sent curls of warmth sailing through her. *One week.* One week with these kids and everything she'd thought she'd known about her life had thoroughly upended.

The house that'd once seemed hollow and heavy was now filled with life.

The memories she'd thought impossible to outrun had fallen behind.

And that dogged sense of dullness—that restlessness inside of her that had fueled her need to find Aunt Lauren, to sell the house, to figure out why the newspaper no longer fulfilled her—she hadn't felt it in days.

"You might want to hurry up and head to the south field. It's a bit of a walk and the kids will get back before you do if you wait too long."

She glanced at Lucas's sister. No, she definitely hadn't been imagining the flicker of irritation in Kit's expression. "Hey, um, sorry for monopolizing so much of your brother's time lately."

Kit only shrugged. "He definitely doesn't mind being monopolized. Not by you." She gave a whistle to Flynnie and moved off.

Leaving Jenessa to wonder why such a blunt statement felt so packed with hidden meaning. Was Kit trying to insinuate . . . ?

No. She turned the direction of the south field, feather-thin clouds barely muting the sun. Lucas would never look at *her* like *that*. She was . . . they were . . . had always been . . . friendly, that's all.

Did Lucas go above and beyond to help her out? Of

course, but that's what friends did. Look at all Sam had done for her over the years. Why, yesterday when she'd had to rush away from that silly auction, he'd bid on four players for her. Refused to let her pay him back. They'd already made arrangements to be at her house by late morning.

Still, it raised the question: Why *was* Lucas single? She'd never really thought about it, but now that she did, it didn't make sense. The guy was kind, thoughtful, and respectful. He was a hard-worker and the opposite of self-absorbed. Any single woman with half a brain in her head—

Her steps came to an abrupt halt at the sight of him, working on a fence just as Kit had said. His hair was pulled into a scruffy ponytail at the back of his head and even from here, she could see the sweat glistening on his brow as he hefted a roughly hewn fence post and shoved it into the ground.

He swiped the back of his forearm over his forehead, the sleeves of his dark green shirt rolled to his elbows. He straightened the post, then lifted the thinner but longer curved plank it connected to.

And that's when he saw her.

He lowered the plank as she started moving toward him again. Why was she nervous all of a sudden? *Because you're here to apologize. Because you were a jerk to him last night.*

Because for a second there, as she'd watched him work under the pale morning sun, she'd suddenly realized that in addition to every other good trait her friend possessed, Lucas Danby was also incredibly attractive.

"Hi." She stopped in front of him. *Don't make this weird.*

Easier said than done considering whatever it was she was feeling right this second. Awareness, that's what it was. And she didn't like it. Not one strange and uncomfortable and unexpectedly intriguing bit. She didn't.

Did she?

"Mornin'." He eyed her with wariness. "I've got a pretty good guess why you're here, Belville, and you really don't have to—"

"Yes, I do. Because I'm really sorry." The words rushed from her. "I didn't mean one word of what I said last night. I was just panicking, and I guess when I panic, I get stupid or something, but that's not an excuse. Any of the kids could've had an accident at any time and it wasn't your fault and I'm sorry."

He leaned his elbow on the fence post. "All right."

"All right? Does that mean you accept my apology?"

"Only if you'll accept mine."

"You don't owe me one." She pushed a fluttering piece of hair behind her ear. "I just said it wasn't your fault."

"At least let me apologize for the text. I mean, I thought I was being succinct, but what did you call it? Offensively unhelpful?"

"'There was an accident,'" she recited. "'Vi's hurt. We're at the ER.' How was that not supposed to induce fear in me?"

Amusement glinted in his hazel eyes. "So you don't accept my apology?"

"Did you ever actually make one?"

How had she never paid attention to his smile before? Honestly, it was downright handsome.

He put both palms on her shoulders. "Jenessa Belville, I am really sorry that I am so bad at texting. I promise to be excessively verbose to the point of obnoxious next time I text you."

"Well." Her voice came out breathless. "I'll hold you to it."

"I don't doubt . . ." His voice drifted as his focus lowered to his bared forearms. His Adam's apple bobbed as he lowered his arms. He lifted his right hand and took hold of his rolled sleeve.

"Don't."

At her single word, he froze.

"I've seen the scars plenty of times." And though she'd wanted to wince each time, somehow she'd always known it was better not to react. Better not to look at all than to stare.

So why was her gaze pinned to them now? They climbed his arms, varying shades of reddish-pink and white, fading away above his elbows. The skin itself might be puckered, but the muscles underneath were well-defined —not bulky but nearly as noticeable as the scars.

"You shouldn't have to keep them covered up all the time. They're part of you."

Any teasing had vanished from his expression. He just stared at her for a moment, the amber hue in his eyes deepening. And then, "Not the nicest-looking part."

She needed to say something light. Rein in a startling onslaught of questions she didn't dare answer. Like why she suddenly felt so flustered at how near to Lucas she stood. Why she felt far too warm and far too aware of each agitated breath. "Well no. That'd be the eyes. Or maybe the hair and beard. Kind of gives an overall Aragorn effect."

She backed up, stumbled over a lowered fence plank she hadn't noticed. Lucas's arm shot out to steady her.

"I should go. The kids. Hayride . . . uh, it'll be over soon. Bye."

She turned, her swift steps swishing through tall grass. *What in the world was that?* Was she actually running away?

"Oh, I'm supposed to invite you to dinner at the Everwood tonight," she called behind her as she kept moving.

"Hey." Lucas's voice rang out. "Didn't realize you were into *Lord of the Rings*."

She looked over her shoulder. The clouds had drifted, freeing a river of sunlight to ripple over his face. "Well, it's a day of surprises for both of us."

Lucas pulled open the front door of The Red Door, the tempting smell of burgers and fries drawing a growl from his stomach. Hopefully Noah wouldn't take too long to get here. He was starving, practically ravenous. He was . . .

Well, he was in a darn good mood, that was all.

Something he wouldn't have thought possible after Violet's accident yesterday. But he'd somehow slowly turned the tide with Noah this week. And he'd had Kit's fence fixed by noon today. Plus, he hadn't had a nightmare all week. All reasons to celebrate.

Or he should stop pretending and just admit to himself that it was Jen's visit to the field this morning that had done a number on him. There'd been something different in that interaction.

Something he liked.

Only thing that could improve his day was smoothing things over with Sam. Which was why he'd picked this particular spot for lunch. Sam almost always had lunch at The Red Door with his daughter on Saturdays. Which meant he'd probably be in a good mood, too. Perfect time to approach him. Lucas hadn't liked the way they'd left things the other day.

His stomach gurgled again as he stepped inside, the stylish interior of the restaurant as pleasing as its expansive menu. He remembered hearing about Beckett's cousin's plans to renovate the old First National Bank years ago. A cool idea, he'd thought, but he never would've pictured this.

Seth Walker had entirely gutted the place, letting wood tones and as much natural light as possible set the atmosphere. He'd used cobblestone from Maple Valley's old Main Avenue to build a counter near the back and included a fireplace in one corner.

"Lucas Danby." The mayor's boisterous voice cut into his thoughts. "Come on over here for a moment, son."

No sign of Noah yet, so he moved toward the table where the mayor sat with several others. Oh, and hey, maybe luck was on his side. Sam was at the table, too. But why wasn't he with his daughter?

Sam's nod was friendly enough. Maybe they wouldn't even have to talk about that conversation the other day. Maybe Sam had let go of his doubts and Lucas could pretend they'd never bothered him in the first place.

"I'm happy to see you, Luke." Mayor Milt placed his napkin on the table beside his empty plate. "I hear you've been helping Ms. Belville with improvements to her property."

He cut another quick glance at Sam. No reaction.

"Uh, yeah. I've got a little landscaping experience."

"Right, and of course, you've worked at your family's orchard for many years."

"True." Why did he get the feeling this was leading somewhere?

The mayor clapped his hands together. "Excellent."

"I don't understand—"

"Bernie Loughlin is retiring from the Parks & Rec Department at the end of the year. We're going to need a new director, and I don't think any of our current city employees have plans to apply for the position. I think you should."

Oh. *Oh.* "A . . . a job with the city?"

"Now, it's not all outdoor work. There's some budgeting

and organizing of children's activities and that sort of thing. But you'd be in charge of city parks, landscaping around city facilities. Bernie always jokes that the job is fifty percent mowing in the summer. How's that sound?"

A full-time job. Here. In Maple Valley.

Before he could formulate an answer, another voice intruded. "Let's not get ahead of ourselves, Milt."

Lucas spotted the owner of the voice. Oh, he recognized that face. He'd been with Sam at that Bible study in the coffee shop the other day. The man with the gray hair. The one who'd looked at him as if . . . as if he had something personal against him.

"I'm not getting ahead of anything, Herman," Mayor Milt countered. "I'm just gauging his interest. Obviously, the council will need to sign off on whoever is hired, so I'm not overstepping my bounds. I just think I happen to know a good candidate when I see one."

Ah, so the gray-haired man was a city council member?

"Actually, fellows, if you don't mind, I'm going to take off." Sam stood. Was he trying to keep Herman from saying anything further? "Luke, got a minute?"

Lucas waited until they were out of earshot to speak. "Did the mayor just offer me a job? And what's that other guy's beef with me? Who is he, anyway? Saw him at the coffee shop with you."

Sam nudged his head toward an empty table and they sat. "Herman Ferris. Been on the council for a few years. He's an okay guy but, well . . ." Sam glanced out the window. "He's a vet. Served in Vietnam. Very, uh, staunch, I guess, and . . ."

The realization was as needling as it was humiliating. The man knew about the dishonorable discharge, of course. Everyone did. But a war veteran would have a special kind of disdain for what Lucas had done.

Sam had said something the other day about wanting to invite Lucas to his Bible study. It was clear now that Herman Ferris was the reason he hadn't.

"You don't have to say any more." He rubbed his palms over his jeans. "So, how's your week been? You'll be at the Everwood for dinner tonight, right? Mara invited everyone. Jen's bringing the kids. Should be a good time."

"Lucas—"

"Where's Mackenzie? Don't you usually spend Saturdays with her?"

Sam's steady gaze didn't leave his face. It was at once both forceful and compassionate. "Anyone who really knows you . . ." He stopped, shook his head. "You know that's not what we see when we look at you, right?"

But how could they *not* see his past when they looked at him? When the reminder was seared into his flesh?

"You shouldn't have to keep them covered up all the time. They're part of you."

There'd been such a honey-sweet assurance in Jenessa's voice when she'd spoken those words. But didn't she see? Yes, the scars were a part of him—a part he despised. A constant visual remembrance of his worst mistakes.

The way Herman Ferris had just looked at him? It wasn't any different than how Lucas viewed himself.

Sam finally broke the taut silence stretching between them, clearing his throat. "Mackenzie's with her mom. Apparently Harper got a job in Omaha. They're looking at houses today."

He looked over at his friend, heard the frustration behind Sam's emotionless explanation. Lucas wasn't the only one with hurts. With pieces of himself he didn't talk about. With Sam, it was a broken engagement. He'd been engaged to Kit, actually, Lucas's own sister. Something Lucas rarely thought about. He hadn't been around during those years, hadn't even known Sam back then other than as a name in his sister's emails.

But Kit had left him at the altar and gone on to marry Beckett years later.

And Sam? In his pain, on what was supposed to have been his wedding night, he'd instead had a one-night stand that had changed his life.

Now he had a daughter he adored but didn't see nearly as much as he longed to and a forever-strained relationship with a woman, Harper, he probably would've married if she'd given him half a chance.

"Man, that stinks. I'm really sorry." A lame attempt at comfort.

"Yeah. Well."

Another stretch of silence. Another throat clearing, this time by Lucas. "About earlier this week, what you said—"

"No need to rehash everything."

"I know but you had a good point. I have been planning to leave. And if nothing else, I at least owe everyone some advance notice."

Sam lifted his eyebrows and folded his arms. "How about the full truth?"

For a moment, he actually let himself consider it. What would happen if he unleashed the whole story? What would it feel like to admit everything? Would Sam be shocked? Angry at Lucas for lying all this time?

Or would he look at him with new respect? Something inside of Lucas ached to know, to let at least one person in.

"I . . . I work for a private military contractor." His words came out monotone, distant. As if it were someone outside his body voicing the truth for him. "I started out as a basic contractor, mainly doing international security and stuff. But now I'm part of an elite team. Kind of like Navy

Seals but we're not connected to the government. Just hired by it."

Sam didn't so much as blink.

He looked up, rushed on, willing his friend to understand. "I've never wanted Kit to know. She already had to deal with me going missing once. Plus, our missions are top-secret."

"What kind of missions?" Sam's voice was low.

"Black-ops, basically. Infiltrating terrorist cells. Busting drug traffickers. High-risk rescues."

No reply.

"Listen, Sam, I know it's hard to believe. And I never meant—"

"You're telling me, six, seven, eight months out of each year you're Lord knows where putting your life on the line? And you've never told *anyone* back home? What if you died? What if you never came home and your sister, Jen, all of us were left wondering—"

"It's not like I haven't thought of that. There's a safety-deposit box. There's a letter for Kit that explains everything. There's—"

Sam lurched to his feet. "A letter. That's how you'd want everyone to find out?"

"Of course not. I'm not exactly *planning* to die."

Sam just stood there, staring down at him. The buzz of voices all around seemed to fade, as well as the music, the clinking of dishes. In his periphery, Lucas saw Noah entering the restaurant, scanning the place.

"Say something, Sam. Please." However he'd imagined this conversation going, it wasn't like this. Not this stark, barren tundra that had him feeling lonelier than ever.

"I don't have anything to say." Sam budged past Noah and stalked from the restaurant.

His appetite was gone. His good mood, vanished.

Noah plopped in his abandoned seat. "What was that all about?"

He couldn't make himself voice his answer, his very real fear. *Possibly the end of a friendship.*

Oh, how she'd missed this.

The Everwood Bed & Breakfast dining room was brimming with noise. All because thirty minutes into dinner Cade had uttered a couple barely discernable syllables that sounded like "wa-wa."

"He's talking. He's talking! I bet it means water. It has to mean water." Violet's eyes were round and she knocked her cast into her glass, milk sloshing over the edge. "Say it again, Cade. Say it again."

At Jenessa's right, Colie set her fork beside her plate. "You don't have to say everything twice, Vi." She glanced up at Jenessa, her dark hair tucked behind her ears. "Do you think it's his first word?"

Across the table, Mara and Marshall were goading Cade on right alongside Violet. Only Sam and Lucas didn't seem as enthralled by the evening's entertainment.

But then, neither one of them had seemed at ease all evening. Was she seeing things or were they flat-out avoiding each other?

Well, she intended to enjoy herself tonight even if they didn't. Today had been a *good* day. She'd had fun with the kids at the orchard. Those football players had made incredible progress on the attic this afternoon, leaving her with only eight or ten boxes of more personal or sentimental items to sort through.

"I think you'd know more than anyone if it's really his

first word, Colie," she said now. "You've been such an attentive big sister."

That kind of compliment to Violet would've earned a beaming expression and probably an impulsive hug. But the half-smile Colie directed to her plate of pasta and alfredo sauce felt just as much of a victory.

Mara must not be worried that they were disturbing any of her guests, because she was currently laughing and hitting her fork and spoon against each other as if that would get Cade to talk again.

Jenessa leaned closer to Colie. "So what'd you think of the secret room?" Just before supper, Mara and Marshall had taken the kids to the den at the back of the B&B and shown them the hidden room they'd found earlier this spring.

Colie tore a piece of garlic bread in half. "It was pretty cool. This house is almost as awesome as yours."

Now Jenessa was the one grinning at her plate. When she looked up, her gaze connected with Lucas, watching her from across the table and two seats down. He nudged his head toward the other end of the table where, oh, Marshall was standing. How long had he been standing? And he was mid-sentence.

". . . so we figured, why wait? Who says we have to spend a year or six months or even one month planning a wedding? So we've decided—"

"Next week." Mara popped up beside him. "We've decided to get married a week from tonight. And we're going to have the wedding right here, out in the backyard."

If the room had been noisy before, it turned downright rowdy now. Jenessa gasped and squealed, hopping from her seat to hug Mara, while Sam and Lucas congratulated Marshall. Cade, apparently unhappy at losing everyone's attention, was whining and Violet was making repeated requests for more pasta.

"I'm so happy for you, Mara. One week? We have so much to do!"

Mara returned her embrace. "Don't be silly. You don't have a thing to do."

"But I can help with decorations and food and—"

"Don't let her," Colie interjected. "Not after what she did to that lasagna."

The group burst into laughter and the noise continued. She found her seat again, her thoughts spinning. Mara and Marshall—a wedding—next week. Oh, if ever two people deserved a happy ending, it was them. After all the brokenness in Marshall's past, all the loneliness and hurt Mara had carried around for years on her own, somehow they'd found their way to each other.

No, they hadn't found their way at all. God had brought them together and they would've been the first to acknowledge that truth. Theirs was such a beautiful story of healing and newfound hope and . . .

Great, she was tearing up. Right there in her chair while everyone around her celebrated, her eyes were pooling with nonsensical tears. *Get ahold of yourself.* She blinked. Sniffed. Glanced down when she felt her phone vibrate. A text? She pulled it from her pocket and snuck a peek at the display.

Meet me in the kitchen.

Lucas?

She blinked again, willing her eyes to dry, and looked around. Lucas was standing over by the doorway, currently shaking Marshall's hand, his phone in his other palm. "Let's celebrate with dessert," he was saying. "Jen and I will get it."

Okay, apparently she was meeting him in the kitchen

and prepping dessert. But why was Sam now looking at her like that? Lips pressed, eyes narrowed.

Everything had gone weird today.

She ruffled Violet's hair as she passed her chair and hurried to catch up to Lucas. He was already pulling a tub of ice cream from the freezer when she entered the kitchen. "You didn't keep your word."

He plopped the tub on the counter. "What?"

"You promised a verbose text. Five words? 'Meet me in the kitchen.' You call that wordy?"

He grinned. "Oh yeah. Forgot about that."

"And why text it when I was right there in the room? Also, what's up with you and Sam? Did you even say hi to him when he got here tonight? Did you purposely pick the chair farthest away from him at the table?"

He opened a drawer, closed it. Opened another and pulled out an ice cream scoop. "Maybe he picked the chair farthest from me. Ever think of that?"

"Why did you want to meet me in the kitchen?"

He pulled the lid off the ice cream tub. "Not to get interrogated, that's for sure. Hand me some bowls, will you?"

She snatched a stack from a cupboard. "Here."

"Thank you." His exaggerated gruffness was a perfect mimic of Sam.

"You're welcome."

"So? Your pitiful excuse for a text?"

He did a miserable job biting back his amusement as he dug the scoop into the ice cream. "You were getting a little teary-eyed in there. Thought you might want an excuse to leave the room." He jerked his head back up. "Why? What'd you think I was thinking?"

What'd *he* think she thought he was thinking? "I don't know, Lucas. I very rarely know what you're thinking and it never used to bother me before."

He let go of the scoop handle and moved around to where she stood on the other side of the table. "But it bothers you now?"

Yes, and she wished she knew why. Wished she knew a lot of things—like why her hands were clammy and how to be a normal person around her friend. Her *friend.*

She moved to the fridge. "I wonder if Mara has any chocolate syrup or caram—" She shrieked when she opened the door. A porcelain doll stared back at her from the top shelf—one of many that used to decorate a guestroom upstairs. They'd been boxed up months ago, but Marshall had kept a few out. He loved pranking Mara with them.

She pulled the doll from the fridge and turned to Lucas. He lifted one brow and smirked. "Those two have a weird way of flirting."

She closed the fridge and returned to Lucas's side. "Why did you think I'd want an excuse to leave the dining room just because I was getting a little emotional?"

He propped one hand on the back of a chair, the edges of his scars peeking out from beneath his sleeve at his wrist. "Because I've figured out something about you in the past week, Jen. You're one of the most upbeat, bubbly people I know. I always sort of thought nothing could faze you. But then I saw you nearly fall apart over that burnt lasagna the other night—"

"It wasn't just the lasagna."

"I know. It was a whole host of things. And last night I saw you panic at the hospital. And all week, I've watched the number those kids are doing on you. What I've figured out is that, for all your cheerful ways, you're someone with really deep emotions. Only you don't necessarily love showing them."

She wasn't sure she'd ever heard Lucas say so much at

once. He'd noticed all that about her? "You say that like it's a good thing. Having deep emotions, I mean."

"Why wouldn't it be?"

Maybe it was the way he was looking at her—as if whatever she was about to say was deserving of his full concentration. Or maybe it was how close he stood—distracting and inviting, all at once. Whatever it was, it made her want to tell him . . . everything.

"My aunt—you know the one I told you about? *She* felt things really deeply. My mom complained about it a lot—called her sensitive and moody and overly emotional. And then, when she left . . ." Her gaze roamed to the window over the kitchen sink. "I lost it, Luke. Like, really lost it. I cried for days. And the worst was when I embarrassed my dad at one of his campaign events. I was twelve—old enough to be on my best behavior, but it was my birthday and I'd been so sure Aunt Lauren would come back for it. I ended up breaking down, crying, and humiliating both of my parents in front of all their important friends."

She rarely let herself return there in her memories. To that stage and the heat of the spotlights. To that one heady, hopeful moment when she'd thought she'd spotted Aunt Lauren in the crowd.

To the moment just after when she'd realized it wasn't Aunt Lauren. When she'd burst into tears right in the middle of Dad's speech.

She hated remembering it, because whenever she did, she felt the same stab of mortification. Worse, the utter abandonment. Not just by Aunt Lauren, but Mom and Dad, too. They hadn't comforted her after that incident. They'd berated her. She'd been in such pain and they'd just pushed it aside.

Like they'd pushed aside any mention of her aunt in the days after her disappearance.

Was that why Aunt Lauren had gone? Had she known how her own sister viewed her? Had she had that same awful sense of simply being too much for the people who were supposed to love her?

"He lost that election," she finished the story flatly.

First one he'd ever failed to win. Dad had ended up insisting she see a counselor for a time, which had taken Mom away from the campaign trail, which had caused reporters to question why his family no longer accompanied him.

Her logical, adult brain knew she wasn't at fault for the results of the race, but the facts of it hadn't erased the feelings.

She wet her lips and found her voice once more. "Anyway, you're right. I don't like to show all my emotions. I don't like to cry in front of people. I like to be put together and in control. That's the version of me I like for people to see."

Which, she supposed, made her more like her parents than she'd previously thought. She'd always compared herself to Aunt Lauren. But really, just like Dad on the campaign trail and Mom with all her social connections, she was more comfortable pretending to be happy than presenting her full self, emotions and all, even to the people closest to her.

Except, lately, around Lucas.

She made herself look up. Something in her needed to know how he would react. Certainly he hadn't expected that long of an explanation. That personal of a story. Did it make her sound pathetic?

He must not think so. Not if he was looking at her like *that*. With such intensity that she'd probably still feel its warmth when she tried to sleep tonight, and oh, she was a fool for ever thinking this man was just a casual friend.

"Well, I think it would be good for you to know that some of us see the other versions of you, too. And we really like those versions. We like every version."

"I . . ." She swallowed. "I think the ice cream's melting." Why was she whispering?

He didn't move a muscle.

Until a clatter of footsteps and laughter came barging in, voices she didn't recognize. And a woman she didn't know threw herself into Lucas's arms.

11

*L*ucas could appreciate what his teammates from Bridgewell were trying to do.

But darn if they didn't have some remarkably bad timing.

Doug's snores rumbled from the bedroom floor, practically rattling the walls of the cottage.

"I really want to know how the heck that guy can legit sleep anywhere." Jamar lifted the cast-iron griddle he refused to leave home without. Seriously, Lucas had seen him whip the thing out at a campsite in Mexico, the night before a raid on a suspected storehouse of weapons. What was that? Two, three missions ago?

It was the one time Lucas actually hadn't lied about being in Mexico when he wasn't in Maple Valley.

"He was asleep on the plane yesterday before the flight attendant even finished the safety talk." Courtney had squeezed into place near Jamar and was currently chopping up a tomato.

Courtney had hugged him last night—boisterously. How in the world was he supposed to take that considering their last conversation? That is, their last conversation up until the previous evening, when the whole group had stayed up past midnight, telling stories to Noah about all their exploits over the years.

And then they'd crashed throughout the house, Court and Mariana taking Noah's bedroom, the guys spreading out wherever they could find floor space in the rest of the cottage. The close quarters hadn't bothered any of them. They'd certainly slept in tighter confines before.

Difference was, Lucas *hadn't* slept last night. At least, not more than a restless hour here and there. Hadn't been able to stop thinking about the look on Jenessa's face when Courtney had embraced him.

Or the utter aggravation on Sam's when Lucas had introduced the team as "old soldier buddies." That it was the truth, vague or not, didn't stop the guilt.

But mostly, it was the echoes of those few minutes in the kitchen with Jen that had pealed so loudly in his head, there'd been no chance of a restful night. She'd been vulnerable with him, and somehow it'd felt like a gift. Like a precious offering she only reserved for . . .

Who? Friends? Had she ever told Mara that story about embarrassing her parents at her dad's campaign thing? How about Sam?

He lifted the coffee mug he'd borrowed from the main house earlier in the week, threw a drink back, and sputtered at the taste. "I guess Kelvin made the coffee, huh? Tastes like I'm drinking sludge."

The rest of them were sipping from red plastic cups they'd grabbed at the mini-mart last night just before closing. That's where the groceries had come from, too. And the paper plates they were about to eat off of.

"If you're complaining about that, wait 'til you see the orange juice he picked out." Mariana lowered onto the couch, one hand on her back. Would it have hurt any one of his buddies to let him know about the pregnancy before she arrived? He'd nearly gawked at her stomach when he'd first seen her.

Noah lifted the orange juice carton from the fridge. "Who buys it with pulp?"

"Kelvin," every other person in the room answered. Even Doug, who'd dragged himself from the bedroom at some point in the past thirty seconds.

They'd come all this way—the team, *his* team—simply to encourage him. To show him he was still a part of the group. Remind him why his work with Noah mattered.

So why couldn't he keep his mind from constantly wondering when he'd have a chance to ditch the cottage, cross the lawn, and stop in at the house?

Courtney had moved on to chopping onions, the scent pungent and each slice of the knife loud. Maybe no one would notice if he slipped outside, just for a second. Grabbed a breath of fresh air.

He gripped his warm mug and let himself out the front door, releasing a sigh into the October breeze. The trees rustled against the wind and a shower of leaves twisted downward. He breathed in deep, tasting autumn and wrapped in the scent of morning.

"Getting a little crowded in there?"

He glanced over at Mariana. "You should be sitting down."

"I've been standing for all of a minute. I'm pregnant. Not decrepit."

He'd thought if someone was going to follow him outside, it might be Courtney. They had a conversation to finish, didn't they? Or maybe not. He'd rebuffed her in the hospital. She'd slighted him over the phone with that remark about going AWOL. Perhaps they were even and there was nothing more to be said.

"You should talk to Court, you know."

So much for that thought.

Mariana eyed him. "I don't think her feelings went that deep. But you stung her pride, Danby. An apology and a handshake would probably go a long way."

If it was someone other than a fellow soldier speaking to him, that might feel like a cold response to the situation. But how much had he wished for one measly handshake from his father when he'd come back to the States? Simple but significant, it could've changed so much.

Maybe he would've found the will to speak in his own defense at his court-martial.

"I hope I never did anything to lead her on."

Mariana shrugged and sat on the front step. "You didn't. She saw something that wasn't there. She's a human—we do that all the time."

Which was exactly why he'd tossed and turned all night. Wondering if he'd seen something in Jenessa last night that wasn't there. Or what might've happened if he'd dared to believe there was.

He leaned against the cottage wall, one palm splayed on a shutter with peeling paint. He hadn't missed the wistfulness on Jenessa's face the other night when she'd said her aunt had picked out the color. But they could use a touch-up. Maybe sometime in between restoring the yard and attempting to mentor Noah and dealing with all his questions and confusions about the future, he could figure out the right paint color and freshen them up.

He lowered onto the step beside Mariana. "Due around New Year's, huh?"

"Yes. Dale insisted on calling our doctor to make sure it was safe for me to fly this late in the game. For the record, if little he or she takes one day longer than expected in making his or her appearance in the world, I swear I will rip open every feather pillow in my house. Can you believe Dale asked me to stop going to the firing range? He's worried about Baby's hearing. I called Dr. Patella about that, too, but would Dale trust his assurances? No sir."

Lucas chuckled. "I think it must take a special sort of guy to be married to a Bridgewell woman."

Mariana paused. "Not a Bridgewell woman for much longer."

He let out a breath. He'd had a feeling that was coming. As soon as he'd seen her last night, he'd assumed that's why Flagg had begun prepping a replacement.

She seemed to read his train of thought. "I think Noah will fit in great."

"He's obstinate. Sarcastic. Pretty much a closed book."

She grinned. "Like I said, he'll fit in fine."

"There'll always be a place for you, you know. Having a kid doesn't disqualify you from serving."

"I know that. But leaving Dale for months at a time started getting old long ago. And besides, I'm forty-one. Might as well make way for the younger generation."

"You just said you weren't decrepit."

"Maybe not, but did you know this"—she pointed to her stomach—"is considered a geriatric pregnancy? I literally watched a nurse circle that word on some form. That might actually be the moment I decided to tell Flagg I'm done. You see someone use the word 'geriatric' to describe you and I'm telling ya, it does something to you."

His laughter joined hers. "Geriatric Mariana. Does have a certain ring to it."

When he quieted, she looked over. "You know, Lucas, if you ever decide that there's something *you* want more than you want this life with Bridgewell, there's nothing wrong with that. Life goes in seasons." Gnarled leaves skittered past their feet. "You've poured yourself into the team. You've sacrificed. We all have. But forever was never part of the deal."

He didn't know what to say to that. Didn't know what she'd seen or not seen to prompt her words. But he knew, sure as autumn's promise of shifting colors and coming cold, he'd needed to hear them.

"You are both geriatric and wise, Mariana."

"I reject the first and happily accept the latter." She struggled to stand and he jumped up, offering his hand as she straightened. She glanced behind her. "Someone else is waiting in line."

Courtney. She padded out the front door as Mariana shuffled in.

"I just want to say—"

"Court, I—"

They started and stopped at the same time. He nodded at her. "Ladies first."

Her posture was as rigid as if they were in line during a morning inspection but she was looking somewhere to the side of him. "I just want to say, it was stupid. It won't happen again. And as for what I said on the phone . . ." She met his eyes. "Cruelty is weakness. And it's not me. And I'm very sorry."

"I could've handled things better."

"Probably." She shrugged. "You could've not gone and got shot in the first place. Then I might not have gotten emotional at the hospital and said what I said."

The ease in her voice filled him with relief. He held out his hand. "Friends?"

She accepted the handshake. "No. Better. Teammates."

Teammates.

Unless, like Mariana, he let himself admit he might want something more.

Somehow she'd done it. She'd gotten three kids dressed and fed and off to church. But paying attention from her seat in the second-to-last row? Apparently that's where Jenessa's mental fortitude had ended.

Because now, as she cleaned up after a Sunday dinner of chicken and fries—thank goodness for The Red Door's carryout menu—she realized she couldn't remember a single word of Pastor Callahan's sermon. Honest to goodness, she had to have fidgeted more than Violet, who'd disturbed the entire back half of the sanctuary halfway through the service when she'd stabbed a pencil down her cast in an effort to scratch an itch and ended up getting it stuck.

But Jenessa was the one who'd turned her printed bulletin into some kind of origami creation. Who'd dropped her Bible when the phone she'd forgotten to silence had blared. Who hadn't even realized until halfway through the closing prayer that everyone had closed their eyes and bowed their heads.

And somewhere between the opening song and the offering, she'd quit denying the reason for her distraction.

What could've prompted five of Lucas's Army buddies to all descend on Maple Valley at the same time? She hadn't even known he kept in touch with any of his old friends from his days in the service.

"My arm's itching again, Jessa."

At Violet's whine from the kitchen doorway, she fumbled the stack of carryout containers she'd been carrying to the garbage can. They tumbled to the floor and scattered.

"Cade, no!"

But he'd already reached the nearest one and plopped one pudgy hand in Colie's leftover barbecue sauce. Where had Colie wandered away to, anyway? Up to her bedroom? She hoped so. They still needed to have that talk about the fight on Friday, and yesterday Jenessa thought she'd come up with what might be a good plan for making it happen.

If she could just get this mess cleaned up. Get Cade down for his nap and find something to occupy Violet.

Keep herself from the constant urge to spy on Lucas and his friends from the kitchen window. Or better still, come up with some casual reason to amble out to the cottage and investigate.

He had a life, personal and otherwise, long before you ever met him. Apparently still had one. And it included that woman who'd hugged him last night. Was she part of the personal or the otherwise?

"It's itching." Violet's frustrated voice pitched.

Maybe the mess in the kitchen could wait. She hoisted Cade and used a wet dishcloth to wipe his palm, then took Violet by her free hand. "We just need to find something to distract you, kiddo."

You and me both.

"Mr. Luke is good at distracting me."

And again, you and me both.

"Well, he's not available at the moment. So what do you say to some arts and crafts? I've got a fun project for us this afternoon, but first, I need to talk to your sister for five or ten minutes. Think you can hang out in your room with Private Teddy and Corporal Barbie for a bit?"

Perhaps the fact that Lucas had Violet addressing her

toys by rank should've been an early sign that his Army days weren't as far behind him as she'd always assumed.

Ten minutes later, she had Cade settled in his crib, Violet settled in her room, and supplies for her afternoon plans lugged upstairs. She knocked on Colie's door and, unlike the routine of rejection in earlier days, received a simple "Come in" in return.

"Hey, you." She peeked her head in to see Colie laying on her stomach on the bed, a book open in front of her. "Whatcha reading?"

Colie held up the thick volume. Some Winston Churchill tome from down in Dad's library. "Wowza. When I was your age, I was reading *Sweet Valley High*."

Colie shrugged. "I like history."

Jenessa left her supplies in the hallway for now and strolled into the room. Had they made enough progress in the past couple of days that it wouldn't be going too far to perch on the bed? Maybe she shouldn't push her luck, not until she gauged how this conversation was going to go.

She pulled out the chair at the white antique desk, the one that had been in her own bedroom for a few years when she was little. At some point, she'd begged Mom for a larger desk where she could spread out to work on her homework.

At least, that's what she'd told Mom. Mostly she'd wanted a workspace like that table of Aunt Lauren's out in the cottage. The one spattered with paint and usually cluttered with whatever materials she'd needed for whatever art medium she'd been into at the time.

"So I guess you want to talk about the fight."

"You're quite astute, Colie Hollis."

The girl sat up on her bed, crossed her legs. "I figured it was coming sometime. You probably would've yelled at me

Friday night if Violet hadn't gone and broken her arm and then I . . ."

Despite the nonchalant look she tried so hard to hold on to, Colie's cheeks turned red. Of course she was remembering her tears in the hospital room. The way she'd cried for her mom, spilling all her hurt and fear.

And staking a permanent claim in Jenessa's heart in the process. How could she feel so strongly about this little girl —about all three of them—so very quickly? The thought that Carmen could call any day, tell them Dustin Hollis had been located . . . she couldn't let herself dwell on it. Had to find some way to focus simply on this little slice of time she'd been given, however long it stretched. An opportunity to lavish these children with a love she wasn't sure she'd even realized she'd possessed before.

"I'm not going to yell at you, Colie. And as for what happened in the hospital, it's okay if you feel a little bit embarrassed about that. I feel embarrassed too when I cry in front of other people."

Please, God, give me the words. The words she'd needed as a child.

"But I sort of think crying can be a really good thing. It's like on a really hot summer day when you're standing on the edge of a swimming pool and you finally jump in and suddenly, you're so happy you did. Maybe it was cold and shocking when you first hit the water, but then it's pure, cool relief. And you wonder why you didn't jump in sooner. That's kind of what crying does, I think."

"Yeah, but it also gives you a headache and a stuffy nose."

"True enough. The thing is, as someone who isn't always that great at showing people how she feels, I tend to think people who do show how they feel are really brave."

Colie fiddled with her sock. "Even if showing it was kind of an accident?"

"Even if."

Colie flopped back against her pillows. "If you're not going to yell at me about the fight, what are you going to do?"

"Well, here's the thing: Yesterday I stopped by Klassen's Hardware and picked out a bunch of paint samples for you to look at. I don't know about you, but I think these pale green walls are super dated. Personally, I'm looking forward to trying out a whole bunch of different colors and I bet Violet would love to come in and help out too." She scooted her chair closer to Colie's bed. "So, I'm thinking we make this whole conversation about the fight as fast and simple as possible so we can get on to the fun. How's that sound?"

That was either hesitant relief or disbelieving doubt on Colie's face. "I guess it sounds okay."

"Maybe we could even save some extra time by skipping all my questions and you could just give me the quick lowdown and we can go from there."

And just like that, the story poured out of Colie. Some silly volleyball drill. A student's unkind words about Colie's old kneepads. The kneepads her mother had given her two birthdays ago.

Colie had pushed, the girl had slapped, the coach had intervened. "I won't do it again. Even if she says something stupid like that again. I'll just ignore it next time."

"You sure? I could talk to the coach—"

Colie sat up so quickly she knocked a pillow off the bed. "No way. That'll only make things worse."

"Okay, I won't talk to your coach if you'll answer one question for me. How are you feeling these days about the whole sixth-grade thing? I know you've only had one day of school so far and with everything that's happened, we haven't had a chance to talk much about it."

Cole gave another of her signature shrugs. "It's not so bad."

"Really?" At Colie's nod, Jenessa stood. "Then I think we can get to the paint samples."

Another pillow dropped. "That's it? You're not going to punish me for the fight?"

"You just told me Coach Bertelli made you run line sprints. You paid for your crime before it even occurred, my friend." She ducked into the hallway and grabbed the mini paint cans and sample swatches. "Ready to play interior decorator?"

She expected Colie to jump off the bed, relieved at the end of their discussion. But she didn't move right away. She opened her mouth, looked away, picked up a pillow and hugged it to herself. And then, "I really loved my mom. I wish she'd talked to me more . . . like this."

The air squeezed from Jenessa's lungs and she dropped her armful on the desk. No hesitance this time. She crossed the room, lowered onto the bed beside Colie. She tucked a piece of hair behind Colie's ear, awed that the girl didn't flinch at the touch.

"I'd love to hear more about her. Anytime you want to talk about her . . . anytime you want to talk at all."

"But we might not always be here. We might have to leave."

What could she say to that? What could she do to provide some kind of assurance to Colie when her own insides twisted and churned at the thought? How could she have known when she'd first asked Carmen to let the kids stay what it would mean for all of them? How fast their hearts might attach to one another until . . .

Until they felt like a family.

Amazingly, Colie let Jenessa comb her fingers through

her hair and then guide her head to her shoulder. "We just can't think about that right now."

Hushed seconds passed, the only sound the thumping from next door. Violet, surely, knocking on the wall. And then yelling, asking if she could come over yet.

"I like blue," Colie finally said.

"Oh yeah? I had a feeling. I think I got four or five shades of blue."

Colie hopped off the bed. "Let's try all of them."

He'd waited all day. Edgy impatience wouldn't let him wait any longer.

Lucas rapped on Jen's back door, a can of pop in his hands. Caffeine after 7:00 p.m. wasn't his smartest move, but he had a feeling his buddies would start in on the pastime reminiscing again tonight and he'd be lucky if he landed on his sleeping bag sometime before midnight.

The cloudless, cobalt sky of earlier today had faded into an opaque canvas overhead. He knocked again, his breath producing a fog of white in front of him.

The door swung open.

"Luke?" Jen's knotted, wet hair flopped to the side. She wore a thick pink robe over a pair of shiny white pajamas, the robe's belt tied loose and lopsided. Was that a streak of blue paint by her ear? "Welp, you've seen the sweatpants and now you've seen the pajamas. You can feel singularly privileged, Danby."

"I didn't say anything."

"You didn't have to. You're practically biting your cheeks to keep from laughing."

"I wasn't going to laugh at how you're dressed. I was

going to laugh at how he's dressed. Or, that is, not."

She whipped her head around, strands of hair escaping from her unruly bun. Cade was crawling across the kitchen, naked as the day he was born.

"Oh, Cade." Her words came out on a groan. "Seriously, what do you have against your diaper?"

The baby stopped at her slippered feet, pulled himself up to a sitting position, and reached his hands toward Jen. Twin dimples framed his untroubled smile. Jen scooped him up with hesitation.

"It's like he *knows*." She stepped aside so Lucas could enter.

"Knows what?"

"That I can't resist those two little bottom teeth. He could pee on me right now, but as long as he's flashing those teeth, I'll be too helpless to muster up even a morsel of annoyance."

"And yet, you get irritated at me for being entertained."

Her expression turned saucy. "Sorry but your teeth aren't as cute."

"I'm offended on behalf of myself, my dentist, and the orthodontist who forced me into braces at age thirteen." He trailed Jen into the living room.

She knelt, laying Cade on his back, reached for a plastic grocery sack, and pulled out a diaper. "Shouldn't you be with your friends, Lucas?"

"They'll survive without me for five minutes." He watched as she secured a fresh diaper, then coaxed Cade's waving arms and legs into a lion-print onesie. She looked surprisingly natural despite her huff of exasperation at Cade's repeated attempts to roll away. "Just wanted to see how everything went today. And, um, well, I noticed when I was here the other day that your security system's broken. I forgot to mention it."

It was the best excuse he'd been able to come up with.

She freed Cade and stood, her laugh teasing her lips. "That security system has been broken for more than a decade."

He took a swig of his pop. "Well, you should really get it looked at."

"This is Maple Valley."

"Crimes do happen here. Remember Mara's stalker? The former Everwood owner's disappearance? And you've got kids living here now. I'm just saying, for the sake of safety, you should see if you can get it fixed. Or install a new one."

Her look turned to one of exasperation. "And when exactly should I do that, Lucas? Because between keeping three children alive and running a newspaper, I'm so lousy with free time. Do you realize I'm basically a single parent right now? Except other parents get eased into this, you know? They have one kid at a time and best-case scenario, there's two adults involved."

Her robe's belt had come loose during her rant and it hung open now to reveal her pajama top buttoned crookedly. But no way did he plan to point that out.

"And don't bring up parents of triplets. Because I Googled it on my phone before I conked out last night. I know the stats. One in a thousand. This is a one-in-a-thousand situation I've found myself in, only I didn't have nine months to prepare."

Shoot, she was in a mood tonight. He liked it. Did she realize she'd grabbed ahold of his arm? Practically had a death grip. And now was really not the time to be enjoying how close she stood to him. "I didn't mean to upset you."

"You didn't." She flung herself away from him and swiped the diaper Cade must've pulled off earlier from the floor. "Anyway, I'm glad you're here because I have questions for you."

Great, here it came. He took a drink of pop just to stall whatever was about to come next. He'd had a feeling last night that his explanation for his teammates' sudden presence in Iowa was lame and unconvincing. Or worse, had Sam spilled what Lucas had told him the other day? Did Jenessa already know about Bridgewell and—

"Why don't you ever go on dates?"

He nearly choked on his pop. "What?"

"I've known you three years and I've never once heard you talk about your love life." She marched to the kitchen and tossed the diaper into the garbage can.

"My *love* life?"

"But maybe you've had one all this time. It'd be just like you." She turned to face him, her expression somewhere between curious and accusatory. "Is it that girl from last night? The one who hugged you, I mean. Not the pregnant one. Oh my goodness, I hope it's not—"

"Geez, Jen, no. Mariana's happily married. Court's just a pal." He didn't know whether to laugh or scowl. "And what gives you the right to talk? You never go on dates either." Not since he'd known her anyway. He knew there was some guy from high school she'd been with for most of her twenties, but she rarely mentioned him. Certainly didn't seem to miss him.

"How do you know?" She crossed her arms. "I went on a date with Sam once."

He should've known not to take another drink. Pop spewed from his mouth. "Don't believe it."

She wrinkled her nose at the splatters that had landed on her pajama top. "I did. How'd you think we met?"

"I assumed you accosted him in some place of business like you did me."

"No, someone set us up and it was awful and awkward and I hated every minute. That is, until Sam paid the bill and looked me straight in the eye and said, 'This wasn't great. Let's never do it again.' And a friendship was born." She cinched her robe over the pop stain. "And I did not accost you."

"I think I should go before this conversation takes any more inexplicably strange turns." He started moving backward toward the door.

She waved her arm. "Go on. Avoid me and my questions."

"I'm not avoiding you."

"You're practically running to the door."

Was it weird that this argumentative version of Jen might be his favorite version? "Just so you know, my friends are staying through tomorrow and we're going to do some training with Noah at a gym in Ames. I'm telling you so that you know in advance I'm not avoiding you. I'm just being a good friend and mentor."

"Fine."

"Fine." He paused. "But we need to go over landscaping plans sometime. The guys are leaving Tuesday afternoon. You got time Tuesday night?" He stepped outside.

"Maybe."

"Yes or no, Jen."

"Okay. Whatever. Sure. It's a date."

Her eyes widened at that last part and he opened his mouth to retort before she could take it back.

But she closed the door in his face.

Which was probably a good thing considering the dorky grin he could feel taking over his expression. Still, he leaned close to the door. "You've got paint by your ear, by the way."

The door muffled her voice. "Go back to the cottage, Danby."

He did. With a newfound energy that assured he wouldn't sleep a wink tonight.

*L*ucas plunged under the river's windswept ripples and into its frigid, unwieldy depths. The water grasped at him, its shocking cold the stimulant his sore muscles needed after that cramped ride to the airport and too many nights sleeping on the floor.

Or probably, more accurately, all those hours at the gym yesterday.

He really had gone soft. He tilted and pushed to the water's ceiling.

"You're insane."

Noah's voice reached him from where he lingered at the river's edge. Lucas kicked his legs, treading to keep his head above the surface. "You were so proud of lifting forty pounds heavier than me yesterday. I'd like to see you try swimming in water this cold."

On the way home from dropping the rest of his team off at the airport, he'd stopped at his old swimming spot on a whim. He'd never had the bulging muscles and brute strength of Doug—or even Noah—but he never failed to outlast the others on a run or in the water. His superpower had always been perseverance.

No, not always.

He hadn't persevered in Afghanistan.

That's why he'd really stopped at the river. Because he'd had the same old nightmare again last night. Because donuts at the bakery with his friends this morning, a cramped ride to Des Moines, half the group in Lucas's truck and the other half in their rental car, handshakes and hugs and goodbyes—none of it had dissolved the aftereffects of the dream.

Not even the thought of spending time with Jenessa tonight had entirely dispelled the nightmare, the images. A blaze, bodies . . . *Tashfeen.*

He dove under again. Shoots of pain sliced down both arms even as they strained against the river's current, his lungs heaving for release inside his chest. He propelled himself upward, just long enough to crash through the surface and gulp for air before plummeting into the murk once more.

The cold stung his skin and seeped inside of him. *This* was an ache he could bear, unlike the memories his nightmares never let him forget.

Underwater, he felt a shake and heard the muted splash of Noah crashing in nearby. Lucas's feet connected with a jagged rock and he pushed himself toward the hazy light bobbing at the surface. He broke through and breathed, blinking the water from his eyes just in time to see Noah rise.

And hear his squawk. "I m-mean it. You're seriously insane."

"Swimming against a current is a better workout than anything you'll get at the gym."

Noah's teeth chattered. "When it's not thirty-five degrees maybe."

"It's thirty-eight." He'd checked the display on the dash in his truck. He pushed a floating branch out of the way. "Race you to that sandy area. See it?"

"Wait—"

But Lucas was already lunging forward, arms laboring against the force of the water. He reached the riverbank a full minute before Noah. But the younger man gained on him the second time. Three more races. By the fifth, their arms reached for the shore at the same moment.

And even Lucas had to admit he was ready for a break. He climbed onto the grass and jutted his hand toward Noah.

Noah grasped it and came out of the water gasping. "C-can you get frostbite from the inside out?"

"Dramatic much?" Lucas shook the water from his hair.

"D-did Flagg put you up to this? One of the guys? Or was this one all you?"

Lucas swiped his shirt from the grass and yanked it over his head. "All me, proud to say. Tell me that wasn't more fun than bench presses."

"It was definitely not more fun than bench presses."

Lucas grinned and started toward the truck. Yes, the windy cold felt like an assault at the moment, but it actually had sort of done the trick. And Noah could complain all he wanted, but Lucas didn't miss the animation in his eyes now. He really did owe Court, Doug, and the rest of them. Yes, Noah had begun to loosen up before they'd arrived, but two days around the team and he'd actually become pretty congenial. Lucas might even go so far as to say he was fun to be around.

Did that mean Lucas was doing an okay job as a mentor? He genuinely didn't know. He'd talked to Jamar about it a little last night after everyone else had fallen asleep. And Mariana this morning. And Doug just before they'd parted ways at the airport.

Basically, any time he'd had the opportunity when Noah was out of earshot, he'd asked his teammates what he should be doing other than, well, keeping Noah busy.

They'd all had the same advice: talk to him.

Not exactly his strong suit.

They reached his truck, and the minute Lucas started the engine, Noah reached out to flick the heat to high. Lucas steered the vehicle toward town.

Talk to him. If only he had the finesse to ease into a conversation about . . . what? Noah's past? His experiences in the Army? Noah had a point last week when he'd said Lucas wasn't his counselor. What did Flagg think Lucas had to offer that a therapist wouldn't?

"So, you've been here a week and a day now. Not as bad as you thought it'd be?"

"Well, sure, until you forced me into ice water." Noah shrugged. "I like the team. What's up with you and Courtney?"

"Nothing."

"I'd already heard a lot about you, but they left out the part about your love life. Courtney, Jen."

There was that phrase again—his love life. When Noah said it, it was just ridiculous. When Jen said it, it was . . .

Interesting. Because it'd come on the heels of her asking why he never went on dates. He should've answered the question honestly just to see how she'd react.

You, Jenessa Belville. You're the reason I haven't looked at a single girl twice in three blasted years.

"Man, you are bad at this."

He yanked his gaze to Noah then back to the road. "At what, having a love life?"

Noah laughed. "No, at getting me to talk. I steered that ship away from me in two or three sentences and boom, you're off in la-la land."

He'd argue but the guy was right. "You're kind of annoying, Noah."

"I don't think mentors are supposed to say that to mentees."

The heater rasped into the quiet between them, welcome warmth flooding over him. Yep, the swim had been a good move. And a hot shower would feel like heaven when they got back.

"Listen, I'm not going to pretend like you owe me your entire life story. Or even parts of it. I don't know if I'd know the right things to say even if you did." He tapped his fingers on the steering wheel. "But the door's open. If or when you walk through it—up to you."

Jamar and Mariana and Doug and all the rest of them might not agree with the approach. Flagg might not either. But then, Flagg had never pushed Lucas to share the details of his time in Afghanistan, explain his desertion, justify his decisions.

A good thing since he couldn't.

Except . . . except sometimes it was worth remembering that, in the beginning, he *had* thought he'd had noble reasons when he'd first made the foggy choice not to go back to his unit. That there'd been a piece of him convinced he was doing the right thing in staying in that little hut. Letting Tashfeen's mother take care of his burns while he tried his best to take care of her.

He'd actually prayed about it. As hours turned into days. When the MPs came looking the first time. The second time. When the burns stopped screaming and the nightmares took their place.

Somewhere in his tortured mind, he'd believed God

wanted him to stay in that village. Maybe he'd heard Him incorrectly, but at least he'd heard something. How long had it been since he could say that?

How long has it been since you tried?

"My best friend enlisted because of me."

His self-focused thoughts vanished as he glanced toward Noah. The younger man's eyes were fixed on the distant lights of Maple Valley. "Oh?"

"He'd gotten expelled right along with me senior year. We were always getting into trouble. When Dad marched me off to the recruiter's, I convinced Abed to come with."

For once, Lucas felt a measure of certainty. He knew to stay silent. To wait.

"It was already seven or eight years after 9/11 by then, but sometimes people still treated Abed like . . . well, you know."

Unfortunately, he did. Even within his own unit, there'd been subtle—and some not-so-subtle—remarks about anyone of certain backgrounds. It was ugly and eye-opening, blatant racism.

"I was such an idiot. So desperate not to go alone that I fed Abed stupid thoughts like, 'Join the Army and people will know you're just as patriotic as the next guy.' So he did." The air in the truck went stagnant. "He died last year. Tanker accident."

Any self-assurance Lucas had felt only a moment ago extinguished now, except for the undeniable knowing that nothing he could say would be adequate. It wouldn't—didn't—matter to Noah that his friend had made his own decisions. That Noah hadn't started the war or caused the tanker accident or even issued the order that had Abed in just the wrong place at just the wrong time.

Logic was no cure for guilt that deep. Shame that painful.

"And you know where I was while Abed was getting smashed? In a freakin' sick bay with the stomach flu and somehow, don't ask me how, a doctor thought he picked up on a heart murmur while I was there and next thing I know, I'm being shipped back home. Turns out the heart thing isn't even a big deal, but I was medically discharged anyway."

Lucas's grip tightened on the steering wheel. "Noah, I wish . . ." That he knew how to react. What to say. "I wish you hadn't had to go through any of that. I wish Abed hadn't."

"Yeah, well, the world's a crappy place sometimes."

He knew that. He really knew it.

But he also knew there was good. There were cold swims that calmed stormy minds. There was hard, satisfying work on a sunny day. There was family—Kit and Beckett and his friends that might not be related by blood but were bound by connection. There was Bridgewell. There was autumn.

There was a God that had talked to him once. Who maybe would again if he could remember how to listen.

There was a beautiful woman with a big heart who, at the drop of a hat, would open a home she hadn't even wanted to three children she'd never even met.

"So." He took a breath. Hoped this was the right question. "What kind of trouble did you and Abed get in?"

At least it didn't seem to be the wrong question. Because a hint of light landed in Noah's eyes. "You ever hear of cow-tipping?"

He looked over with a smirk. "I grew up in Iowa. What do you think? But you don't get expelled from school for that."

"You do when the farmer also happens to be the president of the school board. And he, like, really loved his cows."

"What we know is that Dustin Hollis was fired from his latest trucking job over a month ago. He left his apartment without paying rent three weeks back. And whether he even knows Tessa died this summer . . . it's anybody's guess." Carmen reached for a second chocolate chip cookie from the plate in the middle of the sunroom table. "Thanks for this, by the way."

"Your arrival had good timing." Jenessa cupped her hands around a mug of tea. "I was just pulling them out of the oven."

If the calendar hadn't assured her that fall was in full swing, the wind hurling itself against the house and the rattle of the sunroom windows would convince her now. She'd insisted Colie button up her denim jacket this morning and had sent Violet to kindergarten with an extra sweater for over her *My Little Pony* t-shirt.

Truthfully, making cookies had not been on her agenda for the day—at least not until Colie and Violet got home from school. They'd taken the bus today and should be home soon.

If only Carmen had waited an extra day to call and announce she was making a home visit. Jenessa had been forced to wake up Cade from his nap in the portable crib she'd set up in her office and had left Paige with a half-proofed paper.

She'd made it back to Belville Park just in time to throw some store-bought cookie dough in the oven and do a fast sweep of the house before Carmen arrived. And Cade had fallen back asleep in his crib upstairs easily enough.

This was normal, apparently—unscheduled home visits. Carmen had made it sound like the fact that she'd received a heads-up call in the first place was a favor.

"So what's the next step?"

"In finding the father? We leave that up to the police. Apparently he's not been using a credit card and the last number they can find for him isn't in service anymore, but the police have his license plate number. It's bound to show up on a traffic cam or something soon." Carmen tore her cookie in half and ate a bite. "As for the kids, well, I have to admit I'm a little impressed you managed every single thing on the list I left you last week."

Yes, the house had been thoroughly baby-proofed. Jenessa had replaced the old fire extinguisher. She'd written out multiple fire escape routes and tornado shelter instructions, reviewed them with both Colie and Violet and taped them to the inside of a kitchen cupboard. She'd filled out DHS paperwork and provided copies of everything from her driver's license to pay stubs to her last W-2.

And every night before bed, she'd watched at least two or three foster care training videos, even as her eyelids had dropped and the last of her energy waned.

"I've been wondering about setting up dentist appointments for the kids. I wasn't sure what the protocol is on that. I mean, since they officially have DHS cases open, are they covered by some kind of state insurance?" She probably had an ER bill coming her way soon, too.

"Let's not worry about that right at the moment. Our first priority is finding their father and determining legal guardianship."

"But I asked Colie when they last had a checkup and she couldn't remember. I'm wondering about the eye doctor, too. Violet's still young enough that she'll probably get checked at school but—"

Carmen lowered the remaining half of her cookie to her plate. "I know you're eager to take care of everything. But we're only a week into this. I'd like to keep our focus on the more immediate side of things." She reached across the table to cover Jenessa's fidgeting palm. "I also think it might be good for us to review the . . . temporary nature of this arrangement."

How could Carmen think she'd forgotten? Jenessa had almost gotten used to the subtle but ceaseless anxiety that had become her companion lately. She went to bed with it at night and woke up with it in the morning. The question of whether today would be the last day with the kids. The worry that tomorrow would bring painful goodbyes she wasn't ready for.

Twelve days since Colie, Violet, and Cade Hollis had come into her world. Not even two weeks. But the thought of them leaving now? It was enough to bring on an instant headache. She pushed her lukewarm tea aside. "I know it's temporary."

"Even though the judge's order covered thirty days, if we find Dustin Hollis before then . . ."

"I understand." Her gaze drifted to the sunroom windows. Lucas's truck was still gone. He hadn't returned from dropping his friends off in Des Moines yet. But he'd sent her a text earlier today.

I hope you're ready for detailed garden plans tonight. I've got drawings and an expense list, and I called a guy about an estimate on fixing the fountain, which I think is going to be doable, and I really hope this text is loquacious enough for you because never again will I write this long-winded of a message.
NEVER.

185

She'd laughed out loud and replied immediately. *Loquacious? I'm impressed.*

Thankfully, he hadn't teased her about what she'd said the other night. About tonight being a date. Because of course it wasn't. It wasn't.

Was it?

Focus. Carmen had just asked her something, hadn't she?

She was saved from having to ask her to repeat it by the sound of the door flinging open. "Jessa, we're home! It smells like cookies!"

She grinned. "That would be Violet."

Their footsteps traipsed through the house, telltale thumps letting her know they'd both dropped their backpacks somewhere in the dining room. They appeared in the sunroom doors in seconds.

"You did make cookies!" Violet raced to the table and stood on her tiptoes, attempting to reach the plate.

Colie gave her signature eye-roll but lingered nearby as if awaiting an invitation. Jenessa opened her mouth to call her over when Carmen's gasp stopped her.

"Uh, you didn't have that last week." Carmen's attention sprinted from the cast on Violet's arm to Jenessa.

"Oh, I can't believe I forgot . . ." Jenessa had spent fifteen minutes after the social worker first arrived, filling her in on recent days. How could she have left their ER visit out?

She'd been too busy telling Carmen about all the progress she'd made with Colie. About how Cade had stood on his own in the sunroom the other day, uttered what might be his first word Saturday night at the Everwood. About how well Violet had done her first day in school.

Here she'd worried earlier that she'd sounded as if she was bragging about the victories of the past few days, but now it probably looked as if she'd purposely left out the challenges.

"It happened on Friday. She fell outside, but thankfully it's just a hairline fracture and—"

"Luke took me to the hospital. He speeded." Violet lifted her arm. "Look at all the people who signed my cast."

Carmen gave Violet a tight-lipped smile before looking back to Jenessa once more. "Luke?"

"Oh, he's um . . . he's . . ."

"There he is!" Violet hopped away from the table and pressed her nose against the window, knocking with her good hand.

Even from across the yard where he'd just parked his truck, Lucas must've been able to hear the hullabaloo. Because he waved back, and Noah did too.

"Isn't that the cottage where you found the kids? Those two men . . ."

"Right, um, well, they're staying there at the moment."

"It's a rental property? That would've been important to include on the paperwork you filled out pertaining to your home and—"

"No, they're not tenants, really. They're friends. At least, Lucas is."

With every word, Carmen's posture seemed to stiffen. Oh, this was not going well. "The information you provided was that you are a single woman who lives alone—"

"That's true. Very true. Those guys—they're just doing some work on my yard. A-and yes, Lucas was the one to drive Violet to the hospital, but that's because he was babysitting just for a very short time while I worked and—"

She couldn't very well finish that story. She'd gone to that football auction downtown, which had seemed like a totally logical thing to do at the time, but it would sound awful to Carmen and . . . how had this turned into such a mess?

"A broken arm and a visit to the ER is something you

should've notified me about immediately. That's why I gave you my cell number. I answer at all hours."

"I'm sorry, I . . . I made a mistake." What if this was the kind of thing that could interfere with the custody arrangement? Carmen wouldn't take them away, would she? Her pulse galloped.

"Colie?" Carmen tilted her chair to face the girl. "How are things going for you?"

Jenessa bit her lip, forced herself not to make eye contact with Colie. She couldn't let Carmen think she was trying to do anything to sway Colie's answer but . . . *please God.*

"Good. Things are good."

Carmen looked back and forth between them. "Could I talk to you a few seconds alone, Colie?"

The question did nothing to calm Jenessa's nerves. But she took her cue, reaching for Violet's hand, leading her from the room, and closing the French doors behind her.

"Did I say something wrong, Jessa?" Violet's voice was faint and threaded with worry. The kind of worry a six-year-old should never have to bear. "We don't have to leave, do we?"

Jenessa pulled her close. *I hope not. I sure hope not.*

The doors reopened in scant moments. Colie was seated at the table now, eating a cookie, and Violet joined her.

Carmen came out. She'd gathered her purse, her files. She was leaving? Did that mean . . . ?

"We need to communicate more," she said abruptly. "I'd appreciate a nightly report. Just an email each evening with a few notes about the day. Until further notice."

Okay. She could do that. She'd clearly lost some of the woman's trust, but not enough that it meant losing the kids. *Thank you, God. Thank you.*

But it didn't change the point that Carmen had

attempted to drive home earlier. That this was temporary. That she could be returning the next week or the next day with news that would change everything.

Dustin Hollis wouldn't be off the grid forever.

She sent the social worker on her way, then returned to the girls. "Hey, Colie, what'd you say to Carmen?"

"That I like it here." She finished off another cookie. "And if she tries to take us away, I'll run away again."

He was going to tell her.

Lucas didn't know exactly when and he sure didn't know how, but one way or another, he wasn't walking back to that cottage tonight until he'd told Jenessa.

Everything.

About Tashfeen and the scars and Bridgewell and . . . *everything.*

The warmth of the flames in the outdoor fireplace flickered over him as he took in Jen's profile. Her hair was pulled away from her face, secured with a ribbon that looked like Violet had tied it. She wore the same pink fleece pullover he'd seen her in the other night and long black jogging pants, and she was hunched over the sketch of the gardens, squinting to make out his rough drawing under the subdued glow of the string of patio lights overhead, the fire nearby, a sliver of moonlight.

She seemed so . . . comfortable.

Somehow he'd just known earlier. The moment he'd opened her back door and she'd appeared with a bag of marshmallows in hand, declaring it was the perfect night for a fire, he'd known he'd tell her tonight.

Because Mariana was right. There was something he

wanted more than Bridgewell. But it was something he could never have if he couldn't bring himself to be honest.

And if Noah could share his story with someone he'd only known a week, Lucas should be able to tell the truth to a friend he'd known for years.

"I love what you're planning to do with the different levels and the little rock walls. And it makes sense because the land already slopes a little there." Jenessa propped her chin on her hand, her fleece sleeve pulled over her knuckles.

"Are you cold? We can go inside."

She looked up. "I'm not that cold. Mostly I'm feeling a little guilty for doing a fire without the kids. They would've loved this."

"Yeah, but you probably would've spent the whole time trying to keep Cade away from the fireplace and you'd have ended the night picking sticky marshmallow out of Violet's hair."

Instead, she'd end the night . . . how? As disappointed in him as Sam was?

Or maybe—was it possible?—that hearing his story would open up a new pathway between them? Wasn't that what had happened with Noah earlier today? All the way back to Maple Valley, they'd talked about his friend, his experiences in the Army, the trouble Noah had gotten into over the winter.

How Flagg had found him in a jail cell not all that different from Lucas's.

"So we'll mostly bring in potted plants and flowers for the night of the gala, but you're thinking we can at least plant some hardy grasses and bushes?"

He blinked. Stuffed a marshmallow in his mouth to give himself time to refocus. "Yeah. With it being October, planting flowers is iffy. We'll seed a few areas that'll bloom next spring, though."

Next spring. Did the thought of the future that far down the road bring as many questions to her mind as it did his? Did she think of the kids and where they'd be? Or was there any chance . . . ?

"Lucas?"

He had to stop letting himself get distracted. He'd never find the words he needed to say otherwise. Or maybe she'd help him out and give him the opening he needed. Ask about his scars or his friends or Noah. "Hmm?"

"Want another marshmallow?"

Or maybe he'd have to man up and make his own opening. "Sure." He reached for a roasting stick and plopped a marshmallow on the end. "Am I doing one for you too?"

"How'd you know?" She grinned and handed him a second marshmallow. "You seem quiet tonight."

"I thought I was always quiet." He reached the roaster into the fireplace, dangling it over a flame.

"That's what everyone thinks about you, sure. But I've been around you a lot lately. You can be downright chatty at times. And after that *loquacious* text today, I might go so far as to call you garrulous."

"I feel like you had that locked and loaded."

"I might've used a thesaurus app earlier. But my point is, tonight you seem a little extra pensive."

Well, he'd wanted an opening. "Actually, there's something I wanted to—"

"It's on fire, Luke."

He pulled the stick from the fire, blowing on the marshmallows until the flames died. "That was fast." Two charred, black blobs barely clung to the roaster.

"It's okay, I like them that way." She grabbed one of the

small plates she'd brought out and used her fingers to pry the top marshmallow loose.

"You like them so singed you can taste the ash? No, I'll make you a new one."

But before he could move, she grasped his wrist. "Really. I like them well done."

The scarred skin of his wrist went warm at her touch. "More of a medium-rare guy myself." He fairly rasped the words.

She realized in that moment it wasn't his sleeve she gripped. He watched it dawn on her face, the fire lighting her eyes with awareness and . . . apology? Her fingers slipped away. "Sorry."

"No, actually . . ." He let his scorched marshmallow fall into the fire and set the roaster aside. He wetted his lips. "I thought maybe I'd . . . I don't really have a lot of practice telling . . . so . . . the scars."

Her plate clinked to the cement. "You're seriously gonna tell me about—"

"Just listen, okay?"

"You don't have to, Lucas. You really don't have to. I know you don't like to talk about Afghanistan. That's why I've never asked. Not that I don't want to know. I do."

"Then be quiet for two seconds, okay?"

She opened her mouth again. Closed it.

"What?"

Even in the dark, he could make out her look of embellished innocence. "I was just going to say if it only takes you two seconds to tell the story, then you're not as loquacious or garrulous or effusive as one might hope."

"You finished?"

She pasted on a contrite expression and suddenly, none of this seemed like such a good idea. Couldn't they just go on being silly? Teasing one another? Eating blackened marshmallows while she oohed and aahed over his garden plans and he pretended this was a date even if she didn't know it?

"Luke?"

Just talk.

"It was an IED—improvised explosive device." No, he needed to start further back. "My troop was mainly doing humanitarian work, digging wells, clearing roads, that kind of thing. There was this group of kids that would wander out from one of the villages to watch. Saw them all the time, didn't think much of it."

His gaze fastened on the fire.

"The night of the explosion, just a few days before we were supposed to break camp, the kids had come out again. They were kicking a soccer ball around. One of them stepped in the wrong spot."

"Oh, Luke."

"I was working on a fence in the area—saw the whole thing. Three of the kids were dead, one was alive. I didn't even think, I just picked him up and started running in the direction of the village."

He felt Jen go still beside him.

"Strangers somehow got me to the right house, but by the time I reached it, he'd died. His mother screamed and wept, and I just stood there." While a lifeless body seared his arms and any clear thought of life beyond that moment shattered. "His name was Tashfeen. I didn't know that until three days later. I guess I passed out from the burns. His mother—Kaameh—took care of me. While she was grieving her son, she dressed my burns and . . . and kept me alive."

Jen shifted at his side, reached for his hand.

"And then I just stayed."

That was the part of the story he'd never made it to before. He'd told Kit once of Tashfeen, but he hadn't been able to make himself go further. Even the therapist Flagg had sent him to hadn't heard much about his time living under Kaameh's roof.

"It was probably some kind of shock at first, but eventually I told myself I stayed because Kaameh needed me. Because I could help her. A week passed, two weeks. Then a month. My unit hauled out. I just . . . stayed."

"Because you saw someone in need." Jenessa finally spoke. "Because that's the kind of man you are."

He released her hand. "No. Because I was selfish and cowardly. Because I convinced myself fixing her roof and giving Kaameh food and letting her cry on my shoulder was noble, but really I was just—"

"In shock," she interrupted. "Hurting."

"For almost two years?" He'd let Kaameh mother him in a way he'd missed out on as a child. *Pathetic.*

"You were young, Luke."

"I was old enough to know what I was doing. I *deserted*. I did the worst thing a soldier can do." A log in the fire tipped, sending ash and sparks spattering.

She scooted closer. "So maybe you did. But you paid for it. You went to prison, you were discharged—"

"Dishonorably."

In a move that completely stunned him, she wrenched her hands upward, touched both of his cheeks. "I'm not going to do this. I'm not going to sit here and listen to you talk about yourself like this. I'm not going to just go on letting you act like your decisions in the aftermath of something horrific make you cowardly or dishonorable or any other awful label you want to give yourself, because you're not any of those things. The labels don't fit."

"I hid from the MPs, Jen." Frustration backed each word.

She dropped her hands and scrambled to her feet. "I will walk into that house and leave you out here if you say one more word against yourself." She plucked the bag of marsh-mallows from the ground and marched toward the door. "You are one of the very best, most honorable men I know, and I'm serious, I'm not going to just stay out here while you—"

"What if I've been lying to you since the day I met you?"

She turned. Slowly.

"I don't go to Mexico in the fall, Jen. I go to D.C. and from there, wherever I'm sent. I'm still a soldier. A private one. I work for a company called Bridgewell. Those friends who came to see me—we're a team. Elite civilian specialists who go on dangerous missions and do things we're not supposed to tell anyone about. Things I've never told you or Sam or even Kit about."

Her gaze burned with shock, confusion, disbelief. Too many emotions to separate.

And then, the slam of the door.

She couldn't stop shaking. Why couldn't she stop shaking?

The bag of marshmallows slipped from her hands and she stumbled into the dark kitchen, not bothering with the light.

She was not going to cry about this. She was *not*.

Of course those friends weren't just old Army buddies. Of course Lucas wasn't working on a fruit farm in Mexico half the year. Of course he was still serving and sacrificing and . . . and . . .

"Did you mean what you said out there?"

. . . and he'd followed her inside?

Hot tears pooled in her eyes. Did she mean what?

Couldn't he see she was about to lose it? All because she could still feel the way he'd trembled when he'd told her about that boy who'd died and hear the raw pain in his voice. Because she'd just found out one of her best friends was some kind of international hero, only no one knew.

But he'd told her. Why had he told *her*?

He was standing in front of her now. "Did you mean it?"

"Mean what?" She could barely make out the angles of his face in the shadowy stillness.

"That I'm one of the most honorable men you know. Even after everything I just told you, is there any chance you still . . ."

She felt a tear escape, the mere inches between them charged with something warmer than that fireplace outside could've ever hoped to kindle. "How could I not, you—"

Idiot. That's what she'd been about to say.

But he'd closed the last useless sliver of space between them so quickly she couldn't form the word. And when he took her face in his hands, just as she'd done outside, she couldn't form a thought. Not a single thought save one.

If he doesn't kiss me right now . . .

He kissed her right then.

So softly at first she was worried she'd imagined it. But as his fingers moved to her hair and his other hand drifted down her arm, as he gently moved her backward until only the wall behind her and his hand on her waist held her up, her fears were laid to rest.

This was no moment of make-believe. Lucas Danby was kissing her.

And it was . . . a hundred kinds of perfect. So perfect there was nothing else to do but lean in to him and kiss him back and marvel at the sheer rightness of it all. She slipped her arms around him, breathtakingly certain this was a moment she'd been waiting for her whole life.

She just hadn't known it. Hadn't known it was Lucas who could calm every restless voice inside of her even as his touch, his thrilling closeness sent shivers through her.

"Jessa?"

Not until Lucas broke away did the tiny voice from behind register. And even then, as Violet said her name again, she could barely hear her over the thumping of her heart.

She looked up at Lucas, but it was too dark to make out his expression. Yet she could hear his shaky breath as he backed away and gave her room to slip past him.

What had just happened?

And why oh why did Vi have to pick just that moment to come downstairs?

"*W*hat's the emergency?"

At the sound of Mara's frantic voice out in the newsroom, Jenessa shifted Cade's sleeping form against her chest. Sometime in the past week, her office had begun to resemble a nursery. Portable crib in one corner, toys strewn about the floor, extra diapers in a basket on the windowsill.

But the rolling chair at her desk was not made for rocking a baby to sleep. Her back ached from her angled posture and Cade's warm weight had her nearly sweating. The logical move would've been to tug off her cardigan before he'd nodded off.

But she had no logic today. No focus. No hope of getting a single paragraph written let alone a whole article.

Not after last night. Lucas had *kissed* her. And at some point, she'd gotten over her complete shock and utter awe long enough to kiss him back.

Except no, she wasn't even close to over the surprise of it. Or the absolute perfection. Ten hours later and she could still feel its molten impact. It was as if every sense, every other thought in her mind and her heart, had melted down to one, heady, emotion-filled notion: *Lucas.*

But then Violet had come downstairs and responsibility had ripped her away. By the time she'd gotten Violet tucked in a second time, Lucas had disappeared, though he'd apparently had the presence of mind to douse the flames in the fireplace before returning to the cottage.

And she'd spent the remainder of her restless night swaying back and forth between reliving every millisecond of those moments in the kitchen and wondering whether Lucas was doing the same. Worrying that he regretted it.

Wishing she had the nerve to march out into the cottage in the middle of the night and demand to know what was happening between them.

But she *knew* Lucas. It couldn't have been easy for him to talk about his past the way he had last night. He might need space, time to process.

So she'd settled instead for starting a dozen texts to him . . . and deleting all of them. Until finally, in desperation, she'd sent Mara an SOS ten minutes ago.

Mara, I need you. Are you free? I'm at the office. It's an EMERGENCY.

Her friend appeared in her office door now, and Jenessa had to swallow her gasp to keep from waking Cade. "Are you wearing a wedding dress?" She whispered the question.

"Yes. You know why? Because there I was standing in front of a full-length mirror at Betty's Bridal and my phone dinged and I looked down and the first thing I saw was 'emergency' in all-caps." Mara hissed her exasperation. "What was I supposed to do?"

"Not steal a wedding gown."

"I didn't steal it. Betty saw my face go white and told me to go. I thought something had happened with one of the kids. But no, here you are looking easy as you please, cuddling a sleeping baby."

Jenessa rose and gently laid Cade in the portable crib. "I only look like I'm at ease. Inside I'm freaking out. Completely, totally, and—" She turned back to Mara, gaze sweeping over the ivory gown with its pearl beading, lace elbow-length sleeves, and simple but elegant lines. She took hold of Mara's hand and towed her from the office into the newsroom. "Is this the one?"

Everything in Mara seemed to soften—her eyes, her smile, her voice. "I think it is."

"It's . . ." Jenessa walked a circle around Mara.

"Beautiful," Paige filled in. She rose from her desk in the corner of the office. "I love how understated it is. Not really a tulle girl myself." She slung a camera bag over her shoulder and pointed her attention to Jenessa. "I assumed you'd want me at the county supervisors meeting considering you've got Cade here."

Again. Surely that was the unspoken ending to Paige's sentence. It had to be getting old to her—Jenessa's off-and-on presence at the office, baby in tow more often than not. If not for Paige, there was no chance this week's issue of the *News* would've come out on schedule today.

At some point, Jenessa had to figure out a better way to balance her responsibilities at the newspaper with her role as a temporary guardian. But Carmen's visit yesterday had driven home even more than before the real and harsh reality that the kids wouldn't be with her long-term. The thought of sending Cade to daycare or staying at the office when Colie and Violet were home from school felt like such a loss considering their short time together.

Or maybe it won't be that short. Maybe Dustin Hollis won't turn up. Maybe . . .

Maybe what? Maybe she'd keep the kids forever? Is that what she wanted?

Without warning, without reason, a picture flashed in her mind. Thanksgiving or perhaps Christmas morning. A lit fireplace. A warm house—Belville Park. Three kids in pajamas. And Jen with them and . . .

No, you can't put Lucas in that picture. Not . . . yet. She shouldn't even let herself imagine the kids with her during the holidays.

"Jen? The county meeting?"

She blinked, all too aware that the sudden longing pulsing through her had the power to break her heart. "I owe you big-time, Paige. Seriously, I don't know what I'd do without you."

Paige only shrugged. "It's what you pay me the big bucks for." She flitted out the door.

Mara cleared her throat. "Any chance you could hurry up and tell me why I'm here? You know, before Betty starts thinking I've absconded with the dress after all and puts out an APB on me."

Right. "Do you want to sit?"

"Is there any surface in here where I won't be in danger of getting an ink smudge on the dress?"

"Fair point. Stay standing. I'll make this quick." Except that now that the words were supposed to come out of her mouth, she wasn't sure what exactly those words were. And she'd laid Cade down so why was she still so hot? She slid off her sweater. "Uh, something happened last night."

"And the award for most vague explanation ever goes to—"

"Lucas kissed me."

Mara's jaw dropped and she lowered into the nearest chair. So much for worries about ink stains. "Oh my."

"Yeah, that was my reaction too."

"Finally."

That hadn't been part of her reaction. She rolled a chair over and plopped into it. "What do you mean 'finally'?"

Mara leveled her with a look. "That man has been half in love with you as long as I've known him. Maybe wholly. I mean, it's Luke, so who really knows the full scope of what's going on in his head, but anyone with eyes could've seen this coming from a mile off."

"I've got eyes. I didn't see it coming." Not until those intoxicating seconds right before it'd happened, when her own desire had suddenly grown so potent she could barely breathe.

"So I guess it was good, huh?"

Her gaze shot up to take in Mara's smirk. *It's not as if you can argue.* Except that "good" was a ridiculous understatement. That kiss had been . . . exquisite.

"And now you're blushing." Mara clapped her hands together. "This is a really good Wednesday. I find the perfect wedding dress just days before the big event. I discover my good friend kissed my best friend. And it's not even nine-thirty yet. Tell me everything. How did it happen? How did you react? Are you, like, a couple now or—"

"Wait, back up. Are you telling me everyone has known that Lucas . . . that he . . .?" She didn't even know how to finish that question.

"That he thinks you hung the moon? I don't know about everyone, but within our little circle of friends, yeah, it's been the unspoken secret of note for quite a while."

"I thought Sam's unrequited love for Mackenzie's mom was the unspoken secret of note?"

Mara's eyes widened. "Sam loves Harper?"

"Isn't it obvious?"

"Well, we're not talking about Sam and Harper right

now. We're talking about you and Lucas and how long he's had a thing for you. And I don't know why it's such a surprise to you. You're smart, you're fun, you're loyal. You make everyone feel comfortable and at home, and I think that's a big deal for Luke. He's different around you than other people—more relaxed and open."

She opened her mouth but couldn't find a response. Had she really been so blind?

Yes. And not only to Lucas's feelings, but her own. Because what she was experiencing now—such a rush of affection and admiration for a man with scars and secrets that only added to his wonderful complexity—it couldn't have happened overnight. One kiss, glorious as it was, didn't lead to *this.*

This overwhelming need for more. Of him, of his presence.

Of his kisses.

Yeah, that too.

Mara's giggle interrupted that captivating thought. "I wish I had a mirror so you could see the look on your face."

"Stop."

"You know, Jen, it's not just Luke who's different around you. You're different around him. You don't perform for him."

She felt her expression wrinkle. "What do you mean? You think I perform for the rest of you?"

"I think you try really hard to be happy and upbeat and put-together and that half the time you don't even realize how exhausted you are from the effort of it. I think for all the times you've listened to me and helped me through my struggles, especially earlier this spring, you've never fully given me the opportunity to do the same for you." She shrugged, her smile soft. "I think as much as we've talked about how Lucas never shares about what went on in his past, you never share about what's going on in your heart."

She could only stare at Mara. Every little bit of what she said was true, wasn't it? She let her friends in, but only so far. She pretended with them.

"Mara, you're . . . I'm . . . you're right and I have no idea why I'm like that." Except maybe she did. She'd spent so many years spent trying to be a dignified Belville for her parents. Trying to closet any emotion that might be too much and hide any hint that her faith or her career or her life in general might not be enough.

Had her constant need to be the Jenessa Belville everyone expected stolen her ability to just be . . . real?

Maybe. But not entirely. Because Mara was right about something else, too—Jenessa *was* different with Lucas. She'd showed *him* her heart.

And the kids, too. She thought of Sunday afternoon, of sitting on Colie's bed and having an honest conversation that had been hard for both of them . . . but undeniably genuine.

Mara rolled her chair closer. "I wasn't trying to make you feel bad, Jen. You're not required to bare your heart and soul to everyone. I just want to make sure you know you can if you ever want. With me, I mean." She grinned. "But hey, Lucas clearly offers perks that I don't—"

"Mara!"

"And it's about time, if you ask me."

"Ms. Belville!" Mayor Milt burst through the newsroom door before she could say another word. "I have the most brilliant idea and I couldn't wait another moment to share it."

The interruption couldn't have had better timing. Between all Mara had said and the idea that her friends had known about Lucas's feelings for her before she had, Jenessa's thoughts were a blizzard she couldn't begin to find her way through. Not now. Not without talking to Lucas. But would it even be possible to talk to him without stammering and blushing and eventually asking him to kiss her again just to see if a second time would be as magical as the first?

Great, Mara was back to smirking at her. Was she flushed again?

"Jen?"

She forced her focus to the mayor. "Uh, yes, good morning. You have an idea."

He clapped his hands together, all business. Had he even noticed Mara's dress? "I have the perfect solution for Belville Park, that's what I have."

"I already agreed to host the gala, Mayor—"

He shook his head. "I mean for after. You still plan to sell the estate eventually, correct?"

She did. Didn't she? She hadn't given it much thought in the past few days. Thankfully, the mayor didn't wait for her answer.

"If you still have your heart set on parting ways with the property, I think I have an interested buyer for you."

"Oh."

"Sell it to the city!" His voice pitched high with excitement. "I think we could turn it into a little museum. People love touring mansions, after all. Even if it just generated enough money to cover annual taxes and operating expenses, I think it could be a good investment for the town and a way of preserving history."

She should be ecstatic at the idea. Selling the house to the town would mean she wouldn't need to go through the work of holding an open house and whatever else went along with putting it on the market.

But she couldn't seem to rally the enthusiasm Mayor

Milt clearly expected.

"This could be a win-win for both of us, Jenessa Belville."

So why didn't it feel like that?

Kit's invitation first thing this morning had probably saved Lucas from making a complete fool of himself.

Because if his sister hadn't texted at the crack of dawn to ask if he wanted to meet for coffee before they both got started on their workday, he might've found himself on Jen's doorstep instead. Only question was whether he would've been able to make it through a confession of the thrilling, terrifying depth of his feelings for her without giving up and opting instead to let another kiss do the speaking for him.

Why hadn't he just waited for her last night? They could've talked about . . . *it.*

But the moment she'd disappeared around the corner with Violet, the fear had hit—that he'd moved too quickly. That he shouldn't have moved at all. That he'd just ruined the best friendship he'd ever had.

But she kissed you back.

Oh yes, she had.

He'd replayed it over and over—on the walk back to the cottage, as he'd tried unsuccessfully to sleep, during the drive downtown this morning.

And now, as he stood in line at Coffee Coffee, the smooth and enticing aroma of coffee beans a perfect accompaniment to the sound of rain pattering on the front windows, every memorized moment formed in his mind again.

It'd been better than he could've imagined.

"Whoa, dude, I don't usually get grins like that when I take orders." The barista by the cash register forced him from the memory. "Also, I have a husband."

"Wasn't grinning at you, Meg."

"Well, you were grinning at something." Megan handed him a cup to fill with the house blend, his standard order.

"Maybe I'm just really looking forward to my coffee."

"Or you're just bananas."

"Sometimes I don't understand how you manage to attract repeat customers."

She rolled her eyes. "That all for you today?"

He had to admit, he liked Coffee Coffee's snarky barista, who also happened to be the owner of the shop. And clearly most of Maple Valley did too, considering how packed this place usually was. Of course, it probably helped that she'd married a hometown boy—Eric Hampton, who ran a halfway house across town. Kit had continued the tradition his grandparents had of hiring men from the transitional home to help during the busy season.

"Actually, I'll go ahead and grab—"

"Jen's French roast? Mara's latte? Marshall's espresso? Sam's the wild card so if you're ordering for him—"

"Whoa."

She flashed a smug grin. "And you wonder how I keep customers."

"Got my sister's order memorized?" He held out a ten-dollar bill.

She pressed a string of buttons on the cash register. "Americano. Medium. Unless it's close to Christmas and then sometimes she treats herself to a peppermint mocha. But it's October so Americano it is." She handed him his change.

"You *are* good."

Minutes later, he was seated at a table edged up to a front window. He sipped his coffee, glancing out at the rainy day. Across the street and down a grassy hill, the Blaine River was a dark blue-gray this morning, reflecting the leaden clouds sagging overhead. So much for making progress on the garden today.

But no matter. Maybe he'd swing by MV Garden & Turf on the edge of town after this, put a rush order in for all the items on the list he'd gone over with Jen last night.

"You beat me." Kit dropped into the chair across from him, shrugging out of her raincoat. Which, come to think of it, looked familiar.

"Hey, sis. Is that Grandma's?"

She grinned. "Found it in the coat closet. Can you believe how good of condition it's in? Looks brand new."

He could believe it. Grandma and Grandpa had been nothing if not economical. Which meant Grandma would've gone to extreme lengths to keep a coat in perfect form for as long as possible. She'd probably gone out in the rain coatless numerous times just to preserve the thing.

He pushed Kit's cup toward her. "I miss them." They'd been amazing surrogate parents from the very first day Dad had brought Lucas and Kit to the farm.

"Me too," she said simply. "I really hope heaven's the kind of place where you're allowed to peek back at earth now and then. I'd like them to know we kept the orchard alive."

"You kept it alive, Kit. Not me." He took a drink. "Thanks for texting, by the way. We haven't seen each other much lately."

"Ever since you ditched the orchard for Jen's backyard."

He didn't hear any resentment behind her words, but he felt a prick of his conscience all the same. "I hope you don't feel like I abandoned you. But you've never really actually needed me at the orchard."

"That doesn't mean *I* don't need you."

"So you did feel abandoned? Kit, I'm really sorry. I didn't realize—"

"No, you don't need to say you're sorry. I'm sure Jenessa appreciates your help, and it's not like it was that surprising anyway. To be honest, I'm kind of used to you leaving."

Again, there was no hostility in her voice. No bitterness. So why did his coffee turn tasteless in his throat?

Because it's the truth. He'd left his little sister when he'd enlisted, knowing how hard it was for her already feeling discarded by their father. He'd let his choices and all their consequences separate them for years. Bridgewell took him away from home for months at a time and even when he was home, he spent more time with his friends than her.

"I guess I deserve that."

"Luke, I didn't mean . . ." She shook her head.

"But that's how you feel, right? I've never been the brother you needed. I know that."

"Stop. This isn't why I wanted to meet you today. Do I miss you sometimes? Yeah. Do I wish we had the kind of relationship my husband has with his siblings? Of course." She'd balled up a napkin, but she smoothed it out on the tabletop now. "We've never had a mom, we've barely had a dad. Grandma and Grandpa are long since gone. Each other, that's what we've got left, Luke."

"But you have Beckett. You have that whole Walker clan."

"And I love them. But you're my brother. I guess I just want to try a little harder. I want both of us to try. That's why I asked if we could grab coffee. I want to talk about our lives and our days." She stopped fidgeting with her napkin. "And I want to have the kind of relationship that, when I've got really awesome news, my brother is one of the first people I tell."

He set his cup on the table and met her gaze. He didn't remember Mom very well, but Kit sure looked like the photos he'd seen. Especially now, with that gleam of joy in her eyes. "What news?"

"You're going to be an uncle. Come next spring—early May."

Emotion welled inside him. "Seriously? Kit, I don't even know what to say. Except, congratulations, obviously. And I'm so happy for you guys."

"We're happy for us, too." She laced her fingers around her cup. "We've been trying for a while and—"

"I probably don't need to hear that part."

Her smile widened. "I'm just saying, it's something we thought would happen a little faster than it did. I haven't been that great at trusting God's timing, if I'm being honest, but I know this little one will be worth the wait when he arrives. Or she—he won't admit it, but I think Beckett has his heart set on a girl. He'll be happy no matter what but—I'm rambling, aren't I?"

"You're beaming and it's good to see. Truly, I'm over-joyed for you."

She studied him for a moment before her grin faded slightly. "I'm glad you're glad. I'm a little worried this next part isn't going to sit quite as well with you." She took a breath. "I invited Dad to come for Thanksgiving."

His elation plummeted. "Oh."

"I wanted to give him plenty of advance notice since he usually can't get away."

It's not that he can't get away. He doesn't want to. "Kit—"

"I know it's never worked out in the past. But I can't get over the feeling that maybe this will be the year. And it'd be so perfect because you're home, too. What if we could have an actual family holiday?"

A brick weight pressed on his stomach. Yes, he was home now, but by Thanksgiving . . .

Jen. He'd told her about Bridgewell last night, but only in reference to the past. He hadn't mentioned his plans to return to D.C.

Maybe because he wasn't so certain a return to Bridgewell *was* in the plan anymore. Last night when he'd kissed Jen, that conversation he'd had with Mariana and that bright, bold *what-if* he'd begun to imagine, had suddenly felt within reach.

You could stay. It'd mean finding full-time employment, probably dealing with others like that city council member who'd nixed the Parks & Rec job. But if he could survive Afghanistan, a court-martial, prison, and the numerous Bridgewell missions he'd completed, then he could handle the Herman Ferrises of Maple Valley and carve out a place for himself here. The sort of life that used to only feel like a distant someday.

But the chances of that life including a mended relationship with his father? Next to none.

"You just went from scowling to smiling back to scowling again."

He looked back to Kit. "He won't come." He tried to say it gently, but surely she heard the lurking animosity.

"You don't know that."

"If you feel like I've abandoned you over the years, think about what he did. He dumped us on Grandma and Grandpa. He barely visited, never called as often as he promised he would. He didn't even come to your wedding."

Kit balled her napkin again. "But he's still our father. And he's going to be a grandfather."

"I can't understand why you even want him to come."

He saw the reflection of his frown in the coffee shop window.

"Because I have to at least try." Her expression pleaded with him to understand. "I'm going to be a mom, Luke. And I want to be the kind of mom who shows her kids what it looks like to do hard things—like forgive. And true forgiveness doesn't get to hold on to the bitterness. True forgiveness means having skin in the game."

Yeah, well, this wasn't a game he was keen to play.

But Kit had been so happy minutes ago sharing her news and she seemed so hopeful now. What kind of brother would he be to take that away?

He gave a taut nod and let the subject drop. Might as well hold off the disappointment as long as possible—until Dad inevitably let her down. Like he always did.

It wasn't as if he necessarily needed the excuse. But he'd definitely take it.

Lucas stared at the photo he'd found peeking out from behind the fridge in the cottage. The corners were curled and yellowed, its colors faded. But despite its aged condition, he hadn't needed the scribbled note on the back to know what he was looking at.

The little girl in the picture—Jen. She was probably about Violet's age when the photo was taken, her mop of hair as dark and thick then as it was now. Blue eyes, button nose, same wide smile.

The woman in the photo had to be the aunt Jen had talked about repeatedly. As an adult, Jen was her spitting image. The note on the back read simply *L and J*.

It was reason enough to abandon his work long enough

to go up to the house, especially considering he'd seen Jen's car pull into the drive half an hour ago.

"Thought you were just coming in to grab a water bottle?" Noah's form was a silhouette in the doorway, the sun having decided to show its face after all this afternoon. The ground was still too wet to accomplish much today, but they'd picked up a truckload of stone pavers, landscaping rock, and other supplies after lunch. Most of it still needed to be unloaded.

He supposed he could wait to bring Jen the photo until later but—

"You might as well go talk to her. You're basically useless at this point."

He might glare at Noah if the guy didn't have a point. He opened the fridge, pulled out a water bottle, and took a long drink. "Useless is a little strong."

Noah smirked. "We could've had your whole truck bed emptied by now if you didn't keep looking at the house every two seconds. And since you won't tell me what happened last night—"

"Not a chance." Which Noah should know by now. Obviously he'd seen the fire on the patio last night. He'd joked about how he should've been invited to the pow-wow since he'd helped Lucas complete the landscaping plans. He'd heckled Lucas all the way to the yard store and back.

And Lucas couldn't even bring himself to be annoyed by it. It was good to see the younger man grinning. Good to know he'd done at least something right in his time with Noah.

The Noah leaning against the cottage doorframe now wasn't the same Noah he'd picked up at the airport ten days ago. They'd found a rapport, maybe even the makings of a friendship. A very good thing if they were going to be serving together with Bridgewell . . .

But would they? Or would Lucas follow Mariana's example, make a different choice? Would Noah feel abandoned if he did?

Certainly Kit would if Noah didn't. *And Jen?*

"You've seriously got it bad, man. If nothing else, maybe shut the fridge eventually?"

He tossed a water bottle at Noah, then kicked the door closed. "Soil and seed in the shed. Pavers outside next to it. There's some tarp you can use to cover them up."

With a dramatic flair, Noah stepped aside so Lucas could exit the cottage. "Just ask her on a date, dude. It's not that hard."

"Shut up."

Noah's laughter followed him across the yard, past the garden, toward the sunroom doors.

Jenessa stepped out before he made it across the patio, Cade on her hip and the sound of Colie and Violet's voices drifting from behind her. He could see them through the sunroom windows, set up at the glass table, probably working on homework and having an afterschool snack.

"Hey, saw you on your way over."

Jenessa was still dressed for work—her burgundy dress and burnt orange sweater the perfect picture of the season. But the outfit was no match for her blue-eyed gaze, beautiful and uncertain.

Good, if she'd come out here all perky and confident as usual, it might've meant that kiss hadn't been as weighty a thing to her. He couldn't help hoping the nervous tilt to her smile was a sign she'd spent the whole day the same way he had—barely able to focus on anything but thoughts of last night.

A light breeze lifted the hem of her sweater and combed through the two tiny curls at the back of Cade's head tucked against Jen's shoulder. "Someone looks sleepy."

"Someone needed a longer afternoon nap."

An uneasy quiet unfolded between them. *Man, if you could spill almost your entire life story to her last night, you should be able to come up with something to say now.* Especially considering Noah was probably watching from over by the shed. He'd get laughingly lambasted if the guy saw him awkwardly standing here like a stone statue for too much longer.

"Oh, I found something. It was behind the fridge in the cottage. Just happened to see the edge of it sticking out." He thrust the photo toward her.

Was that amusement gliding through her gaze? If it was, it faded as soon as she looked at the picture, replaced by a look of wistful longing. "That's my aunt and me."

"That's what I figured."

"It's so funny that you'd find this today. I did something kind of silly earlier. Mayor Milt was showing me these fancy, embossed flyers he had printed for the gala. On a whim, I stuck one in an envelope and addressed it to her. I don't know why. She's never responded before . . ."

As her voice drifted, she wore that same look of hope Kit had this morning when talking about Dad and Thanksgiving. What he wouldn't give to make both of their wishes come true.

"You look exactly like her, you know."

Jen lifted one eyebrow. "I've got to be a good decade older now than she is in this photo. I'm already getting crow's-feet by my eyes. Whereas Aunt Lauren . . ." She fingered the photo with her thumb. "She always had the smoothest skin. My mom actually used to complain about it. 'Here I spend a hundred dollars a month on beauty products, while Lauren's probably never used a serum in her life and she looks like that.'" Jenessa glanced up at him and grinned. "I don't think she realized how often I was listening when she talked about her sister. But it's the reason I've stuck with a simple face wash and water routine to this day."

"It's working for you." It slipped out before he could stop it.

Not a bad thing. Not if that was a blush on her cheeks now.

"Lucas—"

"About last night—" Their voices collided.

"You're not going to apologize for it, are you?" She slipped the photo in her pocket and shifted Cade to her other side. "Because if you do apologize, I won't be happy. I'll ... I'll—"

"Do what you did last night?" It was his turn to lift his eyebrows. "Get mad and storm inside?"

"So what if I do? You going to barrel in after me again and ... ?"

Good grief, he wished he knew if that was a challenge or a straight-up invitation. Either way, her deepening flush was just about the best thing he'd ever seen.

But she spoke again before he could manage a single coherent thought. "Will you go to Mara and Marshall's wedding with me?"

Whoa ... what?

"I mean, the kids will be with me, of course, but I was just thinking, you know, it could be fun to all go together. Maybe we would've carpooled to the Everwood anyway, but ..." She gave an exasperated huff. "If you could stop me from babbling any longer and say something, I'd really appreciate it."

"Of course." He blurted the words. "Of course I'll go with you. It's a plan. It's a ... date?"

She released a breath, rewarding him with a smile brighter than the golden sun. "Definitely."

$\mathcal{C}$olie had been staring at herself in the full-length mirror in Jenessa's bedroom for at least five minutes.

"There's only one thing wrong with that dress, Colie."

The girl spun on her heels to face Jenessa, worry pinching her expression. "What?"

Jenessa reached out to brush Colie's bangs to the side. At Colie's request, she'd spent almost an hour using her curling iron on the girl's dark hair earlier. "It makes you look way too old. And beautiful."

The fear seeped from Colie's face, replaced by an unsure half-smile. "I picked the right one?"

Jenessa had taken the girls shopping for dresses for Mara's wedding after school on Thursday. At first, she'd thought to buy them matching dresses. But Colie had naturally gravitated toward more subdued colors like the simple navy blue dress she'd eventually chosen—while Violet had had her heart set on finding an outfit to match her cast. Which meant she was decked out now in a neon pink number that could probably serve as lighting at the outdoor wedding after the sun went down. She was in her room across the hall at the moment, packing a purse with whatever it was she apparently needed for the wedding.

Cade, currently surrounded by toys in the middle of Jenessa's bedroom, was looking just as spiffy as his sisters in a white shirt and gray pants, matching gray vest, and red bow tie. *Like a handsome little man.*

Another handsome man would be knocking on their door soon. The thought was enough to send nervous energy cascading through her whole body. How she was going to survive this night without dissolving into a puddle of absolute delight, she had no idea.

All she knew was that she'd never looked forward to an evening more. In the three days since she'd shamelessly asked Lucas to be her date, she'd pretty much counted the hours.

Her eagerness was likely compounded by the fact that she'd hardly seen the man in the past few days—not alone anyway. She'd been trying to spend at least a little longer in the office each day in hopes of giving Paige a bit of a break, and she'd taken the kids out to the Everwood last night to spend the evening with Mara. Not exactly the bachelorette party her friend deserved, but they'd had a blast giggling the night away all the same.

Lucas and Noah had come over for dinner Thursday evening after her shopping excursion with the girls, but between Violet's chatter and Noah's presence, there hadn't been much in the way of intimate conversation.

That she was even mentally using a word like *intimate* in relation to Lucas still floored her. But she couldn't have denied her growing feelings if she'd wanted to. And she didn't want to.

No, what she wanted to do was explore them. Maybe even get a little carried away in them. Because for days now, there'd been a magical little murmur in her heart, whispering that this might be the best thing that had ever happened to her.

Jenessa gently turned Colie back to the mirror. "I think you picked exactly the right dress. The only thing that would make it better is this." She produced a small gold locket from behind her back. She'd gone looking for it yesterday morning, found it in an old jewelry box at the back of her closet.

She swept Colie's hair over her shoulder and dropped the necklace in place.

"Is it yours?" Colie asked.

"It was. But I think now it should belong to you." She connected the clasp and stepped back. "Take a look inside."

Colie dipped her chin and opened the locket, her eyes going wide. "It's Mom's picture."

It was tiny and grainy, a photo Jenessa had pulled from one of Tessa Hollis's still-active social media accounts. It'd work until they could find a better photo. "I thought maybe you'd like to keep her close to your heart."

Colie whirled so quickly, she stepped on Jenessa's foot. But the impact was nothing compared to the force of the girl's embrace. She threw her arms around Jenessa's waist and buried her head against her body.

And Jenessa's heart lurched. She shouldn't have done her makeup so early. If the tears pooling in her eyes managed to escape, she'd show up to the wedding with mascara stripes on her cheeks. But it'd be worth it.

Because this was the other best thing that had ever happened to her—these kids who, in two weeks and one day, had become her whole world.

She'd heard little from Carmen since that home visit on Tuesday, other than scant replies to her daily check-in emails. Maybe that was a good sign. Maybe it meant

Carmen had forgiven her for not telling her about Violet's arm and for letting two men live in the cottage out back.

One of whom was knocking on her door now. At least, she assumed that was Lucas, his rapping echoing through the house and kindling her already burning excitement.

But she let Colie's hug linger, rubbing her palm over the girl's back and kissing the top of her head. "I'm pretty crazy about you, little girl."

Colie's gaze tipped upward. "I thought you said I looked too old."

Not right now. Not with that vulnerable softness and trust in her emerald eyes. Had Jenessa ever been given a greater gift? "You look perfect. Now, there's a gentleman downstairs waiting for us. I'll grab Cade if you fetch Violet."

Colie toed on her sparkling silver shoes. "Fine, but he's not waiting for us. He's waiting for you."

"Don't be so sure. I have it on good authority that he's a pretty big fan of you Hollis kids."

"Maybe, but he sure doesn't stare at us the way he stares at you." Colie smirked and glided from the room.

Jenessa lifted Cade and paused in front of her mirror. "Does he really stare at me, Cade?" Hopefully he'd like what he saw if he stared tonight. Her dress was an even deeper blue than Colie's. Its sheer long sleeves and neckline meant she'd probably freeze at the outdoor wedding, but she hadn't been able to say no to its graceful style.

She'd kept the rest of her appearance simple too, pulling her black waves into a side bun, her hair's only adornment a silver barrette that matched her earrings and lone bracelet.

Cade kicked his legs against her. "Right. That's his third knock. Let's go." She grabbed his diaper bag from the bed and slipped on her shoes. The girls were waiting for her in the hallway and they made their way downstairs before Lucas could knock again.

With one last frayed breath of anticipation, she opened the door. "Sorry we kept you . . ." She couldn't get the last word out. Not at the sight waiting for her. "I think I need that thesaurus app again."

The corners of Lucas's eyes crinkled as he gave her a lopsided smile. "Huh?"

She needed the thesaurus app because *handsome* wasn't a good enough word. Not even close to how striking he looked in his gray suit and hunter green tie. And he'd cut his hair? It was still lengthy, long enough to be pushed back behind his ears and brush his collar. He'd shaved too, which meant she might very well spend the rest of this night having a giddy mental debate with herself as to whether she liked his attractive jaw better with or without the facial hair. It might be the closest call in the world and . . .

If she didn't stop staring at him, they'd never make it to the wedding. And she was the maid of honor.

Apparently he gave up on receiving an explanation for the thesaurus comment. He stepped forward to take Cade from her arms, glanced behind her. "Colie and Violet, you are probably going to be the prettiest girls at the wedding and that's a fact." He leaned closer to Jen, kissed her cheek, and whispered, "And you'll be the most beautiful woman there, by far."

He picked up the diaper bag, gave her a wink, and reached for her hand.

She'd been right to anticipate this night. Amazingly, wondrously right.

This was the kind of thing Lucas usually avoided—events that required suits and ties and small talk.

But he'd wear a suit every day for the rest of his life if it meant having Jenessa Belville at his side. And she'd been at his side for hours, only leaving him long enough to stand up with Mara for the short ceremony, along with Lenora Worthington, the Everwood's former owner.

And just now, she'd slipped inside the B&B to change Cade's diaper. Otherwise, from the moment they'd arrived at the little backyard wedding, she'd stayed near him. Almost as if . . . as if she was proud to be here with him.

The ceremony had begun just as dusk danced through the sky, leaving a glowing trail of purple and hazy orange. The scent of vanilla, probably from the candles on every table, hung in the air, and it was as if even the trees had dressed to celebrate, leaves having deepened into fiery hues during these early days of October. The sun had ducked into the west by the time the catered meal began after the ceremony, but a full moon now illuminated the yard, along with string lights and paper lanterns.

Someone had turned up the music a few minutes ago and he watched from his perch near a ribboned tree as Colie and Violet danced with several other kids amid a cluster of adult couples.

"They seem attached."

Sam's voice startled him and he straightened. They hadn't spoken much tonight—hardly at all in the past week. Though they'd both stood up with Marshall for the ceremony, they'd managed to avoid conversation.

Had Sam finally grown tired of the stalemate?

"To Jen? Yeah, they love her. You'd think they've been living with her for two years rather than just two weeks." Colie had beamed earlier when she'd shown him the locket Jen had given her. And Violet had been the reason he hadn't been able to sit next to Jen during dinner, insisting on claiming the chair at her right since Colie had already plopped down at her left.

"Not just to Jen."

He wasn't in the mood for Sam's suggestive tone. Not tonight. "If you've got something to say, go ahead and say it before Jen comes back."

"Luke—"

"Yeah, I've spent some time with them. Surprising as it might seem, I'm actually pretty good with kids. I know it's shocking that I'd be good at anything, but it's the truth."

"You know I don't think that," Sam countered. "Look, I never meant for things to get so weird. I just don't like that you've lied to us. I don't like thinking Jen could get attached without knowing the full truth—"

"She does know."

Sam's brow slanted. "She does?"

"I told her everything the other night. And unlike you, she took it well. Really well." Really, *really* well.

Sam's focus reverted to the dancing. "I'd rather not know what that look means."

Luke turned to face him. "Good. I'd rather not tell you. But she's a grown woman, Sam. She doesn't need to be shielded or protected or worried over." She was stronger than Sam realized and deeper than most people knew.

And all he wanted tonight was to give her an evening she deserved, filled with everything good.

Sam folded his arms. "I don't think you're incapable, by the way. I'm not surprised those kids like you. I'm not surprised Jen does. I just can't help wondering what it's going to do to all of them when you leave again."

Jenessa appeared on the patio, Cade in his usual spot on her hip. "Maybe I'm not going to leave."

Sam's head jerked. "You for real?"

"I've been thinking about it a lot. Do you think the mayor was serious about that city job? I know that Ferris guy doesn't like me, but it's not only up to him."

"True enough."

Eyes still on Jen, he was surprised to feel the warmth of Sam's hand on his shoulder. "Everyone will be happy if you stick around."

"That means a lot, Sam. 'Specially coming from you." He peeled his gaze from Jen and shot his friend a smug grin. "A comment like that coming from you is almost sappy."

"I've never been sappy in my life."

"I'm just saying—"

"Go dance with your girl or something."

His girl? He wouldn't have the nerve to go that far just yet. But they *would* dance. And at some point, they'd talk. Actually talk, not just the bumbling starts and stops that'd cluttered most of their conversations since the other night. Since the kiss.

And somehow, someway he'd find the words to tell her what she meant to him.

But first . . . the dance. *Accept the mission. Identify the strategy.*

He left Sam at the tree and threaded with swift purpose through the gathering of tables toward where she stood. Jenessa caught sight of him when he was still yards away, the slow spread of her smile doing ridiculous things to him. Who could they find to keep an eye on Cade for a few minutes?

As if she'd read his mind, Jenessa turned to the closest table and oh, Kit and Beckett were there. She handed Cade to Kit and didn't waste a moment moving away.

They met in the middle. "Dance?" he said.

She nodded and took his outstretched hand. Seconds later, they were at the edge of the crowd of dancers.

Nearby, Marshall and Mara swayed to the music, and Colie and Violet were still having a blast of their own, holding hands and swinging in circles.

Complete the mission.

Before his jostling nerves could hinder him, he pulled Jen close. But he'd moved too quickly and she stumbled, bumping into his chest and laughing.

"Sorry," he rasped, one arm around her waist and the other hand settling on her back. "I don't do this much. Or ever." But at least he'd picked a good time for it, a slow song lulling through the air.

"It's my fault. I shouldn't have worn heels when I knew I'd be standing on grass most of the evening."

Her breath warmed his neck. "You could take them off."

"I would, but now that we're dancing, I'd rather not stop."

Who could blame him for pulling her even closer after a comment like that? "I might be okay with never stopping."

"Lucas?" She lifted her gaze, her fingers behind his collar almost as distracting as the sight of her lips.

"Yeah?" His voice was husky.

"When you said, 'it's a date' the other day, and I said, 'definitely,' we did mean the same thing, right? This is a *date*-date? And you did kiss me and—"

"Yes, yes, and absolutely, unquestionably yes."

She leaned her head on his shoulder, but not before he caught the glimmer of satisfied relief in her eyes. "Good."

"It's also probably important for you to know that, assuming you're amenable and all, I have every intention of a repeat."

He felt her giggle. "The date or the kiss?"

"Both, preferably. Maybe one sooner than the other."

"Well, I'm free tomorrow for another date—"

"Go ahead and willfully misunderstand me all you want,

Miss Belville, but I'll make myself clear soon enough. Again, assuming you're amenable."

She looked up at him again. "When? Right now?"

"And once again, I can't tell whether you're issuing a challenge or an invitation."

Her blue eyes fairly sparkled. "Maybe both."

"We're in the middle of a crowd." He leaned his head toward hers. "All our friends are probably watching us this very moment. And the kids. Think of those impressionable young minds." They were so close now that the tiniest movement would give him what he'd wanted for days. For years, really.

"Are you trying to torture me, Lucas Danby?" Her voice was a breathless whisper.

He tightened his hold, dipped his head . . .

"Jen?"

His sister's voice shattered the moment. *Really, Kit? Now?* He felt Jenessa release a breath as ragged as his own.

"I think Cade has a fever."

All at once his arms were empty as she turned. And then Colie appeared. She tugged on Jen's arm, one hand splayed on her stomach. "I don't feel very good."

Two kids down. One, hopefully, *not* to go.

Jenessa stepped from her steaming bathroom, that hot shower even more soothing than she'd expected, and padded to her bedroom doorway, ears perked for any sound. She'd left her door inched open just in case anyone needed her. Colie had already thrown up twice, and Cade's fever, though thankfully not too high, indicated he must have the same bug as Colie.

Violet, at least, seemed completely fine.

And as of right this moment, five minutes past midnight, all three were still sound asleep if her ears didn't deceive her. She let out a sigh and quickly traded her fleece robe for pink cotton pajama pants and the first tee she pulled from her dresser drawer. She shrugged into a light blue zippered sweatshirt, then stopped in to check on Cade before heading downstairs.

Thankfully, his forehead had cooled. Surely she had prayer and Lucas to thank for that.

Sweetheart that the man was, he'd run to the mini-mart earlier to pick up 7-Up and children's Tylenol. He'd distracted Violet while Jenessa had been in the bathroom with Colie. He'd rocked a feverish Cade to sleep. He'd insisted on sticking around while she showered.

He'd . . . fallen asleep on the couch in the sitting room.

Jenessa paused at the bottom of the stairs, a soft grin crowding out her exhaustion, her worry over the kids, and her regret that their time at the wedding had been cut short by a stupid stomach bug. He looked absolutely endearing, sprawled out like that with one arm flung over his chest and the other dangling from the couch cushion.

Both arms were bare from the elbows down, his suit jacket long since discarded. When had he rolled up his sleeves? She hadn't noticed earlier. But now . . .

She crept toward him, the plush carpet underfoot tickling her toes, and lowered onto the edge of the coffee table in front of him. The kind thing to do would be to wake him up and send him back to the cottage. Or find a blanket and cover him, let him sleep the night away right where he was.

But the pull she felt at the moment was too strong. She watched the rise and fall of his chest for seconds that stretched until she felt herself give in. She leaned forward, elbows on her knees, and brushed her fingers along one scarred arm. His puckered skin was softer than she would've guessed.

She couldn't stop herself from picturing how he'd received these burns, his muscled arms carrying a dying boy's body. It was horrifying. Utterly dismaying.

"Jen?"

Her gaze flew to his face, his eyes now open and fixed on her hand, still resting on his arm. She should move, but she simply couldn't. "How did your hands not get burned too?" She whispered the question.

"I was wearing gloves."

She slid her fingers lower until she clasped his hand. He closed his fingers around her palm, then straightened to a sitting position, tugging her onto the couch next to him.

"The kids?"

"Still asleep. I'd voice my hope that we're over the worst of it, but I don't want to jinx it. I guess time will tell. Do you still feel okay? We probably gave you germs, which I feel awful about."

He released her hand so he could put his arm around her instead. "At the moment, I feel more than okay."

He hadn't made any move to cover his scars. Hadn't even seemed to mind her looking at them, touching them. Who was this Lucas?

And how in the world had it taken her so long to realize her true feelings for this man? Now that she had, there was no going back. "Can I ask you something, Luke?" He'd propped one leg on the coffee table and leaned his head against the back of the couch. "Unless you're planning on falling back asleep."

He smiled with his eyes closed. "I'm ridiculously awake, Jen. It's just I can't look at you too long in those pajamas with your wet hair and you smelling like berries or something."

"That's my shampoo and why not?" She couldn't keep the pleasure from her tone.

"Because you called me an honorable man the other day and I'd like to keep it that way." He fiddled with the damp hair over her shoulder. "What'd you want to ask me?"

"Mara said that you've, um, well . . ." What was the right word? "You've liked me or . . . or had feelings or something for kind of a while. She said basically everyone knew but me." The room's sole source of light, the dim bulb of a lamp, was just enough to make out the red spreading over his cheeks. Was Lucas Danby blushing?

He opened his eyes. "What's the question?"

"Well, is that true? And if it is, why'd it take you so long to say anything?" Not that he actually had said something so much as done something. The thought was enough to make *her* flush.

But then, maybe he'd said more than she'd realized in recent weeks. There'd been that night at the Everwood when he'd said he liked all the versions of her. There'd been countless compliments. She'd just always taken them so casually, as if from a friend.

But Sam was her friend and he hadn't come to check on her that first night when she hadn't gone back to the Ever-wood. Sam was her friend and he hadn't cleared every box from her first floor or taken her out onto the attic balcony or moved into the cottage out back with the sole purpose of helping her.

And he'd sure never looked at her the way Lucas often did. The way he was right now.

"I could give you a thousand reasons, Jen, but I think they probably all boil down into one. I was always scared. I was scared you wouldn't feel the same, scared I'd ruin our friendship. I was scared of telling you all the things I told you the other night." He tucked her head against his shoulder. "And there was always the problem of me leaving every fall."

It was the perfect opening to her next question. The one she didn't want to ask but had to. "And *this* fall?"

His stillness enfolded her. "I don't know anymore."

Hope warmed through her, touching every awakened nerve inside of her. "You know, even if you did go, that wouldn't necessarily mean that this . . . that we couldn't . . . that . . ."

While she tried and failed to find the words, he slipped his arm from her shoulder and shifted so he faced her, his side against the back of the couch and his gaze earnest. "What are you trying to say, Jen?"

She met his eyes and mustered up her courage. "I think you're incredible, Lucas. I've always thought so, even before I knew what you're really doing when you're not in Maple Valley. And now that I do know . . . well, you always come back eventually. As long as you keep coming back . . ."

He'd said his missions were dangerous, though. She supposed his returning was never guaranteed. The thought could just about wreck her.

But then she took in the awe in his ever-shifting hazel eyes as they moved over her face. "I'm the dumbest man in the world."

A surprised laugh escaped. "What?"

"I just never thought that you . . . that we could . . . even if . . . you're amazing, Jen Belville." He stood abruptly. "And I'm done wasting time." He reached for her hand and towed her to her feet. "Mara's right. I've been crazy about you since the day I met you."

"The day I supposedly accosted you."

"Exactly." He hooked his arm around her waist. "You intrigued me, you amused me, you surprised me. Mostly, you took my breath away. As much as I don't think I deserve you, I want you in my life and not just as a friend—"

She was done waiting, too. She rose onto her tiptoes to kiss him.

He gasped against her lips, but it took the briefest, barest second for his other arm to wrap around her. If there'd been a hint of desperation to his touch the other night, it was gone in this moment. Instead, he met her lips tonight with a tenderness that might very well make her cry if she weren't so enraptured by the security of his hold.

He broke away just long enough to whisper her name, then he kissed her again.

She was out of breath when she leaned back, hands on his chest. "I'm really angry at you for waiting this long to make a move, by the way. And I'm angry with Mara and Marshall and Sam for keeping your secret."

Forehead against hers, he grinned. "If this is you angry—"

Another kiss and then she circled her arms around his neck, head tucked under his chin, embraced in the complete certainty that she could stay right here forever and be perfectly happy.

"I hate to say this," he murmured against her hair. "But I'm pretty sure I just heard footsteps upstairs."

"And I heard the bathroom light click on. This is becoming a pattern." She sighed against. "The thing is, as many times as those kids have interrupted, I want them here, Lucas. I want them to stay in my life almost as much as I want . . ." *You. I want you to stay in my life.*

Why she couldn't make those final words eke out, she didn't know. But surely he could hear her longing all the same.

He kissed her cheek and then her forehead. "I'm not going anywhere."

15

It was the crick in his neck he noticed first when he awoke. Then the protesting of every muscle in his back as he opened his eyes.

Then, as he slowly realized where he was—folded like a pretzel into the yellow chair in the corner of Jenessa's bedroom—the sweet, satisfying feeling that he was exactly where he was supposed to be.

His drowsy gaze drifted to the king-sized bed jutting into the middle of the room. Jenessa slept on her side, Violet curled up against her front and Colie sprawled out on her other side.

After Colie had woken up sick again last night, Jenessa had decided to move the poor girl into her own bedroom since there was an attached bathroom and she wouldn't have to walk as far if she woke again.

But as soon as she'd gotten Colie settled, Violet had come out of her room crying, saying she wanted to be with her sister. He'd had a whispered conversation in the hallway with Jenessa at that point. She'd eventually decided

Violet had already been exposed to germs, so she'd let her climb into bed with Colie.

But then Violet had insisted Jen stay in the room with them, too. And when Lucas had tried to leave, she'd started crying all over again, which had turned into worried sobs about Cade being alone.

They were the illogical cries of a little girl still half asleep. She probably wouldn't even remember tomorrow. But regardless, Jen had been too exhausted to resist and knowing her, she wouldn't have wanted to anyway. So he'd urged her in soft tones to go lie down with the girls and had then pushed Cade's crib from his room into Jen's, praying all the way that he didn't wake up.

When he'd finally collapsed in the chair in the corner, he'd only meant to stay until he was sure all three kids were asleep.

But, well, here he was.

And he couldn't bring himself to regret it. Not the soreness from sleeping all night in a chair. Not whatever germs he'd probably picked up from carting the kids from this room to that. Not whatever snide remark he was sure to get from Noah when the guy discovered he'd stayed here all night.

Not with such perfect clarity coursing through him. That *this* was what he wanted more than anything—to wake up in a house filled with people he loved.

He watched Jen's sleeping form, haloed by cascading sunbeams thanks to a large window and the lacy curtains no one had bothered closing last night. He'd wanted her for three years, but somewhere in these past weeks, desire had deepened into an aching need.

But the real surprise this morning was what he felt for those three kids sleeping across the room. How much he'd relished the opportunity to help take care of them last night. He felt such a sense of belonging—as if they needed him and maybe, somehow, he needed them and . . . and what if there was a greater purpose in all of this?

Could God have kept him in Maple Valley longer this fall for a reason? Or was that a foolish thought? After all, he'd once believed God had told him to stay in Kaameh's hut rather than return to his unit. And the fact that he couldn't say for sure where his faith stood these days was likely reason enough not to go around assigning divine significance to his circumstances.

But the point was, for the first time in so, so long, he liked his circumstances. Loved them, in fact. Could happily sit here in this uncomfortable chair watching his favorite people sleep for hours.

Still, maybe it would be better not to be here when Jenessa woke up.

He gave a silent wince at the ache in his muscles when he stood, reaching around to rub his neck then moving as quietly as he could to Cade's crib. Colie never had run a fever. Hopefully Cade's was gone by now.

The baby peered up at him, his Clifford stuffed animal strangled under one arm. Apparently Lucas hadn't been the first one to wake up this morning. He lifted the boy and hurried out of the room before Cade made too much of a sound, waiting until he was on the staircase to whisper, "Morning, little man."

Cade awarded him with a bright-eyed smile.

"You must be feeling a little better." His small body was still warm from sleep, but he didn't feel feverish. Must've just been a twenty-four-hour bug that didn't even last the full twenty-four hours. Hopefully all the girls would wake up feeling okay, too.

He trailed into the kitchen and spent the next few minutes preparing a pot of coffee. He'd thought to head back to the cottage, but that was before he'd realized Cade was awake.

Pitiful, maybe, but he was happy for an excuse to stay.

He'd come to love this house and how comfortable he felt here. After years of feeling like he didn't have a place in Maple Valley, in just two short weeks, Belville Park had staked some sort of claim on his soul.

Of course, more to the point, it was the people inside the house.

Morning sun streamed through the kitchen window, warming his skin. He still had a long way to go before that gala in two weeks, but soon the yard out back would teem with newness. They'd made good progress last week on the small rock walls bordering each level of the garden. They'd begun planting a selection of stronger flowers and shrubs that should survive the current cool temperatures at least until the event. Others would be in place by the gala.

But it was the natural scenery that was most astounding —especially that ancient elm tree near the cabin with its leaves bursting with bright red color.

He kissed Cade's head. "It's a good day, my man. I wonder if Jen's planning to take you to church." He wouldn't argue if she asked him to come along.

He left the coffeepot to percolate and carried Cade to the den. He should probably at least text Noah to let him know where he was. Not that the guy couldn't guess but—

A knock echoed through the first floor. He paused. Who would be at the door early on a Sunday morning? He shrugged and retraced his earlier steps.

He was just entering the foyer when he heard footsteps. He looked up to see Jen coming down the stairs, the sweatshirt she'd worn to bed hanging off one shoulder and her hair adorably tangled. She seemed surprised to see him for a moment before understanding set in.

And then, well, if he'd thought Cade's sleepy smile was cute earlier—

Another knock interrupted. He reached for the door-knob even as he cast a grin over his shoulder. "Morning, sunshine."

"You should've woken me . . ." The happy gaze faded from her face as she looked past him.

He swung his focus back to the door. That social worker —Carmen, was it?—looked from him to Jenessa and back again. And he was pretty sure the same thought running through his head right now was twisting through Jen. *This isn't good.*

If only they'd woken up earlier.

If only she'd come downstairs in time to answer the door herself or, better yet, spot Carmen's car out front and quickly shoo Lucas from the house.

Not that he hadn't done an admirable job of disappearing as soon as possible, but the damage had been done. She knew it by the way Carmen's disapproving eyes followed her around the kitchen as she poured a bowl of cereal for Violet, convinced Colie to try eating a saltine or two.

Cade sat in his high chair, munching on a cracker of his own. Had Carmen decided to make a surprise home visit? Or did she have news of Dustin? *Please, Lord, I'm not ready for that. None of us are.*

She glanced at the girls sitting next to each other in the breakfast nook. Both of them had come trailing down the stairs just minutes after the social worker arrived. Violet had caught sight of Lucas before he'd slipped out of the house, running toward him and insisting on a hug before he left.

Jenessa supposed Carmen had every right to be annoyed. She had assured her only days ago that Lucas was just a friend who was staying out in the cottage as he worked on the landscaping. And now, less than a week later, the woman had found him traipsing around Jen's house, both of them clearly just having risen for the day.

It probably looked . . . like something it definitely wasn't.

"Carmen, would you mind if I ran upstairs to change real quick?" She might be able to handle whatever was about to come a little better if she weren't in pajamas.

But Carmen shook her head. "We really need to talk."

Not a good sign.

"How about in the sunroom?" she added.

Away from the kids? Definitely not a good sign.

Jenessa gave a resigned nod. "Would you like some—?"

Carmen shook her head a second time before Jenessa could finish offering her coffee. So she took a long sip, then topped off her mug and made herself follow the woman.

Carmen closed the sunroom door behind her but at least allowed Jenessa to sit on the side of the table that afforded her a view of the kids.

"I'd really like to set your mind at ease about Lucas," Jenessa started in before Carmen lowered into her seat. "I've known him a long time. He's very dependable. I promise he's a safe person for kids to be around. Two of the kids came down with the flu last night and he was just helping—"

"He's the one who was watching Violet when she broke her arm."

Jenessa flinched. "It wasn't his fault. It could've happened at any—"

"We'll talk about him later," Carmen cut in. "I need to tell you why I'm here."

She could feel her posture go rigid, her lungs squeeze with trapped air.

"Dustin Hollis is working on an offshore fishing boat in Alaska. Apparently that was his line of work years ago."

"You've spoken to him?"

"Not yet, but the company he works for is attempting to get word to him. It seems there was a storm last night and, well, I don't know the specifics on how soon he'll be able to make contact, but his vessel's due in port on Wednesday."

Jenessa let out her breath, but it didn't do a thing to still her edgy nerves. Okay, so they'd found him . . . but he wasn't here. Yet. The kids wouldn't have to leave. Yet. Still, dread gurgled to life. "You think he'll come to Maple Valley?"

"Obviously I won't know for sure until I talk to him, but at this point, he still doesn't know the kids' grandmother has passed. I would think when he finds out she's gone and they're on their own—"

"They're not on their own. They're with me. They're happy here. I know I haven't done everything exactly right, but I'm trying. I don't know much about this Dustin guy, but it sounds like he's barely been a part of their lives. Vi hardly remembers him. So how can you entrust these kids to him just because they're related?"

Any and all patience had completely disappeared from Carmen's demeanor. "You say 'related' as if he's some distant uncle. He's their *father*. And unless there's some substantial reason he's not fit to care for them or chooses not to . . ." She shook her head. "We just won't know anything for sure until I speak with him. But you need to prepare yourself."

This wasn't just alarm now throbbing through her. It was full-on panic. "You don't understand. I . . . you can't . . ."

"Jenessa, how you react to this is going to set the tone for how the children react. If you want to help them through this, stay calm. Stay encouraging."

Stay calm? When three kids she adored—she *loved*—would likely be ripped from her care by the end of the week? "You just can't—"

"We have to."

She searched for another argument, grappled for something, anything to refute Carmen's words. But she'd known this day was coming. She'd known.

The sound of something crashing into glass shattered the silence. Jenessa jumped up from her chair, her gaze bolting to the French doors. A crack splintered one of its square panes.

Colie stood on the other side.

She'd thrown something. She'd heard. How much?

Jenessa raced to the door, but Colie was already running away, her bellowing voice echoing behind her. "We're not going. I don't care what you say, we're not going!"

Lucas had gone to church because he hadn't known what else to do.

He'd lugged Noah along because, well, it just seemed like it might be better for neither of them to be on the property while the social worker was at the house.

But as he sat in a middle row, mindlessly doodling on the bulletin an usher had handed him when he walked in, he could barely stop himself from pulling his phone from his pocket for the tenth time. Carmen couldn't still be at the house, could she?

"You're not setting a very good example, man," Noah whispered beside him.

Frankly, he was surprised Noah was even here. He'd assumed Noah would argue about accompanying him, but he'd been unexpectedly willing to come along.

"If coming to church is your way of making up for spending the night at Jen's, you should at least be paying attention to the sermon."

"Can it, Johannson. And I have nothing to make up for." Except, well, probably years of holding God at arm's length.

Hiding—that's what he'd been doing. Just as shame had kept him at a distance from the people he loved, he'd let it slowly lay brick after brick on the wall between him and the God he'd once sought wholeheartedly.

But Jen, in her acceptance of him, had closed that gap with such beautiful intention. If she could see not just past his dishonor, but through it, to the man he hoped he really was, how much more could God see? Accept? Love?

It'd started, though, with Lucas making the decision to be honest with Jen. To put his wounds and weaknesses on uncomfortable display, come what may. Could he do the same with God? Could he stop hiding?

He ignored Noah's still-smug expression next to him. Left his phone in his pocket. Bowed his head for the closing prayer.

I'm ready to try again, God. I don't really know where to go from here, but . . .

But he was willing to try again. To come out from under the shadow of his shame and into the sunlight.

He lifted his head as the pastor finished his prayer, surprised, soothed, grateful for the tiniest of steps forward.

"So, what now?" Noah turned to him as people started filing from the sanctuary at the close of the service.

Should they risk going back to the house? What if Carmen *was* still there? That couldn't signal anything good.

"Luke."

He glanced over to see Sam moving toward them. "Hey. Didn't realize you were here."

"Got here late. Sat in back. Jen stayed home?"

Sam was just observant enough that if Lucas mentioned Carmen's surprise arrival this morning, he'd most likely jump to the quick and accurate conclusion that Lucas had been at the house all night. Probably best to stay vague. "Uh, yeah, she had a late night. A busy night. With sick kids." He'd just leave it at that. No need to tell Sam about those ten or fifteen minutes after midnight. He'd keep that favorite part of yesterday—er, well, today—to himself.

Or maybe not. Because Noah glanced around from behind him. "Busy. Yep. Sure."

Sam didn't scowl so much as cringe. "Don't want details."

"Unfortunately, I don't really have any," Noah said, pure and vexing nonchalance in his voice. "All I know is—"

"Didn't I say to can it, Noah? And whatever both of you are thinking, you're wrong, so just don't. And what's more, we're in church, for heaven's sake. I think Jen deserves a little more respect—"

"Hey, big brother."

Saved by his sister. "Kit, awesome. Take me away from this conversation, please."

She laughed. "Happy to. Want to come to lunch? Beckett's gonna grill."

Beckett came up behind her. "I'm grilling every chance I get before winter gets here. Burgers sound good?"

Anything sounded good if it got him away from Sam's

glare and Noah's sarcasm. Of course, then Kit went and invited both of them, too. But still. It was shaping up to be a good afternoon.

If only Jenessa would check in. Assure him that things had gone okay with Carmen. That she hadn't received bad news.

But there was still no text as he slid into the truck. He thought about calling, but if Carmen was still there, the last thing he wanted to do was interrupt. But a text wouldn't interfere too much, would it? Jen could just ignore it if Carmen was around.

Noah jumped in the passenger side.

"Yes, I'm texting Jen. No, I don't want any of your dumb comments."

Noah only laughed.

You okay? Any news? I'm really sorry if I messed things up by being there this morning. I'm also sorry if this text isn't long-winded enough. Check in when you can? Going to Kit's for lunch.

"You writing her a book or what?"

He tucked his phone in a cup holder and started the truck. "How many times do I have to tell you to can it before you get the hint?"

"I don't know, but I remember this old Sunday school teacher saying that when something is repeated three times in the Bible, we're supposed to pay extra attention."

He pulled out of the parking lot and onto the street behind Beckett's vehicle. "Gotta say, sometimes you surprise me, Noah. For some reason, I never got the impression church was your thing."

He shrugged. "Because of the tattoos or the sketchy past?"

"Because . . ." He paused. "Actually, I was about to say

because you never mentioned it. But when have I ever mentioned my faith, such as it is, to you?" Or anyone for that matter?

"Used to go with my grandma when I was a kid." Noah shrugged. "And my parents recently started attending. No clue what that's about. Call me curious, I guess."

A comfortable silence accompanied most of the ride through town and out to the gravel lane that led to the orchard. Noah had been to the orchard but not yet inside the house Lucas had spent most of his youth in. Such a strange feeling that old farmhouse gave him—happy memories of his grandparents, the sour impact of his father's absence.

"By the way, Luke, if I went too far in joking—about Jen, I mean—I'm sorry."

Was the guy out to repeatedly astonish him today? "I appreciate that."

"It seems like maybe you have something really good with her."

"Well, it's pretty new." He wasn't even entirely sure what *it* was, except that he liked it. He *liked* it.

"Still, I've kind of gotten to know you, and it seems like you're the kind of dude who treats women with respect. I'd like to think I do the same, but maybe the joking was in bad taste."

He passed the turnoff that led to the main orchard grounds, followed the curve in the road that led toward the house.

"I'd let you off the hook, but if your conscience is bothering you, it's probably smart to listen to it. That'll come in handy if you join up with Bridgewell. So how about, if you feel like razzing me, maybe just pick a different topic next time?"

"We're good, then?"

Lucas pulled into the circle drive in front of the farm-house. "We're good." Huh, had Kit and Beckett bought a new car? A shiny black sedan sat in front of the house.

He pulled the key from the ignition and hopped to the ground. Why were Beckett and Kit just sitting in their truck, looking straight ahead? Maybe that wasn't their car. Was someone else here?

Noah rounded the truck to stand beside him and they watched as a form rose from the sedan. Lucas let out a gasp as recognition dawned.

And then, startlingly, nonsensically, he and Noah both spoke at once. "Dad?"

16

A tide of cold confusion crashed over Lucas, threatening to completely disorient him as he struggled to make sense of what he was seeing, what he'd just heard.

Noah had looked at Lucas's father—was looking at him still—and called him Dad. They'd just had that conversation in the car about finding something new to joke about besides Jenessa. Was this Noah's idea of a funny stunt?

No. There wasn't anything light or teasing in the younger man's expression. He seemed surprised, serious, and . . .

Noah finally looked at Lucas. *Chagrined.* Maybe even apologetic.

What is happening here?

"Dad, what are you doing here?" Kit's voice broke through the waves of jumbled silence.

Dad hadn't moved from his spot beside the black sedan. He stood with the bearing of a soldier—back ramrod-straight and shoulders braced for whatever was about to come. If only Lucas had any idea what that was. What Noah's exclamation meant.

But shouldn't it be obvious? He'd called him Dad.

It can't be.

"I'm sorry to show up like this, Katherine." Dad's focus finally shifted to Kit, where she now stood on Noah's other side, Beckett's arm around her shoulder. "I was going to call, but . . ." He reverted to peering back and forth between Lucas and Noah again. "I wasn't sure I'd be welcome."

"Of course you're welcome. Didn't you get my voicemail about Thanksgiving?" Poor Kit was trying so hard to sound nonchalant and hospitable. But surely her stomach was roiling as fiercely as his own.

This was the man who'd shown not a speck of interest in their lives after dumping them on Grandma and Grandpa. Who'd missed birthdays and holidays and high school graduations. Who called only rarely and hadn't even bothered to show up for Kit's wedding.

And then there was Noah. The apparent truth was only now beginning to sink in.

"You called him Dad." Lucas's voice was barely a muttered rumble. "Why'd you call him Dad?"

"What?" Kit gasped. She must not have heard that part a minute ago.

"I didn't know he was going to come here, Luke. I swear, I didn't know."

He ripped his gaze away from the man who had yet to move another step toward them. "He's your father. You're my . . ." *Brother?* No. It was too impossible to believe.

"I didn't know who it was I was coming to meet until I was already on the plane. At the last second I got a text from Flagg with your full name." Noah's words flew at an anxious pace. "And even then, I wasn't completely sure. But then I saw you at the airport and you looked exactly like him."

Lucas's attention flashed back to his father. He refused to see the resemblance. Kit moved to Lucas's side. "What are you guys saying? You're related to us, Noah? Dad, you have another kid?"

"He has a whole other family." Noah practically spat the words. "Does Mom know about them, Dad? They obviously don't know about us."

Lucas couldn't stop staring at his father. Couldn't make any of this fit together in his brain. Except . . .

Except no, it made complete sense. It made utter, perfect sense. Dad had another family. For decades he'd ignored his first family in favor of his second. When had it started? "Did Mom know?" The question was a growl.

Dad finally moved, just enough to shake his head, inch forward. "It didn't happen until after . . ."

Lucas's bewilderment finally spilled over into outright anger. "You should've just told us. It would've saved us a heck of a lot of wondering why you were never around, why you didn't care."

"Lucas—"

"No, after more than two decades of pretending I don't exist, you don't get to show up now and explain. I don't want to hear it."

Dad's grim expression hardened. "I never pretended you didn't exist. Who do you think sent Arthur Flagg to you when you were in prison?"

Dead weight settled in his stomach.

"Who do you think told him you were elite team material? And before that, who do you think nagged Army officials for the entire two years you were missing? I was tempted to go looking for you myself. Do you know how relieved I was when they found you?"

Long strides propelled him forward. "No. What I know is that you wouldn't look me in the eye or shake my hand when I got dragged home. What I know is you hardly spoke two words to me during the court-martial other than to berate me for refusing to explain myself." Years of hurt-fueled fury rose up in him. "I might've deserted the Army, but you deserted your own children. You're a liar and a—"

"Luke," Noah wedged in. "This isn't the way to—"

He spun on the younger man. "Two weeks and you didn't say a word?" A stream of recollections bombarded him all at once. Noah talking about his father being an Army man. Saying he wasn't always around, but when he was . . . he was fun. *Wheelbarrow races.*

It was pathetic, the jealousy that crawled through him now. And lurking underneath it, the pain he'd tried so hard to push away for so long. "You knew and you didn't bother saying something."

"Hey, don't turn on me." Noah held a hand out toward Lucas's chest.

Lucas thrust it away. He needed to leave. *Now.* Before he did something that would prove true what everyone thought about him.

Not everyone.

Jenessa had called him honorable. An honorable man would walk away before this escalated.

Or he'd stay and work this out. Except what was there to work out? His father was as disappointing as he'd always been. His mentee had played him like a fool for two weeks.

He turned to his sister. "Kit, I can't . . ."

She was glued to Beckett's side, disbelief still etched into every inch of her expression. "It's okay," she whispered. "Go if you need to."

Beckett nodded. "You need space." He directed a hard

glare toward their father. "We all do. Come on, Kit." He steered his wife toward the farmhouse, and Lucas took the offering for the escape it was, stalking to his truck and slamming the door.

Dust kicked up from the wheels as he pulled away from the house, refusing to look back at the two men—his father, his half-brother—left on the lawn.

Jenessa didn't know how to do this.

How many times had she hovered outside of Colie's bedroom door with this same immobilizing uncertainty? This time was worse, though. This time her own broken emotions would make it all the more difficult to soothe the hurting heart on the other side of this door.

But she had to try.

"Colie, can I come in?"

Nothing.

She rapped her knuckles lightly once more and inched the door open. "Could we talk?"

The sticky smell of paint still lingered in the room, along with the Lysol she'd sprayed earlier today. She'd stripped the bed sheets after Carmen had finally left and hadn't replaced them yet. Colie was lying on her side on the bare mattress, her back to the door.

There was a softness to the room since they'd painted last week. Colie's choice of watery blue walls and sheer white curtains seemed another peek into the girl's tender heart. Had she always tried this hard to hide it? Or had her mother's death been the thing to create the hard shell around her.

They'd finally broken through that shell in the past week. It killed Jenessa to think today's news might erect an impenetrable exterior all over again.

If she could just find the right words.

She padded over the carpet to the mattress. It creaked as she lowered beside the girl. She allowed a taut, tentative moment to pass before she lightly touched Colie's shoulder. "You didn't come down for lunch."

"Wasn't hungry."

She rubbed Colie's back. "Does your stomach still hurt?"

Colie shook her head, last night's curls now limp and matted. "A bubble bath always helps me after a hard and fast illness like what you had. Say the word and I'll start running one. I'll even share my favorite lavender bubble bath with you."

"Maybe later."

"Can we talk about Carmen's news? Did you hear most of it?"

Colie rolled over and Jenessa moved her hand before it became trapped underneath her. "She can't just send us away."

Jenessa sighed. "The really unfortunate truth is that she can. By law, your father has a right to custody. That is, unless . . ." She couldn't voice it, the icky hope she'd been harboring for days that he wouldn't be a fit guardian. That DHS would find some reason to take away his rights. She'd actually prayed about it. What an awful thing to hope for.

And even if that ugly prayer were answered, it didn't mean the court would automatically award custody to Jenessa either. Temporary guardianship was one thing, but she'd seen the way Carmen regarded her today.

Apparently it didn't matter that she'd done everything she knew to do to care for Colie, Violet, and Cade. It didn't matter that she'd provided a comfortable place to live, three meals a day, and snacks in between. She'd bought clothing, toys, diapers, formula. She'd put Colie and Violet in school, taken the kids to church.

And she'd loved them. More than any of the rest of it, she'd *loved* them.

Maybe it didn't make sense to feel so engulfed by her role as their guardian. Maybe she'd had no right to become so attached so quickly. Maybe she never should've allowed herself to look in the mirror and whisper a new name for herself, one filled with promise and surprising potential: *Mom.*

Because, yes, this was a maternal love. It wasn't pity for their situation. It wasn't the natural compassion anyone would feel for three kids who'd lost their mother and hardly knew their father.

It was a deep, abiding, nurturing love.

And it'd swept her away before she'd ever known what hit her.

"Unless what?"

When had Colie sat up?

Colie went on. "You said he has the legal right unless . . . what? He's never taken care of us before. So he shouldn't really get to take care of us now, should he?"

"I don't think it's that simple."

"Well, it should be. We like it here. I know he's our dad, but living with him would be like living with a stranger. How is that fair to us?"

"It's not." Oh, she shouldn't have said that. Carmen had made a good point earlier—Jenessa's reaction to this situation would set the tone for the kids' reaction. But she was worried Carmen was expecting a level of stoic maturity from her she didn't possess.

The truth was, everything in her longed to strain toward the same life raft Colie was clearly clinging to now.

You can't. You have to be the strong one.

"You know, even if—when—your dad comes back to Maple Valley, it doesn't mean I won't see you anymore. Who knows, maybe he'll rent the same house you were living in before and that's only a five-minute drive to the other side of town."

"But what if he doesn't stay in town? What if he takes us somewhere else? What if he makes us go to Alaska?" Colie's voice turned frantic. "Please don't let him do that. Please, Jen." She threw herself against Jenessa's torso—not an embrace like last night, but a desperate clutch. "We need you."

Tears that'd been threatening all day pooled behind her eyelids now. She couldn't let herself fall apart. Not in front of Colie. But with every tear she blinked back, another took its place.

"I need you, too." She couldn't hold back the whisper any more than she could her tears.

"So you won't let them take us? You promise?" Colie looked up at her, eyes and nose red.

Don't make a promise you can't keep. Don't do it. "I'll do my best."

Even that was too much. She knew it the moment she saw Colie swipe her arm over her eyes and attempt a smile. She knew it as her own dread mingled with a foolish, stubborn hope.

Logic told her to temper both their expectations. Carmen's voice berated her from afar. But she couldn't bring herself to douse the heightened yearning her almost-promise had fanned into a flame.

So instead, she moved her palm up and down Colie's arm, let herself hold the girl like a mother would until Colie fell asleep. As gently as she could, she shifted Colie into a laying position and stood. Surely the poor thing was still exhausted after last night's illness.

She found a blanket in the closet and covered her, stepped into the hallway. Cade was down for his nap and even Violet had succumbed to sleep after Saturday's late night.

Maybe Jenessa should take a nap, too. Accept the temporary solace of sleep.

But noise from outside drew her to the hallway window. And there, on his knees in the dirt, was the true comfort she needed. She stopped in her bedroom to grab a sweatshirt and started downstairs.

He heard Jenessa coming before he saw her. The shuffle of her shoes over grass still damp with dew, even midafternoon. The swish of her movement.

He didn't know what he expected to see when he looked up, but it wasn't the tear tracks on her cheeks or last night's makeup still smudged under her eyes.

He was on his feet in seconds. "What happened?"

And then she was in his arms, her quiet crying shaking against him. *God, please don't let the kids be gone already.* But that had to be it. Never once had he seen Jenessa cry like this. Or cry at all.

She hates crying in front of people.

So only something truly horrible would cause this. He smoothed his hand over her hair. Why hadn't he gone to the house the minute he'd arrived back at Belville Park?

Because you were too busy pouting. Taking all his indignant ire out on the soil bed. Holding on to his smarting anger as a shield against the resurrection of his childhood pain.

But any and all thoughts of his own turmoil slid away in the face of Jenessa's hurt. The worry tormented him but he waited, holding his questions at bay as he let her cry. Finally, when her trembling began to slow, he leaned back just enough to be able to see her face.

"The kids? Are they gone already?"

She shook her head, and the immediate impact of his relief surprised him. He'd known he would hurt on Jenessa's behalf whenever her guardianship of the Hollis children ended. He'd known he'd feel the sting too.

But the fierce, protective affection he felt for Colie, Violet, and Cade in this moment was enough to knock the wind from him.

"But they found Dustin Hollis." Jenessa's voice was hoarse. "He's on some fishing boat off the coast of Alaska until Wednesday. But Carmen expects he'll come to town when he gets the news."

And then what? The guy would show up in Maple Valley and Jen would be forced to hand the kids over?

Another unwelcome father stepping in where he isn't wanted.

He squelched the bitter thought before it could show on his face. At least, he hoped he did. "But that doesn't necessarily mean the kids will automatically go to him, does it?"

"He's their dad, Lucas." She leaned her head against him once more. "I said something I shouldn't have to Colie. She wanted me to promise that I wouldn't let him take her. I didn't exactly promise, but still."

He felt her take a ragged breath. "And in the midst of a thousand other emotions, I've been feeling guilty. I don't know much about Dustin Hollis at all but I've let myself spend two weeks assuming the worst of him. Worse, I've hoped the worst of him. That's not right—I know it's not."

He was so tempted to counter that. To tell her sometimes men were exactly as flawed and faulty as she might think.

As he'd thought.

And yet, hadn't he been plagued by the same murmurs of guilt all afternoon? Maybe not as strongly as Jenessa, but he'd heard the soft voice at the back of his mind. Reminding him of his own mistakes and how just this morning he'd basked in the thought that Jen, that God, could see and accept, forgive and love *all* of him.

Shouldn't he be able to offer his father the same?

It's different. I've spent a decade trying to make up for deserting the Army. What has Dad done?

Maybe he was trying to do something now in coming to Maple Valley.

Well, Lucas wasn't ready for it. Beckett was right. He needed space. More space than a few hours and miles.

"So the guy's on a boat until Wednesday," he said. "Which probably means the soonest he'd be here is Thursday."

Jenessa nodded against his chest, her hands clinging to his shirt. "That's what Carmen thinks anyway."

"And the kids don't have school Wednesday, right?"

She looked up. "Teacher in-service day. You have their schedule memorized?"

She wasn't smiling and yet, he latched on to the first hint of light he'd seen in her eyes today. "Saw the school calendar hanging on your fridge." He tucked a piece of hair behind her ear. "Let's do something fun with them. Go out of town. Hmm, amusement parks are mostly closed by now, and they've already been out to the orchard multiple times, so the usual fall activities have been covered. Maybe we could find an indoor waterpark or something."

"One last hurrah?"

"Maybe it won't be the last." This must've been how she

felt trying to comfort Colie, desperate to offer some semblance of hope.

"I should get back inside. All the kids are sleeping, but who knows when they'll wake up." She lifted onto her tiptoes to kiss his cheek. "I like the idea, though. It's a plan."

"And a date." He winked just to make her smile.

17

There'd been a time when Lucas might've been bothered by the stares of strangers at the scars on his arms. But how could he bring himself to care with Violet's giggles echoing off the walls of the hotel's indoor pool?

Or the almost timid way Colie looked at him while she climbed up the ladder to the water slide? She hesitated at the top, arms pressed close to her sides, wet hair matted to her cheeks.

Violet was hooked to one of his arms, completely unbothered by his marred skin as she slapped her inflated ring against the surface of the water. Her cast was wrapped in plastic. "Are you gonna go down or what, Colie?" she squawked, sending sprinkles of water at Lucas's face as she hit her float into the water again.

"Something tells me we shouldn't have let you have that second donut this morning, Vi." But both he and Jen had been completely incapable of denying her a sugar high.

Just like they hadn't been able to tear either girl away from the pool until the minute it closed last night. Or say no to a late-night movie in the hotel room. Or refuse the kids one more opportunity to swim before they had to check out later this morning.

Yes, this had been the perfect idea. They'd picked out a hotel in Minneapolis with a spacious pool, and after a string of stressful days, they'd all needed this chance to unwind. To let loose and enjoy themselves. He'd loved every moment with the kids.

But his favorite piece of the trip was that waning hour of the day after they'd finally fallen asleep, when he and Jenessa had lingered at the doorway between their adjoined rooms and just talked.

It's how every night this week had ended so far. Quiet, uninterrupted conversation with his best friend and the only woman who'd ever made his soul feel so free.

He'd finally told her about Dad and Noah late Sunday night. He'd shared more about his experiences with Bridgewell, told her about his teammates, even the awkwardness with Courtney last spring.

She'd shared her own stories about growing up at Belville Park, delved into her hurts. Her father's distance and disease, her mom's addiction, her own search for something to fill her life with meaning. He hadn't been surprised at all when she confessed that her interest in running the newspaper had been weakening for months now.

Helpless impulse carried his gaze to her now where she played with Cade at the shallow end of the pool. Her dark hair was piled in a messy knot on top of her head and the wide smile on her face as she twirled Cade in the water was luminous.

He forced his focus back to Colie, still perched at the top of the water slide. "It's okay if you've changed your mind, Colie. You don't have to go down." Odd that she was fearful, though. Why hadn't he noticed that she'd avoided the slide last night?

"Why's she scared? I've gone on the slide ten times already. And I'm gonna go down it ten more times." Violet's singsong voice bounced off the walls.

"The difference is, you've got all that sugar in you and it hyped you up so much there wasn't any room for fear."

"Really?" She tipped her head and called to Colie, "You should've had another donut. Then you wouldn't be afraid."

"I'm not afraid." Colie stepped aside so another kid could go down the slide in front of her.

The sheen of white in the older girl's cheeks suggested otherwise. And he couldn't handle leaving her up there alone any longer. "Wait just a sec, Colie." At least there weren't many kids lining up for the slide. In fact, unlike last night when the pool area had been jam-packed with people, they only shared the space with a few other families this morning. "Gotta deliver you to Jen, Vi." Still propping her up, he pulled the floatation ring over her head and swooshed toward the shallow end.

Jen stood in waist-deep water with Cade at her front, wet spirals escaping from her bun in every direction. "Oh, someone's finally gonna come keep me company over here?"

He freed Violet and shot Jen a grin. "I would love to keep you company. In fact, I thought I'd made it pretty clear by now that I'm up for keeping you company whenever, wherever, however your pretty self pleases."

He wasn't sure he'd ever get tired of making her blush. Three years of compliments and she'd finally started to figure out he meant them. And the way she was looking at him now . . .

"What's going through that head of yours, Jenessa Belville?"

Cade let out a laugh, splashing his pudgy hands in the water, and Jen's expression was practically electrifying. "Thoughts entirely too inappropriate to voice at the moment."

He gave an exaggerated gasp. "Inappropriate thoughts? You? I hope you know I'm going to have to badger you about that later. For now, I've got our girl to rescue."

Our girl.

The softening in Jen's blue eyes let him know she'd stalled on the same word he had. And the slow fade of her smile reminded him of what he'd been trying to forget since his eyes opened this morning.

The kids *weren't* theirs. They'd be on the road soon, headed back to Maple Valley and all the realities they'd both been avoiding would come crashing back in.

He'd managed to elude Dad since Sunday, staying busy with the landscaping, conveniently heading downtown for supplies or out to the Everwood to hang out with Sam anytime Jen wasn't around. Noah had apparently started staying at the farmhouse. He only knew that because he'd called Kit Monday to find out how she was doing.

"I don't know what to think, Luke. It's like Dad thought he could show up and spark a happy family reunion or something. I know I said all that stuff about forgiving him and I meant it then, but now . . . it's just awkward. We have a half-brother. It still hasn't sunk in."

They hadn't talked long. She hadn't pushed him to come out to the orchard, which both surprised and relieved him. He'd checked in with her again yesterday, and Kit had said Dad was sticking around for the rest of the week.

"We still have a little time." Jenessa's gentle voice pulled him back to the present.

But not much. Carmen had called earlier in the week after finally talking to Dustin Hollis. He planned to make travel arrangements as soon as he was back on shore —today.

He squeezed Jen's shoulder and moved past her, climbing out of the pool and padding over wet tiles to the slide. He made quick work of the stairs and emerged on the metal landing at the top of the slide.

"Hey, you."

"You didn't have to come up here." Colie's teeth were chattering from having been out of the water too long and she hugged her skinny arms to herself.

What was the best way to help her out here? Violet's lack of restraint made it easy to connect with her, but Colie was different. Was she too old for him to suggest going down the slide together? Would that make her uncomfortable?

He was relieved when she spoke first. "I was just thinking about my mom. She was always so busy and stressed out and stuff. Except this one time. I was, like, six or seven or something, and we went to a water park. She was really happy that day."

The urge he felt to put his arm around the girl was almost impossible to resist. But were they close enough for that? He didn't know.

He leaned against the railing behind him instead. "Can I tell you something, Colie? This—well, technically, last night —is the first time I've been to a public pool since my arms looked like this. But last night when I saw you and Violet jump in the pool, I decided to try to forget about the scars and just have a good time. I don't mind admitting it was scary for a second, peeling off my shirt." He lowered his voice conspiratorially. "Especially considering Jen was right there, and I care what she thinks of me pretty much more than anyone."

Colie rolled her eyes. "Obviously."

He grinned. "Thing is, I know Jen would've understood if I'd decided not to swim. Or to wear some long-sleeved shirt into the pool. I had to be ready for it, you know?"

"Yeah, yeah, I know what you're saying. If I'm not ready to go down the slide, I don't have to."

"Yes, and I'm not going to lie to you. I'm pretty proud that analogy worked." He was pleased when she laughed. "I'm sorry things were hard with your mom, though. But I'm glad you have a happy memory of that day. You could go down the slide in her honor now. Or if you want to head back down, I'll walk with you."

She shook her head. "Nah, I'll go." She stepped up to the slide, cast him a side glance. "We could go together."

"Yeah?"

She lifted one shoulder, which from Colie was invitation enough. She squealed the whole way down until they splashed into the water below, and then proceeded to go down three more times by herself.

And he felt almost ridiculously triumphant. He'd found the right words. He'd encouraged her. He'd earned a smile from Jenessa that could've melted a glacier.

But far too soon, he found himself wrapping Violet in a towel and shaking out his own sopping hair, drying off his chest and legs. He slung his towel over his shoulder, then helped Jenessa gather their things, anchored Cade to his hip, and ushered the kids out of the pool area, the scent of chlorine following them to the elevator.

"I don't want to leave."

Colie didn't join in Violet's whining, but he could read the reluctance on her face. It was all he could do to keep his own forced upbeat attitude in place. "We've got all those snacks for on the way home, and I'm sure we can find a fun restaurant to stop at for lunch."

He corralled them into the elevator, punched the button

for their floor, and turned to see Jen watching him. "More inappropriate thoughts, Miss Belville?" he whispered.

"Not if thinking about what a good dad you'd be is inappropriate."

"That might be the best compliment anyone's ever given me."

She was pressed into his side, exactly where he wanted to keep her. He knew what she'd said last week about the possibility of still having a relationship even if he returned to Bridgewell. But he didn't want long distance. He didn't want months apart from her.

He wanted this closeness every single day.

And he wanted her to never stop looking at him the way she did now as she lifted onto her tiptoes just as the elevator door opened. "And as far as earlier"—she kept her voice low—"all I was thinking was that it was a shame you waited so long to take off your shirt in front of me. I might've fallen for you a lot sooner."

She sauntered out of the elevator after the girls, looking back at him long enough to wink.

"Cade," he murmured, not even trying to pretend his shiver was from the wet swim trunks. "Never wait three years to tell a woman you're in love with her, okay?"

He followed Jen into the hallway, but he didn't make it more than two steps before he bumped into her from behind where she'd frozen a half a dozen doors from their rooms.

Water pooled at her feet as she gasped. "Aunt Lauren?"

Jenessa couldn't be seeing what she thought she was seeing. After twenty-three years of silence, her Aunt Lauren couldn't be at this same random hotel on this same random day when Jenessa was. Some things were just too coincidental.

But look at her.

The woman moving toward her walked with the same mix of energy and poise Aunt Lauren always had. That was her same beguiling smile. Her same bold yet elegant style. She was as willowy and graceful as ever.

"Whoa, she came?"

Jenessa's gaze darted to Lucas, who'd come up beside her. Wait, what was he saying? Had he known this was a possibility? *Impossible.*

"When she didn't call back, I thought . . ."

"What are you talking about, Lucas?" The woman—her aunt, that was most definitely her aunt—was nearing.

"I did something, Jen. I hope you're not upset. On Monday I found this drawer full of letters to your aunt that were returned to you and I realized she only lives a couple hours from the Twin Cities and I got Sam to help me find a phone number and—"

"You *called* her?"

His nod seemed frantic, as if he was worried any second she might lose it on him. "But I didn't want to tell you in case she never called back because I didn't want to get your hopes up, and she never did call so I never did tell you." He offered a feeble shrug. "And then I was so annoyed on your behalf that I texted her yesterday morning and pretty much—"

"Reamed me out?" Aunt Lauren stood in front of them, the smile she'd worn a moment ago now faltering and uncertain, with just the faintest hint of amusement as she regarded Lucas.

And then her gaze returned to Jenessa, all softness and light, just like she remembered. "Jenessa Marie."

"What are you doing here? After all this time . . . I don't even know what to say. Just . . . why are you here?"

Her aunt's skin was still smooth and her voice, unchanged. "Because when you get a text that long from a distraught man demanding you stop hurting your niece . . ." Her blue eyes, so similar to the ones Jenessa saw staring back at her whenever she looked in a mirror, filled with tears. "You realize you have to listen."

Emotion clogged in Jenessa's throat. She didn't know what to do, what to say. Didn't even know who to look at, her gaze straying from the woman she'd thought she'd never see again to the man who'd compelled her to come.

A man who watched her with so much gentle care and concern right now, she wanted nothing more than to shoo everyone else away just for a moment. Just long enough to tell him all over again that he was the best man she knew.

But the kids were shivering and Cade was starting to fuss.

And Aunt Lauren was standing in front of her, waiting.

"Jen, if you want to go rinse off and get dressed real quick so you can spend some time with your aunt, I can take care of the kids." Lucas's palm warmed her back. "We still have an hour before checkout."

"There's a coffee shop in the lobby," her aunt added. "I could wait for you there."

She gave a befuddled nod and minutes later, she was standing in a hot shower, washing the chlorine from her hair, but the shock clung to her as stubbornly as her wet swimsuit and the smell of the pool. She hurried through the motions of finishing the shower, drying off, dressing, throwing the rest of her things into her suitcase.

She knocked on the door that joined her room to Lucas's. His muffled voice reached her before he did. "Vi, please stop jumping on the bed. You've already got one broken arm." The door swung open and he appeared, still in his swim trunks, but he'd pulled a t-shirt over top.

He spoke instantly. "I'm sorry if I messed up, Jen. I was trying to do something good, but if I shouldn't have—"

She interrupted his apology with a kiss she'd been saving up for too long. And it wasn't the kiss she wanted to give him—something lingering and unforgettable and packed with a gratitude she could never hope to fully express—but it would have to do for now.

She should've ordered decaf. She was jittery enough without drinking this grande French roast.

But without the coffee, she wouldn't know what to do with her hands. And her first sip or two at least allowed her to stall. Because she didn't know what to say.

All these years of wishing to talk to her again and you can't find a single solitary sentence?

"Nice coffee shop," she finally managed. "I like that it's not a chain. Has more personality. Not as much as Coffee Coffee, of course, but . . ."

Aunt Lauren seemed as uncomfortable as she was. She was seated across from Jenessa, her mug of chai tea steaming in front of her. "Coffee Coffee?"

"Oh, it opened, I don't know, seven or eight years ago. Maybe nine. Long after . . ." *After you left. Disappeared. Abandoned me to an insufferable old mansion and parents who didn't understand me.*

But the mansion wasn't insufferable any longer.

And as for her parents, she'd tried—she'd really tried—to make her peace with their relationship in their final years. It would probably always hurt that they'd set her to the side. That their family didn't have what others did.

But living back at Belville Park now, watching the gardens take shape under Lucas's care—it'd helped her more and more look forward instead of backward.

Clearly, though, she hadn't moved past her questions and longings and tangled emotions regarding Aunt Lauren. She'd sent that magazine and gala invitation last week, after all.

And she was a bundle of fluttering nerves now. *Just ask her.* "Why'd you leave? Why didn't you say goodbye? Why didn't you call or write? And when I found you and tried reaching out—over and over—why did you ignore me?"

The clatter of the coffee shop rose around her—groaning machines, clinking dishes, voices. But her focus didn't leave her aunt's face.

"Jenessa, I . . ." Aunt Lauren's hands shook as she tried lifting her mug of tea. But she gave up halfway to her mouth, set it back on her saucer. "I hate what I did to you," she finally whispered. "I didn't want to leave. I knew I was abandoning you and I hated it."

"So why did you do it? I know you and Mom didn't really get along, but it's not like you lived in the same house. If you needed more space from her, you could've bought a house across town. Or even moved to a new town, but still been a part of our lives." Her fingers squeezed the handle of her tall cup. "A part of my life."

Aunt Lauren shook her head, letting tears spill down her cheeks without bothering to wipe them away. "I promised my sister. I owed it to her after I . . ." She sniffed, closed her eyes, took a breath as if desperate for the resolve she needed to continue. "Jenessa, your father and I had an affair. It was short-lived and tumultuous and by far the worst thing I've ever done."

Every jittering nerve inside her went still.

"Not the worst thing," Aunt Lauren said in a hushed tone. "The worst thing was leaving you."

"You . . . and Dad?"

"Your mom found us and it was horrible." She pulled a napkin from the holder at the edge of the table. "She told me to leave, to never come back. Made me promise to stay out of their lives forever."

That memory came ghosting in—that day she'd come home from school. Dad's yells, Mom's sobs. Aunt Lauren running from the house, never to return. Never any explanation from her parents. Never again the warmth she'd once felt, if not at the mansion, at least in the cottage out back.

Until Colie and Violet and Cade had come to live with her. Until Lucas had moved into the cottage. For days now, weeks, they'd felt like a family. A complicated, cobbled together, *perfect* family.

"That promise included skipping your own sister's funeral? Ignoring me when I tried to reconnect?"

Aunt Lauren looked away, eyes still glassy. "That's what I told myself, but I think the truth is, I couldn't bear the thought of telling you, of confessing." She dabbed her eyes with the napkin. "I'm so very sorry, Jenessa. I've never, ever stopped regretting, wishing . . ."

She had so many questions—about Dad, the affair, why her parents had stayed together in the aftermath. But what did any of it matter? It was too disturbing to think about. A piece of her wanted to rail against her father, but what good would that do?

Aunt Lauren was here. She could rail against her.

But how did a person lash out at someone whose sorrow was near tangible? It wasn't that she didn't feel a degree of anger toward the woman, but it was mixed in with so many other emotions, she might not have known how to express it if she tried.

"How was it that Lucas could convince you to meet with me and I couldn't?"

Aunt Lauren looked back to Jenessa. "I couldn't take it anymore—wondering about you, missing you." She offered a thin smile. "And in his first voicemail, he said something about how he'd prayed all day before calling. He sounded so sweet and endearing. And every maternal feeling I'd ever had toward you as a child reared up in me so fierce, I just had to come. I had to see you and meet this man who's obviously head over heels in love with you. I had to make sure I approved."

Her first instinct was to tell her aunt she didn't have the right to approve or not approve anymore.

But she couldn't. Not when there was finally one emotion clambering to the surface, doing its very best to drown out all the others. A childlike yearning to be safe and loved and secure. "I missed you so much." Her voice broke.

She gave in and let herself cry.

"What is it with fathers?"

Lucas said it so quietly he wasn't sure Jen had even heard it above the humming heater and the closing credits of the cartoon playing on the DVD system in the back. Cade had been asleep for an hour and Violet for at least the past thirty minutes.

He glanced in his rearview mirror. Colie leaned against the window, eyes closed.

"My dad, your dad." His gone for most of his childhood. Jen's physically present but emotionally distant. And after what Jen's aunt had told her today—well, his father wasn't the only one who shielded a tight secret. "I know we're trying to keep an open mind about the Hollis dad, but fathers in general just aren't looking so good in my book these days."

Jen held out a bag of Twizzlers. He'd lost count of how many he'd eaten twenty miles ago.

"I happen to know there are some spectacularly good dads out there," she said. "Look at Sam. He never gets all the time he wants with Mackenzie, but he pours himself into the relationship as best he can. He'd give anything to have full custody."

She was right. And Marshall used to have a daughter. She'd died two years before he'd come to Maple Valley. Lucas had no doubt the man had loved her more than his own life. And if Marshall and Mara ever had kids, they'd be incredible parents.

"Look at your grandpa," she added. "He might not have technically been your dad, but the way you talk about him makes him sound like he was everything a father should be—supportive, loving, hard-working."

"And he loved my grandma. Not in a boisterous, showy way or anything, but just by quietly standing beside her through whatever came their way."

Wispy clouds drifted over the evening sky, the waning rays of a burnt amber sun reaching out as if through flimsy gossamer. They'd made this trip stretch as long as possible. When he'd met Jenessa in the lobby of the hotel, her aunt had asked if she could treat them all to lunch. He'd looked to Jen before agreeing, wanting to make sure she was comfortable with it. Though traces of earlier tears had still been evident on her face, she'd nodded.

And he'd watched all through lunch at the restaurant as a timid hope bloomed in her. He could see it in the way she slowly opened up to her aunt, sharing about her college years, her stint as a paralegal, her efforts at the newspaper. She'd mentioned that high school boyfriend who she'd been with for too many years—shooting him a glance and grinning when he scowled.

When the kids were finally full and their table a disaster, he'd rounded them up while Jen hugged her aunt. It wasn't the full, comfortable embrace he knew she was capable of, but still—there'd been fresh tears in both of their eyes. Her aunt had promised to come visit.

After that, they'd taken the kids to the Mall of America, let them spend a couple hours on rides before finally loading back into the SUV and hitting the road for home. They were about forty minutes from Maple Valley now, moving down I-35 and soon to turn onto Highway 30 and head west into the sunset.

He couldn't help thinking it'd be nice to just keep going. Take these kids who didn't belong to him and this woman who did—he really hoped she did, hoped she knew he belonged to her—and just keep driving.

Except that'd be kidnapping.

And Jen had the newspaper and he had the final touches to make on her garden before the gala, not to mention a father and half-brother who might still be waiting for him to acknowledge them.

Unless they'd given up and Dad had ditched town. But Kit would've said something.

Then again, maybe she had. He didn't know when he'd last looked at his phone. For all he knew, she could've texted anytime today to say Dad had tired of lingering in Maple Valley. But he'd given his phone to Violet somewhere on the other side of the Iowa–Minnesota border so she could play a game and who knew where it was now.

"You sound a lot like him."

"What?" He spared Jen another glance. Her dark hair was a riot of wind-blown waves and orange sunlight traced her profile.

"Your grandpa. Quietly standing beside your grandma. A person could describe you the same way."

"I did quietly stand beside Grandma a lot. Especially in church during hymns, but then she'd give me that look that meant business and I'd finally start singing."

Jenessa tapped him with a Twizzler. "You know that's not what I meant."

For all the strangeness of this week—knowing Dad was just a few miles outside of Maple Valley, dealing with the knowledge that he'd have to say goodbye to these kids soon, processing the fact that he had a brother and wondering how long they'd go on avoiding each other—there'd been this one ceaseless and wondrously bright spot.

Jenessa Belville had become the everyday presence in his life that gave new purpose to his days. She knew his secrets. He'd glimpsed her deeper emotions. Had he ever felt so connected to someone?

"I have to tell you something, Jen."

She shifted in her seat, let the bag of licorice slide into the console between them. He steered onto the exit ramp.

"I made a decision. I'm not even sure when. It's just that at some point it stopped even being a question to me." He wished he could park the car and look in her eyes as he said this. But maybe it was enough to sense her gaze and savor the familiarity of it. "I'm not going back to Bridgewell."

He heard her quick inhale. Glanced away from the road long enough to see the joy-filled smile she tried to contain.

"It's okay. You can be happy about it. I'm happy about it."

"Seriously? 'Cause, Luke, anytime we've talked about it, you've worn this look of pride—a good kind of pride, I think. You're obviously good at what you do or else you wouldn't have made the elite team. I don't want to be the reason you lose something important to you. It'd be way too selfish of me."

He freed one hand from the wheel and reached across to grasp hers. "But I'm not losing it. I'm giving it up for something better."

She stopped attempting to hold in her elation. It glowed in her face and danced in her eyes.

Or, no, wait . . . that twirling light wasn't only the brightness of her gaze. With a groan, he looked in his rearview mirror. "I think I'm getting pulled over right now. What a way to ruin the moment."

But Jen was still smiling even as he released her hand and pulled onto the shoulder. "A speeding ticket can't ruin this, Lucas. Not a chance."

He braked. "Yeah, but I don't think I was speeding." And why was there a second police car now angling in front of him, hemming in their vehicle?

Trepidation gathered in his throat and made a slow trek through him. He had his window down and his wallet out by the time the first officer reached his door. For a moment, the cop didn't say a word—just flashed a light in his face, in Jen's, then toward the back of the vehicle.

The officer gave Lucas a grim stare as he lifted his walkie-talkie. "Yeah, Rogers, this is Bloomdale. I'm reporting in on that attempted kidnapping."

18

"This is completely insane."

Jenessa started around the counter in the police department in Ames, but one look from the officer in charge and she halted. How in the world was this happening? *Kidnapping?*

At least the officers who'd "escorted" them to the station, even the cop frowning at her now, all seemed to believe her story. Which wasn't a story at all—just the truth. But apparently Carmen was the one she had to convince, and the social worker hadn't arrived yet.

"If we were going to kidnap the Hollis children, why would we have been on the way back to Maple Valley when you pulled us over?"

The officer in charge, Captain Rogers, leaned over the counter. "We'll get this cleared up as soon as Ms. Rodriguez arrives, I'm sure. I have a feeling the whole thing was a misunderstanding, but surely you can understand that we needed to take a report of missing children seriously."

"I don't see how they can even technically be considered

missing since I'm their temporary legal guardian. They're with exactly the person they're supposed to be with."

"Jen." Lucas's soft voice called to her from the row of chairs where he sat with the kids. Cade was sound asleep on his lap and Violet nearly so beside him. Colie, though, was wide awake on his other side. "Come sit down," Lucas murmured, one hand splayed over Cade's back.

She took the chair beside Violet, placing an arm around her and smoothing the girl's hair. "How can you be so calm about this? It's outrageous."

"I know, but hopefully Carmen will get here soon and—"

The glass door nearby pushed open and the woman herself hurried in. She took one look at Jen and Lucas, the kids gathered around them, and sighed. "Hi. I apologize that this got blown out of proportion."

"Blown out of proportion?" Jen was on her feet again in an instant. "You told the police we kidnapped—"

"No, that's not how it went." Carmen glanced at Colie, sitting up straight and taking in every word. She turned to Officer Rogers. "Is there a room where I can talk with Ms. Belville and Mr. Danby?"

Since when did she know Lucas's last name? Had Jenessa mentioned it?

"Don't you think the kids have been through enough by now?" Jen argued. "I'd like to get them home—"

"We're going to talk first. The kids will be fine out here for a few minutes." Carmen's voice brooked no argument.

Lucas's slow exhale indicated his resignation. He stood, touched Colie's shoulder, silently communicating. She moved into the chair beside Violet and opened her arms for Lucas to lower Cade.

They followed Officer Rogers down a hallway and into what looked like a conference room. He gave Jen a look of apology before closing the door. Lucas lowered into a chair, appearing composed and ready for whatever was about to come.

But Jenessa couldn't just sit down and take whatever Carmen was about to throw their way. This was so *wrong*. Every little bit of it. "How could you possibly think—"

"You didn't send your nightly check-in email last night," Carmen interrupted. "I called this morning and you didn't answer."

Jenessa's mind raced. It was true—in the busyness of packing a bag for each of the kids, hitting the road, and then swimming at the hotel, she'd completely forgotten the email last night. And she'd seen Carmen's call lighting up her phone this morning, but she'd been with Aunt Lauren and . . . once again, she'd just forgotten. They'd gone out for lunch and then Lucas had given his phone to Violet so she could play a game, and Colie had asked if Jen had any games on her phone. Only spider solitaire, which had been enough for Colie, who'd announced an hour later that the phone's battery had run out.

That was a good two hours ago. She explained it all to Carmen, but the woman wasn't even close to satisfied. Apparently, Sam too had tried calling and texting both Jenessa and Lucas after Carmen had contacted him.

"I went to your house this afternoon. Then your office. And your reporter said you'd taken a couple of days off. She said something about you going out of state."

"And you automatically translated that as we *kidnapped* the children?"

Carmen shook her head. "I never used that word. But when I spoke to the police, I did have reason to believe that you'd left town because you wanted to avoid turning over custody to the children's father and—"

"They didn't have school today." Jenessa finally let

herself sit. "We just wanted to do something fun with them. We were on our way home." *Home.* Except it wasn't Colie or Violet or Cade's home. Tears filled her eyes and Lucas reached for her hand, gave it an assuring squeeze.

"I truly am sorry for how out of hand this got. But please try to see where I was coming from. You left town on the day Dustin Hollis was scheduled to catch a flight to Iowa. You're with a man who"—she turned her focus on Lucas—"has his own criminal history."

"He doesn't have a criminal history." Jenessa felt Lucas's grip tighten.

"Jen—" he started, but she interrupted.

"He served a prison sentence for an Army-related issue, yes, but that's not a criminal history. You're making him sound like he's a repeat felon when the truth is, he's upstanding and noble, and if you knew what he's been doing in the years since then—"

Lucas interjected, "Jen, please."

But when she looked to him, he only shook his head.

Carmen filled the silence. "I looked him up, Ms. Belville. I know his history. I know he doesn't stay put in one place for long." She spoke as if Lucas wasn't sitting right here, listening to her degrade him. "He's done drastic things before, including things that led to a dishonorable discharge from the military. It wasn't all that big of a stretch to think the both of you had become attached to the kids and each other and decided to do something drastic together."

Lucas's hold on her hand went slack. It was as if she could feel any sense of assurance or worth draining from him. *Say something, Lucas. Tell her she has it wrong.*

When he didn't speak, Jenessa wetted her lips. "That's quite an imaginative conjecture. And it's completely inaccurate. I've only ever tried to do what's good and helpful for the kids. I adore them, and yes, I'm obviously attached. But I know what's coming. I wasn't running away from it."

"I understand that now. And again, I apologize for the misunderstanding." Carmen tapped her glasses farther up the bridge of her nose. "My job is to look out for the children's safety and wellbeing first and foremost, but I realize that in my concern and distress over their whereabouts, I misconstrued the circumstances."

"Can we leave now?" Lucas finally spoke again.

Carmen only spared him a brief glance. "First we need to talk about what will happen tomorrow. I've spoken to Dustin twice now. He's got a red-eye flight tonight. He won't arrive in Iowa until early tomorrow morning. He's going to catch some sleep in a hotel and then come to my office in Ames."

Then it was really happening. What she'd known was coming was less than twenty-four hours away.

"I'm going to spend some time talking with him. But unless there are any immediate red flags . . ." She waited until Jenessa met her eyes. "We'll come together to your house to pick up the children. I'll text you before leaving. Please have everything ready and packed."

"Do you know where he'll be taking them from there?"

Carmen nodded. "The rental they were living in before is still available. He was able to make arrangements to pay a deposit. That's a small but good step in the right direction." Carmen folded her hands atop the table. "But the DHS case will still be open for some time. I'll be meeting with Dustin regularly, checking up on the situation to make sure the kids are taken care of."

Jenessa knew she was only setting herself up for false hope if she asked the question, but she couldn't stop herself. "If . . . if things don't go well, if it turns out Dustin Hollis ends up needing to go back to Alaska or decides he doesn't want to be responsible for the children, is there any chance . . . I just need you to know that I would open up my home to those kids at any time. For however long." *For forever.*

For the first time since they'd walked into the conference room, Carmen's regard came close to softening. "I know what you're asking, Jenessa. And we just don't know what the future will hold. I always like to see families restored, but I also know that sometimes families can be knit together by something other than blood relation."

She must've known Jenessa would latch on too tightly to that last sentence because she went on quickly. "But I can tell you that any sort of longer-term custody arrangement would come with many more complications and requirements than a temporary emergency situation."

Why did Carmen's gaze flick to Lucas just then? What was she trying to say?

"There's no point, though, in ruminating on any of that now. Not when we don't know how things with Dustin Hollis will play out."

Lucas was so still beside her. So painfully quiet, even for him. Carmen stood, perhaps sensing they needed a moment alone. But when she silently left the room, Lucas only stared at the top of the table.

"Luke, the things Carmen said . . ." She touched his arm and he flinched.

"Let's just go home." He rose, reached for her hand. But it didn't comfort her the way it should.

A sleepless night was only going to make this conversation more difficult. But Lucas had put it off long enough.

Through his windshield, Lucas stared at the age-worn

farmhouse where he'd spent so much of his childhood. The pale light of morning washed over its faded gray siding and windows. Kit kept saying one of these days she was going to scrape off the peeling paint and freshen up the place, at which point Beckett usually chimed in and said it'd be easier to hire out the job.

And then the both of them would lapse into contented sighs, acknowledging they cared more about their fifty acres of land and nearly five thousand trees than the exterior of an old house.

Their conversations had never failed to fan the flame of his desire for that kind of belonging, home, family. Too often in the past, his longing had flickered down into mere sparks. But the past weeks had been so packed with fresh kindling that now he was afire with hope and even something like certainty.

And when he'd told Jenessa last night that he was giving up Bridgewell, he'd truly believed his future burned bright and promising.

Until a new storm doused his optimism. It wasn't the police or even the shock of what Carmen had assumed. It'd been what the social worker said. And then what she didn't say but clearly implied.

That if there was any lingering chance of Jenessa having a future with the children, his presence was a complication.

Even now, the realization, the pain of it, twisted and clenched inside him. He'd tried praying last night, but the silence that had filled his years in Afghanistan, in prison, revisited him now.

I know I said I was going to try, God. But what's the point if You won't speak to me? Help me?

He pushed open his truck door. He had as little optimism for this conversation to come with his father as he did his other worries. But the one thing he'd known this morning was that he couldn't keep avoiding it. Even if only for Kit's sake, he needed to step up.

And he needed to get it out of the way first thing so he could be back at Jen's side when Dustin Hollis showed up.

The first frost of fall had visited overnight, leaving a glassy white sheen over the hardened grass underfoot. At least he'd thought to cover the gardens with tarp before he and Jen had left town the other night. Only a week and a half until the gala, but it felt part of a distant future. Too far away to dwell on with all the concerns of the present.

Kit must have seen him coming. She appeared on the porch steps, cup of coffee in hand, but she promptly set it on the wide railing and pulled him into a hug. "I'm really glad you're here, Lucas."

"I feel bad that I abandoned you with him for this long."

She pulled back, not quite smiling, but not frowning either. "Honestly, I think it's for the best. I have a feeling he could only handle the reactions of one of his adult offspring at a time."

"Yeah, but he deserves to face both—all three—of us."

Surprisingly, Kit chuckled. "He does. But Luke . . ." She handed him the mug, nodded to let him know she'd meant it for him. "While he's made awful choices, if there's one thing that's become clear to me in the past three days, it's that he's been facing the consequences of the choices day after day for years. He's been punished by guilt and regret and, believe it or not, even a sense of loss."

Lucas lifted one shoulder. "Good." He probably sounded spiteful, but he was too tired and too churned up to care.

"I'm not saying I'm over it," Kit went on. "Or even that I'm ready to have some kind of relationship with him. But my wise husband reminded me the other night that carrying the burden of feeling like it's my job to see that he's suffered enough for his choices is just pointless. Keeps me from processing my own emotions and reactions."

"Beckett is pretty wise." But Beckett also had a father whose love was so evident the whole town looked to the Walker family as a paragon of kinship and togetherness. "Anyway, you don't have to worry that I'm going to go in there and give him a black eye or anything."

She laughed again. "Hey, don't think I didn't want to. Or that Beck didn't. Or Noah especially."

"How is Noah?" Lucas had gone from a mentor with good intentions to probably a complete failure. And the guy was his half-brother? He still couldn't comprehend it.

"He's . . . quiet." She leaned on the porch railing. "You know, now that I know who he really is, I can see some resemblance. Dad's ears, your nose." She paused. "Again, I'm not saying I'm suddenly in a great place with all of this. But I do think there might come a day when we look back and realize that at least one good thing came from it. We know our half-brother now. I used to wish I was from a big family like the Walkers, and yet, my own family is bigger than I realized."

Except it wasn't exactly *their* family. It was Dad's *other* family. But what good would it do to point that out to Kit? She'd handled this whole thing with so much more grace and maturity than he had.

"Sometimes I can't believe you're the younger sibling, Kit. Beck's not the only wise one in your marriage."

She squeezed his arm. "He's in the kitchen—Dad, I mean. There's leftover waffles from earlier if you haven't eaten yet. Beckett's already at the orchard, and he took Noah with him."

Good. He'd need to talk to Noah eventually, but one difficult conversation at a time suited him just fine.

"Thanks."

Kit moved down the porch steps. With a sigh of reluctance, he let himself into the house. The aroma of breakfast —maple syrup and coffee—engulfed him as he tugged off his shoes and started for the kitchen.

He found his father just where Kit said he would, sitting at the table with an empty plate and empty coffee mug, this week's issue of the *Maple Valley News* open but disregarded in front of him. "Morning, son."

Son. "Uh, Kit mentioned waffles." He looked to the counter, opened a cupboard, and grabbed a plate just so he wouldn't have to look at his father yet.

"I'm glad you're here."

Same thing Kit had said, but it was filled with more awkward intensity than any one sentence should be able to hold. Lucas didn't respond. Instead, he took his time adding a waffle to his plate, slathering on butter, syrup, walnuts. As if he had any appetite at all.

Finally, when he couldn't find any other reason to stall, he walked to the table and sat across from his father.

Dad didn't wait more than a moment. "I don't have any excuses, Lucas. But I can give you the facts if that'd help. I met Nancy Johannson three years after your mother died. She was a nurse on the base. You and Kit were still living with your aunt at the time."

Lucas cut a square from his waffle but didn't bother lifting it to his mouth.

"Eventually Noah came along. We weren't married and Nancy wanted him to have her last name. She doesn't have siblings, wanted to keep the Johannson name going. I didn't argue. And . . . and I suppose I became comfortable with things as they were, thinking of my life in two parts."

Lucas couldn't avoid meeting his father's gray eyes any longer. "Except there wasn't really two parts. There was the family you actually cared about and invested in and the family you didn't."

"I did come visit, Lucas. When I realized you'd be better off with your grandparents, I moved you here. I thought it was the right thing at the time." He rubbed his jaw, frustration in the movement. "I know I was—I am—a pitiful excuse for a father."

"What I don't get is why." He cut into his waffle again, but once again, only pushed the bite around his plate.

"Why didn't I tell you about Nancy? Or Noah? I wish I had an explanation that makes sense. At first, I think I felt guilty for being happy with Nancy but later—"

"No, why you left us in the first place." Was it the accusation in his brash words that seemed to steal every last ounce of rigidity from his father's bearing? Or the hurt he wished he could've concealed, the rasp in his voice surely giving him away?

Dad shifted in his seat, one hand clenching the edge of the table, the other rubbing his chest. He opened his mouth, closed it, swallowed. "It was a mistake."

"Obviously."

"It was . . . it was the horrible decision of a man who didn't know how to exist without his wife."

"If you expect me to feel bad for you—"

"I don't. Lord knows, I don't expect anything from you."

Lucas finally gave up on his waffle and abandoned his fork. "Then why are you even here? Did you know Flagg was sending Noah and you suddenly got worried we'd all discover the truth? Or . . . ?" He saw the shift in his father's eyes, realized what it meant. "Oh. Right. Of course. You were playing chess with Noah's life just like you did mine. *You* sent him to Flagg. Probably even suggested to Flagg that he send him to me."

Dad didn't argue.

"So maybe you wanted us to figure out everything. Wanted some kind of relief from your guilt."

His dad looked him square in the eye. "Yes, maybe that. But maybe I've also seen enough of my firstborn's life from afar to know he's what my youngest son needed. Lucas—"

He stood so swiftly, he bumped the table, sending his fork clattering to the floor. "No. If this is going to shift into some conversation where you tell me you admire the man I've become, I don't want to hear it. If there's anything honorable in me today, it's not because of you."

He sounded wilted and bitter, he knew. More like an angry teenager than an adult who just last Sunday had felt the blossoming of a renewed faith. Who just yesterday had reveled in Jenessa's whispered assertion that he'd make a good father.

But he was really just a wounded son.

And he wasn't ready for this.

"Dad, I don't have any more to say right now."

"I have one more thing to say—"

He started toward the door. "I'm not in the right head space for this."

"It's not about me or the past. It's about your future."

He halted.

"I've been talking to a JAG officer about appealing your dishonorable discharge."

He turned. Slowly. "That's impossible. There's a time restriction—"

"The review board makes exceptions in special circumstances, and we've already convinced them these are special circumstances. They're going to grant you a hearing, Lucas."

He could only stare at his father, speechless, numb.

"I have to leave tomorrow morning. Can we talk about this again before I go?"

"I don't . . . I . . ."

His father's gaze turned almost pleading. "You had PTSD. That wasn't taken into near enough consideration during your court-martial. And the JAG who was assigned to your case didn't have a clue what he was doing. We can get that dishonorable off your record. Son, if you'll just—"

It was that word again—*son*—that shoved into him with such force he nearly stumbled as he spun and walked away.

Jenessa would not cry in front of the kids.

No matter the jagged edges of her broken heart, piercing her from the inside out, she would not cry in front of them.

She knelt in front of Violet in the entryway, helping her shrug one arm into her fall coat then pulling the other sleeve carefully over her little cast. Outside the window, the wind howled and the nearly white sky seemed braced for snow. Looked more like a Thursday in December than October.

"I don't remember what he looks like." Violet still had a trace of frosting on her lips from the sprinkled donuts they'd been eating thirty-five minutes ago when Carmen had texted to say she and Dustin Hollis were on the way. It was more than Jenessa would've normally given the girls for a snack but on this, their last afternoon to sit in the sunroom and talk about the school day, she'd splurged.

She licked her finger then smudged away the frosting on Violet's lips. "Didn't Colie show you that photo of your mom and dad this morning?"

She could feel Colie shift her weight from one foot to the other where she stood behind her.

"Yeah, but you can only see the side of his face in it and I can't even tell what color his hair is. Do you remember what color his hair is, Colie?"

"Brown." Colie's voice was flat.

"Is he nice?"

Jenessa looked over her shoulder in time to see Colie's limp shrug. The older girl wore the locket Jenessa had given her. It peeked out from the same faded jean jacket she'd worn the night Jenessa had found the kids in the cottage, the one with the too-short sleeves that bared her wrists. Jenessa had bought her a new coat last week, but maybe something in the girl had needed to wear the old thing. Needed the hint of familiarity.

I don't even know what to pray anymore, God. I know I need to pray that Dustin Hollis is a good man. That he fills their house with love and joy.

But it felt like all the love and joy was about to leak from *this* house. And it was breaking her.

She turned to Cade. He'd already managed to unzip his coat and pull off his hat. His car seat and Violet's sat nearby, along with the diaper bag, suitcases, folded-up Pack 'n Play, tote bags full of toys and books. The better part of a month's worth of life together represented in a pile of belongings.

It made her think of her parents' things. Of all the boxes that used to clutter this house. Things that had lost their meaning somewhere along the way.

Would there come a time when Colie looked at the locket Jenessa had given her as just a necklace and not a memento of this time together? Would Violet eventually forget these weeks the same way she'd forgotten the color of her father's hair?

I'll never forget. Couldn't even if she wanted to. And deep down, underneath the heartbreak, she didn't want to.

287

Painful as it was to part ways now, she wouldn't have traded this experience for anything. She stood, lifting Cade with her, kissing his cheek. "I hope you guys know how much I'll miss you. These have been the very best three weeks."

She felt Lucas's warm hand on her shoulder. He'd been here for the past hour. Had eaten donuts with the girls and changed Cade's diaper and quietly helped Jenessa pack the last of their things. He'd gone to see his dad this morning, but she knew he didn't want to talk about it. Knew too that things were still a little off after that conference room conversation with Carmen last night.

But they both seemed to sense without words that these final minutes were simply about this goodbye. Everything else could wait.

As if on cue, the rumble of an engine let her know a vehicle had pulled into the driveway. She looked out the window by the front door, recognized Carmen's car, and behind it, a blue four-door sedan that must belong to Dustin.

"He does have brown hair," Violet said.

Colie stepped up beside Jenessa and took her hand. "I'm going to miss you too."

Was it her sister's words that unleashed the emotion in Violet or just a sudden realization of what was happening? Either way, abrupt emotion erupted from her. She broke into loud sobs and threw herself against Jenessa.

With a helpless look toward Lucas, Jenessa handed Cade over and bent down to pull Violet into her arms. Violet's loud cries apparently upset Cade because before she knew it, he was crying from his perch in Lucas's hold.

And that was the scene Carmen and Dustin walked in on. Two crying kids. The third trying so achingly hard to be stoic. The next minutes passed in a blur as Carmen introduced Dustin and they went about loading the kids' things and arranging car seats in Dustin's car.

Jenessa finally managed to calm Violet long enough for her whispered words of comfort to be heard. "Remember how much you told me you liked your old bed in your old room? That's where you get to sleep again tonight. You'll have Private Teddy with you and Colie will be there. She's such a good big sister to you."

She looked up at Colie, the tears in the older girl's eyes almost enough to make her forget her promise to herself. *You will not cry in front of the kids. You won't.*

She hugged Violet one more time, rose to kiss Cade's cheek, and left Lucas to say his goodbyes to the younger two. She moved to Colie, drawing the girl into a tight hug. "I'll never forget the day I found you in my cottage, Colie Hollis. It was the best surprise I've ever gotten."

They couldn't prolong this any further. Dustin Hollis had been pure politeness during their introductions, but his uncomfortable impatience was beginning to show now. He kept shifting his weight from side to side, attention darting between Lucas with the younger two children and Jenessa and Colie's embrace, the brackets around his thin lips deepening with each strained second that passed.

It was time.

"Violet already has an appointment to get her cast off next week." She almost handed the appointment card to Carmen, but at the last second held it toward Dustin instead. "Colie has a math test on Tuesday."

Dustin nodded, running one hand over his buzzed hair. "I appreciate what you've done for my kids. Thank you."

"You're welcome." It felt like the paltriest conversation she'd ever had. Traded words that couldn't possibly capture the intensity or emotion of this moment.

And then it was just . . . over.

The kids were in the car. The car was pulling from the driveway. Carmen was saying goodbye and leaving as well.

And Lucas was pulling her close. "You held it in long enough," he whispered. "Go ahead and let it out now."

His shirt was already wet with her tears.

19

*E*ven with this many people packed around Jenessa's desk, her office felt too empty. None of Cade's toys littering the space. No portable crib in the corner.

But her friends were here. And that was something.

With only two spare chairs in the office, Mara looked only too happy to be perched on her new husband's lap as she talked about the ten-day honeymoon they'd spent at a cabin in Canada. "Autumn is pretty in Iowa, but up there with the lake and the trees—"

"And the lack of other people," Marshall cut in with a grin.

Mara didn't miss a beat. "It was absolute perfection."

Sam grabbed a second pastry from the bakery box in the middle of Jenessa's desk. "We're going to have to look at pictures, aren't we?"

Mara shot him a playful glare. "Not until tonight. We're going to have a good old-fashioned Friday pizza and movie night. Everyone in?"

Jenessa nodded. She knew what her friends were doing

and she loved them for it, even if she was having a hard time latching on to the comfort and cheer of their presence.

It'd been a week and a day since the kids left with Dustin Hollis. She hadn't seen them since. Colie had called once over the weekend and it'd been clear it was a supervised call. She'd heard Dustin's voice in the background urging her to end the call after about ten minutes.

Jenessa was back to putting in longer hours at the newspaper, but if she'd begun to lose her vigor for the work before the Hollis kids came along, she was entirely bereft of it now. She couldn't seem to rally any excitement for tomorrow night's gala either.

Still, she forced a happy tone. "We should save a pastry for Paige. I owe her for all the extra work she's put in the past few weeks."

"I think that might be our cue," Marshall said, gently nudging Mara off his lap and rising. "Jen, you'll pass on the movie night invite to Luke?"

Sam barked a *harrumph*. "As if she needs to. He follows her around more than ever." He stood and stretched, turning to the newlyweds. "There have been, ah, developments since the wedding."

Marshall smirked. "Way I heard it, there were developments before the wedding."

From somewhere underneath her rainy spirits, Jenessa unearthed the closest thing she had to a light-hearted expression and directed it Mara's way. "I guess now that you're married, it means all girl talk gets passed on to him."

Mara moved around the desk. "Well, you didn't tell me *not* to tell him." She hugged Jenessa as the guys filed from the office. "I'm sorry again that we weren't here last week. I know it's been hard."

"Mara, I told you before, you can't apologize for being

on your honeymoon. You were right where you were supposed to be."

"I'm just glad Lucas has been here for you."

He had. And yet . . .

Mara stepped back. "Uh-oh, what's that look mean?"

"Nothing." Or more accurately, a something she didn't want to talk about. Because it might all be in her head. Lucas was around, of course. He'd worked long days finishing the landscaping, putting the final touches on the garden, installing the new fountain. He'd come up to the house each night when he was finally ready to crash.

But instead of long conversations into the early hours of the morning like last week, more often than not they'd settled in front of the TV. He didn't seem distant so much as distracted.

But then, he was missing the kids too while also dealing with the fallout of his own family situation. Noah had gone back to staying at the cottage, but from what little Lucas said, though they worked together, they'd lost the easy rapport of earlier days.

"It's just weird. We can't seem to get past the awkwardness of it all. And I still don't understand why he didn't say something sooner."

"Things just feel a little off with Lucas," she finally said to Mara. "But I'm sure after the gala everything will settle down and we'll get back to how we used to be." Except there hadn't been a *we* before the kids.

Mara picked up her coat from the back of a chair but after a glance at Jenessa, she set it back down and lowered into the chair. "How are you really doing, Jen?"

The same old urge nearly prompted the same old response. *I'm fine. It's a hard season, but I'll get through it. I'm a Belville, after all.* A forced hopefulness. A hollow grin.

A pretense. *No.* She dropped into her chair. "Awful,

that's how I'm doing. I'm depressed about the kids being gone. I'm scared Lucas is pulling away. I can't bring myself to care about work. And I can hear any number of admonishing voices in my head telling me to have faith and trust God, and frankly, I want to tell every one of them to leave me alone."

She didn't wait for a response from Mara. Now that she'd started, she couldn't stop. "I don't know if I can talk myself into rebounding this time. Losing Aunt Lauren as a kid wrecked me. Feeling abandoned by parents—that messed with me, too. I have struggled to feel any kind of true purpose or belonging for *years*, and when I tried to think of what I wanted my life to look like, it was always just this blurry 'someday.' And then finally—*finally*—everything comes into focus. Those kids land on my doorstep. I realize I'm basically in love with my best friend. But in a blink, it's all gone and . . . and why in the world are you smiling right now?"

Mara flattened her expression. "I'm not smiling."

Exasperation pricked her. "I thought this is what you wanted! I'm baring my heart and soul. I'm admitting I'm depressed. I'm ticked at God. I've got like every ugly emotion going on at once. And you have the gall to be amused?"

"I'm not amused. It's just you said you were in love with your best friend and I couldn't help—"

"That can't be the only part you heard. Why aren't you telling me I should be grateful for what I have? Trying to cheer me up? Giving me a sermon? Trying to convince me that even though things feel awful and bleak today, I'll see God's hand in it all someday?"

Mara reached over Jenessa's desk and covered her hand. "Because I don't think that's really what you need right now."

"I know. What I need is for everything to work out exactly the way I want."

Mara squeezed her hand. "Don't we all."

Quiet seconds ticked by. "But if you were going to give me a sermon, what would you say?"

Mara studied her for a moment. "I'd probably say don't be afraid to wrestle with your faith. God's not going to ditch you the moment you get real with Him. I think He'd rather have your honest emotions any day over plastic smiles or some rote performance." Mara gave her hand a second squeeze. "The same goes for your friends, by the way. Thanks for being honest with me."

Sam and Marshall's voices drifted in from the newsroom. And someone else's voice. Jenessa glanced out the window. Noah? What was he doing here? "I'm glad you're home, Mara. I missed you more than I realized."

"Just don't give Marsh any credit. I had to drag him back. Turns out he might be even more of a hermit than Lucas."

"Or he just really liked having his wife to himself."

Mara's cheeks pinked. "A definite possibility." She stood again, glancing out the window. "Looks like someone else is here to see you. I should go." She reached for her coat once more. "About Lucas, though—*he's* not gone, Jen. He's not part of some unattainable, distant someday. He's right here today. And if you really do love him—"

"You're not going to let me forget I said that, are you?" Not that *she* could forget. She loved him. She loved Lucas Danby and she had no idea what to do with that.

"I'm just saying, as long as you're in baring-your-heart-and-soul mode, maybe consider telling him."

295

Lucas poked the last of the brushed nickel solar lights in the ground just as the approaching shadow overtook him. "Where've you been?"

He rose to face Noah, wishing the question hadn't come out so gruff. Wishing he knew how to bridge the tense distance between them. They were headed toward a confrontation one of these days, but with every day that passed, setting his world to rights felt more and more unlikely.

Between Noah and the phone calls from his father he continued to ignore and the ache in his gut when he thought of the Hollis kids, he was tangled in so many knots he didn't know which one to focus on first.

And threaded through the whole mess was what that social worker had said. He couldn't get her words out of his head. *"I can tell you that any sort of longer-term custody arrangement would come with many more complications and requirements than a temporary emergency situation."*

He was the complication. He knew it. And the requirement? Probably that if Jenessa were to have a partner in raising the children, it would need to be someone without a prison record. Without dishonor literally attached to his name.

He shouldn't let it bother him so much. The kids were gone. The chances of them returning were slim anyway.

But even without the kids in the equation, what did he *really* have to offer Jen? Look at how Herman Ferris had reacted when the mayor had mentioned that city job. What if Lucas never could find actual steady employment?

Sure, he'd always had a job waiting for him at the orchard, but it'd only ever been part-time and seasonal. He had no doubt Kit would stretch it to a year-round, full-time position if he asked, but no way would he do that—not when she and Beckett had a baby on the way.

He had plenty of savings from his time at Bridgewell, but it wasn't the money or income or job that bothered him. It was that feeling he couldn't shake that Jen deserved more. That even if his ugly past didn't faze her, his unpromising future might eventually become a drain on their relationship.

Or maybe just a drain on him. Which would, in turn, affect her.

"You're doing that la-la land thing again." Noah broke into his reverie.

He bent down to straighten the solar light he'd just placed. "You never answered my question. Where were you?"

"Running an errand."

It'd been like this for days—stilted questions and vague answers. Maybe he should just bite the bullet like he'd finally done with Dad. Except look where that had gotten him. More confused than ever. Dad wanted him back in D.C. in November. He assumed he was still going back to Bridgewell.

Flagg assumed the same, and he'd apparently talked to Dad. This, he knew, from a voicemail the man had left just yesterday. Lucas had been nearly as reluctant to talk to Flagg as he was his father. After all, the man had kept his acquaintance with Dad a secret for ten years now.

Was anyone *not* keeping secrets?

He leveled Noah with a look. "Should we just do this? Right now?"

Noah didn't have to ask what. "Go ahead. You gonna throw a punch or—"

"Why didn't you say something when you first realized who I was? Why lie for two weeks? What ulterior motive could you have possibly had?"

Noah stepped onto the stone path they'd laid last week.

"An ulterior motive? Dude, you do remember that I was basically sent here against my will, right? Unlike you, I *knew* Dad had pulled strings to get me a meeting with Flagg but—"

"Right. Because you actually have a relationship with him. Because he did things like wheelbarrow races with you. He—gasp—lived in the same house with you most of the time."

"That's not my fault." Noah paced the path. "I have no clue why he did what he did. I have no clue why we're the family he picked. But what's the point in taking it out on me?"

Lucas reached for another solar light, knelt to the ground, and stabbed it into the dirt. Too deep. "I'm not blaming you for his choices. I'm blaming you for your choice to not tell me the truth of who you are."

"You're really one to talk. How many years did you spend lying to all your friends about Mexico?" He made air quotes with his fingers on the last word. "Have you told more than one or two people how you got those scars? How about your court-martial? You weren't exactly shining rays of truth during that."

"You don't know what you're talking about." Knees still pressed to the ground, he avoided looking up.

Noah stopped in front of him. "If you get a pass for taking years to spill your secrets to the people who know you best, maybe I should get one for not knowing how to tell a stranger a secret I'd only just discovered myself." He kicked a light Lucas had just placed. "And you know what? I'm sick of hearing you complain about Dad not being around. It wasn't exactly easy *with* him around either."

He veered from the path and stalked to the edge of the garden.

"Noah—"

"Maybe Jen can talk some sense into you."

Lucas jerked to his feet "What?"

"Yeah, I stopped at her office. Go ahead and be mad at me for that, too. But she knows about the review board now. Maybe you'll listen to her." He marched away.

For a few hours, she'd almost been able to forget the hole in her heart.

The laughter with her friends, the coziness of the Everwood, Mara and Marshall's honeymoon pictures and stories . . . all of it was warmth to comfort the cold, empty spaces inside her. The spaces that should've been filled with the kids.

With Lucas.

She slid him a glance from the passenger seat of his truck. He'd let a hint of a beard shadow his face again and the dark green shirt he wore under an open flannel buttondown was one of her favorites. Under the low lights of the Everwood's den, the color had brought out the olive specks in his eyes.

But here in the truck, it was too dim to make out his mood by the shifting hues in his eyes. Still, she knew there was a storm brewing under his silence. She'd seen it so many times over the years. But she'd thought they were past the secrets.

Until Noah had come to the newspaper office today and spilled a new secret.

"I just think he should at least consider talking to my—our— father," he'd said. *"I know how much that discharge bothers him. It's okay if he's still ticked at Dad—believe me, I get it. But to not*

jump at that kind of chance just because it's Dad who's pulling the strings?"

Noah had asked her to talk to Lucas about it.

But why hadn't *Lucas* told her what his father was trying to do for him? Did he think she'd try to talk him out of going to D.C.? Or into it?

Was this just Lucas Danby doing his normal Lucas Danby thing? Quietly processing his thoughts until he was ready to share? Or did the fact that he hadn't mentioned this mean something more?

Stop. Lucas was about to show off his work in her backyard. He deserved her smiles and appreciation, not questions and overwrought emotion.

He pulled into the driveway by the house and cut the engine. "Can you wait just a minute? I'll go turn on all the lights so you get the full effect."

Whatever his hidden thoughts, his nervous eagerness to show her the gardens was evident enough. It was something to latch on to. "I can't wait to see it." It was mostly the truth, save the small piece of her that wondered if it'd be strange seeing Mom's gardens restored to their former glory. Would it stir old hurts? Or heal them?

He gave her a light kiss on the cheek. "Sit tight and I'll come back for you."

Silent seconds passed and she missed the warmth of the heater. But soon enough, he returned, opening her door for her and offering her his elbow once she stepped out.

"May I escort you to your own gardens, Miss Belville?"

It was the first glimpse of his playful side she'd seen in days. She hooked her arm through his elbow. "As you wish, Mr. Danby."

Bright moonlight peered from an inky black sky lavish with glimmering stars. A hushed wind hurried her steps through the side yard, or maybe that was Lucas's long strides. "Is this why you were distracted all evening at the Everwood? Anxious to show off your hard work?"

He laughed and oh, she'd missed that sound. Maybe this was all they'd needed in these last stressful days. Moonlight, stars, the magic of an October night. Her breath was white in the air and she should've worn a coat, but no matter. She was with Lucas.

Everything will be okay.

They emerged into the backyard and a gasp flew from her lips, the sight before her so stunning, so gorgeous she dropped her hold on Lucas's arm. "Oh my." Lights and lanterns illuminated the garden and the gentle trickling of the fountain in the center was lulling background music to the pure enchantment of what she was seeing. Three levels of garden beds spread over the yard, blanketed by tall grasses and plants, interspersed with potted flowers and lawn ornaments.

Lucas and Noah had pulled up the old brick path that cut through the gardens and replaced it with winding stone walkways bordered by lights. The area was dotted with benches.

"The whole place will look a little more cluttered tomorrow when Leigh and the event committee show up." Lucas's voice cut into her awe. "They'll add a big tent and tables here and there. I'm glad you're getting to see it like this first."

"I'm glad too." A shiver curled through her.

Lucas peeled off his flannel shirt and helped her shrug into it. "Outdoor space heaters will make a difference tomorrow."

"It's beautiful, Lucas. Every little inch of it. It's remarkable. I can't believe you did all this in just a few weeks. That you could take a neglected, overgrown yard and turn it into this . . . absolutely magical space." *You would've loved this, Mom. And Dad, too.*

For once, the thought of her parents didn't hurt. No, the Belvilles hadn't often been a happy family. But this would've made Mom and Dad happy. And there was a surprising amount of comfort in that.

She looked up at Lucas. "It even smells good."

He took hold of her hand and tugged her forward. "That's probably more the fountain than the plants. I got this stuff you can put in the water to add a scent. I like the honeysuckle, but there's also lavender, vanilla, maybe a rose one. Not sure how long it lasts."

She leaned close. "Actually, I think what I'm really smelling is your shirt. I don't know if it's soap or cologne or what, but it drives me crazy."

He eyed her.

"A good kind of crazy," she amended.

He slowed as they neared the fountain. "Good. A guy can't have his girl thinking he stinks."

She giggled and then gasped all over again when he pulled her into his arms.

"Sorry, it's just been too long since I kissed you, Jenessa Belville."

The cold she'd felt only moments ago was pushed away by a perfect, poignant warmth. "You just kissed me in the truck."

He leaned so close his nose touched hers. "That hardly counts."

And the moment his lips touched hers, she knew he had a point. A really, *really* good point. In fact, if he wanted to go on making his point indefinitely . . .

He pulled the barest breath away. "I've missed this," he whispered. "I've missed you. Ever since the kids left . . ."

She touched his stubbled cheek. "I'm sorry. I know I've been overly emotional and mopey and—"

"No." She felt his jaw move under her hand. "You have every right to hurt. The depth of your feelings is one of the things I love most about you."

Love. It was the first time he'd used the word, but somehow she knew it wasn't the first time he'd thought it. He didn't stumble over it or even seem to realize he'd said it.

He *loved* her. He'd shown it in a thousand different ways.

And she returned that love with an intensity that scared her. Mara had told her she should tell him and if ever there were a perfect moment . . .

But those weren't the words that came out. "Noah came to see me."

Lucas took a breath, one hand sliding from her back to her waist. "I know."

He knew? "So he told you he talked to me about your dad? Some appeal or review board or something? He said there's a hearing and maybe your discharge could get changed and—"

"Do we have to talk about this now?"

She removed her palm from his cheek to join the other at his chest. "I know how much your record bothers you. When Carmen mentioned it the other night—"

He took a step back and her hands slipped away from him. "Yeah. Carmen."

"I hate how she dredged all that up but—"

"But she had a point." Regret shown in his eyes. "Jen, if there's even the tiniest chance that things don't work out with Dustin, that those kids could have the opportunity to come back here . . . I'm a complication."

She shook her head so vehemently she felt her ponytail loosen. "That's not true. If Carmen knew the whole story, if she knew you . . ." A thought hit. "Or if you go along with your dad and get that dishonorable off your record—"

"So you want me to go to D.C.?"

"I don't want you to go anywhere. But what if it could change everything?"

He turned away, raking his fingers through his hair. "Jen, if I go to that hearing, I'm going to have to relive Tashfeen's death and how I spent the next two years all over again. Everyone wonders why I didn't defend myself at the court-martial. It's because I *have* no defense. I deserve the punishment I received."

"But everything you've done since then, everything you've sacrificed—"

"What did I sacrifice? What did I give up to join Bridgewell? I had nothing at that point. Kit was in London, Dad wanted nothing to do with me. I had no purpose, no direction. Bridgewell saved me." He turned back to her and the pain in his eyes—a dull shade not even the moonlight could brighten—nearly undid her. "And what's that review board going to say when I admit I might be quitting Bridgewell now?"

Might be? Oh, why did those have to be the two words that rang so loudly?

"You're right," she whispered. "We shouldn't be talking about this now. Can you show me more of the garden?"

It was the cowardly way out of a conversation she wished she'd never begun. And for a moment, she thought he might refuse. She braced herself for whatever heartbreak might come next.

But he only reached out to tuck a piece of her hair behind her ear, a regret she wished she didn't see in his soft gaze. "Come see how the fountain works."

20

"Oh, my stars, Jenessa Belville. Your mother would be so proud."

Mayor Milt's boisterous words carried across the garden, drawing Jenessa's gaze from the cottage. Why hadn't Lucas joined the gala yet? Wasn't as if he had far to travel.

A cozy warmth permeated the grounds of Belville Park thanks to the half-dozen heaters set up around the space, and a beautiful, burning sunset created the perfect backdrop to this night that should've had her awash with energetic anticipation.

Instead, her every cheery smile and round of small talk was hobbled and artificial.

"Mr. Mayor, so good to see you. And I really can't take credit for any of this. Lucas and his friend Noah did all the yard work and landscaping. Leigh Pierce and her committee handled all the actual event coordination." She tugged the shimmery green shawl she wore over her black evening gown closer. "I just showed up."

The mayor ran his palms over his red sweater vest. "You

did more than that. You provided the space. You agreed to put off the sale of your house. Speaking of which, I have an invitation for you."

"Oh?" She waved at Raegan McKinley as she passed. Raegan was a hometown girl, sister to Beckett Walker. Her husband, Bear, was currently up on a small wooden platform providing tonight's music alongside the oldest Walker sibling, Logan.

Mom always used to hire a stringed quartet for these events, but the choice of soft acoustic guitar was perfect. And the most enthusiasm Jenessa managed to conjure today was when the two brothers-in-law had shown up early for a soundcheck. Having bought the newspaper from Logan, she knew him a little better than Bear, but it was fun to see both of them back in town for the weekend.

Mayor Milt pulled a folded paper from his pocket and handed it to her.

She opened it and felt her forehead wrinkle. "An agenda for next month's city council meeting? But I'm already at every meeting—or if I can't be there, Paige covers it."

Mayor Milt's grin burst as he said, "You didn't look closely enough. I'm not asking you to be there as a member of the press, but as a local property owner." He poked a finger at a line halfway down the page.

Discussion Item 8: Potential purchase of Belville Park

"Oh, uh . . . oh."

"Surprised?"

"Yes, definitely."

"I've already talked to the city treasurer. If the council approves a proposal and budget amendment, we might actually be able to take Belville Park off your hands."

Off her hands. Only a month ago, that's exactly what she'd wanted. Now?

Her gaze wandered over the gardens and the townspeople and friends milling about, then to the back of the house. The sunroom where Colie and Violet always sat with a snack after school, where Cade first stood on his own. The patio with the stone fireplace where Lucas had bared his deepest wounds and secrets.

"You *are* still planning to sell, aren't you?"

"To be honest, I don't know." But without the kids here, she was back to being a lone woman who couldn't possibly need or use all that space.

Unless Lucas and I . . .

What? Got married and had a bunch of kids? Why did that feel like such a fuzzy picture in her mind? *If there's such a thing as soul mates, Lucas Danby is mine.*

Yet the same dread she'd had in those final days with the kids, desperately wanting to hold on to something she feared was slipping away, simmered in her now. Last night they'd skirted around the topic of the future without any finesse whatsoever. But they couldn't put it off forever.

The buoyancy in the mayor's expression gave way to a fatherly kindness. "Well, if you've had a change of heart, we'll all understand. I love the idea of preserving the history of Belville Park, but it was a home first. And if it can be a home again, that's something to celebrate." He patted her shoulder. "Now, I need to find that writer from *Iowa History*. And where's Lucas? I want to commend his work on this place."

I wish I knew. She glanced at the cottage again. There was a light on now. "I'm sure he'll be here any minute."

"Hey, Mayor Milt, Jen."

Jenessa turned. Logan? Since when did he leave the stage? "Bear's doing a solo act now?"

Logan grinned and tugged his wife to his side. "Amelia just got here, so I granted myself a break. And there's someone I want to introduce you to."

She noticed the bundle in Amelia Walker's arms then. "Oh, my goodness. There's another Walker in the world?"

Logan fairly beamed. "Adoption was just finalized last week. Meet Sadie Flora Walker."

"Oh, you guys, she's beautiful. Where's big sis?"

Logan laughed. "Running around somewhere, probably convincing her doting grandfather to let her eat way too many appetizers."

"Last time I talked to you, you were thinking about moving back to Maple Valley. Is that still happening?"

They talked for a few minutes more, though Jenessa cast repeated glances toward the cottage. What could be keeping Lucas all this time? Mayor Milt eventually moved away, though she could hear his booming voice even at a distance as he congratulated Leigh on her event planning.

"How's everything at the paper?"

She blinked, forcing herself to focus on Logan. "It's good. I finally hired another reporter this summer."

Logan looked at her for a moment. "You're bored with it."

"What?" It was the same thing Sam had said weeks ago. But she was around Sam nearly every day. She hadn't seen Logan Walker in months.

"Listen, I was grateful when you bought the paper. For one thing, Amelia would've had my head if I'd sold it to a chain." Amelia elbowed him with a laugh. "But no one says it has to be your baby forever."

Her baby. It was just a phrase, a saying. It shouldn't sting her so.

But as she watched Logan and Amelia wander off, join Logan's dad and their oldest daughter, the frustration simply became too much. Any picture she'd ever had for her future had gone out of focus when the Hollis kids came into her life, replaced with a new image she'd come to love, to so desperately desire.

It'd been ripped away and she was helpless to do anything about it.

But she could do something about Lucas Danby. Mara was right—he was still here. They *could* make this work. She skirted around a cluster of people and strode past the tent, away from the garden, across the grass, the light in the cottage window drawing her like a beacon.

She lifted one hand and knocked, pulling her shawl tighter now that she was away from the space heaters. "Lucas? It can't be taking you this long to get ready." She knocked again. "I hope you're not shaving. I think I finally decided the five-o'clock shadow look is my favorite."

Still no answer. She tried the knob. Unlocked.

"Of course, if you did shave, then kisses are less scratchy." She shrugged and opened the door. "So either way it's a win for—"

She froze.

"Jessa!"

The only three faces she could've wanted to see as much as Lucas's stared back at her. Colie, Violet, Cade—what were they doing here?

And *where* was Lucas?

"I know I said swimming is a good workout. But not alone when it's almost dark."

Lucas approached the riverbank, moonlight rippling over the surface and a cold wind shuddering through him. The relief he'd felt moments ago when he'd spotted Noah's hunched form sitting on a fallen tree trunk at the river's edge clung to him.

He hadn't thought too much of it when Noah hadn't come back to the cottage last night. Had figured he'd gone back to the farmhouse to stay or maybe booked a room at the Everwood.

But for some reason, panic had set in this afternoon. He'd tried to brush it off. Noah was a grown man, and if he'd decided to ditch town, ignore Lucas's calls and texts, fine. That's what he'd kept telling himself as he helped with the final gala set-up—pulling the tarp off the plants and flowers he'd covered last night, putting fresh batteries in all the lights that weren't solar- or electricity-powered. But when he'd gone back to the cottage to get ready, the worry had gotten to him.

So he'd gone looking. He just wished he'd thought to check here sooner. By now, the gala was probably in full swing and Jenessa would be wondering where he was.

"Do I look like I'm about to go swimming?" Noah didn't move his gaze from the water.

"No, but you do look cold." What the heck was the guy doing out here in short sleeves?

"If you're thinking about peeling off that suit jacket and handing it to me, don't. I'm your brother, not your girlfriend."

Brother.

Just one word. It was like a gust of wind, blowing over and scattering all the emotion, the questions, the tumult of the nearly two weeks since he'd learned the truth of Noah's identity. Of his father's life.

He sat on the tree trunk beside Noah. "You were right yesterday. I've been taking out my anger at Dad on you."

"Well, I did the same thing to you the first week I was here."

"So, you really didn't know anything about Kit and I before? Flagg didn't prepare you at all?"

He shook his head. "He put me on a plane to Iowa with hardly any details. I went along with it because what else was I going to do? My life was going nowhere and here I suddenly have this chance to join an elite team and do something crazy and cool. If I had to go spend a few weeks in Iowa first to prove I was ready, well, okay."

"But then you got a look at me and suddenly put it all together?"

"Well, he texted me your name while I was on the plane. And I knew I'd heard it before. Back during your court-martial. I was just in high school, but I remember sort of jokingly questioning Dad about it and asking him if you were a distant relation."

"I don't think I want to know how he answered that."

Noah glanced over at Lucas for the first time. "He didn't deny it, just artfully dodged the question."

Hmm.

"But anyway, yeah, when I saw you, the light bulb went on. That day I disappeared on you, I was on a fact-finding mission. Called Dad, got the truth out of him, hung up on him." He shrugged. "So he knew I was here for a while before he showed up. I guess when he got that invitation from Kit, he realized I hadn't spilled his secret and decided to come do it himself."

"As weird and dysfunctional as this whole thing is, so much about Dad finally makes sense to me now."

Minutes passed, only the water's soft lapping at the riverbank's edge filling the nighttime quiet. Finally, Noah spoke again. "I called Flagg. I decided not to join."

Lucas lifted his head. "Really? Wow, I'm surprised."

"I don't think I was ever soldier material. I joined because of Dad. I was considering Bridgewell because of

311

Dad. Heck, I'm here right now because of Dad. I'd like to do something because of someone other than him for once." He looked over again. "How about you?"

He was the one to shrug now. "I had completely decided to resign. But then . . ." He hadn't been able to bring himself to talk about this with Jen last night. He'd known where their conversation was headed, and when she'd offered him an out, he'd taken the escape. But at some point, he had to face the truth.

He spent the next several minutes telling Noah about the explosion in Afghanistan, about Tashfeen and his mother.

"Everyone back home thought I was missing, but there I was, living in Kaameh's house. I was pretending to be a Good Samaritan, but the truth is, I turned my back on my duty because Kaameh made me feel good. She mothered me in place of Tashfeen. And I . . . I just ate it up. I selfishly took everything she offered—comfort, affection, friendship— without giving anything of real value back. After enough time passed, it actually felt like home."

He traced the path of the river to the darkening horizon. "I'm worried I'd be doing the same thing to Jen if I stay. That it's selfish." It was the first time he'd faced his misgivings with true, aching clarity.

Noah gave him a thoughtful look. "How do you know you didn't give anything back to that boy's mother? Taking care of you might've been the one thing that kept her sane after he died. Being in her home might have kept it from feeling as empty as it would've otherwise."

"Maybe." But it didn't change the fact that, deep down, he hadn't stayed for her. He'd stayed for him. And in doing so, he'd let down his unit. He'd let down his family. He'd let down himself.

If only he could cast off the feeling now that no matter

what he decided, whether he stayed or he left, he was about to let down Jen, too.

"So . . ." He looked to Noah, all at once in desperate need of a change of subject. "Hate to break it to you, but I'm not exactly an award-winning older sibling."

"Actually, I stayed in the farmhouse long enough to know Kit thinks the world of you. She's pretty cool too." Noah quirked one corner of his mouth. "And I haven't totally hated working alongside you."

"Speaking of, we're supposed to be enjoying the fruits of our labor right now." He stood, stretched out his hand. And despite his unsettled future flurrying like a blizzard inside him, he managed a grin—or at least a half-smile—for Noah. "Since we're not potential colleagues anymore, I say we start over."

Noah clasped his hand and rose, the gesture turning into a handshake. "Brothers?"

He nodded. "And friends."

They started toward their vehicles, but Lucas paused when his phone beeped. "I'm guessing that's my lecture for being late to the party." He pulled his phone from his pocket.

And froze as he read Jen's text.

Where are you? The kids are here. Or were. Vi and Cade still are, but Colie ran and I don't know where she is . . . please just get here.

"I know you're freaked out, Jen, but I need you to try and explain to me again what happened because I didn't get it all the first time."

Sam's usual gruff demeanor was nowhere to be found, his calming voice almost taking the edge off her panic.

Almost.

Jenessa held Cade against her chest, his warm body heavy in her arms where she stood in the middle of the sunroom. Violet's pattering footsteps clattered through the house as she ran through the place, excited to be here and heedless of the seriousness of her sister's disappearance.

She paced the length of the room. "I went to find Lucas, but I found the kids in the cottage. They said their dad had gone out—again. Apparently he's been doing that most nights. He left them alone and they got it into their heads to run away and come here and . . ."

And the moment she'd seen them, she'd dropped to the floor of the cottage, gathered them into her arms. If she just could've stayed there, if she hadn't forced herself to do what she'd known she had to do.

Through tears in her eyes, she'd told Colie they had to call her dad.

"I would give anything to keep you here, but I can't. Not unless your dad says it's okay."

Colie had refused to give her Dustin's phone number, so she'd ushered the kids through the crowded garden and into the house and called Carmen. But she'd made the mistake of walking into a different room to make the call.

And when she'd returned, Colie was gone.

Somehow she made it through the explanation in less than a minute, bouncing Cade against her hip as she spoke. Sam knew the rest. She'd come rushing out to the gala, hoping to find Colie among the crowd.

But that was fifteen minutes ago and she still hadn't been found.

"I can't just stay in here waiting, Sam."

"Violet and Cade need you to be with them. We're going

to find her any minute, Jen. She can't have gone far in this short of a time. And if Dustin Hollis or the social worker shows up—"

"Jen!" Lucas burst into the room. "What's going on?"

She spun to face him, Cade's weight heavy in her arms. "You'd know if you'd been here." It was her fear spewing the unhelpful words, forming hot tears in her eyes. "The kids came back to the cottage, which is where I thought you were."

Sam touched her shoulder. "Let's focus on Colie now. Can you think of any spots where she might go? Even any hiding spots here in the house where she could be? I know you looked already but—"

"Ross, we've got something." The voice came over Sam's walkie-talkie.

Eyeing Jenessa, he lifted it to his mouth. Lucas took Sam's place at her side, but his hand on her back felt cold.

"Whatcha got?" Sam spoke.

"Looks like there was a hit and run over on Beach Street. I think it's the Hollis girl."

The last of her courage drained from her as her whole body went cold.

21

*L*ucas would give anything to be what Jenessa needed right now—a hero in the middle of a crisis.

But all he could do was stand helplessly at her side as the doctor spoke.

"Our immediate concern is the splenic rupture caused by one of the broken ribs. We've already done an ultrasound to determine internal bleeding, and she's being prepped for surgery now." The doctor looked around the gathered crowd as if not entirely certain who to address as the main family representative.

His confusion was warranted considering the packed room. Dustin Hollis had just arrived minutes ago, but he stood alone several feet away from Carmen Rodriguez. Violet was hooked to Jen's side and Lucas held Cade, his free arm around Jen. Sam was here, and Mara and Marshall had texted that they were on their way.

"Splenic rupture . . . that's a ruptured spleen?" Jen asked, allowing the doctor's attention to settle on her. He nodded. "So . . . what? Are you removing it or—"

The doctor interrupted. "It'll be one of our surgeons, Dr.

Henson, completing the operation. He's reviewing the ultrasound now, and I'm sure he'll come out to speak with you before he begins. But it does appear to be a small tear, so he may be able to repair it without removing the organ."

Lucas tried to pay attention as the doctor explained what would happen with the other injuries—the two broken ribs, the cracked wrist. But the words were fuzzy in his head, the heaviness of the past hour cloaking him in fear and exhaustion.

"But again, our main concern is stopping the internal bleeding as soon as possible." The doctor attempted a reassuring expression. "With that under control, chances for a full recovery are very good."

Full recovery. Very good.

There. Those were the four words he'd focus on. Jen and the others asked a few more questions, and soon the doctor was turning and disappearing down the hallway. He felt Jen's ragged exhale under his palm and pulled her to him, her head landing against his chest near Cade and Violet's arm curling around his knee.

"A full recovery," he murmured against her hair. "She's going to be okay."

"She has to make it through the surgery. They have to stop the bleeding."

"They will."

Her tears were hot through his cotton shirt, but he was glad to feel them. They were better than her stone-cold shock of earlier. Her frozen silence on the way here. They hadn't even been able to leave for the hospital right away, not without car seats for the kids. Jenessa hadn't wanted to leave Violet and Cade behind.

Thankfully, someone from the gala had offered up a vehicle already outfitted with car seats.

"Violet, would you like to sit with me?"

Lucas looked up to see Dustin Hollis standing nearby. The man's face was haggard with worry. He might've left the kids alone tonight, but at least he'd come here as quickly as possible.

Violet shook her head. Dustin's shoulders dropped.

Jenessa slowly pulled away from Lucas. "Um, if you'd like to take Cade . . ."

It had to have cost her to say the words, and his already bruised heart pulled with pain for her—for all of them. Lucas handed Cade to Dustin as Jenessa knelt to hug Violet. "I think we're going to have a long night, kiddo. Should we try to get you comfy?"

They spent the next few minutes arranging two chairs into a makeshift bed, spreading a blanket and helping Violet settle. Mara and Marshall arrived right as Violet's eyes began drifting closed.

All it took was a look toward Marshall and he picked up on Lucas's silent communication. "If you two want to stretch your legs, grab something at the vending machines or whatever, we can stay with Vi."

Jen gave a slow nod and relief flooded Lucas when she took his hand. They were barely out of earshot of the others when he spoke. "I should've been there. I was with Noah. I was worried about him. But I should've—"

She squeezed his hand. "No, Luke. I was scared. I didn't mean what I said."

They slowed as they neared the vending machines. The fluorescent lights overhead highlighted Jen's ashen pallor, and the poor woman was still wearing her dress. If they were anywhere else, if this were any other circumstance, he'd take the opportunity to tell her how beautiful it looked on her. Instead, he shrugged out of his jacket and slipped it over her shoulders.

"This is getting to be a habit," she said with a sad smile. "You're very gallant, Lucas Danby."

He could offer her the warmth of a coat but not what she really needed. Security, the promise that everything would be okay if they could just get through this awful night.

He tipped her chin up so she was looking up at him. "She's going to be okay."

She watched him for a moment, a glassy veil over her eyes. "But are *we* going to be okay?"

He opened his mouth but no words came out, his pause stretching so long that she eventually slipped free of his hold.

Her heels clicked on the tile floor as she took two steps backward. "For the record, I love you."

A cloud of desperation fogged over him. He pressed his palm against the humming vending machine. "I love you, too."

She crossed her arms. "But I keep getting the feeling that's not enough for you. It's like you think you need to be some perfect man with some perfect past and some sparkling, bright future without any question marks. But all I need is your love, Lucas. And your friendship. And just . . . you."

"Jen—"

"Lucas." A voice bounded in. "Oh, uh, sorry. I'm interrupting."

Lucas spun. What in the world? Arthur Flagg stood in the hallway. What was he doing in Maple Valley? Again?

He heard the click of footsteps and turned once more, just in time to see Jenessa disappearing down the hallway.

319

Even if Sam hadn't recognized the man who'd come to see Lucas, Jenessa would've eventually figured out his identity just from the way he carried himself—from the way Lucas straightened to attention at the sound of his voice.

At first, she'd thought it might be his father. But Lucas's look of surprise had quickly turned to relief. Not his father, in that case.

Which left the man she'd heard Lucas talk about many times since he'd first told her about Bridgewell.

Over an hour had passed since Colie went into surgery. Violet was sound asleep in the chairs next to her. At some point, Dustin had passed a sleeping Cade to Mara. He sat in the opposite corner at the moment, talking quietly with Carmen. Sam was in the chair Lucas had used earlier.

"I don't know how to convince him, Sam."

He shifted and straightened in his chair. Had he started to doze off? "Uh, might need a little more context."

"I don't know how to convince Lucas that none of it matters to me—his military record, his prison record, the secrets he's kept, the wounds that still hurt him, his father. It doesn't matter to me. It doesn't change how I feel about him."

He didn't say anything at first, just rubbed his cheeks and crossed one leg over the other. Then seemed to think twice, planted both feet on the ground, and turned so he faced her. "Can I say something you might not like?"

The TV droned in the corner, and the whir of the revolving door let in a blast of cold air. "I'm not a wilting flower, Sam."

"Well, okay then. All those things you listed—they matter to Luke. They're burdens he carries, and you can't just talk him into putting them down and walking away." He exhaled. "Can't love him into it either."

"I accept him exactly as he is, burdens and all."

"But you have to let him *be* who he is, too. Think about it. He went to war after 9/11 because of the sense of personal responsibility he felt toward his country. It's the same code of ethics that kept him from speaking up for himself during his court-martial because he believed he deserved to pay for his desertion. And all the secretive work he's done since then . . ." He shook his head. "Lucas's drive to serve and sacrifice and look out for the needs of others, whether it's on some mission or here with you, that's a part of who he is."

Sam shifted again, appearing uncomfortable with his own words. "If he's pulling back right now, then maybe the way to show you care is by giving him the space and time he needs to wrestle with whatever it is he's wrestling with."

"You're right. I don't like hearing that." She slunk farther into her chair, suddenly aware that Sam had recognized in Lucas what she hadn't. Last night in the garden and again just minutes ago, she'd seen a man sinking into the shame of his past.

But Sam had seen a man filled with integrity, with the desire to do the right thing in the present.

And asking Lucas to somehow find instant clarity because of *her* feelings, *her* acceptance of all he carried with him—well, it wasn't all that different than her parents expecting her to set aside her emotions at their demand. She needed to walk through her emotions, not just around them.

Lucas needed to walk through all that pulled at him now. And maybe, much as it hurt her, he needed to do it without her.

"I don't like it when you're more discerning than me, Sam."

He crossed his arms. There was the Sam she knew.

"But you know I have a point, and you're grateful I

spoke my mind as a friend of both you and Lucas and blah blah blah, right?"

She elbowed him.

"Jenessa." Carmen stood in front of her. "Could I talk to you for a minute?"

A fresh dread wound through her. Colie wasn't even out of surgery yet. Surely the lecture she was about to receive for whatever she'd done wrong this time could wait. But Carmen was already moving off toward a second waiting area walled off by glass, Dustin on her heels.

Jenessa rose. "Guess I'd better go. But Sam?" She waited until he looked up at her. "Thanks."

He nodded.

She joined Carmen and Dustin in the smaller waiting area, Sam's words resounding in her mind, realization and hurt mingling in the aftermath. And fear . . .

Fear that she was going to have to trust Lucas enough to let go. Trust God enough to meet her in the pain of it. Do some wrestling of her own.

I don't think I can do it, God. I'm tired of trying to hope someday it'll all work out.

She looked to her hands clasped in her lap.

Then just trust Me for today.

Her breathing hitched and her gaze lurched upward. No, that hadn't been an audible voice but—

"Jen?" Carmen's serious tone cut in. Both she and Dustin were staring at her.

"Uh sorry." She shook her head, tried to focus. But those words, that whisper in her soul—hadn't come from her. "I-I did call as soon as I found the kids in the cottage. As soon as I got them up to the house, I—"

Carmen placed a hand on her knee. "You did the right thing. I'm very glad you called. And what happened after, the hit and run, I hope you're not blaming yourself for that."

Oh. She hadn't expected that. She'd gotten so used to making mistakes in front of the social worker, she'd just assumed . . .

Carmen looked to Dustin and he cleared his throat. "I'd, um . . . I'd like to speak to you about custody arrangements."

Jenessa's fingers stilled on her armrest. *Trust Me.*

Carmen waited a beat before picking up where Dustin left off. "Dustin has expressed to me that the past nine days have been difficult. He doesn't have much experience with full-time parenthood, particularly being a single parent to three children."

She had a feeling Carmen was putting things diplomatically. If what Colie had said tonight was true, that he'd disappeared each evening and hadn't returned until the early morning hours, it was likely he wasn't ready to give up a lifestyle he'd previously lived.

But she wasn't going to sit here and judge him. She barely knew him. She didn't know what challenges he might've faced previously.

Dustin rubbed his hands on his faded jeans, coughed. "I thought it would be different. Figured I owed Tessa since I was never around and didn't really do a good job sending money." He lowered his head.

Carmen folded her hands on her lap. "Dustin and I have been talking for the past hour. I told him I was worried he was making a rash decision during a traumatic night. He's agreed to take a few days to think more about this. But in the meantime, if you'd be willing, we'd like to send Violet and Cade home with you."

Could they hear the erratic thrumming of her heart? "I'm willing. Very willing. A-and of course, I'm happy to talk about the future if . . . whenever you'd like, Dustin."

He nodded, stood, then walked away.

"I don't know what to say." She slid her shaking hands

down the armrests.

"You need to understand he could change his mind. I didn't even want to bring it up with you tonight, but he insisted."

"But if he doesn't change his mind, is there truly a chance I could be granted custody of the kids? Not just temporarily but—"

"I really don't want to get too far ahead of ourselves."

"Please. I need a hope to hold on to tonight."

Carmen let out a long sigh. "Yes, there's a chance. If he's serious, if you're serious, if there aren't any major obstacles in the way, there's a chance."

She stood. "Thank you, Carmen." She angled to return to the main waiting room but paused. Lucas was just outside the glass, his gaze centered on her. How much of this conversation had he just heard? She cast him a trembling smile.

How could so much sorrow linger in the smile he sent back?

She moved to go to him, but a nurse interrupted. "I have an update for Colie Hollis's family."

"Shouldn't you join them, son?"

Flagg's hand was warm and heavy on Lucas's shoulder where they stood several feet away from the crowd gathering around the nurse.

But he'd heard what he needed to hear. The operation was nearly over already and Colie had pulled through just fine. The surgeon hadn't needed to remove her spleen. Had done something called an arterial embolization to stop the bleeding and was now finishing the procedure.

"Luke?" Flagg prodded.

"Oh, uh, no. I'm good over here."

He still couldn't believe the man was here. Apparently, after Noah had called Flagg this morning with his decision not to join Bridgewell, he'd immediately booked a flight.

They'd spent the past hour talking quietly in the chairs near the vending machines. He'd spilled his guts to the man —about Dad and Noah and the kids and finally, when Flagg pushed him, Jen.

"I sound unstable," he'd said when he'd finally reached the end of the whole saga.

Flagg had chuckled. *"No, you sound like a man who's tired. Who's had his world tilted one too many times in different directions."*

"You never told me you knew my dad. You didn't tell me about his other family. And Noah—you sent him here knowing we'd eventually figure things out. What was the purpose in that?"

Flagg's expression had gone almost apologetic. *"Yes, your father and I had a passing acquaintance and yes, he's the one who first contacted me about you. He checked in now and then, asked how you were doing. As I got to know a little more of him and his story, I struggled through the years with what to do. I prayed about it. I thought about telling you—so many times. But every time, something stopped me. A still, small voice I've learned to listen to."*

"You're saying God told you to lie to me?"

"I'm saying that with my limited, human understanding, I sensed Him telling me to wait on His timing."

"And you were that confident you heard Him correctly?"

Flagg shook his head. *"No. But I was—I am—that confident that His grace, guidance, and compassion are bigger than any mistakes I could make. I don't think it's nearly as much about whether we hear everything correctly all the time as whether we're still listening."*

It sounded nice, but Lucas had tried listening. Ever since that morning in church, he'd tried. One of the things he'd prayed about was whether to contact Jen's aunt and for a while, he'd felt so good about how that had turned out.

But since then, it felt like his prayers were hitting a concrete ceiling and then simply dropping. And he was left to pick up the scattered pieces, clueless what to do with them.

"I don't think I have the kind of faith you do, sir. Too much has happened. I've drifted away."

Flagg had appeared to ponder his admission for a few quiet seconds. *"Personally, son, I happen to think a weathered faith is a good faith. It means you've been through a storm and back. Or maybe you're still in it—still fighting. Maybe your belief is battered and weak. But that just means you're in a prime place for a rescue. For a miracle."*

But since when had Lucas been the kind of man who received miracles?

Flagg stood then, plunked a handful of change into the vending machine. Bought Lucas a pop and a bag of candy. *"What's your girl's favorite candy? Might as well bring her some."*

His girl.

His girl who'd just been told there was a possibility the kids she adored might be able to have a home with her after all.

If there were no "major obstacles" in the way.

Jen was asking the nurse a question now, wondering how soon she'd be able to see Colie. She still wore Lucas's suit jacket, its sleeves far too long for her arms. She'd swept her hair over to the side for the gala, but tendrils had escaped throughout the harrowing events of the night.

He let out a tattered breath, turned to Flagg. "I think now might be a good time to slip away."

Flagg's brow creased. "You sure?"

He nodded and started toward the revolving door before he could change his mind. Chilly night air entrapped him when he stepped outside. He had no concept of what time it was and the half a can of pop he'd chugged churned in his stomach. He'd have to ride with Flagg, so Jen could have the vehicle they'd borrowed.

"Lucas!"

He closed his eyes. Turned.

He should've known Jenessa would see him leave and chase him out.

Flagg patted his back. "I'm in the blue Jeep at the far end of the lot. I'll wait."

Jen's heels clicked over the cement as she hurried to him, the lights of the hospital glowing behind her against the dark night. "You can't leave now."

"Jen—"

"They said we can see her in an hour or so. At least stay until then. She'd want to see you. Not that she'll be awake, but . . ." A frantic edge laced her voice. "Please don't go."

"I heard Carmen's news. And I won't do it, Jen. I won't be the reason those kids don't get to stay with you long-term. I'm not going to be an obstacle to that dream coming true for you or for them." *Please don't argue.* If she did, he didn't know how he'd make himself leave.

As if she could read his thoughts, she didn't speak. But the tears in her eyes were worse than any words. She slowly took off his suit jacket, held it out. Only when he accepted it did she move any closer. She leaned up to kiss his cheek.

And pierce his heart with her whisper. "I'm just not as noble as you, Luke. I'll let you walk away now, but I refuse to say goodbye."

She pulled back, wiped the back of her hand over her eyes, and turned away.

22

*J*enessa stood on the cottage doorstep, drawn here by an undeniable beckoning in her spirit.

And the pang in her heart of missing Lucas.

She twisted the doorknob and let herself in, rusty hinges and scuffed floorboards creaking. She'd realized this morning that other than those hasty minutes of finding the Hollis kids here—both the first and second time—she hadn't really stepped more than a few feet into the little house.

For some reason, this chilly early November morning, with the wind lulling and colorful leaves turning and twisting like ornaments, she'd needed to do this.

Five weeks and three days since I found the kids the first time.

And one week exactly since Lucas had flown back to D.C. with both Noah and the man who'd come to the hospital. He'd come to see her, at least, before leaving for the airport last Monday, though it'd been little more than a repeat of that night in the parking lot. Few words, each one dripping with sadness and regret. A hug, a kiss on the cheek, unanswered questions clogging her throat.

But Sam's wisdom wouldn't allow her to voice them. For once, she'd decided to be the quiet one. To let Lucas do what he felt he needed to do.

At least in the pain, there'd also been the incredible joy of having the kids back in her house. Violet had been ecstatic to return to her pink bedroom and Cade had settled back in as if he'd never left. Three days later, Colie had come home, too.

Home.

Jenessa moved into the middle of the cottage's main room. The coffee mug Lucas had borrowed from the house still sat in the sink at the middle of the kitchenette. Was it her imagination or did the cottage smell like him? Like a stomach-warming mix of pine and mint and—

The table.

Her feet carried her to the rectangle table over in the corner, still splotched with paint and pen marks, wonderfully nicked and scraped. She ran a hand over its surface and smiled. Maybe she should move it to the main house. The kids could use it for homework or crafts.

She plopped into one of the table's mismatched chairs and pulled out her phone. She probably should've made this call before now, but with all the busyness of the past week, she simply hadn't had a chance. There'd been meetings with Carmen, with Dustin, with a lawyer who would walk her through the numerous hearings and paperwork and steps to come.

There was still a hint of anxiety lurking underneath all the activity. The process for Dustin to officially give up his rights and allow Jenessa to eventually adopt the kids would likely last months, and he could still change his mind.

Yet he seemed resolute. There would be more court dates, more legal steps to cement her role in the children's lives. But things were moving forward, however slowly.

Jenessa was still trying to discern how to talk to the kids about their father's decision. It was the kind of thing that could affect all of them in mental and emotional ways they might not even realize until later in life. She was determined to help them process and adjust and heal. She'd already sought out a counselor, asking Carmen for resources.

In the midst of all the upheaval, at least one thing, one decision, had cemented in her mind.

"Good morning, Ms. Belville," Mayor Milt finally answered.

"Morning. How's everything at city hall today?"

"Splendid." He lowered his voice. "Although Joanna—you know my secretary—thinks I need to cut back on caffeine and only made half a pot of coffee today. We'll see what she says when I fall asleep at my desk come midafternoon. But methinks you have a reason for calling other than to hear about my coffee woes."

"Actually, I do. It's about Belville Park, Mayor Milt. I've decided not to sell."

His chuckle sounded in her ear. "Well, of course. I already heard from Joanna who heard from Barney Jeeves, the trash man, that you threw out the *For Sale* sign last week."

"I should've known." She leaned her chair against the wall. "Well, I do apologize. I know you'd started thinking about museum opportunities and such."

"Jenessa, this town already has a heritage railroad and depot museum, a family orchard, thirteen antique stores, and at last count, forty-four different fairs, festivals, and events on the community calendar. It's entirely possible we've gone as far as we can go."

"You really do need to talk to Joanna about that coffee situation. Never in a million years would I have thought you'd say such a thing."

They talked for another couple of minutes before ending the call, and Jenessa stood, turning one more slow circle around the cottage that housed so many of her earliest, happiest memories.

But no longer would her sense of warmth and family only happen inside these walls. The main house was a home now. And Colie and Violet would be wondering what was taking her so long. Cade might wake up at any minute.

She walked to the sink and retrieved Lucas's cup.

"I forgot how adorable this cottage is."

She whirled. "Aunt Lauren?"

Her aunt's grin was wide and wondrous. "You loved surprises as a kid. I hoped for the whole five-hour drive here that was still the case. But if I should've called—"

She lowered the mug to the counter and moved to embrace the older woman. "I'm so glad you're here." They'd talked on the phone several times since meeting in Minneapolis, had even started texting on a daily basis. "You abandoned the art gallery for the day?"

Aunt Lauren laughed. "Oh, Tony can handle it. He's an excellent fill-in in a pinch, in addition to being a stand-out husband."

She'd heard plenty about Tony during their calls. The couple had met in their late thirties at some charity fundraiser, and he'd been wildly supportive of Aunt Lauren's dream to open her own gallery.

"And you're here because . . ." she prompted.

"Because I wanted to see my niece and those cute kids again. Technology is nice, but it only goes so far." She looked around the cottage. "I hadn't considered I'd get the perk of seeing this place again, too. I stopped at the house first. Colie sent me out here."

"Did you see the shutters?" She'd made that discovery

for herself on the same day Lucas had left. He must've spent his last hours in Maple Valley freshening them up with a new coat of paint the exact shade of blue her aunt had chosen years ago.

"I did indeed." She wandered to the table in the corner, running her fingers over its surface just as Jen had done. "How can I be so overjoyed at our reunion while at the same time still so pained at all I've missed?" She met Jen's gaze with tears in her eyes.

"I was just thinking about that—about the tension of complicated and conflicting emotions. I'm over the moon about the kids being here but . . ."

Her aunt stood in front of her, her rose-scented perfume mingling with the smell of the cottage. "But you miss that man who writes the crazy-long texts."

Except he hadn't written any crazy-long texts lately. Lucas had called her twice and texted a few times, caring but quiet as ever.

It wasn't enough. And she couldn't shake the desire to chase him down and beg him to come home.

"Everyone says he needs space. And I know that's true. He's had so much to process lately." Aunt Lauren had already heard it all. "I just didn't know it was possible to miss someone this much. Weeks ago, I started picturing . . . oh, this sounds ridiculous, but I started picturing him as part of my family. I had thoughts of Thanksgiving and Christmas and the kids in pajamas. Part of that picture might actually happen. But it just doesn't feel complete without him. And I still haven't figured out how to be okay with that."

Aunt Lauren tilted her head. "Who says you have to be okay with it?"

She managed a laugh. "I'm trying to do this whole thing where I trust God. Just, like, one day at a time."

"Jen, you can trust God and still wish things were different. Faith doesn't mean you stop dreaming about the future or desiring something you don't yet have. God cares about the things that matter to you." Aunt Lauren took her hand and led her to the table once more. She sat and motioned for Jen to do the same. "Do you remember when I first taught you to use watercolors?"

"Yeah. Your painting stint lasted from when I was seven to almost nine. It was ceramics before and photography after."

Her aunt gave a breezy laugh. "Wow, good memory. Well, I was so excited to get started—I had paper and paints and plans to go all Bob Ross on you. Teach you brushstrokes and whatnot. You wanted to paint the cottage, but you insisted on drawing it out first. I think you went through half a sketchpad."

"What can I say? I was a perfectionist."

"No, you were scared. I figured it out quickly enough. I'd told you how unforgiving watercolors can be, and I think you worked yourself into a lather of worry about splotches and accidentally mixed colors."

Jenessa traced a streak of paint on the tabletop. "You're saying I'm scared of what will happen with Lucas if I push him or crowd his space?"

"I'm saying there comes a point when you have to just paint your picture." Aunt Lauren leaned forward. "You've already seen the image in your head, dear niece of mine."

She had. She'd seen it in vivid, bold color. The most beautiful of dreams.

A dream she wouldn't have even known to imagine for herself months ago. Before the kids showed up at the cottage. Before Lucas trekked his way into her heart. Before the house she'd planned to leave had bidden her to stay.

What could any of that be, it struck her in this moment,

but the handiwork of a God who loved her? Who saw her heart even more clearly than Lucas did. Who'd known what she needed when she'd been restless and uncertain.

Who knew what she longed for even now.

She'd been working on trusting Him with each day. Could she start trusting Him with her tomorrows, too? Enough to take a scary step forward?

"Take it from someone who waited far too long, Jen," her aunt said. "When you know what you want, it's worth mustering up the bravery to go after it."

"That sounds lovely, but Lucas has it in his head that he's an obstacle to my situation with the kids." For all she knew, she could follow Lucas all the way to D.C. only to have him tell her to go home.

Aunt Lauren propped her elbow on the table. "Yes, well, I've had some things in my head for years. Faulty things that kept me from you. Lucas is the one who doused me with common sense." She grinned and shrugged. "I say you give him a taste of his own medicine."

One week back in D.C. had stretched into two.

Lucas fingered the collar of his oxford, wishing for the freedom to loosen his tie. It was one thing to get decked out in a constricting suit for Jenessa's sake—for a wedding or a backyard gala. But an appointment in a lackluster office building with beige walls, plastic plants, and elevator music hardly seemed worth the effort.

And yet, as Dad and Flagg and his own common sense kept trying to drive home, it was important to make a good impression on the JAG officer who'd agreed to represent him at the review board hearing.

He glanced across the waiting area to where Dad sat with an open magazine on his lap. He hadn't turned a page in ten minutes.

Nor had they shared more than polite small talk. Not today. Not in any of the days since he'd returned. *But I'm here, aren't I? Isn't that enough?* The only sound other than his own constant shifting in his chair had been the ding of Dad's phone a few minutes ago. A text message he'd barely glanced at.

Lucas fidgeted with his tie again. Why he'd felt the need to show up thirty minutes early was beyond him. Probably because he'd known Dad would—some infernal Army promptness. Strange how there were some memories even decades of distance from the man couldn't erase.

"I read Flagg's reference letter."

He blinked, his gaze jutting upward at the surprise of Dad's voice. "Oh, uh, okay. I haven't read it." Nor had he read any of the letters from his teammates that would go to the review board alongside Flagg's recommendation and his own written testimonial.

Which he had yet to write. He'd told himself he might as well wait until after this appointment, during which they'd discuss the verbal statement he'd make when he appeared in front of the board in December.

But mostly, the thought of sitting at the empty desk in his empty D.C. apartment, working on a testimony about his past when his present felt so burdened and his future hazier than ever before, just felt futile.

And how was he supposed to focus on the task anyway when his thoughts were so crowded with all he'd left behind in Maple Valley? He missed Jen so much it was nearly a physical ache, as intense as the burns that had marred his arms. He missed the kids. He even missed that tiny little cottage.

At least he'd managed to paint the shutters before leaving. One last feeble attempt to let Jenessa know how much he cared. He just wished he knew where to go from here.

Flagg had told him he was in the prime place for a rescue—a miracle. Maybe that's what this chance at an appeal was. But why didn't it feel like it?

"It was a good letter." Dad's voice jutted into his thoughts. "Flagg said . . . good things."

"I guess that's . . . good." Could a conversation get any more stilted? "Are you writing a reference too?"

Dad closed the magazine and set it aside. "I wasn't sure you'd want me to. But I'd like to."

It seemed overly warm in here. Lucas shrugged out of his jacket. He could put it back on whenever the lawyer made an appearance.

Dad cleared his throat. "Actually, I've already written it. I have it with me if you'd like to take a look at it."

Did he want to read it? *Do I even want any of this?* He'd once craved freedom from the label of dishonorable more than almost anything. Now he stood on the precipice of gaining that freedom, yet weariness dragged his every step forward.

Dad stood, crossed the few feet between them, and pulled an envelope from his pocket. Only when Lucas accepted it did Dad sit—this time in a chair directly across from him. *If this wasn't spectacularly uncomfortable before . . .*

He stared at the envelope between his fingers. The words inside wouldn't change anything that'd happened in the past. They wouldn't change the hurt, the distance, nor the secrets that had caused it all.

But Dad was making an effort. He had to at least attempt to do the same. He slid his thumb under the flap and pulled out the folded letter, a single page. His gaze slid past the date and salutation to the body of the missive:

This letter will be brief, because to my personal shame, my presence throughout much of my son's life has been brief. Fortunately, a person does not need to spend inordinate amounts of time with Lucas Danby to believe with conviction that he's worthy of a change in his discharge status.

You will read letters from others that detail Lucas's dedicated paramilitary service in the past ten years, so I don't need to dwell on that. Nor do I need to give you a list of his attributes—you'll see them for yourselves when he stands before you.

Instead, I'd like to tell you about my other son—Lucas's half-brother, Noah. Noah served two tours in the Army, but he has struggled since being medically discharged more than a year ago. Over the past 12 months, I've witnessed a pattern of negative choices, irresponsibility, and dangerous behavior, and as a father, felt helpless to know how to address it.

Noah recently spent a month with Lucas in Iowa. During that time, they worked side by side as Lucas sought to mentor Noah. Since Noah returned to Washington, D.C., here is what I see in him: A renewed commitment to his veteran's support group. A heightened sense of responsibility and accountability. A willingness to invest in his own potential. And a determination not to let his past dictate his future.

I credit my son Lucas with the transformation I've witnessed in Noah. And I ask you not to let <u>his</u> past dictate <u>his</u> future. Not when his present is filled with examples, including Noah, of lives impacted for the better. Whatever your decision, I remain a proud father of the man my son Lucas Danby has become.

Thank you.

Lucas's hands shook as he stared at the letter, sentences blurring together in front of him. Straightforward and powerful, it pierced a place so deep inside of him that even if he were a man of a million words, he'd never be able to express the eddying impact of what he'd just read.

"I don't know what to say, Dad." Couldn't even make himself look up to meet his father's eyes.

"I've made so many mistakes, Lucas. And I know reconciliation isn't as simple as an apology. Or a letter. I just want you to know that whenever you're ready, whatever it takes, I'd like to try. I'm ready to try."

I'm ready to try. They were the same words he'd whispered to God back in that pew in Maple Valley—knowing he was a mess, knowing there was no reason God should accept his feeble attempts.

Other than a love that was bigger than his mistakes.

This man sitting before him, his father, needed the exact thing Lucas had needed for so long. To be seen as a man not cloaked in shame, but covered by grace. Lucas had only just begun to see himself that way before everything had turned upside down back in Maple Valley. Only now, as he looked at his father, did he realize all over again that he had a *choice.*

A choice he might have to make daily. To see himself as a man of honor. Not because of anything he had or hadn't done, anything he might or might not do in the future. Not because of how Jenessa saw him or even how he now knew his father saw him.

But simply because he was loved by the God who'd created him. A God who saw his tattered faith and stayed anyway. A God who'd watched him walk away and had chosen to follow.

The truth seeped into him now, emboldening and undeniable—*this* was the miracle he'd been waiting on. He'd lived so many years of wishing he could be a hero for others. But his own Rescuer was even now swooping in, giving him the grace to see his father in a new way.

He finally looked up and met Dad's uneasy gaze. "I'm ready to try too."

Just one sentence but, weighty with significance, it somehow spanned decades and distance. He stood, crossed the few feet to Dad, and held out his hand.

And maybe it shouldn't have affected him the way it did when his father rose and grasped his hand. Maybe the rush of emotion was out of place in this stark, drab office building.

But at least he wasn't alone. Because Dad's eyes pooled with tears as he shook Lucas's hand.

"Lucas Danby?"

He cleared his throat, blinking, turning toward the woman who'd checked them in when they arrived. She rose from behind her desk. "I can show you into the conference room now."

Lucas nodded and reached for his suit jacket, but his father grasped his arm before he could pull it on. "I think we have somewhere else to be."

Lucas lifted his eyebrows. "What? Dad, we've been sitting here for almost half an hour. If you need to go, that's fine. I can handle it on my own and—"

"Is this really where you want to be right now, Lucas?"

"Uh, I don't under—"

"Do you even want this?"

It was the same question he'd just asked himself ten or fifteen minutes ago. He hadn't had an answer then. He wasn't sure he had an answer now. But there was a sudden urgency in his father's eyes. "You said there's somewhere *we* need to be?"

Dad pressed his lips together, nodded, reached for his

briefcase. He threw a glance at the receptionist. "Apologies." He practically hauled Lucas from the building.

They were settled in his father's Lexus when he tried again. "Are you not feeling well or something?" He twisted to drop his jacket in the back seat then pushed up his sleeves.

"Look, I got a text from Flagg when we were sitting in that waiting area. I was going to wait to address it until after the meeting, but I changed my mind. For now, that's all you need to know."

"All I need to—Dad, what is going on?" And why did his father look almost . . . excited?

He tried three more times in the twenty-five minutes it took to escape the metro, twice more as they veered toward his suburb apartment. At least, he assumed that's where they were headed.

He'd assumed correctly. Forty minutes after they'd abruptly fled the law office, he found himself walking up the hedge-lined sidewalk to his building. The one that had never felt like home and probably never would.

Do you even want this?

Out here in the fresh air, with the wind rustling through brittle leaves and an autumn sun that made him think of golden fields and fall in Iowa, he could answer that question.

Changing the status of his Army discharge might bring a momentary satisfaction. Like the relief of a first breath after plunging into a cold river.

But he wanted more. He wanted the thrill of an upstream swim. He wanted the work and the wonder and the exhilaration of everything he'd left behind in Maple Valley. He wanted a real home where he could live his messy life—all of it—in the bright light of day, no more secrets.

He wanted Jenessa Belville.

His father pulled open the door that led into the building's lobby but didn't follow him inside. He looked over his shoulder. "Dad?" Why didn't he—?

"Mr. Lucas!"

His gaze whipped around, any stunned words he might've somehow found behind his utter shock lost to the noise erupting around him.

Violet's squeals. Cade's shrieks. Some soft greeting from Colie he couldn't make out through the echoes bouncing off the walls.

And best of all, one little, beautiful word from his favorite person in the world. "Hi."

23

*J*enessa could hardly chastise Lucas for taking so long to speak when she couldn't bring herself to move. No, she just stood there, heart thumping so loud he and every resident of every apartment on the first floor could surely hear it.

She wet her lips. "We would've been here a week ago, but I had to get DHS permission to take the kids out of state and—"

"What *are* you doing here?" Lucas had one arm around Colie, his other hand ruffling Violet's curls. Somehow in the hullabaloo, his shirt had come half-untucked and his sleeves were pushed up to his elbows. And though it was almost a shame he'd shaved today, she was irrationally happy to see he hadn't cut his hair.

Cade was pulling himself up into a standing position against Lucas's legs now.

"I . . . we . . ."

"Come, Miss Belville, surely you can be more loquacious than that."

Sudden, sweet impatience swept in and her legs finally

moved. She marched toward him until she was close enough she could smell that maddening scent of his, and she leaned over Cade and around the girls to hug him. "We're here to ask you to come home with us."

It almost scared her to say it. He might argue. He might say no. He might tell her all the reasons it wouldn't work.

But she had to ask. She had to hope.

Because when she hadn't known what to imagine for her life, God had imagined for her. He'd already given her Colie and Violet and Cade. He'd given her Aunt Lauren. He'd given her enough trust for today and enough hope for the days to come.

Say something, she mouthed.

But before Lucas could speak, a voice from behind glided in. "Aw, a family hug. Someone take a picture."

She felt Lucas's sharp inhale of surprise as he realized what he apparently hadn't until just then. That Kit was here too, along with Beckett.

Chin pressed into his chest, she tipped up her gaze to meet his. "I thought I might need reinforcements. And I think Kit wanted to see your dad again."

"Jenessa Belville." The wonder in his eyes was unmistakable, but it was the love and longing she saw there that stole her breath. "I hope you know if it weren't for all these kids, I'd be hugging you back right now."

Was that her answer, then? "I would hope you'd be doing more than that."

With a brisk movement that reminded her of the night they'd first danced together, when he'd pulled her toward him so fast she'd nearly lost her shoes, he stepped back, bending to steady Cade against Colie. He gave each of their heads one more ruffle, then reached for Jen's hands, looking behind her to Kit and Beckett. "You're on kid duty."

And then, before her glee could escape in a laugh, he towed her into the hallway.

"Where are we going? Is your apartment here on the first floor? Do you know how hard it was to get ahold of Flagg or any of your teammates to get this address?"

He didn't reply, only tugged a key from his pocket, and twisted it into the door they'd stopped in front of. He pushed into the door and barreled into the room.

"You should really get better at making sure people have emergency contact info and—"

He cut her off in one smooth motion, pulling her into his arms and kissing her. And if there'd been any lingering worry that she shouldn't have come, that he needed more space, more time, it melted away as she melted into him.

She didn't know how many seconds, minutes, passed before she leaned back, breathless and giddy. Now *that* was an answer. "I have to tell you what I did last week. I marched into Carmen's office. I told her if we're going to move forward with these custody arrangements, I had to make one thing super clear."

He kissed her lips again, followed by one cheek and then the other.

"Pay attention, Lucas. I said while I know I'm capable of taking care of the kids on my own—"

"Of course you're capable." His lips tickled her ear.

"—part of what made them so happy and content and secure at my house in the first place was having you around too. And that it would be ridiculous to think you're an obstacle when what you really are is one of the best things that's ever happened to them." She was the one to kiss him now—soundly. "And to me."

She clung to him, out of breath and out of words, but so full of warmth and delight she wasn't sure how any moment could possibly top this one right now.

But that was the thing—there'd be more moments like this. There'd be more kisses and merriment and love that kept growing. How did a person ever come to grips with this kind of joy?

"And what did Carmen say?" he finally whispered against her hair.

"Oh, well, after I ranted for a good twenty minutes, she said, 'All right, let's talk about what this looks like. Calmly.'"

He chest rumbled with laughter. "And what does it look like?"

"Well, we talked through a number of scenarios. I explained that you have a rather low-profile but high-intensity position that takes you away from home sometimes—"

He stilled her with a shake of his head. "No. I'm done at Bridgewell."

"But—"

"I'm done and I've known it for a long time. I just got confused for a minute."

"It was more than a minute. You've been gone for two weeks. Pure torture."

His arms tightened around her. "The other scenarios, Jen. What'd they look like?"

She stood on her tiptoes to press one more kiss to his lips and then, "A family, Lucas. They all looked like a family."

She pressed the picture in her mind of his joy-filled smile just then. Of the rich, swirling sheen in those ever-shifting hazel eyes of his that spoke of longings fulfilled. Of all the bright and beautiful somedays to come.

And his low, perfect voice matched the whisper of her heart. "Let's go home."

EPILOGUE

THANKSGIVING

"*J*en, Jen, JEN! Hurry up."

At Lucas's excited shout, Jenessa stopped filling her coffee mug halfway and jammed the carafe back into place. "Hold your horses."

The smell of the caramel rolls they'd devoured hours ago still clung to the air, along with the cinnamon Violet had gone slightly overboard with as they'd prepared the pies for later.

Flour dusted Jenessa's pajama top, and probably her hair too, but who had time to care, let alone look in a mirror, on a morning like this?

Within a couple hours, Belville Park would fill with so many of the people she loved most. Mara and Marshall and Sam, who was overjoyed to have Mackenzie for the day. Aunt Lauren and Tony. Kit and Beckett. Paige. Noah and even Lucas's dad and Nancy.

Dustin Hollis was the only wild card. They'd invited him, but whether he'd show was anyone's guess.

But the people she loved the *most*-most were already

here, the drifting music of their voices and laughter sweetening the air around her even more than cinnamon.

Lucas bounded into the kitchen, exaggerated impatience in his warm gaze. Violet had been playing with his hair again—it was pulled back with a scrunchie into something halfway between a ponytail and a bun. He took the mug from her hand and plunked it on the counter.

"Hey, we're playing host to a thousand people later. I need that extra caffeine."

Wasn't he cold in just a tee and gym shorts? "But you're going to miss it."

"Miss what?"

Apparently he decided it was too much to explain. He gave a huff and swept her off her feet. Her shriek turned to laughter as he carried her into the family room, where all three kids were gathered on the floor.

He plunked them both onto the couch. She landed next to him, arms still around his neck and legs sprawled over his. "Well, I guess when someone wants his wife's presence, he gets his wife's presence." She tried to sound scolding and failed entirely.

Lucas's stubble scratched her cheek in that way she loved when he kissed her. And for what was surely the millionth time since they'd married in a short and simple courthouse ceremony last weekend, she thanked God they'd decided to copy Marshall and Mara. Forgo some pointlessly lengthy engagement.

Lucas had stayed out in the cottage until the day of the wedding, and Noah had too. They'd found a brotherly closeness as they tossed around the idea of opening a landscaping business together. Of course, Mayor Milt was still trying to talk Lucas into applying for that city parks job. She was glad he didn't seem in a hurry as he weighed his options, especially considering his upcoming appeal hearing in D.C.

She'd been surprised when he'd decided to move forward with it. But when he'd told her why, she'd only fallen more in love with him. *"I was going to let it go. I'm done letting my record define me."* They'd been standing in the hallway upstairs when he'd said it, having just tucked in the kids. *"But Dad went to a lot of work making it happen. Besides, I have my heart set on adopting these kids so if getting my discharge downgraded would help—"*

She'd interrupted him with an embrace. As for her part, Jenessa's hours at the paper had dwindled down to almost nothing, with Paige taking on more and more of the daily operation.

"Trust me, you'll be glad I fetched you," Lucas said now. "Okay, guys. Let's see if he does it."

Tucked against her husband, she watched as Colie coaxed Cade into standing. Thankfully, her injuries from the car accident had healed smoothly. Violet scooted into place several feet away from her older sister.

"He's only ten months old, guys. That's awfully early to —" She interrupted herself with a gasp as Cade took one tottering step and then another.

"Told you," Lucas murmured in her ear.

Violet squealed and clapped, and Colie's beaming expression was the perfect picture of a proud older sibling. After a few more steps, Cade plopped to the floor, giggled, and clapped for himself.

They repeated the setup several more times, Colie and Violet positioning Cade and holding their arms out as he made his wobbly way back and forth.

"This is exactly what I pictured, Lucas."

"Hmm?"

"A holiday morning. All of us together. Pajamas."

His arms tightened around her. "About that last part, though. We might want to consider getting dressed. People could start showing up anytime. My dad has this thing with being ridiculously early to everything."

She shifted so she could face him. "How are you feeling about him coming?"

"Fine. More than fine, actually. I think things are only going to keep getting brighter and better." He gave her a quick peck and stood, securing her before she toppled from his lap. He clapped his hands. "All right, crew, we've got company coming soon. Time to make ourselves presentable."

Violet saluted and Colie rolled her eyes. Lucas scooped up Cade, and Jenessa followed her family from the room.

An hour and a half later, the house teemed with people, the front door opening every five or ten minutes with new arrivals. A burly wind whooshed outside the windows and sent curled leaves skittering in the door with each guest.

She was just finishing lighting candles on the dining room table when Lucas peeked into the room. "Hey, you might want to come up to the entryway."

The creak of the oven door sounded from the kitchen. Hopefully Noah was following her instructions on the pies. "You're not going to waylay me this time? Sweep me off my feet and carry me to whatever it is you want me to see?"

A flirty glint danced in his eyes as he waltzed toward her. "Well, you have to admit I'm pretty good at sweeping you off your feet."

"Literally, figuratively, and otherwise."

The teasing in his eyes sparked into something deeper as he pulled her to him. "Part of me says I should stop giving in to the temptation to kiss you literally every time I'm in the same room as you, especially now that our friends are here. But then I remember what we've had to put up with from Mara and Marsh for months."

"Hey!" Marshall and Mara exclaimed together from the kitchen.

"For the record, some of us would still like to have an appetite for Thanksgiving dinner," Sam growled.

"Ignore him and kiss me, Lucas Danby." She wound her arms around his neck. "We're newlyweds and we can get away with it."

"Oh, I plan to get away with it long after we're newlyweds." He gave her a quick kiss, then tugged her from the room. They passed Lucas's father lounging in the sitting room, a copy of *Iowa History* in his lap. Mayor Milt hadn't stopped raving about the two-page spread featuring Maple Valley for days—nor the photo of the Belville Park gardens on the cover.

They arrived at the entryway in time to see Dustin Hollis walking up the sidewalk.

He'd actually come. What would the kids think? She'd asked Colie and Violet how they felt about a week ago. Dustin had moved down to Des Moines earlier in the month after officially signing away his rights, and they didn't hear much from him. But both girls had said they were okay with seeing him on the holiday.

And they appeared okay now as Dustin came in. He seemed uneasy and uncertain, but there was no mistaking his soft smile when Colie said she was glad he'd come. She led him farther into the house, showing him around.

"Do you think we did the right thing inviting him?" Jenessa whispered as she watched the man interact with the children he'd chosen to give into her—into *their*—permanent care. Such a gift.

Lucas slipped his arm around her. "We prayed about it."

"I know. But the whole thing is a little messier than it

would be if we'd opted for a clean break." Cold seeped through the front door, the waning breaths of autumn making themselves heard in the rustle of the trees outside.

But she couldn't possibly feel warmer, her husband close to her side and this great big ridiculous house finally anything but empty now.

"What I know, Jenessa Danby, is that I'd rather have a messy life with you than any neat and orderly existence without you." He kissed the top of her head and led her into a room packed with liveliness and laughter.

And she knew Lucas was right. Things were only going to keep getting brighter.

THE END

ACKNOWLEDGEMENTS

Writing *Some Bright Someday* was so . . . weird. For real. I spent nearly nine months trying to write Lucas and Jen's book, but couldn't get past the opening chapters.

But then, in a whirlwind two weeks in September, this story and these characters suddenly came spilling onto the page. And I knew without a single doubt that the wait (and yeah, the tears—is it silly to admit that?) were worth it. Because while I have needed every story I've ever written, I think perhaps this is the one I've needed most of all. (So far, anyway.)

So first and foremost, I'm thankful to God. Not only for helping me write *Some Bright Someday*, but for speaking in a language I can hear—through the voice of my characters and the heart of this story.

Many thanks also to:

Mom and Dad—for all your encouragement and prayers and love.

*My grandparents, siblings, and the rest of my awesome family—*for being a constant reminder that real people are even better than fake ones. (Special shout-out to my sister Nicole for listening to so much of my frustrated whining when I was struggling to write this.)

Courtney Walsh—for so many brainstorming voxes and so much empathizing and such great friendship.

Amazing and supportive author friends—including my GLAM girls (Gabrielle Meyer, Lindsay Harrel, and Alena Tauri-ainen) and the MBT crew (Susan May Warren, Rachel Hauck, Beth Vogt, Lisa Jordan, Tari Faris, and Alena, again!)

Editor extraordinaire Charlene Patterson—for making this book shine!

Nancy Parlapiano and Terri Simmons—for finding my typos and forgiving my complete lack of care about Oxford commas.

Jenny Zemanek—for this gorgeous cover!

NEEDTOBREATHE—for being the best band ever and releasing the best album ever right before I went into writing seclusion in September. Your music is magic and I am a fangirl for life.

The goats at the Airbnb where I wrote a huge chunk of this book—they were cute. :)

Readers—I will never stop being grateful for you. Thank you for letting me put my heart in your hands time and again.

ABOUT THE AUTHOR

MELISSA TAGG is the Christy and Carol Award-winning author of swoony and hope-filled small-town contemporary romances, including the Maple Valley series, the Walker Family series, the Where Love Begins series, and the Enchanted Christmas Collection. She's also a former reporter, current nonprofit marketing strategist, and total Iowa girl. Melissa has taught at multiple national writing conferences, as well as workshops and women's retreats. When she's not happily lost in someone else's book or plugging away her own, she can be found spoiling her nieces and nephews, watching old movies, and daydreaming about her next fictional hero. Connect with Melissa at melissatagg.com.

- 🅕 facebook.com/authormelissatagg
- 🅨 twitter.com/melissa_tagg
- 🅞 instagram.com/melissatagg
- 🅐 amazon.com/author/melissatagg
- 🆂🆂 bookbub.com/authors/melissatagg
- 🅖 goodreads.com/melissatagg

Sign Up for Melissa's Newsletter

Keep up to date with Melissa's book news and more by signing up for email list at melissatagg.com.

You May Also Like . . .

Meet the Walker siblings in Melissa Tagg's critically-acclaimed Walker Family series! Set in Maple Valley, four close-knit siblings grapple with their careers, relationships, and faith as they learn what it means to take risks, chase dreams, and fight for their futures.

CPSIA information can be obtained
at www.ICGtesting.com
Printed in the USA
LVHW030005091121
702796LV00005B/118